THIRST
NO. 3

ALSO BY
CHRISTOPHER PIKE

THIRST NO. 1

THIRST NO. 2

REMEMBER ME

THE SECRET OF KA

THIRST
NO. 3

THE ETERNAL DAWN

Christopher Pike

Simon Pulse
NEW YORK LONDON TORONTO SYDNEY

This book is a work of fiction. Any references to historical events, real people, or real locales are used fictitiously. Other names, characters, places, and incidents are the product of the author's imagination, and any resemblance to actual events or locales or persons, living or dead, is entirely coincidental.

SIMON PULSE
An imprint of Simon & Schuster Children's Publishing Division
1230 Avenue of the Americas, New York, NY 10020
First Simon Pulse paperback edition October 2010

For information about special discounts for bulk purchases, please contact Simon & Schuster Special Sales at 1-866-506-1949 or business@simonandschuster.com.
The Simon & Schuster Speakers Bureau can bring authors to your live event. For more information or to book an event contact the Simon & Schuster Speakers Bureau at 1-866-248-3049 or visit our website at www.simonspeakers.com.
Designed by Mike Rosamilia
The text of this book was set in Adobe Garamond.
Manufactured in the United States of America
10 9 8 7 6 5 4 3 2 1
Library of Congress Control Number 2010931392
ISBN 978-1-4424-1317-7
ISBN 978-1-4424-1318-4 (eBook)

For my father, my first and greatest hero

The author wishes to thank Paul Dorado
for the brilliant songs he contributed to this novel.

ONE

The dawn, seen through the eyes of a vampire, is supposed to be painful. But since I have never embraced the myths told about my kind, I find the morning sun delightful. The hour before the sunrise is my favorite part of the day, although I suppose I'm at my deadliest in the depths of night.

I am, after all, a creature of darkness. I kill when I wish, and whoever can commit such a ghastly act, again and again, and never get caught can pretty much rule the world, or at least a small corner of it, as I rule mine. The power to take life is the second greatest power in the world, after the power to give it. It is with this perhaps unhealthy but unquestionably accurate point of view that I patiently await a chance to exercise my power once more.

My victim-to-be is a rapist. As a five-thousand-year-old

female—who cannot honestly be classified as "the weaker sex"—I admit to hating men who force themselves on women. History has paraded the cruel act too often before my eyes. I remember my early days, when I was only a few centuries old, how I would react when I came upon a rape. The sight would cause me to burn with rage until I had cracked the assailant's neck, or else torn off his genitals, or . . . well, both. I suppose, one could say, that I was overreacting, but I didn't feel that way then and I wonder if I will feel any different today.

I look forward to playing with my victim.

His name is Daniel Boford, although friends call him Danny Boy. He does not fit the classic rape profile. He is rich, intelligent, from a good family, a senior at Truman College—in whose stadium I presently sit. Danny is finishing up a full athletic scholarship as a gifted football receiver and an NCAA champion sprinter. The NFL is near drafting this year, and national sportswriters expect him to go in the first or second round. He has a bright future, our Danny Boy does, or I should say he did.

Now he will have no future at all.

What was it that initially drew my attention to the guy? Several things. The local news had reported an unusual number of rapes the previous year in Truman Village, a small town in north Missouri that was named after the thirty-third president of the United States, the first and last person on earth to order the use of nuclear weapons against human beings.

The second point that caused Danny Boy to catch my attention was the fact he was an athletic hero, and as a result had almost unlimited access to the school's female population. When I added this fact to a whiff of blood I noticed when I came near him, then you can see why I thought I had my man.

Ah, you might wonder how I noticed the blood and knew it was not his. Don't. I'm a vampire, I know everything there is to know about blood. Even if the guy had showered under an ice-cold waterfall after committing his dastardly deeds, I still would have smelled his victim's blood on him. My nose is extremely sensitive. Plus I smelled the blood on Danny Boy down low, from his crotch area.

Yet neither the rape reports, his hero status, nor the blood was enough to absolutely convict the guy. To do that I had to study how he interacted with women, which I began to do, from a distance. Did I mention that I see better than most people? Even better than most telescopes. Watching Danny from across the courtyard as he flirted with females, I saw several signs I have come to associate with rapists. His pupils would swell, his breathing would accelerate, and his neck and fist muscles would tense—all at the same time.

From long experience, I knew this last sign to be the most significant. Why? The neck tenses because the rapist's brain is cooking, and his hands keep gripping the air because what they really want to do is grab the woman in front of him.

Sigh. There is so much I could teach the FBI.

For example, their agents say rape is not a crime of sex, but one of control and dominance. My answer to that is *all* good sex involves control and dominance. Personally, I have to admit, I do like it rough, but I have to be careful in bed lest I paralyze any man brave enough to make love to me.

Suddenly there is a faint light in the east. Birds begin to sing, and fast-moving footsteps begin to approach the cinder track. I sit in the stands, at the fifty-yard line, in the tenth row, and watch as Danny jogs toward a point in front of me, near the starting line. Although Danny is a gifted sprinter, his coach has recently moved him up to the quarter mile, probably to improve his chances of winning another NCAA title. I can only assume there's more competition at the shorter distances.

As a result he has to do a lot of endurance work. His coach has him running several miles of interval training before the rest of the team arrives. Often he sprints a hundred meters, jogs a hundred, then sprints two hundred meters, jogs two hundred, and finally sprints a full lap, before resting for a few minutes and starting the cycle over again. For a rapist, he has remarkable self-discipline.

This morning, he completes three cycles of his interval training before he notices me. He probably didn't see me earlier because I wear black leather pants, a coat, and black boots. I hide most of my long blond hair in a ponytail I have tucked under my collar. In the dim light, I'm almost invisible.

He waves when he sees me and says hi. As he walks toward

me, I see his pupils dilate. He probably thinks I'm another fan, he has so many.

"You're up early," he says. "What are you doing here?"

"A friend of mine's on your team—Teri Raine. Do you know her?"

"Sure. Teri's a good buddy. She runs a mean mile."

Teri Raine also has an athletic scholarship, running cross-country in the fall and distance events during track season. Although it has only five thousand students, Truman College has a strong sports program. Teri more than contributes. As a freshman, just nineteen years old, she's gone the whole year without defeat. Her major is premed. She wants to be a surgeon, and the reason I know all this, and even care, is because we're related.

I'm confident I'm her SUPER-GREAT-grandmother. Teri is three hundred generations removed from Lalita, my only human child, but during the centuries, I have gone to great lengths to keep track of the female side of my family tree. Of course, when it comes to the male side, it has been next to impossible to know for sure if a boy is related to me. Long ago I abandoned that particular record-keeping, although I must admit I still occasionally pass a man on the streets—with blond hair and blue eyes and a certain gravitas—and wonder if he belongs to me.

Teri's genes are remarkably similar to my own, although I have twelve strands of DNA while she has the usual two. However, the human aspects of my DNA are almost identical to hers. A month ago, while she was sleeping—a sleep I enhanced by blowing my breath across her face—I took a swab from inside her cheek and sent it to a lab. I was not surprised to discover her silky blond hair, piercing blue eyes, and strong, flexible limbs are the result of my lineage.

In a sense, she's my child, and because I have seen that Danny favors her over the other girls on the team, I can't postpone killing him. I suspect he will attack her immediately after the school year ends. And he's no fool. He knows he can't simply wear a mask like he has done with some of his other victims, and let her live. She's spent too many hours training beside him. She knows his body too well. He won't just rape her.

Danny is struck by my resemblance to Teri Raine. At the mention of her name, he gushes, "You look like her sister!"

I stand. "Did she ever tell you she had a sister?"

"No."

"Then I must be someone new."

"I haven't seen you around. Do you go to school here?"

"I'm taking a few classes. People tell me you're about to graduate."

He grins. "You've been asking about me. Not fair, I don't even know your name."

I smile. "Alisa."

He comes up the steps and offers his hand. "Daniel Boford."

"Pleased to meet you, Danny Boy."

He's suddenly in heaven. His pupils go wide; any larger

and they'd blot out the whites. He breathes rapidly, his neck muscles tense, and his palms, why, they squeeze the air in front of him. His boldness impresses me. He's just raped a girl and now he wants me so bad he's willing to risk being bad all over again. It must be my resemblance to Teri.

"You're a sly one. What else have you heard about me?" he asks.

"Oh, that you're a ladies' man."

"Not so. Who told you that?"

"No one."

"Seriously, I want to know."

"You know us girls, we stick together. I can't reveal my sources."

He crosses his biceps across his chest and thrusts his hip forward. He's powerfully built, his brown hair long for a jock. Sweat seeps through his gray T-shirt, and although he has washed since his last victim, I smell her perfume on him. Ecstasy. Is that what he promised his victim, before he hurt her? Michelle Cornwick is still in the hospital, her mental wounds deeper, no doubt, than her physical ones.

Danny takes a step closer. He's too close; most people would feel he had entered their space. "I want to know who said that," he insists.

I shrug. "It doesn't matter."

"But it does, Alisa. Lies like that, they spread."

I stop and stare at him. "Michelle Cornwick."

He stops. "How is Michelle doing?"

"As far as I know, she's fine. Why do you ask?"

"She was raped. You must have heard. The talk is all over campus."

"Like I said, I'm a part-time student, I'm not here much. But God, that's terrible about Michelle. Do the cops have any leads on who did it?"

He shakes his head. "None."

"How can you be sure?"

"I know the local cops. During the fall, they come to all the football games. You must have heard I'm something of a celebrity."

"Bragging, Mr. Daniel Boford?"

"What can I say? I know I'm good." He moves closer still, to where I can feel his breath on my face. He wants to grab me, to take me now, but a part of him senses something's wrong. I don't back away from him. I don't flinch from his gaze. I don't do anything his previous victims probably did. That both excites and confuses him. He stares me in the eye. "Is your name really Alisa?" he asks, his tone changing.

"Yes."

"You're serious?"

"Don't I look serious?"

"I'm not sure." He glances around to make sure we're still alone. "There's something about you I don't get." He pauses. "Are you a cop?"

"I thought you knew all the local cops."

"Answer my question."

"No, Daniel Boford. I'm not a cop." I slowly smile. "Just a fan."

"Then you must have seen some of my races."

"I've seen a lot of them." I actually came to the track meets to watch Teri run, but I don't tell him that. "I saw you win that amazing double in the Lynwood Invitation."

"You mean, when I ran the hundred and the two hundred?"

"Gimme a break! You ran the two hundred and the four hundred meters. You won both races. And you anchored the four-by-four-hundred-meter relay." I pause. "Trying to test me?"

"Maybe."

"How am I doing so far?"

"Pretty good. You want to go for coffee?"

"Right now? Is there a place open?"

"Sure. I know a place."

"Don't you have to finish working out?"

"I'm done." He touches my arm. "Don't you want to talk some more?"

"Sure. But—"

"But what?" he asks quickly, and in an instant I realize his antennae are still up. I have underestimated him, not that it will affect the final outcome.

"All right. I'll have coffee with you. Where do you want to go?"

He squeezes my arm. "Where do you want to go?"

"Like I told you, I'm sort of new to this—"

"Are you sure you're not a cop?" he interrupts.

I stop, act worried. "You just asked me that."

"Yes, but since you lied the first time, I thought I'd ask again."

I casually shake off his hand and pull a badge from my back pocket. "No, not a cop." I open the badge. "FBI."

The ID is real—I paid someone high in the bureau to make it for me. I enjoy such toys, they come in handy. However, it doesn't impress Danny. He studies it but acts unconcerned. I don't know what to think. He's either very cool or very stupid.

"Why is the FBI interested in me?" he asks.

"Michelle Cornwick."

Finally, I get a reaction out of him.

"That's bullshit! She told everyone that the guy who raped her had on a ski mask. I talked to her parents."

"How nice. You've met Mom and Dad."

"Quit screwing with me, lady." He looks me up and down, no doubt searching for a gun. But he doesn't see one, because my snub-nose Smith & Wesson revolver is under my shirt, near my lower spine. I have a blade, too, in my right boot. He adds, "The guy who raped her wore a condom."

"Condoms break."

He fidgets, finally showing some fear. "You here alone?" he demands.

"No. I have backup."

"You're a liar. You couldn't have matched my DNA to anything found on her. Mine isn't on record."

"How do you know?"

"I've never been busted. I've never had a sample taken."

"Lisa Gonzales," I say flatly.

"What about Lisa?"

"You're doing her, in between a few others. Once I explained this to her, Lisa—with her doctor's help—was only too happy to give me a sample of your semen."

"Lisa's a friend! She would never stab me in the back!"

"She probably wouldn't stab good old Danny Boy. But we're talking about a rapist here. Lisa's no dummy. She understood how important your sample was to our case."

"What case?"

"The case of the federal government against Daniel E. Boford. In other words, we know who the rapist is. And I'm here to take you in."

"You're arresting me?"

"Yes."

He is an interesting specimen. His fear is genuine, but I sense his hatred is stronger. "Where's your backup? I want to see their badges."

"Why?"

"Because I think you're a fake. If the FBI was interested in me, the local cops would have given me a heads-up."

"You're wrong. You've assaulted women as far off as New Orleans. You've crossed state lines. That's what brought you to the FBI's attention. Face it, buddy, you're busted."

He snorted. "Busted? I'm going to be picked in the first round of the NFL draft next month. That's who Daniel E. Boford is."

"He's also just another asshole who doesn't know when to keep his dick in his pants." I stop and pull handcuffs from my coat pocket. "Turn around. Place your hands behind your back."

"What for?"

"Because you're under arrest and I'm going to cuff you. Do as I say."

He makes no move to obey. He keeps scanning the area. The stadium looks empty; it sounds empty too. Except for the birds singing there's just the two of us—that's what he's thinking. I can tell by the change in his body language, the growing confidence in the way he holds himself, that he doesn't believe I've brought backup. He thinks he can take me.

"No," he says. He waits to see if I draw a gun, and even that will not stop him, because he believes he's close enough to disarm me. I play into his fantasy and draw my weapon. I purposely move too slow, and as I bring it around, he grabs my right arm and points the revolver at the sky, squeezing my wrist. He smiles.

"Didn't they teach you anything at Quantico?" he asks.

I struggle. "Let go of me! Sanders! Tanner! He's resisting arrest!"

No one appears, and his smile widens. "Looks like your

backup slept in, Alisa." He rips the gun from my hand and turns it on me. He can see the side of the five-round chamber and knows it's loaded, but he's not sure what kind of bullets the gun holds.

I glare at him. "They're sharpshooters, and right now they're taking aim at your head. If you want to live, give me back my gun."

My gun. I sound like I'm pleading. He laughs.

"Drop it, there's no one here except us. But I'm confused. Why did you decide to take me alone? Did you want all the glory?" He lifts the gun and points it at my head. "Answer me."

I hesitate. "Harold Proveman."

"Who's he?"

"The father of Linda Proveman. One of the first women you raped." I pause. "He posted a large reward for the capture of the man who defiled his daughter."

Danny nods in understanding. "You thought you'd collect the reward rather than take the 'well done' pat on the back the FBI will give you?"

"Yes."

"Liar. You're not FBI at all. You're some cheap down-on-her-luck private eye. No trained FBI agent would act as clumsy as you." He cocks the revolver. "Does Mr. Proveman know who I am?"

"Yes."

He puts pressure on the trigger. "Are you sure?"

"He knows you go to school here. But I never gave him your name."

"Because you wanted to be sure to get all the reward first?"

"Yes."

He smiles and lowers the gun. "How much am I worth, by the way?"

"A hundred thousand dollars."

He whistles, impressed. "What did Mr. Proveman plan to do with me once you turned me over to him?"

"You don't want to know."

He smiles some more, before yanking the cuffs from my hands and spinning me around. "Put your hands behind your back."

I do as he commands. "You don't want to do this, Danny."

"Why not?" He cuffs me and drags me down the steps toward the parking lot. The light in the east has grown, but the track is still empty. I speak in a pitiful voice.

"I have a plan that can make both of us a lot of cash. I have another suspect that fits the profile of Linda Proveman's assailant. I can turn him over to her dad and collect the reward and split it with you."

"Why would Mr. Proveman believe this other guy did it?"

"I can use your semen sample and tie it to him. That's all the proof the man needs. He's connected, Mafia, a real hothead. He'll murder whoever I bring him. I swear, by noon today, you can have fifty grand in your pocket."

"No."

"At least think about it!"

He slaps my head with the gun. "I'll be worth a hundred times that in a month. And I don't trust you. You plan on lying to the guy who hired you, which means you're probably lying to me right now." He pauses. "I'm sorry, babe, but you've got to disappear."

He drags me toward his Honda Accord, which is the main reason for my charade. I don't want to kill him and dispose of his body using my own car, not with all the new techniques for uncovering evidence that modern-day cops have at their disposal. Better Danny drive me to his own dumping ground in his vehicle. Wiping away my prints will only take seconds. I'm new to the city, he has lived here for years. He knows the area better than me. He'll know the perfect spot to make a body disappear.

I knew ahead of time he was not simply a rapist, but a killer. I could refer to a dozen signs he gives off that make it obvious. But the simplest answer is best. A killer knows another killer, and I have killed thousands.

He doesn't shove me into the trunk but forces me to drive. There are holes in my story, and he senses them, like any dangerous man would. He wants to know everything he can before he kills me. He doesn't want any surprises messing up his draft day.

In the car, he cuffs me to the steering wheel and digs the

gun into my ribs. Yet I refuse to talk unless he lets me listen to the radio.

"What the hell?" he mumbles. "Are you nuts or something?"

"I like music. Don't you?"

"Alisa, look, I don't think you grasp what's going on here."

"Do you want me to turn right or left at the corner?"

"Left." He shakes his head. "You are one weird bitch, you know that?"

"I like to think I'm unique."

"How did you catch me? The truth."

I glance at him and let my voice go cold. "You'll see."

He shifts uncomfortably at my sudden change in tone. He keeps the gun in my side, but there's a tremor in his grip. My cold tone can be like ice to mortals. He no longer feels in complete control.

But he still intends to kill me, and rape me, I'm not sure in what order. We drive far into the countryside before we turn down a dirt road that leads through a patch of thick trees. I smell the swampy water before I see the green pond. He's buried bodies beneath its surface. I smell them as well.

But my nose is more sensitive than a bloodhound's. The spot is perfect for murder. Totally isolated, with a lake deep enough to hide a hundred corpses and wash away an endless number of fingerprints. Danny disconnects me from the steering wheel but keeps me cuffed. He orders me out of his car.

Now that he has me alone, his confidence returns. He forces me to the edge of the pond. The grass is tall and thick; it clings to our legs. The air is humid, filled with the faint buzz of insects. I can tell he's excited, but I don't need my vampiric skills to know that. His pants bulge.

He points the gun at me. "Strip," he orders.

I hold up my cuffed wrists. "With these on?"

He cocks the gun. "Do it!"

"No. I'm . . . shy."

He shakes his head in disbelief. "You're shy? Do you see what I'm holding? Do you know what it will feel like if I put a cap in your belly? Trust me, you don't want to find out."

"I couldn't afford real bullets," I mutter.

"Huh?"

"The gun, it's loaded with blanks."

"You're bullshitting me again."

"Go ahead, shoot, I don't care."

"All right then." He raises the gun, takes aim at my stomach and fires. I feel the wad of the blank's paper spread over me like dry rain as the noise from the shot echoes through the woods. Yet I know, with my extraordinary hearing, that there's nobody within ten miles of us to hear the shot. Danny probably knows the same. He's not worried we'll have company soon. But he stares at my gun in disgust.

"You were going to drag me to a Mafia hood with a gun loaded with blanks?" he asks.

I slip out of the cuffs as if I were Houdini. But I don't snap them in two. I need them. Taking a step toward him, I let him see more of the real me. My eyes, I feel their heat and I know they must burn. He suddenly has trouble looking at me.

"What the hell," he whispers.

"You see, I've just been acting the fool to fool you. All along I wanted you to bring me to this spot, to where you dump the girls you don't let go. Only I didn't know where it was. That's why I let you give me directions."

I have allowed my voice to change further, to take on the timbre of my true years. People, when they hear how ancient I really am, usually do one of two things. They freeze in awe or shake with fear. Danny isn't in awe of me, not yet, but he begins to pale.

"Who are you?" he mumbles.

I reach into my black boot and remove my blade.

"Death," I say as I come closer.

He holds out a trembling hand. "Wait a second. This has all been a misunderstanding. I'm not going to really hurt you. I was just playing with you. Honestly, I'll drive you back to school right now."

"No. Your school days are over with. You won't be running any more races, and the NFL isn't going to draft you next week." I gesture to the lake. "You're going to die here, and you're going to stay in this pond with all the other people you left to rot here. The fish and worms and insects will find their way into the interior of your car, to your body, and over the next few months they'll munch on your skin and muscles and organs until all that's left of you is a slimy skeleton. Eventually even that will dissolve, and it will be like you never existed, Danny Boy."

He trembles with fear. He has tears in his eyes. My voice, my words—the power in them shakes him to the core. His own voice cracks as he tries to convince himself he's not going to die.

"But you're just a chick. You can't hurt me."

"Then why are you so scared?"

"Because of that knife. Put that knife away and we can talk."

"Where exactly would you like me to put it?"

"I don't know, just put it—"

He suddenly stops talking, because I've shifted into high speed and thrown the knife so hard and fast it's sunk up to its hilt in the center of his right thigh. He gazes down at it in horror as a thin line of blood trickles over his sweats. In the blink of an eye I'm standing beside him. I pat him on the back in a poor imitation of comforting him.

"You don't want to pull it out," I warn. "There's a large artery that runs through each leg, and I'm afraid I just severed one with my knife. Pull out my knife and your blood will gush all over the place. You'll be dead in two minutes, maybe less."

He's suddenly sad. "Can you help me?"

"I'm not a doctor."

His whole body trembles as he points to his car. "Alisa, please, drive me to a hospital. My family has money. They'll pay you. They'll pay you whatever you want."

"I already have money. Besides, that's not what I want."

He is heartbroken. "No?"

"No. But I'll help you back to the car and I'll tell you what I do want."

He limps weakly as I assist him to his car. He doesn't protest as I shove him into the passenger side. A part of him still thinks I'm lying, and that in the end I'm going to save him.

I climb in the driver's side, close the door, and cuff his left wrist to the steering wheel. I do it so fast the deed is done before he realizes it, and his face is suddenly filled with the awe I have been waiting for. Yet his fear is greater.

"You're not human," he whispers.

"True. I'm not."

"Are you an alien?"

I smile. "You know, over the years people have called me all kinds of things, but that's a first. You should be proud of yourself, Danny Boy."

He stares down at the knife impaled in his leg. Moving him to the car has caused the blood to flow faster, and his sweats are soaked red. He puts his hand on the hilt of the blade.

"You don't want to do that," I say.

"It hurts."

I stop smiling. "Rape hurts. Did you stop and think of that when you hurt all those women?"

He shakes his head as tears roll over his cheeks. "Please, you're making a big mistake. You have the wrong guy."

"Two minutes ago you pointed a gun at me and ordered me to strip. Why would you do that if you weren't going to rape me?"

He sobs. "All right, I did it, I'm guilty. I'll tell the police I did it. I swear. Just please take me to the hospital."

I reach over and stroke his hair. "I'm sorry, you have to stay here with all the women you wanted so badly."

"No! God, no! I can't die!"

"Shh. Calm down, you won't suffer long. And to make sure you don't, there's something I'm going to do for you before I say good-bye."

He gazes at me with sudden hope. "What?"

"Oh, just have a little drink is all." Before he can react, I reach over and remove the knife and press my mouth to the gushing blood. He must eat a healthy diet—his blood tastes particularly good. Or maybe it's because I have gone a long time without feasting. Ever since my maker, Yaksha, and my daughter Kalika gave me their powerful blood, I have discovered that I don't need to feed on humans to survive.

Yet old pleasures die hard. Danny Boy is white as a ghost before I'm through with him, and I can hear how his heart struggles with so little liquid to keep it beating. As an act of kindness, I slip the knife back in his leg and close off the leaking artery.

"There," I say. "How do you feel now?"

He gasps for breath. "Scared."

"I bet your girlfriends felt scared too."

He stares at me. "Please stop."

"Stop? But we're just getting to the fun part. It's going to be like in the movies. I'm going to start the car and steer it toward the pond and jump out before it hits the water. But I'll close my door if you want so you don't get wet." I pause. "Of course, this car isn't a hundred percent waterproof. I'm afraid the water—and all those nasty creatures I told you about—will eventually get inside. You might be dead by then, you never know. If you're not, you'll get to feel what it's like to drown."

"No . . . Please."

"Come on, show some spirit! I bet you drowned plenty of your girls. It's only right you should experience everything they did."

He weeps quietly. "I don't want to die."

I lean over and kiss his cheek.

I spare him my favorite farewell remark.

But I keep my promise. Starting the car, I accelerate rapidly and turn in the direction of the pond. At the last moment, I leap out my side and slam the door shut. The car has plenty of momentum and belly flops far from the shore, before it slowly begins to sink.

To my surprise, Danny thrashes vigorously inside, even though I have drained him of all but a couple of pints of blood. As I wipe off my hands and listen to the noise he's making, and to the hissing and bubbles the car gives off as it sinks below the surface, I think of his last words and consider how often I've heard them over the years.

Turning, I race toward the main road. It does not matter how fast I run. Behind me, I still hear him screaming.

TWO

A long-distance truck driver gives me a ride back to Truman. He is taking a shortcut through the back country, on the downside of a sixty-hour stretch of road that reaches from LA to Miami. When I climb into his tobacco-rich cabin, he looks plum exhausted but perks up with my vivacious company. He wants to know how a pretty little thing like me got stranded in the middle of nowhere.

"Just ditched a no-good boyfriend," I say.

The guy slaps his knee. "You don't sound bitter about it."

"I'm not."

"That's good, real good. Where'd you ditch the bastard?"

I smile. "Where the fishes swim."

He thinks that's pretty funny, and we laugh together. I don't worry he will hear or read about Danny Boy. The man is just passing through and is so tired he hardly knows what state he's in.

Back at Truman College I have a change of clothes in my car that I keep for such emergencies. My ride didn't notice, but there's blood on my shirt and pants, and I know Teri's much more perceptive than your average truck driver. I'm actually signed up for a few classes and have campus privileges. After a quick shower in the locker room, I slip into fresh black slacks and a white blouse before returning to the stadium.

The track is a beehive of activity, with most of the team present. The coach is smart; he likes to get in the hardest workouts before the heat of the day hits. Teri is running quarter-mile intervals, the coach calling out the time for each lap she completes. Teri would not be able to match Danny Boy's times, but she is the fastest woman on the team, and once again I'm surprised at the pleasure it gives me to see her doing so well. That Proud Mom feeling, it's been ages since I experienced it.

I sit in the same place in the stands where I sat when approached by Daniel and wait for Teri to finish her workout. My ears hear everything. The head coach and his two assistants wonder where Daniel is but are not overly concerned. They figure he finished his workout early and is probably at home taking a nap. No one on the field gives me a second look, and that is important. It was always possible someone saw me get into the car with Daniel. But no, he's gone, gone for good, and his body will never be found.

The women of Truman need fear no longer.

An hour passes, and Teri is finally done with her laps and

is alone and heading for the showers when I approach. To my surprise I feel my heart pound—it's almost as if I am nervous. I need to talk to her soon, before she disappears back home for the summer. But if everything goes according to plan, she'll stay in Truman.

Naturally, I worry my appearance might startle her, we look so much alike. But I've fixed my makeup to alter the lines on my face. And I have on dark sunglasses, so she can't see the deep blue of my eyes. I don't want her feeling like she's looking in a mirror. Plus I wear a baseball cap, which hides my long blond locks. Later, if I sense my looks still bother her, I can dye my hair.

"Teri Raine?" I say.

She glances over and jumps slightly. My face has startled her, but she recovers quickly. "Yes?" she says.

I offer my hand. "Alisa Perne. I got your name from the job-placement office. They told me you're looking for a summer job."

Her grip is firm. "That's right."

"Well, I think I have something you might enjoy."

"What company do you work for?"

"I work for myself. If you took the job, you'd be working for me."

"What kind of job are we talking about?"

"They told me you're a premed major."

"Yeah. But I've only been here a year."

"I know. You're only nineteen, but with all the advanced courses you've taken, you're technically a junior. They let me peek at your transcript. You've already finished a year of organic and inorganic chemistry. You're done with most of your biology, physics, and calculus. It looks to me like you'll be in medical school by your twenty-first birthday."

Teri is guarded, not a bad thing. "I'm surprised they told you so much about me."

I had put a vampiric spell on the woman in the employment office, but I'm not going to tell Teri that. "I need someone right away, and I'm willing to pay three times what you could get anywhere else in town."

"Doing what?"

"Research, mostly. I'm a writer, I'm working on a major medical thriller, and there's a hundred and one facts I don't have the time or the inclination to look up. It makes sense to just hire someone to do it for me. Interested?"

"Are you a published novelist?"

"I've published numerous short stories," I tell her honestly. "But this will be my first big book."

"First novels usually don't pay much. If you manage to sell them."

"Oh, this will sell. And I'm independently wealthy. I don't have to worry about the size of the advance."

"Must be nice."

"Money is always nice."

"How many others are interviewing for the job?"

"A few. But on paper you're my main candidate."

"Why?"

"Your record shows you're aggressive. I like that. And your grades are high, so you're smart, and I like that, too."

She is unmoved by my compliments. "What kind of salary are we talking about?"

"Thirty bucks an hour. Or a hundred dollars a day even if I only call you in for an hour."

"With that kind of cash, you could hire a full-fledged medical student."

"I'd be hiring his ego as well. Look, I don't want someone who has all the answers. I want someone who doesn't mind looking for the answers."

Teri nodded. "It sounds very interesting, Ms. Perne."

"Alisa, please."

"I'd like to talk to my boyfriend about it."

"That's fine."

She thinks I don't approve, tries to explain. "I'm hoping to live with him this summer. So in a way he's my landlord."

I tease lightly. "Does he know you want to move in?"

She smiles and her guard drops. "I'm not a hundred percent sure. The last nine months, with my track scholarship, I've been sleeping in the dorms. So we've had plenty of space between us, which has been good. But moving in together is another thing."

"But you feel too old to go running back to Mom and Dad just now."

I know Teri's mother—I once spoke to her forty years ago, when she was twelve. I bought her a vanilla ice cream cone, and she told me she wanted to be an astronaut when she grew up. But she married young and sort of retired. She doesn't have Teri's fire.

"You're a mind reader. Yeah, I miss them, but I talk to them every week. I mean, I don't miss them that much. And I hate the idea of leaving Matt right now." She pauses, shakes her head, embarrassed. "I can't believe I'm telling you all this stuff. You must be thinking this is no way to interview for a job."

"You're being yourself—that's the best way to make a good impression." I pause. "Is your boyfriend a student here?"

Her remark about being a mind reader strikes home. I am a telepath, but I have to focus hard on a person to read their thoughts. For that reason, I seldom use the ability, and almost never on people I like. It feels too much like being a peeping Tom to me. Also, to directly implant a suggestion in someone's mind is exhausting, particularly if they're strong-willed.

"No. Matt's, well, it's hard to say what he is. He's from Europe—he's a bit of a drifter. But he's a brilliant singer-songwriter. Right now he's got two gigs. He plays the Gator Friday and Saturday nights. And this club in Prudence, the Black Hole, hired him part-time during the week. Are you familiar with these clubs?"

"I know the Gator. It's in town, isn't it, off Main Street?"

"Yeah. The place used to be a library, if you can believe that. Now it's the loudest spot in town. Matt's playing there tonight. Two shows—one at nine, the other at midnight."

"I'd love to meet him. If that's all right with you."

"Sure. But—"

"I was just thinking he might have questions, if he's the protective sort. It might be good for the three of us to meet socially, see if we can stand each other."

For the first time I feel Teri studying me. She's good—she does so without being too obvious. But she senses I'm coming on strong, and she's careful. Once again, I don't mind. In fact, I approve. No one knows as well as I how cold and cruel the world can be.

"I'm sure Matt would be happy to meet you," she says.

"I'll swing by tonight." I offer my hand again. She shakes harder this time.

"I'm seriously interested. Oh, could you bring a few of the stories you've written tonight?"

She wants to know if I am for real, or just a hack.

"Sure," I say.

My house is as far out of town as the spot where I buried Daniel, except it's in the opposite direction, due west of the campus. I could just as easily have rented a place as bought one, but I prefer to purchase because I'm a privacy fanatic and dislike sleeping in a place not equipped with high-tech security equipment. I have a past. I have enemies. I cannot be too careful.

My home sits all alone in the center of a spacious grass field that gently slopes down to a large lake. On the other three sides are trees, thick as a jungle, but when I say the field is huge, I'm not exaggerating. There's a half mile of open space in every direction around the house. With that much land on all sides, I can always see who's approaching. The property alone cost twenty million—a reasonable amount for someone who started saving five thousand years ago.

I notice a pot has been knocked over on the walkway that leads to my front door. I have a team of gardeners who come once a week and take care of my plants and flowers. But they come on Mondays, and today is Friday. The pot is heavy; the wind could not have disturbed it. Besides, the breeze that wafts off the lake is gentle this time of morning.

For several minutes I stand and study the situation. My nearest neighbor is ten miles away—one of the few families I know in the state—but by chance they are in Europe. They would not visit anyway, not without first calling. Also, I don't take any mail at the house, but use a PO box in town. There's no reason for someone to visit.

My hearing spreads out like invisible sonar. I hear rabbits, squirrels, and possums in the woods, baby birds squeaking in their nests, but I don't detect the telltale rhythm of a human hiker. Of one thing I'm sure: No one drove up to my property in the last few hours. I would be able to smell the odor of their car fumes.

Yet I do smell something foreign, and I squat beside the broken pottery and bring it near my nose. Whoever bumped the pot was sweating, as if they had walked to my place from a great distance. However, I see no prints in the grass.

The mystery deepens when I go inside and check the recordings of my video cameras. The cameras are an important part of my security. They scan inside and outside, and I've arranged them so there is no blind spot. I find one of the cameras has gone dead, the very camera that was pointed at the broken pot. But when I pull it from its place beneath the eaves, I can find nothing wrong with the camera. The damage is internal, beyond the scope of my senses. I don't smell any sweat on the camera, nor do I see any fingerprints. If someone did handle it, they wore gloves.

I check the large walk-in vault I keep in my master bedroom, hidden behind a heavy chest of drawers. Inside the vault is an assortment of weapons: Glocks, semiautomatic .45s, old favorites of mine; AK-47s; two laser-guided Barringer sniper rifles, which are accurate over a mile.

I also have ten million in cash on hand, in various currencies. I never know when I might suddenly need to travel. I have passports and credit cards that allow me to assume a half dozen different identities. The IDs are not just expensive fakes. They are the real thing—I have built up the identities over decades.

Indeed, I purchased this house under the name Lara Adams, and that's the name I go by around town.

It was just a slip of the tongue that I told Teri my name was Alisa. It's not my real name, of course. At most, a handful of people know me as Sita, the name my father gave me long ago. But Alisa is a favorite alias; for some reason I wanted Teri to know it.

I'm still upstairs in my vault when I hear a car approach up my long driveway. I seldom get guests. I assume the people who have come to visit are the same ones who knocked over my pot. I know without looking that there's more than one person in the car. I hear a man and woman talking, idle conversation:

"Do you think she's home?"

"How much should we tell her?"

I close my vault, but I exchange the Smith & Wesson I took with me to dispatch Daniel and replace it with a powerful Glock .45. I'm not paranoid, but I am always careful. It's probably the main reason I'm still alive.

The couple—she's in her late twenties, he's at least five years older—drive a rented Camry. I can tell it's rented by the Hertz sticker in the window. I study them through the window as they park and ring my doorbell. She does not look threatening, although I can tell she is nervous. She has an academic demeanor. She talks with her hands and uses big words when small ones would suffice.

I already know her partner's a cop. He has the look, and he's carrying a gun, although it's well concealed beneath his pants, above his ankle. I can tell they're lovers. He touches her arm lovingly as she waits anxiously for me to answer.

I finally do.

"Hi," I say as I open the door. "What brings you two all the way out here?"

"Hello," the man says. "My name's Jeff Stephens and this is my friend Lisa Fetch. We hope we haven't caught you at a bad time?"

Jeff is portly, on the short side, with a receding hairline, a brown mustache, and a friendly face. Yet I can tell he works out; he's nimble on his feet. Lisa is the same height as her boyfriend, but thin, with red hair and tired green eyes. There are shadows beneath those eyes. There's no doubt she's under a lot of stress.

I smile. "I suppose that depends on what you want me for."

The woman returns my smile. "Are you Alisa Perne?"

Damn, I think. They know my old alias. They must know a lot about me to have come across that name. Yet neither of them smells like the person who knocked over my pot. Hmm.

"Yes," I say. "May I ask where you got that name?"

Lisa answers. "An old boyfriend of mine was doing some research on the firm I currently work for. He came across your name."

"What's the name of your firm?"

"IIC. Infinite Investment Corporation. They're based in

Malibu, California. Their primary business is investing in the stock market."

"They cater to private investors?" I ask.

"They pretend to," Lisa says bitterly. "But they mostly cater to themselves."

I'm curious. I open my door wider. "Please come in and tell me all about it." Yet I stop Jeff as he comes through the door. "I'd rather you left your gun in the car."

He's impressed. "How did you know I'm carrying?"

"'Cause you look like a cop."

"Really?"

"It's a compliment."

Minutes later they are sitting in my living room. I offer them fresh coffee, which they gladly accept. For a vampire, I'm unusual—I drink more coffee than blood.

Unless I'm mistaken, they are both "nice people," and I'm not afraid they intend to harm me, at least not directly. A superficial scan of their minds has told me that much. But the fact they know my old alias is not good. They could damage me by talking about me with the wrong people. A few years ago I had a serious run-in with the FBI—and the U.S. Army, for that matter—and I doubt they've quit searching for me.

Once we're comfortable, I cut to the point.

"I assume when you say your old boyfriend was researching the firm you work for, you mean he was hacking into their computer files," I say to Lisa.

My insight surprises her. "How did you guess?"

"What better way to get dirt on a company?"

"Why do you assume they're dirty?" Jeff asks.

"Your tone when you speak about them. You sound angry." I turn to Lisa. "What's the name of your old boyfriend?"

Lisa is uncomfortable. "Why is that important?"

"He's snooping around files that contain information about me. I deserve to know his name."

Lisa replies, "Randy Clifford. I only asked him to look into IIC because I noticed highly irregular patterns in their investments."

"Why isn't Randy with you today?" I ask.

"He disappeared not long after we asked him to hack into IIC's system," Jeff explains.

"When was the last time you spoke to him?" I ask.

"A month ago," Lisa says sadly.

"But you say this is an investment company. They hardly sound like the type that would have people whacked. I assume it's staffed with stockbrokers and lawyers and accountants?"

Lisa nods. "Yes. And one mathematician. Me."

"What sort of work do you do for them?"

She spreads her hands helplessly. "For the first six months I wasn't sure what I was doing. They'd hand me reams of papers filled with numbers and order me to search for patterns. It took me a while to realize they were records of their investments. For some reason, in the last two years they've begun to make only ten percent a year on their money, rather than their usual twenty-five percent."

I almost choke on my coffee. "There's no investment firm in the world that gets that kind of return on their money."

"IIC does. Or at least they did," Lisa said.

"Did you figure out why their returns have dropped?"

Lisa hesitates. "No."

She's lying, or at least she knows more than she's willing to say.

"This is all very interesting, but what brings you here?"

"We told you, your name came up when Randy hacked into their system," Jeff says. "IIC even had this address. That's how we were able to find you."

I've lived in Missouri only two months. No one should have my address. "In what context was I mentioned?" I ask.

"Randy was looking into that when he vanished," Jeff says. "All we know is that IIC considers you 'a person of interest.' That's how you were described in their files."

"Where does Randy live?" I ask.

"Manhattan," Lisa says. "He works for an investment firm on Wall Street, Unlimited Investments Incorporated, or UII. But here's the real kicker. After he hacked into IIC's system, he realized it was indirectly connected to a half dozen investment firms, his own included. In fact, that's how he was able to break through IIC's firewall. It was familiar to him."

"Are you saying all these companies are really one and the same?"

"Yes," Lisa says.

"Aren't there laws against such things?" I ask.

Jeff nods. "Sure. But as far as Randy was able to tell, IIC and their partners are simply fronts for a single gigantic investment firm."

"Which is called?"

"That's the point. It doesn't have a name. It's not supposed to exist," Lisa says.

"This sounds like it has all the makings of a complex conspiracy story. But I still don't see what it has to do with me."

"Surely you must be curious why IIC is interested in you?" Jeff asks.

I'm extremely curious, but I respond casually. "I'm a person of some wealth, although I prefer not to advertise the fact. I'm sure, like any other investment firm, that IIC keeps a record of wealthy individuals."

"You weren't just on a list," Lisa says. "They had a whole file on you."

"Why didn't you say that at the start?"

"I'm saying it now!" Lisa snaps, and I can tell she's not angry at me, but at her company for making her old boyfriend disappear.

"What else was in my file? Besides my name and address?"

"We told you, Randy was looking into it when he vanished," Lisa says.

"Randy did say the file spoke of you as having a 'lengthy history,'" Jeff says.

"What does that mean?" I ask, but it's easy for me to imagine the true answer.

"We don't know," Jeff replies.

Lisa leans toward me. "You don't appear to be worried that IIC is obsessed with you. Frankly, I'd be very worried."

"Because of what they did to your old boyfriend?" I ask.

"That's the tip of the iceberg," Jeff says. "The more we dig into IIC and their partners, the more we discover how big and powerful they are."

"They may be the richest company in the world," Lisa says.

"And no one knows their name," Jeff adds.

I shake my head. "How do they make so much money on the market?"

Lisa hesitates. "We don't know."

"Are you still working for them?" I ask her.

"Yes."

"That must be risky." When Lisa does not respond, I add, "Don't you have some idea how they make their money?"

I've finally asked the question that matters. Lisa and Jeff exchange an uneasy look. "Have you heard of the Array?" Lisa asks.

"No. What's that?"

"We're not sure, not yet," Lisa says.

"But it's clear from the info Randy dug up that the Array allows them to invest with remarkable accuracy," Jeff says.

"Is it an advanced software program?" I ask.

"It might be," Lisa says. "We know it deals with computers."

"Did you come all the way to Missouri hoping I'd know about this Array?"

"We were hoping you would know something," Jeff says.

"Whoever you are, you're important to IIC," Lisa says.

"I promise you, I know nothing about the Array or IIC." I suddenly stand, signaling that our meeting is over. The fact I don't know about the investment firm doesn't mean I'm not going to find out everything I can about them. Lisa and Jeff get up reluctantly. They don't want to leave. Lisa offers me her card.

"Please call if you hear from IIC," she says. "Or anyone else that worries you."

"I will," I promise. "But may I offer a piece of advice?"

"Please," Jeff says.

"Be careful who you discuss this matter with. If they made Randy disappear because he hacked into their system, they can make you two disappear as well."

"We've tried to be careful," Lisa says. "But we thought with you, we could—"

"We thought we could trust you," Jeff completes her remark.

I like them. I give them a quick hug.

"I assure you I'll keep our talk confidential." I give them each a card of my own. "Keep in touch. I'm very interested to hear more about this Array."

When they're gone, I call two separate agents who are employed by the FBI but who really work for me. I tell them what I know about IIC and ask them to learn more. I instruct them to look into Randy Clifford's disappearance while they're at it. The two agents—who don't know each other—agree to get on the case right away.

I also hire two private detectives to look into the matter—again, a man and a woman who don't know each other, but who once worked for the CIA. These four people I pay handsomely, and I have every confidence in their abilities and their discretion. I trust them and they trust me. I warn them the job could be dangerous, and to call if they feel the least bit threatened. I like to think I take care of my own.

But it's at times like this that I wish I had a true confidante, someone I could open my heart to without hesitation. In five thousand years I've known only a dozen people I could totally trust. I don't know if that's a testament to my nature or to human nature. I just think it's sad. Now, in this age, the one person I know I could trust above all others, Seymour Dorsten, doesn't even believe I exist.

Oh, Seymour knows about Alisa Perne. He even knows my real name is Sita. But he sees me as a fictional character, an amazing immortal vampire who exploded in his mind one day and who didn't give him a moment's peace until he wrote down the story of her life. He thought I was a product of his muse, when in reality I was in deep telepathic contact with him.

Now, this instant, I write my own story, but at first I let Seymour do the job. One might wonder why. Well, it was not something I planned—my mind just found him one day, and I discovered I couldn't let go. So rich was his imagination, so deep were his feelings. For these reasons alone, I thought he should be the one to tell my tale. Plus the telepathic link between us was almost flawless.

I suppose a part of me felt I had been led to him by a higher power. I was sitting alone by the ocean, thinking of Krishna and his dark blue vastness, when my thoughts first intertwined with Seymour's. I feel it was fate that brought us together. However, even though he knows me better than I know myself, we have never met in the real world.

But that is going to change. Soon.

I can hardly wait to see the look on his face.

THREE

I arrive at the Gator early and sit in the back in the corner. The club is small, it has a maximum capacity of a hundred. Conservative Truman is not exactly a huge drinking town. I notice the stage is equipped with only two instruments, an acoustic guitar and a piano. The amplifiers are modest. I understand where the owner of the club sees Matt in the scheme of things. Matt is there because the boss needs somebody on stage. Otherwise, the owner wants his patrons to be able to talk during the show. People like to talk when they drink, and they like to drink when they talk. The boss knows his business. No singer, no matter how talented, is going to slow down the bar.

Teri and Matt are not visible, but that doesn't stop me from getting to know them better. They are in the back, in the dressing room, and I can hear them as clearly as if they were sitting beside me. Few people understand the subtleties of vampiric hearing. Simply by focusing on them, I can negate every other sound.

Teri is telling Matt about meeting me.

"She's a fascinating woman. When she first introduced herself, I thought she was my age. But after we talked for a few minutes, I realized she was a lot older."

"Is that when you noticed the wrinkles around her eyes?" Matt replies in a rich voice. He has an accent. I hear German, Norwegian, and shades of British. He's well traveled.

"Shush. She doesn't have any wrinkles." Teri pauses. "Actually, she's one of the most beautiful women I've ever met."

"I thought you said she looks like you," he teases.

"She does. She's me times ten. She has an aura about her."

"Does she have money? That's all that matters."

"I saw her car. She drives a Porsche."

Matt sighs. "I don't know."

"What don't you know?"

"Her whole story sounds fishy. Why would she hire you to do medical research when she can afford someone with a lot more experience?"

"I told you, she finds most doctors and med students to be egomaniacs. And I can't say I disagree."

"That's a hell of a generalization."

"We all make them, sweetie."

"If she's such a big-time writer, how come we've never heard of her?"

"She never said she was big. She went out of her way to say this is a first novel. But she's been published, and she's going to bring samples of her work tonight."

"I'll believe it when I see it."

Teri sounds annoyed. "Why are you so down on her? This could be a big break."

"That's what worries me, that you've got your hopes up. There's no reason she should pay you that kind of money in a hick town like this. I only get fifty bucks a night, and I've got to put on two shows."

"You get tips as well, and you've got me to come home to."

"That's the only reason I'm playing this dump."

Teri's tone changes to worried. "Is it getting to you?"

"Kind of. American audiences aren't as sophisticated as Europeans. You just like to hear covers of popular songs. I can hardly squeeze in any original material. That should be the only reason a guy like me plays this small a club."

"You play here because I live here." Teri pauses. "But if you want to move, I'll understand. I'm not going to stop you."

"Teri, please, don't start that again. I'm here because I want to be here."

"But you bitch about it all the time. Maybe you should head off to New York or LA, give yourself a real chance."

"Like you would follow me there."

"You can leave and come back. It doesn't mean we have to break up."

"Really? You know any long-distance relationship that works?"

"No."

"That's why I'm not leaving."

Teri sighs. "Why do I hear a 'yet' in that remark?"

"Because you're paranoid."

"I'm not paranoid."

"And you don't know how much I love ya."

I hear Teri smile. "Do you love me?" she asks.

I hear them kiss. Ah, to be young again. My vampiric brain has endowed me with perfect recall, and yet I can hardly remember the last time I was in love. There was Rama, five thousand years ago, and then Ray, fifteen years ago . . . but no golden moments in between. Maybe I've blocked out my sentimental memories because they all ended so painfully.

It sounds like my job is not finished. If I want Teri to stay in Truman, then I still have to win Matt over. However, if he rejects me, it might be a blessing in disguise. The truth is, I shouldn't be getting involved in Teri's life.

My motive is selfish. I'm feeling lonely, and Teri reminds me of myself when I was young. But no one knows better than me how dangerous I am to be around. Take for example the matter of the broken pot, and Jeff and Lisa's visit this morning. Who knows where any of that might lead?

I sense a strong intuition in Matt. That quality alone might warn him against me. I tell myself that if he doesn't welcome me willingly, then I won't use any vampiric tricks to seduce them.

The club begins to fill up for the nine o'clock show, and fifteen minutes later Teri appears and waves to me. I stand when she reaches my table and squeeze her hand. She wears a white skirt and a yellow blouse and has a red rose tucked in her blond hair. I wear black slacks and a gray top and have a Glock—a nine-millimeter—tucked beneath the back of my belt. I gesture for Teri to sit and take the chair beside her.

"Did you have trouble finding the place?" Teri asks.

"Nothing in Truman is hard to find. You just have to stand in the town square and slowly spin. You see everything there is to see."

"It's kind of sad, isn't it?"

"No. I like small towns."

"Really? You seem like a big-city woman to me."

"You don't know me. I'm practically a recluse."

"That must help with your writing."

"It does, when I'm writing."

"Do you suffer from writer's block?"

"Procrastination. A close cousin."

"Did you bring some of your short stories?"

"Just the few pieces I've published. Why don't I show them to you after your boyfriend sings?"

"That's cool. He should be out in a minute."

"I've been listening to the audience. They like him."

"Wherever he goes, he quickly collects a fan base. It's not just me saying it—he's the real thing."

"You think he's going to be big?"

Teri's eyes shine. "I know he is."

"I admire your faith in him."

"Thanks. I just hope, you know, that I don't stand in his way."

"You won't do that."

"I might without intending to." Teri gestures to the small club. "Look at this joint. It's nice, but he's not going to bump into a talent agent here. He needs to leave."

"And you don't want him to leave?"

"I'm torn. My scholarship's here—I have to stay. But if I'm honest with myself, I know he's just killing time here. He should say good-bye and not look back."

"If he had one hit, he could send for you, and you could go to school anywhere."

Teri looks doubtful. "Guys who get on the radio don't often send for the girl back home."

Our conversation stalls. I choose not to argue with Teri, because what she says is true. Most guys who become rock stars and hit the road find plenty of girls to keep them occupied. Yet, in the short time I listened to them talk, I felt Matt cared for her. He was definitely protective, which is always a good sign.

The lights dim and there's applause, but still Matt doesn't appear. I listen to the background chatter of the crowd and am not surprised to hear Danny Boy mentioned. Apparently his disappearance has been noticed. Teri nods to the audience.

"Can you hear what they're talking about?" she asks.

"Some guy called Danny?"

"Daniel Boford. He's on the track team with me, but he's mainly known as a big football star. He didn't show up at practice this morning or this afternoon, and no one can find him."

"Are you worried? Is he a friend?"

Teri frowns. "I hope nothing's happened to him, but I wouldn't call us friends. To be honest, he kind of gives me the creeps. He's always hitting on me, even though he knows I have a boyfriend."

"Let's not worry about him, then."

"Agreed."

Matt suddenly appears, and I suck in a breath. If I looked familiar to Teri, he looks familiar to me, and I haven't the faintest idea why. He's tall, with broad shoulders and shaggy brown hair. His eyes are dark brown, but I hesitate to call them warm because there's an intensity to his expression, to his overall demeanor, that causes the small crowd to focus on him. He clearly has ingredient *X*, whatever the hell that is. He's charismatic and extremely handsome. Now if he can just sing . . .

He does not say hello to the audience. Instead, he picks up his guitar and begins to play a melody I don't recognize. It must be an original. The piece has a Latin feel to it. I'm reminded of brilliant but unknown guitarists I've heard in tiny clubs in Mexico and South America.

He begins to sing, and I draw in another breath. He's not

merely good—he's wonderful! He's obviously well trained and has superb range. But more important is the feeling in his voice.

She's not just a pretty face,
A pretty face, in a pretty place,
Something's not quite real,
I pass this way every day,
But today I've learned to feel

In a book I've seen the best,
Lady Godiva and the rest,
But none compare to this new song,
Next to you I'll soon belong

And if you say you'll love me too,
To be as one and say we're true,
I'll have your pretty face to see,
It's me with you and you with me

She's not just a pretty face,
A pretty face, in a pretty place,
Something's not quite real,
I pass this way every day,
But today I've learned to feel

She's singing my song la di la di la di

She's not just a pretty face,
A pretty face, in a pretty place,
Something's not quite real,
I pass this way every day,
But today I've learned to feel

"Pretty Face" is an unusual song to open with. Besides being unique, it has layers of meaning to it most beer-drinking fans wouldn't care about. But maybe I underestimate the audience because they give him a big hand as he switches to the Beatles song "And I Love Her." It's only then I realize how much he reminds me of Paul McCartney. It may sound silly, after having lived so long, but I've never found a group I love as much as the Beatles.

Matt plays five songs on his guitar before he even speaks to the crowd. By now he has them in the palm of his hand, and they applaud everything he says, even though he just talks about what a boring day he had. Once again he drips charisma—he can do no wrong.

I'm in for another surprise when he switches to piano. He's a superb guitarist, but I can tell from the moment he touches the keys he's been playing since he was very young, and that he's classically trained. The first song he plays on the piano has no lyrics, and it needs none. I came to cast a spell on Teri and her man, and now I discover myself falling beneath his magic.

In the middle of the set, Teri leans over and asks if I like him. I shake my head and smile, but she's not offended, because she understands. To say yes would be too trite.

The hour set goes by too quickly, and even though Matt performs an encore, like the rest of the audience I find myself wanting more. At least I get to talk to him after the show, since he heads straight for our table. Teri stands and gives him a passionate hug, and I have to restrain myself from doing likewise. When he does shake my hand, he stares deep into my eyes.

"Teri's told me a lot about you," he says.

"But we just met. Does that mean she's been spying on me?"

Teri blushes. "Matt, you promised not to embarrass me."

"I put that poorly," he replies. "I just meant that Teri was impressed with you. She says you're a writer?"

"Among other things, yes. I brought three magazines I've sold stories to. I'd be flattered if you'd read them and tell me what you think. You've obviously got a way with words."

Matt shrugs. "They don't let me play my best material in a place like this. Hey, would you like a drink? The bar's open to me and my friends."

"Sure. Coke and Scotch. Tall and strong."

"Great. That's my favorite drink," Matt says, gesturing to the waitress. He puts in our order and automatically asks for a ginger ale for Teri. Matt wants to hear about the stories I've written and isn't put off when I tactfully tell him that later would be a better time to talk about them. His persistence is no surprise; I know his doubts about me.

"Very well," I say, taking out a *Playboy* magazine from the previous year. "I sold a horror story to the Big Bunny last year. It's kind of dark. It's about a man who gets marooned on an island with a werewolf and a vampire. The tale revolves around which monster he's going to decide to change into."

"They won't let him remain human?" Matt asks, as Teri sits quietly.

"The vampire would. But the werewolf won't. If he stays human, the werewolf will see the man as food."

"I'm surprised he's given a choice. They should both see him as food."

"You misunderstand my monsters. They were crossing the ocean—before their boat sank—for a reason. They're both lonely and searching for more of their kind."

"So what does your hero choose to do?" Matt asks.

"He prefers to be a vampire. But if he does, the werewolf says he'll become his enemy. So he changes his mind and says he wants to become a werewolf. But the vampire's smart—he has more wisdom. He knows they're stronger together and doesn't feel the need for them to be enemies at all."

Matt's interest jumps up a notch. "They'd be stronger together because the werewolf can go out in the sun? While he's really only a supernatural being once a month, when the moon is full? Is that what you mean?"

"That's what the werewolf assumes the vampire means. But this vampire—even though he dislikes sunlight—doesn't turn to ash when the sun's rays fall on him. He keeps this quality a secret, though. He knows he's about to have two enemies on the island instead of one. Because even though the human trusts the vampire, he's afraid of the werewolf."

"I'd be afraid of the werewolf," Teri says.

"I'd let the vampire change me," Matt says.

"Why?" I ask him, although I'm pleased at his remark.

"It's clear the vampire has more up his sleeve. I'd trust him as my master more than the werewolf."

"The human is not choosing either one as his master," Teri tells him.

"But he is," I say. "These are ancient beings, and they know only a master-disciple relationship. When he chooses to become a werewolf, the man knows he must obey his maker or else be destroyed. But that's the choice he makes. Almost immediately after his transformation is complete, the werewolf tells the man they have to hunt down the vampire and kill him. The man doesn't want to. The vampire has done nothing to them. But the werewolf says the island isn't big enough for two masters, and he threatens the man. In the end, the two seek out the spot where they believe the vampire rests during the day. They soon find it, too soon. The ease should have made the first werewolf suspicious, but he's too intent on killing the vampire. He puts a stake to the vampire's heart and goes to pound it in. But suddenly the vampire leaps up and breaks the werewolf's neck. Then the vampire is alone with the man, who's only been a werewolf for less than a day. The man begs for mercy, and the vampire says he would let him live but he can't." I pause. "Do you know why?"

"Because werewolves and vampires are natural enemies," Teri says.

Matt disagrees. "No. That's not the point of the story. At the start the vampire says there's no reason they have to be enemies. That it's foolish." He nods to himself. "But I know why the vampire has to kill the man."

Teri glances at both of us. "Why?"

I nod to Matt. "Tell us."

"The vampire's merciful but wise. He knows to show mercy twice—to someone who's already rejected it—would be foolish. Because the man didn't understand the vampire's mercy to begin with, over time it's inevitable that he'll begin to doubt it again. For this reason the vampire has to kill the man."

I silently applaud Matt and open the magazine to the last paragraph of my story. There, I let them read my vampire's reasoning. It's identical to what Matt has just said. Teri doesn't know who to be more impressed with.

"I absolutely love that story," she says.

"It was good," Matt has to admit.

"Not great?" I tease him.

"Maybe," Matt says. "There's one point I didn't like. You changed the rules of the mythology. Vampires can't function during the day. If you're going to do something like that, I think the werewolf has to know ahead of time. To be fair."

"But I was fair. At the start I said the vampire was wise, and you interpreted that to mean he had an ace up his sleeve he wasn't showing. You were right. The werewolf and the man underestimated their foe. And that's why they both died."

"I wish the vampire had let the man live," Teri complains.

"The man made himself the vampire's enemy," Matt said, staring at me with fresh appreciation, nodding. "You're right, Alisa, it's a great story."

"Thank you," I reply.

Teri smiles. "I guess it takes a genius to recognize a genius."

Matt continues to stare at me.

"That's true," he says, and I know I have won him over.

FOUR

On the ride back home, I feel the effects of the six Scotch and Cokes I drank. I have to focus on the road to stay on it. But a much more powerful cocktail plagues me: the mixture of happiness and guilt I feel in my heart.

Sitting with Matt and Teri, drinking, talking, eating, listening to Matt play his music, simply being in their company, made me feel like I was with family. What a strange and wonderful experience. It created a mysterious bubble. Even though the club was packed, it was as if the three of us spent the evening alone around a delicious fire. Most of all, it made me feel we belong together.

So says my heart, while my head shouts, *Beware!* Nothing good can come from interfering with their lives. Plus there is nowhere for the relationship to go. In the end my energy would overwhelm them, my money, my immortality. I am too much of a boss—long ago I recognized this flaw in my character—to hold back from directing their lives. Already I want to call people I know in the entertainment industry and arrange auditions for Matt. He has the talent—he just needs a break.

How easy the fantasies roll inside. How rich his life would be if he was able to work full-time in a field he loved, producing beautiful songs, selling millions of copies while making millions of dollars. Teri wouldn't have to sleep in a dorm, but could have a house of her own. She could go to Harvard for her undergraduate degree and then go on to Yale Medical School.

Yet all the glorious things I imagine I can do for them are exactly why my brain shouts for me to stop. A young man like Matt could lose his inner confidence by not struggling for success. And Teri's humble beginnings molded her into the sensitive human being I love. It is difficult for most people to realize, especially parents when it comes to their children, but suffering is often a great gift, not the curse most humans assume it is. The people I admire most have all suffered.

There is a spiritual dimension to struggle as well.

Krishna once said that few people focused on him intensely except when they were in pain. Of course, the remark was impersonal. Krishna was not referring to his form, the events of his life, or even his words when he spoke of himself. He was not a god in need of praise. His idea of worship was infinitely flexible; he saw all deities as himself. Nevertheless, he felt pain gave humans the greatest incentive to focus on the supreme.

It helps me, simply to remember Krishna.

I suddenly feel more balanced.

I come to a compromise inside. I'll see Teri and Matt for a few years, maybe ten, no more, and then I'll vanish from their lives before they realize I'm not aging. Under no circumstances will I ever let them know who I really am. Also, I'll limit how much I spoil them. They'll never enjoy their success if they don't have to fight to get it.

By the time I reach home, I feel I can make the relationship work.

I'm fifty yards from my garage when I hear a faint whistle sound.

I throw myself lengthwise across my front seat.

My back and front window explode in a shower of glass. The bullet must have been unusually powerful. The windshields are supposed to be made of bulletproof glass. If I had moved a hundredth of a second later, I would have been missing a head. And even I, Sita, who have the blood of Yakṣha and Kalika pumping through my veins, could not have survived such a wound. The person who just fired must know that. He must know exactly what it takes to kill me.

Bullets pound my car. Several hit the windshield. Many more are aimed at the trunk. The sniper is using armor-piercing rounds and is hoping to penetrate the length of the car and kill me that way. He doesn't know that, by wild chance, I bought a large amount of tools yesterday and have yet to remove them from my trunk. For the first time in my life, my laziness has saved my life.

I want my assailant to think I've been hit, so I take my foot off the gas pedal and let my Porsche roll toward the garage door. Fortunately, it veers slightly to the right, bringing me closer to the safety of the house wall. I decide not to press the button that will open the garage door. Instead, I let the front end of the car hit the wall before I leap through the passenger door and make a beeline for the side of the house. My path leaves me exposed for a mere ten yards, and since I can move fifty times faster than any human being . . . I should be safe.

Yet I'm only halfway to the corner of my house when the back of my right thigh suddenly feels like a mass of liquid fire. Somehow the sniper has shifted his aim from my car to my leg in a thousandth of a second. It might be a lucky shot on his part, but I seriously doubt it.

I have to throw myself around the corner of the house. But that doesn't stop his insane barrage. His bullets are not merely armor-piercing, they must be made of some kind of exotic metal—purified uranium perhaps. They blast through the plaster as if it were made of butter. It's only when I near the side door that the contents of my garage—another half dozen vehicles—begin to act as a shield against his weaponry. Finally, he must realize he no longer has a shot at me, because he suddenly stops firing.

I open the side door and limp inside the garage.

I collapse on the floor. Blood pools around me in the dark. His bullet has not merely hit my leg, it's torn away a chunk of flesh twice the size of my fist. By blind luck, he missed the major artery that runs down my leg. Yet he's pulverized my sciatic nerve, and even I, who can heal instantly from almost any wound, will need time to rest and replace a major nerve. Until then I'm crippled, and he's still out there, probably closing in on my position.

I force myself to quiet my breath so I can hear what he's doing. He's in the woods—I can tell that much right away. But I'm surprised to hear him stay in the trees and not press his advantage. Then I realize just how smart he is. He doesn't know for sure I'm wounded, and even if he can see my blood, he can't know the extent of my injury. No doubt he's afraid to expose himself by crossing the open field that lies between my house and the trees.

I stop breathing altogether and am able to ascertain his exact position. He's southwest of my house, two hundred yards into the woods. Again, I have to congratulate him on his caution. Even if I had a sniper rifle in hand, he would be a difficult target. It would be hard to get a clear shot through so many trees. But because he's the one in the woods, and has no doubt cut away clear angles to my house, the reverse is not true. At present, he has the advantage.

I can't hear anyone else in the forest. Good.

I can tolerate a tremendous amount of pain, but my ruined leg is pushing me to my limit. The tissue struggles to knit back together, but there's simply too much missing. Ideally, I need a series of transfusions to speed up the healing process. But I doubt my assailant will let me take a blood break.

I think of my upstairs vault. My only hope is to get to my weapons. It's agony to stand, but I force myself to my feet. My world spins. There's a cabinet nearby, filled with bathroom supplies, and I grab a roll of toilet paper and hastily wrap it around my wound. Blood immediately soaks through the paper, and I reach for another roll. The bleeding finally begins to slow. It's not much, but it's something.

I limp into the house, trying to move as silently as possible, and take a flight of stairs to my bedroom. I'm surprised he continues his cease-fire. I keep expecting his exotic bullets to slam my west walls. Perhaps he wants me to feel hopeless before he spends any more ammunition.

My hope is crushed when I see my chest of drawers lying facedown on the floor and my vault door sitting wide open. The vault's been raided. He left the ten million in cash but removed every single gun.

That vault was supposed to be impenetrable.

And I didn't even sense he had been in my house.

Who the hell is this guy?

A mass of bullets suddenly strikes my west bedroom wall.

I'm fortunate I hear them coming—otherwise, I would have been cut in half. My foe's switched weapons. It seems his armor-piercing sniper rifle's no longer good enough for him.

He's turned a Gatling gun on me.

The invention of the Gatling gun goes back in time to the battle of Gettysburg and the Civil War, which surprises most people who see it demonstrated on the deck of an aircraft carrier or a navy destroyer. The weapon's so impressive—most people assume it must be a modern creation. The first time I saw it in action, I wanted to buy one. I love dangerous new toys. But I never was able to find a seller.

Basically it's made up of a long barrel that's continually fueled by a dozen or more revolving ammunition chambers. It can easily fire a thousand bullets a minute. The navy uses them to create a wall of flying lead that can detonate any missile launched at their ships. A modern Gatling gun is one of the most deadly weapons on the planet.

Now, to my great misfortune, I have the same wall of lead aimed at my comfy two-story house in the normally peaceful Missouri countryside. As I rush to my stairs, I see a three-foot circular hole rip open behind my bed. It takes an instant to transform my mattress into a dizzy cloud of down feathers. The bullets soar the length of my room and ricochet inside my empty vault. That's where my assailant assumed I was standing.

I have one chance. I have a second, smaller vault hidden beneath the carpet in my living room. It doesn't contain as many exotic weapons as my upstairs compartment, but it's lined with lead, and it's possible my assailant missed it when he was inside my house.

Dragging my wounded leg downstairs, I tear away the carpet with my nails and hastily spin the dial on the floor vault. I've lost so much blood, I have to struggle to remember the combination. But when I finally pull open the door, I feel a wave of relief.

A break at last! My foe has overlooked this vault. I take out a couple of .45 semiautomatic Glocks and stuff them in my belt, along with three throwing knives. But my eyes feast on the one Barringer sniper rifle I have left. It has a powerful sighting scope that's equipped with a laser, which works well with my superhuman vision.

I grab as many clips of armor-piercing bullets as I can carry, a dozen. Since each clip holds twenty rounds, I figure I'll have 240 chances to kill my foe.

He must suspect I'm no longer upstairs, because he suddenly shifts his Gatling gun to the living room. Once more, I'm fortunate my ears are able to anticipate his change in attack. Before the bullets even strike the living room, I shove a sofa and china cabinet against the wall to give me a brief umbrella of cover. Then I retreat back to the garage, essentially putting the house between me and him.

I have to go on the offensive. I'm pretty sure he knows I'm a vampire, because chances are he's a vampire.

It's the only thing that makes sense. No human being should have been able to hit me when I ran from the car to the house. Sure, it could have been a lucky shot, but what are the odds of that? Just the fact he was able to drag a Gatling gun into the woods indicates how strong he is. The weapon weighs a ton. No, he has to be a vampire.

But who made him? Yaksha would never have done so. He would never have disobeyed his vow to Krishna. And as for Eddie Fender—who for a time had access to Yaksha's blood—I destroyed him years ago. The only source of vampire blood that seems remotely possible is the U.S. Army.

Joel Drake—an FBI agent I'd changed into a vampire—was the unwilling guest at a secret government facility outside Las Vegas. It's true I wiped the damn place off the face of the earth with an H-bomb, but it was always possible the general in charge of the camp had shipped vials of Joel's blood to the Pentagon before I exploded the bomb. Certainly the government connection would help explain where the vampire in the woods had obtained a Gatling gun.

Still, I have my doubts. I even have doubts about climbing on the roof, which would give me my best shot at the guy. My reasoning is simple—he will expect me to go up on the roof. If I fail to take him down with a single shot, he can casually spray the roof with his Gatling and splatter my guts over the grass, all the way down to the lake.

No, I must outwit him. I have to do the unexpected. I'm a

sitting duck as long as I'm stuck in the house and he has plenty of ammunition for his supergun. I have to get to the woods, that will even the odds. I assume I know the area better than he does—after all, I live here. If I can reach the trees, I might even swing the odds in my favor.

True, my leg's healing at a phenomenal rate, but I'm still crippled. I'll need at least a minute to reach the trees, and he'll spot me long before that. Unless . . . what? Can I create a diversion of some type?

A minute of frantic concentration gives me a plan.

Stage one—I have to transform my house into a big firecracker. I have materials that can do the trick: natural gas, a propane tank, the gasoline in the cars parked in my garage. But the key, the trigger, will be the propane tank. Unfortunately, I know enough about the gas to know it won't explode—like such tanks always do on TV—simply by hitting it with a bullet. My trigger will need a trigger.

The powder in my sniper bullets is not ordinary gunpowder. It's been soaked in nitroglycerin—that's what causes the bullets to fire at such a high velocity. Working quietly, I unload two clips of bullets and spread them on an oil rag on the concrete floor. My hands are strong—I'm able to pull the caps off forty rounds without effort. Once I have a pile of powder available, I tie it into a ball and soak it with oil so it will stick to the side of the propane tank that stands outside my garage.

Next, I creep into the kitchen and turn on all the gas

burners in my stove and oven. But I kill the pilot light, so the smell of gas begins to fill the room. At the same time I listen to what my assailant is up to. It sounds like he's using the pause to reload his guns. He probably figures that I'm dead meat—that it's only a question of time.

Back in the garage, I siphon off the bulk of the gasoline in the tanks of my cars into empty Sparkletts water bottles. The bottles hold five gallons each—I have only four. But I have over a hundred gallons of gasoline at my disposal, so I have to make several trips, back and forth, to spread the gasoline all over my house.

However, I leave each car with at least a gallon in its tank.

The cars are the trickiest part of my plan. When the time is right, I plan to launch them away from my house at different speeds and directions. They are a major part of the diversion I'm trying to create. I use rope and a complex combination of knots to rig the steering wheels to the gas pedals. I'm not worried my Porsche will block the way of the escaping cars. Just before I jumped from it, the Porsche veered to the right of the garage door.

Ah, the garage door—it is almost time to open it. Unfortunately, I have to launch the cars as soon as I open it or else he'll just blow the vehicles up inside the garage. For that reason, I start all six of the cars before I open the door. It's a delicate balancing act. The cars are in gear and ready to go. It's only the closed door and the cramped space that keep them in place.

Once more, I stop and listen to what my opponent is up to. He appears to be doing likewise. He must have supernatural hearing to know I've started the cars, more proof that he is a vampire.

I stuff what clips I have left into my coat pockets and swing my sniper rifle over my shoulder. At last, I'm ready to make my dash for the woods. I have no idea what my odds are, but I like the many layers in my plan—the levels of deception. If I do die tonight, after walking the earth for almost two million nights, then no one can accuse me of not putting up a good fight.

I push a button and the main garage door opens. The cars take off like hungry rabbits, all in different directions. I've rigged each steering wheel separately. Some are pulled to the right, others to the left, some to the far right, and so on. Watching them race away, I'd swear they were driven by six different drunks.

I run out the side door, near where my blood covers the floor. My assailant immediately begins to fire on the cars, using his Gatling gun. He can't see me leaving the house, not yet, because I'm still in its shadow. The steep outline of the roof protects me, and I know I'll remain invisible until I reach a small rise three hundred yards away. Yet that's only a third of the way to the trees, and I know he won't take long to slay all six cars and realize they were nothing but a ruse.

Yet, for the moment, he seems quite happy to blast away at my vintage models. A glance over my shoulder shows me the mess he's making of my Mercedes. The black sedan finally explodes when he hits the gasoline tank, and I watch as he shifts his aim onto my Ford Expedition that I use to haul supplies in. For now, he is pretty confident I'm in one of the vehicles.

My limp is clumsy, but I can still run twice as fast as most people. I'm fortunate to reach the low rise on the ground just as his supergun falls silent. Another five feet and the house will no longer shield me. Plus he has finished with the cars. The six burn like smoldering tanks on a lost battlefield. He has not been fooled. I can feel him scanning the area. He knows I'm not dead.

I drop to one knee and take aim at the propane tank, specifically at the wad of gunpowder I have attached to it. By now, a choking cloud of natural gas has filled the house and mingled with the fumes of the hundreds of gallons of gasoline I have soaked into the floor and the furniture. My firecracker is ready—I have only to light the fuse.

I put my laser scope on the oily ball and fire.

One shot, that's all I need.

The house explodes in a red and orange mushroom cloud.

I turn and run toward the trees.

The size and glare of the exploding cloud gives me further cover. But my foe has already guessed what I'm using it for, and he rakes his bullets through the smoke and fire. He can't see me, not yet, but he can guess where I am and where I'm going. For that reason I don't make a beeline for the woods. Instead,

I veer slightly to the left, taking a path that's longer but hopefully safer. Almost instantly I have confirmation of the wisdom of my course. Off to my right, the ground erupts as the Gatling gun seeks my flesh.

I feel the anger in my foe. Feel it in the way he fires.

He knows he has been tricked, and he does not like it.

I almost make it. Once more, he may have gotten off another lucky shot, or else my bright mushroom cloud burned too fast and left me exposed. I suppose it doesn't really matter how he's able to hit me. All I know is that when the bullet slices through my right side, through my liver, I'm in serious trouble.

Like normal people, the worst place for me to get shot is in the head or the heart. I'm not sure if I could withstand such a blow. A bullet through the liver is almost as bad. The reason is the large number of arteries and veins in the organ. The blow to my thigh has caused me to lose a lot of blood. But this hole in my liver has turned me into a red geyser. I'm just entering the woods when I'm hit. It's all I can do to run another twenty yards and collapse behind a thick tree.

The pain is worse than before. I feel burning, like the leg wound, but also an immense amount of pressure. I struggle to remain conscious. I know I must slow the bleeding, but it's hard to move. Eventually, I manage to wiggle out of my leather coat and tie the arms over the hole. But the wound is on both sides, the front and the back, and I know his bullet has torn at least one major artery. It makes me sick to think of how scrambled my insides are, and I realize I cannot count on my body's ability to heal itself.

Pulling my coat slightly down, I reach up and stick my fingers directly into the hole. I want to be sick, but I fear if I vomit, I'll throw up a piece of something that I need. My fingers are not steady; they shake as they probe for the lacerated artery.

But eventually I find it and pinch it shut on both ends with the tips of my nails. Almost immediately the massive blood loss stops. I keep telling myself, if I can just stay alive a few minutes, I might be able to heal enough to where the shredded ends of the artery mend.

I'm doing surgery on myself. With my fingernails as scalpels.

God, how I wish I could black out and wake up in a hospital.

Sitting against the red-smeared tree, I concentrate on three things. First, I have to keep my fingers steady. I literally will them to stop trembling. Next, I focus on my breath. Long, deep breaths are best. They slow down my metabolism. Finally, I listen for my opponent. He probably knows he hit me; he may even be able to follow the trail of my blood to this very tree. Yet I'm deep enough in the woods to prevent him from using the Gatling on me. He would just waste his ammunition tearing apart trees.

I'm not surprised to hear him come to the same conclusion. I know because I hear him begin to hike toward me.

He's cautious, this guy. He doesn't consider hiking across the open field to reach me. He knows if I'm still alive I can shoot him dead from a mile away. No, he stays in the trees, in the shadows, steadily circling around the field and my burning house.

My place continues to blaze like an insane asylum's bonfire. The townsfolk probably didn't hear his guns, but I'm sure somebody must have heard the house explode. We'll probably have company soon in the form of police and firemen. I don't know if I should root for them to hurry. Chances are my foe will kill them the second they arrive.

He's halfway to my position when I feel the two ends of my torn artery finally fuse together. It may sound gross, but it's a delightful feeling, because it tells me I will live. At least until he shoots me again. I'm grateful to be able to take my fingers out of my liver and tighten my coat sleeves back over the wound.

With my liver healing, I'm able to sit up and listen more closely to his movements. I note how often he stops to listen, how unsure his step is. I still believe he's a vampire, but I know already my hearing is superior to his. I can hear his breathing, his heartbeat. Yet at best I think he has only a vague idea of my location.

My big ears don't make me cocky. I'm still seriously injured, and if we end up fighting hand to hand, he'll probably win. The fact he's coming after me means he's confident he can finish me off. Once more, I feel my best hope is to do the unexpected.

I decide to climb a tree.

With my side leaking and my thigh burning, it's the last

thing I want to do. Also, once I'm up in a tree, if I fail to kill him or seriously injure him with my first shot, then I'm doomed. But my gut tells me to take the chance, and I have learned to trust my gut, even when it has a hole in it.

Quietly, oh so gently, I slip off my boots and use my sniper rifle to prop me up. I can't climb the tree I'm leaning against—it stinks of blood. But I can't go far, I'm weak and nauseous. Besides, the more I move, the greater the chance he'll hear me. Yet I deliberately head deeper into the woods, which will directly place me in the path he's following. I soon find an old fern that looks promising.

I wrap the strap of my rifle around the barrel and bite down hard on it so there's no chance the weapon will sway and bump a branch as I climb. Holding the gun this way keeps my arms free. I'm lucky my hands and feet are unharmed. I'm able to scamper up the tree fairly quickly. It's the tallest tree in the area, and I don't stop until I'm two hundred feet above the floor of the forest. I snuggle inside a handful of tightly placed branches, hoping the raw wood will offer some protection. Because I assume he has infrared equipment, I use the damp leaves to smear my bare skin with as much liquid as possible, trying to reduce my heat signature. I concentrate on my head; it gives off the most heat.

My view of the woods is vast, but I cannot see my opponent, not even using the infrared feature on the rifle's scope. Still, I can hear him approach, and I notice he's veered in the direction of my previous position. My blood, I think, he must smell my blood.

That's good—he's heading toward a spot I have a clear shot at.

The waiting seconds are hard on me, and I wonder if I've grown soft in my old age. I keep flashing back to Teri and Matt. If I die tonight, I'll never have a chance to get to know them, and they'll never know what became of me. I've no doubt my foe is anxious to collect my body and my blood.

He's two hundred yards from my previous position when he stops. I note how he slows his breath. He's probably trying to scan the woods with a similar infrared scope. I wish I had more water to soak in. I wouldn't be surprised if he's stopped along the way and drenched his entire body in a stream. He's still not showing up in my scope.

But I can still hear him. I know when he starts to move again. To my surprise, he's now heading directly toward me! Chances are he has better heat-sensing equipment than I do. He must have caught a glimpse of me in the tree. Very slowly, I turn in his direction, trying to catch even a flicker of him in my scope. All I need is one shot. . . .

I catch a glimpse of his foot, but it quickly disappears behind a tree before I can take aim. The move reassures me. He's moving like a hunter who knows approximately where his prey is, but I doubt he's seen me in the tree. I have chosen my spot well. The damp compactness of the branches is also dispersing my heat signature.

I make a bold decision. I turn off the laser sighting on my scope. I can aim better with it on—like most people—but I fear he'll spot the laser even at its lowest setting.

For a long time, he stands behind a tree, then he suddenly leaps behind another. He moves too fast for me to get off a shot. I continue to follow his movements more with my ears than my eyes. I assume he knows in which direction I wait, because he's careful not to let a vulnerable limb stick out. Still, there's a huge difference between knowing my general direction and knowing my actual position.

He continues to head straight toward me!

The gap between us shrinks. A hundred yards, fifty yards, twenty yards . . . He stops thirty feet from my tree, and it's obvious he still doesn't know where I'm hiding. But I can't see him! I can't get off a shot!

However, his close proximity makes me rethink my strategy. From the start I've only been interested in killing him and surviving. Unfortunately, his death will tell me nothing about who sent him. But if I could disarm him, take him alive, question him, I might learn a great deal. I need information; I especially need to know who he's working for.

My knives. I love knives, and I applaud my wisdom in removing three sharp ones from my vault and tucking them in my belt. If my foe truly does not know where I am and he steps from behind the tree where he's standing, then I'll have a clear shot at him. I can easily take his head off with my rifle. But to use my knives, to have full use of my arms, I'll have to stand.

He's so damn close he'll probably hear me.

The decision weighs on me. Should I just kill him and survive the night, or should I risk dying but maybe find out how to survive the next year? It's really a question of how quietly I can move and how sensitive his ears are.

I decide to risk it. Slowly standing, I jam my rifle against a nearby branch. I'll reach for it the instant I release the knives. Of course, if the knives don't stop him, the rifle will do me no good. There's no question his reflexes are as good as mine. He'll shoot me before I can reach for the gun.

I hold a knife in either palm. Right-handed, left-handed—both hands work the same for me. My goal is to cut the nerves between his shoulders and his arms. If I'm successful, he'll lose control of his hands and be helpless. The armor-piercing bullets in my rifle are too powerful for such delicate surgery. A hit with one round would blow off his arm. The knives it must be.

Quietly, I suck in a breath and raise my arms over my head.

I stand still as a statue.

A minute later he tries slipping between two trees.

I let the knives fly. He hears me move, there's no question, and I'm pretty sure he hears the knives approaching. But he hesitates a fraction of a second, and that's all it takes. The knives catch him on the front side of both shoulders. The blades are long, eight inches each, and I've thrown them with such force that they sink all the way through his body and poke out his back.

But he's a fighter, this guy, I have to admire that. Even with the knives cutting off his nerves, he tries to twist his body so his rifle's pointed at me. He almost succeeds, but before he can fire, I have my rifle in hand and blow out his left knee. The bullet almost amputates his leg. The combination of wounds, to his upper and lower body, sucks the life out of him, and he drops his rifle and falls to the ground. Still, he reaches for a weapon in his belt.

"Stop!" I shout from the tree. "Move and I'll take off your head!"

He freezes. Quickly I climb down, but I'm not in such a hurry that I relax my aim. He's clearly an experienced killer; he's still dangerous. Once on the ground, I circle cautiously, my rifle held ready, keeping a distance of ten yards.

He's tall, extremely well muscled, with bronze skin and dark hair cut close to the scalp. His thick black eyebrows and eyelashes remind me of someone from another time and place. He's dressed completely in black. He sits on the ground with a hand pressed over his wounded leg. He'll have to possess my rejuvenating powers not to lose his leg.

His expression's difficult to read. He breathes heavily; he must be in terrible pain. Never mind his leg, the knives piercing the nerve bundles in his shoulders must be agonizing. Yet he doesn't moan or whimper. He shows almost no emotion. He's spent half the night trying to kill me, but to my surprise I feel a wave of sympathy for him. I admire a worthy adversary, and he's one of the finest I've come up against.

"Who are you?" I ask.

He doesn't answer. I notice an unusual watch on his left wrist. At first I assumed he was trying to stop the flow of blood with his left hand, but now I realize he's trying to keep the dial of the watch pointed at me. Could it be a weapon?

"Raise your arms, now!" I snap.

He tries to follow my order, but his arms flap uselessly. Still, his odd watch is no longer pointed at me. I move closer and sniff the air. The shock I experience right then forces me to take a step back.

He's not a vampire!

How do I know? He doesn't smell like one. All vampires—even the disgusting Eddie Fender—have a faint smell of our creator, Yaksha. This man smells more human than anything else.

There's another reason I know he's not a vampire. This close, I can hear the subtleties of his heartbeat, things I could not hear at a distance. A vampire's pulse, even under stress, is extremely regular. One might say the sine wave never wavers. This man's heartbeat is slightly erratic. True, his heart pounds with a strength much greater than an ordinary mortal's, but the rhythm is more akin to a human's. The same with his breathing. It's not as smooth as it should be.

"What are you?" I ask.

He glares at me. "Kill me."

"Are you so anxious to die?"

"Kill me."

"No. I want to talk. You owe me that."

He sneers. "I owe you nothing."

I cannot place his accent. His English is perfect—the majority of people would assume he's from England. But I hear other lands in his words.

"Why the hostility?" I ask. "You attacked me."

"With good reason."

"What have I ever done to you?"

"I know what you are."

"Maybe you do. But whoever you are, I mean you no harm."

"Liar!"

"I speak the truth. You can hear the truth, can't you, when it's spoken? I honestly don't know who you are."

My remark surprises him. He chews on it a moment.

"Can I rest my arms?" he asks.

"Yes. But keep your watch pointed away from me."

His arms drop to his lap. "Can you pull out the knives?"

"I will if you answer a few of my questions. Agreed?"

He shakes his head. "It's not allowed."

"Allowed? You say that like you report to someone. Who?"

He shakes his head. He won't answer.

I move closer. "Look, I'm serious when I say I mean you no harm. But someone sent you here to kill me, and frankly, that pisses me off. If you don't start cooperating, I'm going to do things to you that will hurt a lot worse than that leg and those knives."

He lowers his gaze, his eyes focus on his watch.

"I's toad bein, jar?" he whispers softly.

I recognize the language, but only because I spent time in ancient Egypt. That was back in the days of Suzama. I doubt my attacker and whoever he's talking to know that. My foe just said, "It is her, is it not?"

A voice replies via the watch, in the same forgotten dialect. "There's no doubt. You've done well."

"Can I end it?"

"Yes. Now return to the Eternal Goddess."

"All glory to the Eternal Goddess."

The words are no sooner out of my assailant's mouth than he twists his jaw to the right side and bites down. I hear a tooth inside his mouth—it can't be a normal tooth—explode. Instantly I catch a whiff of something acidic in the air and leap back. A glowing cloud of red gas expands around his body as he exhales. The fumes are extremely corrosive. Within seconds his face melts away, his clothes catch fire, and his body begins to burn with a ferocity I've never seen before.

The blaze is as short as it is fierce. A minute later it's gone, and so is the man. All that's left is a pile of ash. Whatever he used to kill himself belongs to a technology more advanced than anything I've encountered.

Yet somehow he's connected to ancient Egypt. The clue gives me small comfort. I still don't know who or what these creatures are and why they want me dead.

FIVE

Four days later I wait for Teri and Matt to visit my new home. For obvious reasons, I rented it in a hurry. The place is closer to town and lacks the security system my original home had. But since the system proved useless in the last attack, I don't fret over its absence.

I have learned little about my assailant since he burned to death. I was able to retrace his steps and find his Gatling gun, and from there I was able to follow his path back to a van parked at the end of a road that lay about three miles from my home. A search of the van turned up nothing: no ID, fake or otherwise, no money, no hotel keys, no maps, not even a round of ammunition. Yet it's clear the van was a rental, and I've passed its license plates on to the same FBI agents and detectives that are working on the IIC mystery.

I feel the two mysteries must be connected. They entered

my life at the same time—the same day—a remarkable coincidence, and I have never believed in coincidences. So far everything Lisa Fetch and Jeff Stephens told me about IIC has proven to be accurate. Although my sources have been unable to discover how the firm excels in the market, they have uncovered proof linking it to other investment companies. It appears IIC and its partners are quietly accumulating a trillion dollars without anyone knowing about it.

Lisa had spoken of the disappearance of an old boyfriend, Randy Clifford, who vanished into thin air while hacking into IIC's computer system. My friends in the FBI have been able to determine that a certain "Marko" visited him the night he vanished. Marko is known to the FBI to be a highly paid hit man with Mob connections. My people tell me his price is high for the best of assassins—a million even. It seems he can charge so much because he has the ability to make his "marks" disappear without a trace. I can only assume that's how he earned his nickname.

I plan to visit Marko soon.

After all the noise on my property, I had to act fast to keep the local police and a stream of higher authorities from investigating too closely. I managed to keep my privacy the old-fashioned way—by paying exorbitant bribes through my East Coast attorneys. The money has worked so well, not a single person in town has asked why my house just happened to explode.

But even people who have been paid to remain silent inevitably talk, and I fear such talk will get back to Teri and Matt.

But since I never gave them my address in the countryside, they have no reason to connect me to the rumors going around town about the "house that got hit by the meteor."

I sort of like that rumor.

I wonder who started it?

My new home is a single story, a spacious rectangle, also located in the woods but hidden in the trees, with no view of a lake. It already possesses a lead-lined vault, which I have stocked with enough weapons to repel a small army. By coincidence, I now own a Gatling gun that is identical to the one that destroyed my original home.

Sigh. That was one toy I could not bear to let the police take.

Teri and Matt arrive on time, at three, on a Tuesday afternoon. We have a late lunch of swordfish, which I grill out back beside my Olympic-size pool. Now that I no longer have a lake to leap into, I enjoy the pool. Swimming is my favorite exercise. Naturally, my liver and leg wounds have totally healed. I don't feel so much as a twinge when I do my hundred laps each morning.

I have told Teri and Matt to bring their bathing suits, and it turns out Matt is every bit the athlete his girlfriend is. He could never compete against me, of course, but I note how hard he has to swim to get out of breath. He is competitive when it comes to Teri. The two race before we eat, and he makes a point of winning each lap. Teri sees it all as good fun, but I notice he doesn't. The guy does not like to lose.

I soon find that to be true when it comes to arguments.

Teri's eyes often stray to his well-muscled body, and I must say I find myself looking at him longer, and more often, than I should. There are no two ways about it—the guy is hot.

I'm careful not to let Teri catch me looking.

After we swim and eat, Teri tries talking Matt into singing a new song he's working on. He refuses; he won't play without an instrument. But when I just so happen to find a guitar in my closet, he has no excuse. He tunes the instrument with his feet in the water but then stops.

"I didn't know you played," he says to me.

"I dabble."

"This guitar is tuned perfectly. You have a good ear."

"Thanks. What's your song called?"

"'Mystery Mind.' But it's rough."

"It's fantastic," Teri mutters.

Matt strums a few chords and begins to sing:

You've moved through time,
And left behind the masses in your wake,
You loved me then, you love me now,
You're always there to take

A diamond is an easy find, compared to what
I'm calling mine,
The ages leave the smallest clue,
To roads untouched, but never true

Where to find this mystery mind? The Gods
confide in you.
I need your answer. Call my name. Abandon
guilt, Abandon shame,
And when you take my outstretched hand, by simple
nod or love's command,
I'll wrap you in eternal flame, our hearts to fuse,
one and the same

I tire of my shattered pace,
I reach to feel love's one true face,
I fear I failed to take heed of your first and final signs

Walk with me, at least pretend,
To hell's back door around the bend,
We'll crush the darkness as it sleeps,
And leave the waking world to mend

Where to find this mystery mind? The Gods
confide in you.
I need your answer. Call my name. Abandon
guilt, Abandon shame,
And when you take my outstretched hand, by simple
nod or love's command,
I'll wrap you in eternal flame, our hearts to fuse,
one and the same

When Matt finishes, Teri applauds and gives him a kiss. I see how much he looks to her for approval. But I can only gaze in silent amazement. I feel the song is about me, for I often feel trapped in an endless mystery of time, in Krishna's own mind.

"Awesome," Teri exclaims. "I love how you changed around the second chorus. You didn't just repeat the first round."

"I changed it while driving here," he says, before turning to me. "What did you think? You can tell me the truth. I know it's rough."

"I think it should be played on every radio in the country."

"Me too," Teri adds.

"Get off it," Matt snorts.

"I'm serious." I suddenly stand. "I know people in New York and LA. At three of the majors: Atlantic, Sony, Geffen. I bet I could get you an audition with that one song."

I make the offer knowing I've already vowed not to help them with their lives. So much for vows—I'm much too impulsive to take them seriously.

"Why should they audition me?" he asks.

"Because I know them," I reply.

"How?" he persists.

"I've got money. Money opens every door. Look, I'm not trying to trample on your male pride. I can only help you get your foot in the door. Your song still has to knock them over."

"Would he have to record it first?" Teri asks.

"It wouldn't hurt to walk in with a demo of what we just

heard. But it's not necessary. You've got charisma, Matt. They'll see it. If I was you, I'd let me make a few calls and then get on a plane tomorrow."

He shakes his head. "The song is brand-new. I can't go into a major label with it. It needs work."

"You have a dozen songs you've worked to death," Teri says. "Take Alisa up on her offer."

"I'll think about it."

Teri gets impatient. "What's there to think about?"

He gives her a look. "Lots of things."

I hold up a hand to stop the argument from happening. "Just tell me when you feel ready," I say.

Matt continues to fiddle with the guitar. I can tell he loves it. Later, I'll have to figure out a way to give it to him. While he strums the instrument, I ask Teri to take a walk with me. The official reason is to explain her job responsibilities, but I can feel she wants to talk. We hike through the nearby woods. They feel so peaceful, yet I keep alert, listening for the slightest sound that would tell me we are being followed.

"I don't know why he cut you off like that," Teri says after we've hiked maybe a quarter of a mile. "I hope you didn't feel he was being rude."

"Not at all. He wants to make it on his own. I respect that."

"Matt's a hard one to do favors for. He's super independent."

"So are you."

She blushes. "What makes you say that?"

"No one's helping you pay for college."

"I was lucky to get my track scholarship."

"It wasn't luck that allowed you to win so many races in high school. You worked your butt off."

"I did, but . . ." She doesn't finish.

"What?"

"Running comes easier to me than most people. It must be my genes. Sometimes I wonder if I could run in the Olympics."

"The metric mile? The fifteen hundred meters?"

"Yeah."

"Tell me about it."

Teri stops walking as she struggles to find the words. "I train mostly on the track because the coach expects it. And I'm good at running intervals. I know it's a quick way to build strength. But I feel at home when I go out for longer runs, alone, either late at night or early in the morning. Sometimes I slip into a rhythm—it's hard to describe—where I don't get tired no matter how fast I run. At times like that I feel I could break the world record in the mile."

I understand perfectly. But then, I'm not human.

"So you want a gold medal and you want to graduate medical school before you're twenty-five. Anything else?"

Teri laughs. "You're making me sound like Ms. Super Achiever."

"There's nothing wrong with fulfilling your desires."

"What if there are ones you feel you'll never fulfill?"

"You're talking about Matt again."

"No. Yes! How did you know?"

"You can control what you do. But you know you can't control him." I pause. "By the way, that was brave of you to encourage him to audition."

"He has so much talent. You're right, I can't hold him back."

"But it scares you just the same."

"Sure. You saw the way the girls all cheered when he came on last Friday. If he gets his foot in the door, he'll hit it big, and then he's going to get hit on by every chick between New York and LA."

"Do you want my advice?"

"If you have some to give me, sure."

"Actually, I usually hate giving advice. People never listen to it. In the end, they just do what they want to do."

"I'm listening . . . Alisa."

"Trust."

"Trust in what?"

"Just trust."

"You mean, trust in his love for me?"

"That's part of it. Trust in the big picture as well."

"What's the big picture?"

"No one knows. That's why you have to trust in it."

Teri considers for a moment, then smiles. "How did you get so wise?"

"Oh, I've been around."

We walk for another hour without talking. I enjoy the

exercise, but I'm also looking for places to set up monitoring devices to increase my security.

Back at my house, we find Matt reading a short story that I wrote for a sci-fi anthology. It's a personal favorite; I left it out on purpose. It follows the observations of K-8-P—or Kap—the name my hero goes by while he's on earth. Matt reads it aloud to catch Teri up.

Although from another planet, Kap is a low-level grunt who, along with his partner, has been assigned the job of destroying the earth. Kap's own world is only a few centuries further along than earth, but it belongs to an advanced galactic civilization that has been monitoring earth's TV and radio programs for decades, and that has determined we are far too hostile a race to be allowed to expand out into the galaxy.

My story begins with Kap and his partner spraying a ten-mile-long asteroid with a special type of black paint that reduces its albedo ratio—its ability to reflect light—to near zero. Then the two outfit the asteroid with rockets that fire for a month and slowly alter its orbit so that it will intercept the earth in three years. Because it's so dark, earth astronomers won't notice the asteroid until it's days away from destroying our home.

The job done, the two enter a deep freeze that will keep them asleep for a decade while they cruise home. Only Kap sets his hibernaculum so that he awakens as soon as his partner is asleep. He turns their ship around and heads for the earth. He is curious to meet humanity. This is the tenth planet he's destroyed, and he wonders what criteria the top dogs in the galaxy are using to decide who lives and who dies.

The story takes off when Kap takes a shuttle down to earth and is fired upon by America's missile shield. His shuttle is damaged, and he crash-lands a couple of miles offshore, near San Francisco. The shuttle is equipped with a device that instantly gives Kap amnesia, lest he accidentally or intentionally warn any backward planet that it is about to be destroyed.

Kap survives the crash and is rescued by a fishing ship.

The rest of the story deals with Kap's innocent observation of human life. In one sense he sees everything with a child's eyes. But in another sense his observations are profound because they're completely unbiased.

I called the tale "Eyes of the Stars," and it won both a Nebula and a Hugo award for best sci-fi short story of the year. Like most of my work, I published it under the name Lara Adams.

"Why do you use a pen name when you write?" Matt asks as he finishes the story.

"Don't be so nosy. Her reasons might be private," Teri scolds.

"I do it to maintain my privacy," I say.

"I don't believe that," Matt teases. "Most people, when they're nobodies, talk about how they wouldn't mind the money fame brings, but they'd hate to have people chasing after them taking their picture. But I think everybody wants fame."

"Not me," I say flatly.

"Come on," Matt insists. "Wouldn't you love to have your

picture taken by paparazzi and splashed all over the magazine covers?"

"Paparazzi are vultures. They're the last people I'd want near me."

"I couldn't agree with you more," Teri says. "Our society suffers from celebrity addiction. So much reality TV gives people the impression that the only way to be happy is to be famous."

"Hear, hear," I mutter.

"Would Kap agree with you guys?" Matt asks.

"You know he would. You just read my story."

Matt disagrees. "Kap's observations of mankind are confined to small things. How people push ahead of each other in checkout lines. He never reads a paper while on earth. He doesn't study our politics. He doesn't go after the bigger picture of why we're a danger to the rest of the galaxy."

"Remember, for the bulk of the story, Kap's lost his memory—"

"I don't know why you set it up that way," Matt interrupts, a bad habit of his. "Kap's observations would be more interesting if he could mentally compare his home world to earth."

"Kap's observations are worthwhile because they're innocent," I say. "He focuses on the small things we do because they're the most telling. When he sees a herd of cattle being rounded up for slaughter, it's his gut reaction that makes the story ring true."

"The truth is most of us would be vegetarians if we saw how animals are killed," Teri says. "Matt, remember that chicken farm we drove past in Kansas? After they gave us a tour, that was it for me. I haven't been able to eat chicken since."

"You're a hypocrite, darling. You still eat steak."

"Once a month. To keep from getting anemic."

Matt gestures to the swordfish. "You ate meat right now."

"Fish is not meat," Teri says.

"Tell that to the fish just before you chop off his head."

"Krishna used to say that fish were swimming vegetables," I say.

"By Krishna do you mean the Hindu god?" Teri asks.

"Yes."

"I didn't know you were into Eastern thought," Teri says.

"I like to study what every tradition has to offer."

"According to Kap, humanity has nothing to offer," Matt says.

"Not true. In the end he tries to save the earth," I reply.

"So what? Ninety percent of his observations of us are negative. The one place where you do deal with a larger issue is when it comes to money. You portray everyone who's rich as evil."

"Kap never uses the word 'evil.' He just notes that the distribution of wealth on earth is insane. Kap never gets angry at the rich. But he can't help feeling their behavior is illogical, because such unfairness cannot be sustained forever. At one point equality is either achieved or a culture falls apart due to internal pressures. History has taught us that much."

Matt laughs. "Bullshit. America's the most powerful nation

on earth. But ninety percent of the wealth of this country is held by one percent of the people, and America shows no signs of faltering. It grows stronger with each passing decade."

"China grows stronger with each passing decade," I say. "They're the ones who pay the interest on our national debt."

"I knew, I knew it," Matt jeers. "You're a left-wing liberal."

"You could not be more wrong." I hold up both my hands and flex them. "I believe only the strong survive."

"Then you're a Republican, like me," Matt says.

"I despise Republicans," Teri mutters.

"I'm neither," I reply.

Matt misunderstands me, of course. Having lived so long, I can't tell the difference between the two political parties. They both sound like broken records that started skipping after the founding fathers died. Now there were some real men!

Matt continues—he still wants to win the argument.

"At the end of the story, when Kap's partner returns to find Kap and restores his memory, he makes an impassioned argument why violent races cannot be allowed to spread across the stars. I assume that was you talking. It sounded like it came from your heart."

"It's true, I did speak through his partner."

Teri is hurt by my remark. "Do you really feel there's no hope for humanity?"

I find it hard to lie to those I care about.

"I feel the road we're on leads nowhere. Yet part of me is

an eternal optimist. I feel if we can change direction, we can survive."

"Why hire Teri to help you write a medical thriller?" Matt asks. "Your heart is clearly with bigger themes. Write a novel that focuses on a dystopian society."

"You mean, a novel that takes place after the bomb drops?"

"That's already been done," Teri says.

"Alisa will tell you that everything's been done," Matt says.

"True. It's how you do it that counts," I say. "But as far as my thriller being a small story—you have to understand it deals with our genetic code. I think our genes are the keys to our existence. They can either be our greatest wealth or our worst curse."

"How does it start?" Matt asks.

"With someone dying from a mysterious cause."

Matt smiles. "I look forward to reading it."

"I hope I can help you with it," Teri adds nervously.

"You'll help, trust me. I'll give you more work than you can handle."

Matt leans over and puts his arm around his girlfriend. "Let me tell you a secret about my girl that took me a long time to discover. She's tougher than you and I put together."

He lowers his head and kisses her, showing no inhibitions. Teri, aware that I'm watching, breaks away. But I feel the heat of her body. Naturally, I feel my own heat. The guy has sex appeal enough to sell by the pint.

I give Teri a list of books I want her to hunt down and

buy. My next novel is not just an excuse to get to know her. I honestly think it can warn mankind about what's coming next.

The books I want Teri to find are not easily available. A few were self-published. All deal with the human genome. I give her cash to purchase the material and she promises to bring me receipts.

Matt squeezes me tightly and whispers in my ear. "There's something about you," he says, so softly Teri cannot hear.

The remark strikes me deeply. I wanted to have lunch together to get to know them better. But when I look back, I realize it was Matt who did all the probing. I suspect his teasing was all a charade. That he's like me, and has no political views at all. It makes me wonder what he really thinks.

"Do you know what it is?" I whisper back.

"Something. Something."

SIX

Over the next week, I have them out to my house twice. The first time they come together. The next time they come separately. They both say the latter happened accidentally, but I feel they're trying to feel me out. I don't mind, I enjoy their company in either form, although I realize it could be a mistake for me to be alone with Matt. The guy has ingredient *XYZ*—if there is such a thing. He's so damn sexy! If I didn't love Teri so much, I'd have already jumped him. Even if he put up a fight, I wouldn't have cared.

But the trouble is I do care.

The day after I visit with them alone, I check my e-mail and discover that my female FBI agent, Claire Mason, has tracked the van's license plate number—the van the assassin used to haul his Gatling gun in—and has discovered that a Claudious Ember rented it a week ago from a Hertz in Manhattan.

A further examination of his whereabouts shows he flew into Los Angeles the previous week, before flying to New York.

His original point of departure? Zurich, Switzerland.

It probably means nothing, but one of Yaksha's men, Slim, told me that Yaksha worked out of Switzerland. I tell Claire to fly to Zurich and expand her search. Once more, I warn her to be cautious, to mask her trail, to be wary of strangers.

I only send Claire after Claudious. She made the breakthrough—it's her right to follow up on it. She knows how well I reward success. Besides, if I sent my other FBI agent to Switzerland, and the two detectives, they would get in each other's way. Worse, they might call attention to themselves. Claire is the smartest in the group. I trust her to be careful.

Claudious was not careful enough. Whenever I leave the country, I carry several passports and frequently change my ID. Also, he should have removed the license plate on the van, or swapped it with another, and filed down the identification number on the engine. To give the guy his due, he was probably confident he would kill me without much trouble.

It continues to puzzle me why Claudious's organization sent only one assassin after me. Perhaps they wanted to demonstrate what just one of their people could do. It's possible it was a test. Perhaps they wanted to see what I could do.

The information on Marko gnaws at me. I hate that he's out there, especially when Lisa Fetch is still working at IIC. Even if she had quit her job and moved to another city, I would be uneasy about her chances for a long life. Her connection to Randy Clifford is too tight; it was while doing her bidding that he was killed by the hit man. I feel it is only a matter of time before Marko pays Lisa and her boyfriend—the cop, Jeff Stephens—a visit.

I ask myself why I should care. Of course, I have practical reasons to be concerned about IIC. They have a file on me. They know my address. They refer to me as a "person of interest." Worse, they say I have a "lengthy history." Does that mean they know I'm a vampire? I don't know, but I have to find out.

Still, none of this explains my concern about Lisa and Jeff. The truth is, I just like them, and I would hate to see something bad happen to them, especially when I can prevent it. I don't decide who I care about—I don't know if anyone does. But I like Lisa and Jeff enough to bump up my visit to meet Marko.

The contract killer lives in Iowa, of all places, in a small town named Fairfield. At least he is centrally located. My source tells me he owns a thousand acres of land outside of town and grows feed corn—for pigs, cows, chickens, not for humans, although people consume it indirectly in the form of corn syrup. He has two residences, one in town, the other out on his land. He sits on the city council and attends church every Sunday. He has a wife and two young children. Talk about a great cover.

I fly to Cedar Rapids. A package is waiting for me at the airport, outside the secure area. In the package is a Glock .45, with two spare clips and a silencer. I'm one of those fortunate billionaires that have set up teams of gofers all over the world, people who are only too happy to deliver to me whatever I want, when I want it.

I rent a car and take a leisurely ninety minutes to reach Fairfield. By now the sun is setting, and I have only to swing by Marko's farm to know he's staying there with his family. "Damn," I swear quietly. I would prefer not to have the wife and kids around—they might cramp my style. But I'm confident I can lure him outside.

For ten minutes, I study the family through an open window. Marko sits with his wife and children, watching a new science fiction TV series. A fire burns under a chestnut mantel and the house smells of roasted turkey and homemade stuffing. There are numerous biblical paintings on the walls. The man himself—who's known in town as Joe Henderson—is forty-five, thin but wiry. He is six-two, and when he stands to get a cup of coffee for his wife from the kitchen, I notice how fast and smooth his movements are. No doubt he has the reflexes of a cat.

Mrs. Mary Henderson is fifteen years younger, pretty and plump. She wears a tiny gold crucifix, similar to my own, and a cheap store-bought dress that hides her legs. She has a boy and a girl. Both are cute, with red cheeks and bright smiles, and I can tell by their happy faces they don't have a care in the world.

It's clear family life suits Mr. Henderson, yet at the same time I note his constant alertness. There's no question in my mind he was trained by some branch of the military in special ops, and a quick peek inside his mind reveals a cold darkness I have seldom seen in a human being.

But I don't recoil in disgust. He is a curiosity. On the outside, Mr. Henderson looks like the perfect family man, but if his interior life could be displayed on a poster, it would probably be blank. He's unlike Danny Boy, the rapist, who took pleasure in taunting his victims. In a sense Marko is a consummate professional—he kills for money, nothing more, and when he's with his family, he's able to block his secret life out so well he hardly thinks about it.

He's like a robot with two sets of hard drives that he uses for memory. Two storage units that seldom connect. The guy would undoubtedly fascinate most psychologists. At some time in the past a switch must have broken inside him and cut him off from his humanity.

He does not appear to mind.

To draw him outside, I use a simple approach. His kids might have better hearing than their father, but it's Daddy who's been trained to listen to every tiny noise. Gathering a handful of pebbles, I stand near a window on the other side of the house from the living room and gently toss them at the glass. I throw four stones, each one a minute apart, until I finally hear him rise from his chair.

"Is something wrong, dear?" his wife calls.

"The pigs are squealing," he calls to her as he climbs the stairs. "I just want to have a look."

"Should we stop and tape the show?"

"That's okay, hon. I won't be gone long."

Upstairs, I see him move to the window, and I hide by pressing my body against the house wall. He doesn't turn on the bedroom light, but I know why he's upstairs. He opens a desk drawer, with the help of a key, and takes out a semi-automatic. I can tell the type of weapon by listening to what follows. He loads it with a clip, screws on a silencer, cocks it, and slips it under the back of his belt.

He's outside a minute later, standing on the porch, listening to the night. In this respect he is like me—his first line of defense is his hearing. I let him hear my footsteps as I scurry away from the house and into the nearby cornfield. He dashes around the side of the house, but already I'm invisible in the tall stalks. There's no moon—the night is black as ink. I have to admire his patience, his courage. He knows he has a visitor, and in his line of work he knows that can only mean bad news. But he doesn't turn on any lights, nor does he run back inside and call the police. He doesn't want to alarm his family, and he's confident he can deal with the situation.

I wait and listen as his heartbeat slowly accelerates from

ninety beats a minute to a hundred and twenty. Fortunately, I can see as well in the dark as in the daytime, and I'm able to follow his every move. He probably has infrared goggles in his private arsenal, but he did not bring any with him. I understand. How would he explain them to his wife if she stopped him leaving the house? Still, with each passing minute I note the frustration on his face, the tension, the smell of sweat on his skin.

My goal is to lead him deeper into the field, farther away from the house. I don't want to involve his family any more than he does. After five minutes of sitting, I shake a branch and dash another hundred yards deeper into the corn. He does not hesitate but follows quickly, making almost no noise. He's an experienced fighter, on all terrains. He has wisely removed his shoes. Any leather shoe or boot, no matter how broken in, makes a faint squeaking sound. I, too, am barefoot.

We play the same game for the next ten minutes, with me pausing to let him catch up, and then dashing away again. I never let him get close enough to hit me with a lucky shot. But I know the game is stressful for him. His heart jumps to a hundred and seventy beats a minute. He has begun to pant, and sweat drips from his forehead. His well-lit house, only a half mile away, must look a lot farther in his eyes.

I crouch low and let him come within twenty yards of my position.

"Had enough, Marko?" I say casually.

He freezes, then scans the area in my direction, his gun held ready.

"My name's Joe Henderson," he replies. "What are you doing on my property?"

"Randy Clifford. New York."

He sighs faintly. He knows now that he's the contract. It must be a novel feeling for him, to be on the other side of the equation. His heart is a hammer in his chest. He's scared.

"What do you want?" he asks.

"Information. In exchange for your life and the lives of your wife and children."

"You're a professional. You won't kill them."

"Not if I leave here with what I want to know. By the way, I have you in the crosshairs of a sniper rifle. The scope is infrared. If you reach for a match or cigarette, I'll shoot." Although I have no need of a scope at this distance, he's expecting me to give him these instructions. The flare of a match in an infrared scope would blind the person who's using it.

"You sound close," he replies.

"I am."

"Maybe too close for safety."

"Be my guest, go ahead and take a shot. Just as long as you know I'll take a shot of my own and you'll be missing your right knee."

He considers this for a moment, then lowers his gun.

"You have the advantage," he admits.

"Drop your gun. Now, on the ground."

He drops his gun.

"Kick it away from you."

He does as he is told.

"Randy Clifford," I say. "Who hired you?"

"The contract came to me over the Internet. I didn't ask who was behind it. Like you, I never do."

"I'm not like you, and your answer is unsatisfactory."

He speaks quickly. "My broker can be contacted at redsplash1@fastmail.com."

"That link will just lead to another link. It won't help me."

"That's all I have."

"I'm warning you, seriously, you don't want to lie to me again."

"My broker's a very private person. We've never met."

"Not true," I say, and I know this for a fact.

"It is true. There's no reason for us to meet."

I shoot his right kneecap with my silenced pistol. A .45 is a powerful round for a handgun, but it cannot compare to the armor-piercing bullets Claudious Ember and I were using a few nights ago. Marko lets out a muffled cry and drops to one knee. His wound isn't fatal—nor will he lose the leg—but he's bleeding freely. I speak to him in a sympathetic tone.

"I know what you're thinking, Marko. It doesn't matter what you tell me, I'm going to kill you. You're also thinking that if you hold out a bit, then break down and give me something, anything that's useful, I might at least spare your family. To be blunt, all of this would ordinarily be true. But you're wrong to think I'm an assassin and someone has hired me to kill you. I hate professional hit men, and when I cross paths with one, I usually kill them. Also I've studied your family, and your wife and children, and they appear to love you, although they would be hurt to know what little love you're capable of."

"I care for my family," he says, breathing heavily. He does think I'm going to kill him.

"Fine. Right now—before your wife gets worried and comes looking for you—I want to talk business. Tell me the name and address of your broker."

He hesitates. "Rita Centrello. She lives in New Jersey, a small town called Olive. 2112 Oates Drive. She's an old broad, in her seventies, harmless as a fly."

"Mafia?"

He shrugs. "It's not like you think."

"If you warn her that she's going to have a visitor, I'll come back and kill your family. Understood?"

"Sure."

"IIC. Have you heard of them?"

He hesitates. "Yeah. Before Randy, they gave me a contract for a woman in the Bay Area who worked for them. Michelle Ranker. They've given me regular jobs over the last five years. Always paid top dollar. It made Rita and me wonder, you know. To be blunt, Rita doesn't know anything about them.

Believe me if you want, I don't care. But I asked Michelle what their big secret was."

"Right before you killed her?"

"Hey, she was in a talkative mood. She told me she'd tell me if I promised not to kill her. What the hell. She didn't understand how this business works. I told her what she wanted to hear and she swore to me that IIC was working for the Antichrist. That they were preparing the way."

"How?"

"By making truckloads of money. She said they were spread all over the world, and had controlling shares in more companies on Wall Street than you can imagine. But she said no one knew about them, not really. They were strictly behind the scenes."

"How do they make their money?"

"I asked her that. She babbled on about something called the Array."

"What's the Array?"

"I don't know. She started crying then, begging me not to kill her. I got impatient and hit her. That was a mistake. She started talking crazy stuff. The kids, she said, she was the one who paid the kids. A hundred bucks a month, that's all IIC paid them."

"Who were the kids?"

"Beats me. It sounded like they were a bunch of normal kids. They weren't psychic, and they knew nothing about the stock market. But Michelle did say they were all from the third world. She acted like she was their mother. She said she made sure they got their checks each month. But then she started sobbing. She said that was her big mistake, that she had talked about them once in public. That's why they had sent me to kill her. She got real hysterical at the end, I don't think anything she said was reliable." He pauses. "You're not just busting my balls? You really might let me go?"

"You sound like Michelle."

"Don't screw with me."

"Relax. Did you question any of IIC's other contracts?"

"No."

"Did you question Randy?"

"I wanted to, but he had a gun. I had to move fast."

"Was he your last hit?"

"Yeah."

"Do you have a contract for another?"

"Yeah. It's IIC-related. The . . . well . . ." He doesn't finish.

"You were going to mention the file. I want to see that file."

He speaks with force. "It's in a vault in my office. Go in there and you'll run into my wife or my kids. I can't risk that."

"I can be in and out in a minute if you give me the combination to your vault. And I can promise they won't see me."

"No one can promise that."

"See how easily I hid from you? Mr. Marko the Magnificent. Tell me what I want to know. This is a deal breaker."

He sighs. "The vault's behind a painting behind my desk. Sixteen right. Nineteen left. Three right. Four left. Then spin the dial clockwise three times to clear it before you try to open it. Otherwise, it will trip an alarm and tip off Rita."

"You sound like you care for the old broad."

"She's been good to me. We've been good for each other."

"Do you work for any other brokers?"

"No. I make enough with Rita."

"Good. Because Randy was your last job."

"You can't be serious?"

"I'm very serious."

"What if I promise to turn down all IIC jobs from now on?"

"Promise all you want. But know if you leave town in the next thirty years—for any reason whatsoever—I'll hunt you down and kill you and everyone in your family. If you doubt my sincerity, test me and take a drive to Cedar Rapids next month. Your son will be dead the next day."

"These conditions are highly unprofessional."

"I told you, I'm not a professional."

"You can't set up a wall around this town."

"I don't need a wall, just a few informants. Besides, you saw how easily I found you. It'll be just as easy to track you."

He considers. "I was thinking of retiring anyway."

I hear truth in his words. "The kids?"

"Yeah."

"Tell me what Michelle meant by the Antichrist."

"How should I know? She was raving. She knew she was about to die."

I can't argue. "I'm going to give you two names: Lisa Fetch and Jeff Stephens. If you hear of a contract that's been put out on them, you're to alert me immediately."

"What's in it for me?"

"A large check."

"I prefer cash."

"Fine. Call this number." I have him memorize a private phone line I keep for such purposes. "Are we clear about everything?" I ask when we're done.

"I still don't want you in my house."

"That's the least of your worries. You'll see a light go on in my car when I'm about to leave. It's parked at the end of your driveway. Don't speak to your wife until I'm gone."

"I can't believe you're going to let me live."

"Miracles never cease. Two last points. Did you see any data files Randy had in his possession? Ones that related to IIC?"

"No. But I was given strict instructions to destroy his computers. He had six."

"What kind of security does Rita keep?"

"She lives with her boys—the three youngest: Mad Max, Slim, Fats. They're not professional. They catch you and they'll skin you alive. Please, if they do catch you, don't . . ."

"Don't mention your name, I got it. How's the leg?"

"I'll live."

"That's right. You'll live in Fairfield until the day you die. Capisce?"

"Capisce," he agrees. Then he asks, "May I ask a question?"

"Yes."

"Who the hell are you?"

I stand in the dark and begin to move away.

"Someone you don't want to meet twice," I reply.

Back in Cedar Rapids, in the airport parking lot, I study the file I stole from Marko's house. The contract is on a seventeen-year-old girl from India named Shanti. She was born in Madras but now lives in San Antonio, Texas. There's a picture of her in the file. That's what catches my attention first.

Shanti's face is horribly disfigured.

Apparently she was the victim of a crime that has become all too popular in my home country. Forced into a marriage arrangement when she was but a child, she tried to get out of it two years ago, when she was fifteen. Her suitor-to-be didn't approve of her decision. Instead of being a gentleman and letting her go, he bought two car batteries, drained the sulfuric acid into a steel cup, and threw the corrosive liquid in her face. Clearly, if he couldn't have her, he didn't want anyone else to have her.

From the photo, it is obvious Shanti is blind in the right eye, and her file states she has only limited vision in the left. I find it hard to study the picture and not feel sick and angry.

Half her face has been melted away. The file contains her street address and a note that says, *The mark is helpless, devoid of security of any kind.*

Yet the file contains another note. *It's important Shanti be killed as soon as possible.* It makes me wonder.

I have suddenly lost interest in Rita and her boys. Inside the airport, I alter my return ticket so that I'll arrive in Texas in the middle of the night.

SEVEN

The next morning, I sit outside Shanti's house in a fresh rental and contemplate how I should approach the girl and her uncle, Shivam Garuda, who appears to be her sole guardian. Since I don't have time to cultivate a friendship with the girl, a blunt introduction seems best. I have a fake FBI badge that my contacts in the agency will back up, should the uncle call and check on me. I'm now Special Agent Jessica Reese.

The house is small, with at best two bedrooms, in a poor section of town. I have arrived early enough to catch the uncle before he leaves for work. I don't imagine Shanti will answer many questions without him present. According to Marko's file, she's alone from nine in the morning until six at night every day. Her injuries keep her from attending school.

I do a sweep of the area before I knock. There don't appear

to be any assassins near the house. Why should there be? IIC has assigned the job to Marko, the best hit man in the country. When I do knock, Shanti's uncle is quick to answer.

"May I help you?" Mr. Shivam Garuda is only forty-five but looks older. He's extremely thin, to the point of malnutrition, with white hair and a bump on his spine that forces him to bend slightly forward.

"Hello. My name's Jessica Reese. I'm with the FBI."

I'm wearing a black pantsuit and skillfully applied makeup, both of which make me look at least in my mid-twenties. But it's the tone of my voice, the way I flash my badge, my whole manner, that makes me appear older. Mr. Garuda studies my badge closely.

"What can I do for you?" he asks, guarded.

"I'm here to speak with your niece, Shanti. But I understand you're her guardian and wouldn't mind if you sat in on the questioning."

"What is this about? Is Shanti in trouble?"

I nod sympathetically. "She may well be in trouble, but not with the U.S. government. Please, if I could come in and have a few minutes of your time, I think we might be able to help each other."

My tone reeks of sincerity. Plus, I look harmless. He relaxes a notch and lets me in the house.

"Shanti is sleeping. Do you mind waiting a few minutes?"

"Not at all."

"Would you like some tea?"

"Tea would be nice. Thank you."

He brings me up a cup of warm chai and heads for the back of the house. The taste brings back old memories. On the wall are paintings of Lord Krishna—as a child, with his mother Yashoda, and as an adult, playing his flute for the gopis. Of course, I knew from their names that the Garudas were probably Hindu, but it warms my heart to see they worship the same God as myself. If only they knew that I once met Krishna . . .

Mr. Garuda reappears a moment later. He looks uncomfortable. "My niece is getting dressed. She won't be long. But I want to warn you—"

I interrupt gently. "I'm aware of her condition."

He's relieved I know but nevertheless nods sadly. "She was the prettiest girl."

"I'm sure she was." I pause. "Has she had reconstructive surgery?"

He gestures to his poor abode. "It's all I pray for. But right now, there's no money for doctors."

"I understand."

Shanti appears a few minutes later, wearing dark sunglasses and a simple white dress. In person, her disfigurement is even harder to bear. The acid did not just take the right eye but also her right nostril and a large portion of her right cheek. A large gap extends away from her mouth, revealing stained molars and a mass of scarred gum tissue.

Yet she doesn't hesitate to take a step forward and shake my hand.

"My uncle says you are Special Agent Jessica Reese," she says.

"Call me Jessica, please. You're Shanti?"

"Yes." She gestures. "Have a seat, make yourself at home. This is exciting for me. I watch *X-Files* reruns all the time, but I never dreamed that I would one day be visited by a real-life FBI agent."

Like most educated Indians, her English is excellent, but unfortunately there is a faint hissing sound to Shanti's words. It's due to the large hole in her cheek, and perhaps nerve damage to her tongue. Otherwise, I'm sure, she would have a delightful voice. I vow right then I'll get her the finest plastic surgeons in the land, once I know why the IIC wants her dead.

I chuckle at her remark. "This might surprise you, but that show is one of the reasons I became an FBI agent."

"Have you been one long?" Mr. Garuda asks. I've done my best to make myself look older, but he's sharp-sighted and no fool.

"I'm only two years out of the academy in Quantico. You may have heard of it. It's back in Virginia. Before I graduated, our instructors used to joke that all the newbies would be sent off to Texas. It turned out I was the only one."

"You must feel isolated," Shanti said.

I shrug. "Sometimes."

"Have you made any new friends?"

These are questions I should be asking her, the poor dear.

"None that I would take home to Mother," I say with a smile. Then I change my tone, getting serious. "I should explain the purpose of my visit. I must warn you ahead of time it will shock you."

"In a good way or a bad way?" Shanti asks innocently.

"I'm sorry, I wish I was here with good news." I lift up the file I took from Marko's house and pass it to her. "Shanti, can you read?" I ask.

"Yes. With these glasses on."

"What is that you're giving her?" Mr. Garuda asks.

"Once again, please brace yourself. This file was taken off a notorious hit man known to the FBI as Marko. He has a reputation as a killer for the Mob. But in this case, for reasons unknown to us, he's been assigned to kill you, Shanti."

Mr. Garuda gasps in fear, but Shanti remains remarkably calm.

"What did I do to him that he would want to kill me?" she asks.

"You misunderstand. He's been hired by a third party to kill you. He's a professional. He murders people for a living. He has no personal interest in you."

Shanti holds up the picture. "This must have been taken recently."

"How recently, do you think?" I ask.

"The dress I'm wearing in this photo—I only bought it last month."

"Are you saying this Marko is going to come to our house?" Mr. Garuda demands.

I raise a hand. "There's no danger of that. Marko has already been taken out of action. He won't be harming anyone else. But we still have a problem. We don't know who hired him to kill you." I pause. "Do you have any idea why someone would want you dead, Shanti?"

She slowly shakes her head. "No. I mean, there's Juna. He's the one who . . ." She has trouble finishing the sentence.

"He's the man you were engaged to?" I say carefully.

She nods. "But that was two years ago, in India. Juna's a poor shopkeeper who makes his money rolling bibis all day."

"Cigarettes?"

"Yes. How did you know that?"

"I've traveled in India. So you feel Juna is an unlikely suspect?"

"Yes."

I turn to her uncle. "Mr. Garuda, do you have any enemies?"

"None that I know of." He stops to wipe at his eyes. "I'm sorry, this is very disturbing. Shanti has been through so much, and to think there is someone out there who wants to hurt her again . . ."

Shanti strokes the man's arm. "Don't worry, Baba. The FBI is here to protect us. Nothing bad is going to happen."

The girl's calm courage impresses me.

"What Shanti says is true," I say. "I'm going to assign a team of agents to this house so that Shanti will be guarded 24/7. Should a second contract be taken out on her life, no harm will come to her. Any professional hit man who approaches this house will quickly see how well she's guarded and immediately leave town."

"Why do you think there will be a second contract?" Mr. Garuda asks.

"Because they arrested the man who was supposed to kill me," Shanti explains to him before turning to me. "Is that true, Jessica? Whoever wants me dead will just hire someone else?"

"Yes. Assuming they're anxious to have you killed. And that appears likely given the fact they hired Marko at the start. Until he was caught, he was considered one of the deadliest hit men in the country."

"I must be more important than I realized," Shanti says.

"To someone," I say. "We come back to our original question. Is there anyone you can think of that would want you dead?"

"There's no one." She gestures to her face. "Because of my injury, I seldom go out. Never mind enemies, I hardly have any friends."

"Do you work, Shanti?"

She hesitates. "No."

"You don't have a part-time job that you might do from home?"

She glances toward her uncle. "There's a small job I have, but I'm not supposed to talk about it."

"Why not?"

Mr. Garuda interrupts. "The company that employs her has a strict privacy policy. I'm sure you can understand."

"On the contrary, I can't think of a single American company that warns its employees not to talk about the firm they work for." I pause. "We're talking about IIC, aren't we?"

Shanti and her uncle look surprised. "How do you know about them?" she asks.

"Let's just say the FBI is very interested in them. In fact, we suspect IIC might be behind the contract on your life."

"That's impossible," Mr. Garuda says. "They're an investment firm. They have done nothing but help Shanti. I can't believe they'd want to kill her. It makes no sense."

"It makes no sense to me, either. But then, I don't know what your niece does for IIC." I pause. "How do they help you, Shanti?"

She hesitates. "They send me a check for one hundred dollars every month."

"Why? Because you're handicapped?"

"It has nothing to do with my face." She stops and puts a hand to her wound. "At least, I don't think it has anything to do with what Juna did to me."

"Explain."

She lowers her head. "It's silly."

"Tell me anyway."

She raises her head, yet this time her eyes don't go to me, but to one of the paintings of Krishna on the walls. She stares at it a long time before she answers.

"When Juna threw the acid in my face, the pain was unlike anything I had ever imagined. I felt as if someone was holding a blowtorch to my head. The burning wouldn't stop, even when my friends washed away the acid. It just kept burning and burning. They took me to the doctor and he bandaged me and gave me pills for the pain, but still the burning stayed. I felt I would go mad. I couldn't see then, nothing, and the doctor told me the blindness would be permanent. I didn't know what to do. My mother and father—they felt sorry for me. Yet they also felt I had disgraced our family by refusing to marry Juna. My own father had the nerve to say that what Juna had done to me was my karma."

"Damn him to the deepest hell," Mr. Garuda whispers.

"Please, Baba, don't curse. It doesn't help."

"He's my brother, and I'll curse him till the day I die."

"He's still my father. I have to respect him. I owe him that."

"You owe him nothing. In this life or the next."

It appears to be an old argument between them. Shanti shakes her head. "My whole life was pain and darkness. I didn't know what to do. I couldn't eat. I could barely drink. I thought I might die, and a part of me prayed for death. But then . . . this will be hard for you to understand."

"Not at all. Then you started to pray to Krishna."

She stared at me. "How did you know?"

"I pray to him as well."

"How? I mean, why?"

"I'm not from around here, but that's a long story. Please continue."

"It's hard to explain. In India we have what we call mantras. The mantra of a deity is supposed to be identical to the deity. Just saying Krishna's name is supposed to bring his blessing. But we have a sacred book in India called the Bhagavatam that contains secret mantras that Krishna taught those close to him. One has always been very dear to me. I would repeat it for hours even before Juna attacked me." She pauses. "This must all sound like eastern mysticism to you."

"Om Namo Bhagavate Vasudevaya."

"That's my mantra! How did you know?"

"I've studied the book you refer to."

"But it has other mantras in it. How did you know I use that one?"

I shake my head. "I don't know, maybe Krishna told me."

Shanti continues to stare at me. "You are not like a normal FBI agent."

"I'll take that as a compliment. Go on."

"What happened next was a miracle. The vision in my left eye returned, and I was able to move around without help. And the pain began to go away. It didn't stop completely, but then, I didn't pray for everything to heal." She smiles. "You must think me stupid."

"Not at all. You found that when you were suffering, it was easy to think of Krishna. You were afraid that if all your suffering was taken away, you would no longer think of him as often."

Shanti is astounded. "How can you know these things?"

"Let's just say I have suffered as well."

"And you worship Krishna?"

"'Worship' is such a big word. I think of him, that's enough for me."

Shanti nods. "I'm happy the FBI sent you instead of another agent. Maybe Krishna had something to do with your coming. When I was healing, and the IIC man came to my door, I thought perhaps Krishna had sent him."

"Why?"

"Because he told me I could earn a hundred dollars a month doing next to nothing. If you've been to India, you must know how much money that is there. Suddenly I had enough money to take care of myself, although my father tried to claim it for himself."

"The bastard," Mr. Garuda muttered.

"Baba!"

"He's a thieving bastard!"

"I'm afraid I must agree with your uncle on this point," I say to Shanti. "But you keep dancing around my question. What do you do for IIC?"

"I close my eyes and answer questions."

"What kind of questions?"

"I don't know. They don't really make sense. Usually the man on the phone will spell out a list of letters and then ask for a yes or no. But I don't answer by speaking aloud. I just push one for yes and two for no."

"If you don't know what the question is about, how can you answer at all?"

"I asked that when they hired me. They told me not to worry about what was being asked. They said I should just say what came to me in the moment."

"How often do you answer their questions?"

"Once a week."

"Always on the phone?"

"Yes. They gave me a special phone with headphones so I can listen to the questions without having to hold the phone to my ear. They said that way my arm wouldn't get tired." She pauses. "It's real easy to do. Most of the time I feel like I'm doing nothing. The only hard part is when it goes on for a long time. Then I get restless. But that doesn't happen too often."

"Let me get this straight. Once a week they call and you put on your headphones and listen to a series of questions that make no sense. And you answer yes or no by pushing either one or two on your phone?"

"Yes."

"Could these strings of letters be stock symbols?"

"I thought of that. I've never recognized any of the groups of letters. But that doesn't mean anything. I don't know much about the stock market."

"Shanti, have you ever heard them talk about something called the Array?"

"No. What's that?"

"We're not sure yet, but it's somehow connected to IIC."

"They always send the check on time," Mr. Garuda says. "They're never late. To be frank, the money has been a blessing. Without it, I wouldn't be able to take Shanti to physical therapy."

"Whoever comes on the phone is always friendly," Shanti says. "It's hard to believe they would want to hurt me. I mean, I could see why they might want to fire me. I don't know if I get many of their questions right. But why would they want to kill me?"

"I have no idea," I say honestly.

We have reached a standstill. I don't know what else to ask, because I have no idea what IIC's up to, other than accumulating tons of money and targeting people for assassination. It appears unlikely Shanti has anything to do with their Array or their success in the market. Likewise, it seems ridiculous to think Shanti poses a threat to them.

Yet they want her dead.

Plus they see me as a threat, or at least as a "person of interest." It's possible—likely in fact—they sent the superhuman assassin to take me out. However, if they have access to killers like that, why do they hire men like Marko to do some of their dirty work? It's difficult to see a pattern in their behavior. They're clearly rich, powerful, but they seem to be kind of crazy.

I stand and check my watch—eight forty-five a.m. I have already made up my mind. I'm going to California, to Malibu, to have a talk with the principals at IIC face to face. It's a weakness of mine, this impatience, to suddenly barge in where angels fear to tread. But I can't help myself.

"I told you I'm going to assign agents to guard this house," I say. "If you go out, Shanti, they'll follow you at a discreet distance. They'll work in shifts, and I'll make sure they introduce themselves to you when they first arrive so you know who they are. But after that you're to ignore them. Don't feel you have to feed them or to let them use your restroom. These people are professionals. It's their job to take care of you. They'll be armed, but don't let that intimidate you. They're all highly trained. Like I said before, if a hit man checks out this block, he'll see how well guarded you are, and he won't be able to get out of town fast enough. You will be in absolutely no danger."

Shanti also stands. "Will you find out why someone wants to hurt me?"

An overwhelming need to protect her sweeps over me. I'm not sure why. I squeeze her shoulder as I speak next. "I'm going to do nothing else but work on this case. I promise you, I won't rest until it's solved."

Shanti hugs me. "Thanks, Jessica, and go with Krishna's love. I feel he's the one who brought you into my life."

I remember how Krishna spared my life five thousand years ago.

"You might be right," I say.

EIGHT

It's noon before my flight lands at LAX. I rent a car—a Mercedes SL—and drive toward the Pacific Coast Highway and head north into Malibu. The day is bright and warm. The sea breeze feels invigorating. Along the way, I dial Lisa Fetch, the woman who visited me at my house and first told me about IIC.

I actually called her a couple of days ago, just to make sure she was all right. We ended up talking for hours. She's a fascinating woman—she might even be classified as a genius. She's at her best talking about mathematics. Since the subject has never been one of my strong points, I'm intrigued by people who have an instinctive grasp of its subtleties.

For example, Einstein's theory of relativity cannot be understood without an insight into the mathematics behind it, and Lisa is the first person I've ever met who was able to explain the necessary math formulas to me in a few short minutes, and in such a way that I could understand them. Her vision of how numbers and time and space all fit together opened a fresh door in my mind, and here I thought there was nothing else for me to learn. Lisa is as much an artist with her equations as Matt is with his music.

Unfortunately, today, the instant she answers I know she's in trouble.

"Alisa," she says, sounding tense. "I was just going to call you."

"What's wrong?"

"It could be nothing. I've been unable to reach Jeff today. You remember him, he came to your house with me."

"Of course, the policeman. Do you two live together?"

"We spend a lot of nights together, but he has his own place. Still, we talk every morning no matter where we sleep. We were supposed to have breakfast together. He never showed up, and he's not answering his cell."

"Have you been in to work today?"

"Yes. I felt too restless to stay. I'm worried about him—I don't know what to do. I feel like I should call the police."

"Don't call them yet. I just arrived in LA—I might be able to help you. But it's important that you stay away from work the rest of the day."

"You're really here?"

"Yes."

"What are you going to do?"

"I want to talk to the person in charge of IIC. Who should I ask for?"

"There are several principals. Tom Brutran is the president of the firm, but everyone knows his wife, Cynthia, is the real boss. I doubt either of them will see you without an appointment, and they won't give you one on such short notice. They're busy people."

"I think they'll see me. Remember, I'm listed as a 'person of interest' in their files."

"That's true. Should I go there and help introduce you?"

"No. That would be a mistake. Under no circumstances do you want to connect yourself to me. You haven't spoken of your visit with me, have you?"

"No. Jeff hasn't either. Oh, God, do you think something has happened to him?"

"I can only hope he is okay. The more I learn about your company, the more they disturb me."

"What do you mean?"

I want Lisa afraid. Her fear may be the only thing keeping her alive.

"I looked into the disappearance of your ex, Randy Clifford. He was killed by a notorious hit man named Marko. The man usually works for the Mob, but IIC paid him a large fee to make Randy disappear. He also wiped clean all his computer files."

"Where did you get this information?"

"My sources are impeccable. I strongly recommend that you come down with a serious case of the flu and don't return to work for the next week. I need time to figure out what IIC's up to."

"I told you what they are up to. They're making tons of money on Wall Street and funneling it through dozens of dummy corporations."

"That doesn't explain how or why they're doing it. Lisa, do you know a girl named Shanti Garuda? She's originally from India but she now lives in Texas."

"No. Who is she?"

"Someone I had an interesting conversation with this morning. Have you found out any more about the Array?"

"No. I finally asked a few friends at work about it."

"What did they say?"

"It's what they didn't say. They clammed up fast."

"Interesting. Listen, I'll be at your firm in a few minutes. I'm going to go now, but I promise to meet you afterwards."

"Wait! I can't just sit around here and do nothing."

"Lisa, you're the one who came to me and told me IIC was dangerous. Since then I've done plenty of research on my own and discovered they're more dangerous than any of us realized. Stay away from work and stay away from Jeff's house."

"What's wrong with Jeff's house?"

She's too strong-willed to simply obey. I have to use the

power of my vampiric voice. Even before I speak, I let the tendrils of my will stretch out and envelop her. I speak in a clear but soft voice.

"Under no circumstances are you to go there until we meet up. This is very important. Do you understand?"

By her sudden change in tone, I can tell my words have penetrated deep into her psyche. "I understand," she mumbles. "I'll wait for you."

"Good girl," I say, and hang up.

IIC is located deep in Malibu, far north of the business heart of town. The area is mostly empty grass hills with an occasional twenty-million-dollar mansion thrown in for good measure, lest one forget the cost of local real estate. The firm is situated in a beautiful but modest-sized structure two miles from the coast, atop a manicured hill with views of the Pacific so wide I wouldn't be surprised if Hawaii were visible on a clear day.

I admire the architecture because it breaks every rule in the book and somehow remains standing. Virtually solid glass, it stands four stories tall on a series of white support beams that make up an interlocking collection of rectangles, squares, pyramids, and yes, remarkably, spheres. Which leads me to believe it was designed by a model maker on acid. The building is not merely modern; it is from a generation not yet born. If IIC is trying to hide their money, they're not trying too hard.

I park and casually enter the building. The welcoming

secretary sits beside a busy switchboard. I say hello and tell her I'm there to see Cynthia Brutran. She asks if I have an appointment.

"Just tell her Alisa Perne is here," I reply.

The secretary puts the call through, and I'm mildly surprised that my name alone does the trick. The woman tells me to have a seat, Ms. Brutran will see me in a few minutes.

The few minutes stretch into twenty, and I grow restless. I'm about to stand and strengthen my demands when a young woman with a three-year-old child enters the building and asks to speak to the firm's official president, Thomas Brutran. She is also told to take a seat and ends up sitting across from me. The woman's little girl is ridiculously cute, and I find my impatience evaporating.

"What's her name?" I ask the mother.

"Athena," the woman says. "Her father is obsessed with ancient Greece." Mother has red hair like her child, green eyes, but whereas Athena will grow up to turn every male head in a room, Mom is still struggling with her postpregnancy fat and appears stressed. Indeed, we are talking less than ten minutes when she excuses herself and says she has to use the restroom. Standing, she gestures to her daughter and looks at me.

"Can you watch her a minute?" she asks. "She seems taken by you."

The request is a little odd. Athena is trading grins with me, true, but we haven't exactly bonded. The woman is showing a reckless amount of trust by turning over her child to someone who is essentially a complete stranger. But hey, this is Malibu—the woman probably needs the privacy of the restroom to swallow her half dozen prescriptions.

"No problem, I'll take good care of Athena," I say.

The woman collects her bag and hurries away.

"You must have a trustworthy face," the woman at the switchboard observes, reading my mind.

"I thought the same thing," I reply, following Athena out of the corner of my eye as she wanders toward the painting on a nearby wall. The art, like the architecture, is so modern that the artists apparently feel no need to learn how to draw or paint. Nevertheless, the bright colors appeal to the child. She points at a bright canvas.

"Heaven," she says.

"Is that what heaven looks like to you, Athena?" I ask.

"Daddy's gone to heaven."

The secretary and I exchange a worried look.

"I'm sure he's okay wherever he is," I say.

Athena nods. "I miss him."

"It's okay to miss him. It just means you love him."

Athena's face darkens. "Mommy says he's gone. That we'll never see him again."

The remark is so painful, I hardly know how to respond. "Wherever your daddy is, I'm sure he's thinking of you, Athena."

The remark appears to comfort the child, but it's been a

long time since I played the role of mom. I might have said the wrong thing, because one second Athena appears to be enjoying the brightly colored paintings and the next second she grabs a glass vase holding a rose from beneath one of the pictures and lifts it over her head. Before I can stop her—without switching into hyper mode—she breaks it on the glass table where it previously stood.

Athena howls in pain, her tiny fingers covered with blood and pieces of glass. Feeling like the world's worst babysitter, I rush to her side. With my vampiric sight, I quickly identify five slivers of glass that have penetrated her skin, even through her blood. I'm picking them out, scratching myself in the process, when I hear the hysterical voice of the child's mother.

"What have you done to my daughter?" she screams.

"Nothing. She broke a vase and cut herself. It looks worse than it is. If you'll give me a minute, I can pick out the last few pieces of glass."

"Get your hands off of her!" the mother cries, and runs over and yanks the child from my hands. The woman behind the desk stands.

"It was nobody's fault," she says in my defense. "Your daughter grabbed the vase before either of us could stop her."

"Shut up!" the mother snaps.

The young woman frowns. "Pardon me?"

"You heard me," she says as she turns for the door. "Just be happy I'm not suing you both. And tell your goddamn boss to shove his gold leaf investment program up his ass."

The young woman goes to swear at her but manages to control her temper. She swallows. "I have bandages in the other room. If you could please give me a moment to fetch them . . ."

"To hell with you both!" Athena's mother shouts before storming out the front door. The secretary and I exchange amused looks.

"I hope she didn't upset you," she says.

"Not at all."

"You know the old saying: No good deed goes unpunished."

"That's the story of my life."

The woman points to my bleeding hand. "You're the one who needs the bandage."

I held Athena firm while picking out the glass, but a wounded child is one thing I've never learned to totally control. My fingertips are more badly scratched than I realized. Yet they are healing rapidly.

"That's not necessary," I say, raising my hand to decrease the blood flow into my fingers. "I'll just pop in your restroom a minute. I'll be fine."

The secretary shakes her head as she strides away from her desk.

"A couple of bandages will keep the cuts from getting dirty."

"I'll take them when I get back." Cradling my injured hand with my other hand, I try to keep my blood from spilling on the floor. It is an old habit of mine, to guard my blood. Once in the restroom, I let the hot water wash over my cuts. Already they have sealed; nevertheless, I'm careful to wash away the faintest sign of my blood.

When I return to the front desk, and the secretary, I hide my healed fingers beneath a paper towel. I gratefully accept the woman's bandages and casually wrap them around my fingers. The secretary is a polite soul.

"I'm really sorry you had to be subjected to all that."

"The child moved so fast. I don't know if it was the talk about her father, or if she hated that painting."

"Did you see her face just before she broke the vase?"

"No. She was looking away from me."

The secretary frowns. "Her eyes suddenly blazed. Something set her off. I don't know, that kid kind of spooked me."

"She seemed sweet," I say, but my words lack conviction. Something about the kid bothered me as well.

Ms. Cynthia Brutran calls for me a few minutes later. The secretary directs me to take the elevator to the fourth floor. At the top of the building, I'm met by what appears to be Ms. Brutran's personal secretary—a young man who couldn't look more sexy if he was naked. He flashes a warm smile, apologizes for my having to wait, and directs me to the boss's office.

Ms. Brutran sits behind a beautifully finished walnut desk

crowded with keyboards and computer screens. To say the lady multitasks would be an understatement. She's forty but looks ten years younger. She's had work done to her face and neck by an exceptional surgeon. It would take my eyes to spot it.

Her short brown hair has a bright sheen. She wears a single piece of jewelry, a diamond ring encircled with a dozen tiny rubies. The central stone is exquisite, without significant flaws, and is no doubt worth more than most people make in a lifetime. She has on a beige pantsuit. Her overall look is professional but relaxed. I'm dressed in a black skirt and a red blouse, and hopefully project the feel of a hunter.

Yet Ms. Brutran isn't truly relaxed. Her gaze is intense, and she does not hesitate to let me feel its heat. It's probably an old habit—to intimidate weaker souls in business meetings. She doesn't know exactly what I am, but she knows something about me. She's guarded but not fearful. I smell steel and gunpowder coming from the drawer on her right. I find it interesting she keeps a loaded weapon so close at hand.

"I hear you had a little accident downstairs," she says.

"News travels fast in your building."

"To me it does. Are your fingers okay?"

"Just scratched, thank you."

"My receptionist said your name is Alisa Perne, and that you need to speak to me. May I ask the nature of your business?"

I stare at her and allow a measure of my power to enter my gaze. She blinks under my invisible and extremely subtle assault but does not back up or try to look away. For the first time I notice how disciplined her mind is. I don't get an immediate sense of her thoughts, although I reach for them. It's as if she wears a psychic helmet over her head. I'm intrigued.

"Simple curiosity," I reply.

"I'm afraid I don't understand."

"Please, let us dispense with the innocent act. You agreed to see me—a complete stranger off the street. Who made no appointment ahead of time. Whom you have never met before in your life." I pause. "You must have a reason."

She hesitates, then nods. "I ran your name through our database. It says you're a person of interest."

"Does your database explain why?"

"Of course. Our company research has identified you as one of the wealthiest women in America."

"That's extremely confidential information. How did you come across it?"

"Frankly, I don't know. In my daily business I often use our database, but I don't spend time creating it." She pauses. "May I ask how you've managed to stay so completely out of the public eye?"

"Through great effort. But now you and your firm have invaded my privacy. I want to know why."

"We're an investment firm, one of the most successful in the country. It's only natural we should seek out people such as yourself with a large amount of wealth."

"Is that what you do? Manage other people's money?"

"It's one service we offer, yes."

"Because I heard different. I heard you manage your own money. So well that IIC is worth trillions of dollars. Trillions that no one knows about." I turn the tables on her. "May I ask how you've managed to keep these trillions out of the public eye?"

She smiles stiffly. "I fear you've been misinformed. Our firm is rich, true, but not on that scale."

"You're lying," I reply. I still can't read her thoughts. She blocks me somehow. Yet I sense hidden depths behind her walls. This woman must be handled carefully. I cannot simply snap her neck, much as I might want to. I sense she would not let me, although I have no idea how she would stop me. My intuition tells me only a part of her story.

However, she doesn't have the supernatural heartbeat of the man who came to kill me. She doesn't have his speed, muscle control, powerful eyes and ears, nor his extraordinary strength. She's human, only she's a highly evolved human. Suddenly, I feel her struggle to scan my mind, and I block her by keeping it blank. As blank as my expression.

The puzzle deepens, as my curiosity soars.

"We've just met," she says. "Don't you think it's foolish to start with such insults?"

"I apologize."

She nods. She accepts my apology.

"Now tell me why your company's keeping a file on me. The real reason. And don't tell me it doesn't exist. Randy Clifford discovered it before you had him killed."

There, I've gone and done it; once again my impatience has overridden my caution. I've thrown down a challenge I can't take back. Now Brutran realizes I know about the dark side of IIC's business deals. I sharpen my focus, using all my senses, to see how the information affects her, and again I'm stunned by her control. Her expression remains impassive.

"I'm afraid that name doesn't ring a bell," she says.

"Does the name Marko?"

"Who's that?"

"The hit man who murdered Randy. IIC paid for the contract on him."

Ms. Brutran is amused. "I'm sure you have proof to support these wild accusations?"

"Of course. I never leave home without a pocketful of proof."

"Ms. Perne—"

"Alisa, please. If I may call you Cynthia."

"I prefer Cindy."

"Cindy it is."

"Alisa, I agreed to see you because of the reason I stated. You're wealthy, and my firm is interested in investing your wealth. But as to these wild accusations you're making, I must say they seem beneath a person of your stature."

Slowly, I turn up the power of my gaze. Brutran doesn't flinch. Indeed, I feel an odd power radiating back from her, one I've never felt before.

"Who are you?" I whisper.

"I told you who I am."

"What do you want with me?"

"I told you that as well."

"But you're lying, we both know that. Why the games?"

"I'm a businesswoman, Alisa. I don't play games." She leans closer. "It's important you understand this clearly. This meeting is important to our whole firm."

She's trying to tell me something without saying it aloud. There's also power in her words. She's trying to implant a suggestion inside me. Because I'm aware of the psychic trick, I'm able to block it. But I struggle to figure out her hidden message.

"Then tell me the true nature of your business," I say.

She smiles. "Why should I?"

"Perhaps I can help you. Perhaps we can help each other."

She shakes her head. "Honestly, I doubt you would help us. At least not willingly."

Us.

"You think I need to be motivated," I say.

"Yes."

"Then you must know who I am," I reply, straining with my mental antennae to pick up even a fragment of her thoughts. But I get . . . nothing.

"We have some idea."

I scan the room, searching for hidden cameras, listening devices. I see nothing, but that means nothing. They could be built into the very walls. Yet there's a strange dead sound to the room. Our words hit the walls and don't bounce back. I assume she employs an exotic form of soundproofing.

She has referred to "us" and "we." She's telling me our conversation is not private. She might also be warning me that if I try to attack her, I will be cut down.

"Tell me what you want with me," I say.

"Maybe later."

"I didn't come here to harm you."

"Then why did you come?"

"For information."

For the first time, I appear to have said something the woman did not expect. She frowns, and I finally realize she's listening to an implant buried deep in her ear. Yet the technology must be advanced. I can't hear what her associates are telling her.

"You can always put them on speakerphone," I taunt her.

She gestures, as if to brush aside my comment, or else the ones in her head, I'm not sure. Then she points to the door. "I think it would be best if you left. Now."

Since she has implied that there are guns trained on my body, I take her advice. But I don't want her to think I fear her. Quite the contrary.

"Shanti Garuda," I say. "You've taken a contract out on her as well. Due to conditions beyond his control, Marko won't be assassinating her or anyone else anytime soon. And I'd advise you not to hire another assassin."

Nothing surprises this woman. She reacts as cold as ever.

"How is she any business of yours?" she asks.

I stand. "She's a friend of mine. I want her left alone."

Brutran also stands. "This is my building, my company. I give the orders here."

She is definitely threatening to kill me. This instant. I'm forced to back down, a feeling I despise. "You're right, Ms. Brutran, this is your place. I'll leave you now."

"Later, Alisa."

"Definitely."

NINE

Lisa Fetch answers the door of her condo after peering through the eyehole. At least she's displaying some caution, but I doubt she's ready to hear everything I have to tell her. She hastily invites me inside.

"Did you meet with Ms. Brutran?" she asks.

"Yes."

"How did it go?"

"Before I answer, I'd like to know if you've heard from Jeff."

"Not a word. I'm so worried."

"Take me to where he lives."

"Why?"

"I want to examine the place. Let's go now."

"Shouldn't we call the police?"

"No." It's a hard no, difficult for her to resist.

Fearful, reluctant, Lisa nevertheless climbs in my rental

and we speed over to her boyfriend's place. My driving scares her; she worries I'll get a ticket. She doesn't know all I have to do is smile at a policeman and he'll walk away.

Jeff lives in an actual house. I ask Lisa to remain in my car while I go inside. She resists, naturally, she wants to come along, but finally gives me a key to open the door. I tell her to shout if anyone approaches the car. Yet I feel we're safe, for the time being. I know we weren't followed. That was one reason I drove so fast.

I smell the blood the instant I enter the house.

I remember Jeff's smell from his visit. It's his blood.

A bloodhound would sense the odor, perhaps, but not a human. And I suspect the people who came for Jeff have not left traces of blood that can be detected by special chemicals or lights. Nevertheless, his blood is in the air, infinitely tiny particles, and it is fresh.

There's a strong odor in the bedroom. But I'm not surprised that my nose leads me farther on, to his bathroom, to the drain in his tub. I'm able to see the scene as if it were playing out live before me. They surprised him in his bedroom, probably while he slept. They struck him on the head and cut him slightly. Then they carried him into the bathtub and butchered him alive with a sharp knife. It doesn't matter how long they ran the shower. I can smell the amount of blood that's gone down this drain, and it's enough to fill a body.

I notice there's no computer in the house.

Lisa told me he owns three.

I return to the car. Lisa waits anxiously.

"Did you learn anything?" she asks.

Putting my hand on her arm, I gaze into her weary green eyes.

"Jeff's dead. He was killed last night. IIC sent their people to kill him."

Lisa struggles to keep up. "You don't know that. You can't . . . I was in his house this morning, and there's nothing there that shows he was attacked."

"That's because the people who killed him were professionals. But in my own way, I'm a professional. I know a crime scene when I see it. Jeff is dead, and your life's in danger. Frankly, I'm not sure why they didn't kill you last night. I can only assume you're still of value to them."

"You don't know any of this!" Lisa screams.

I lock my gaze on her eyes and force the truth into her brain.

"He's dead. IIC killed him. I'm sorry, but you have to accept that."

In response, she collapses, sobbing, in my arms. I hold her a long time. Although I've killed thousands, I've never forgotten the feeling of what it's like to lose a loved one. Lisa truly loved Jeff, he was a fine man, and I know she'll miss him for a long time.

I drive her back to her condo and order her to pack. She

obeys as if in a trance. I make sure she brings with her all the computer records or written files she has on IIC. Apparently, she has a load of information on her laptop, which I keep with me as I store the rest of her things in my trunk. We get on the 10 freeway heading east.

"Where are we going?" she mumbles.

"Where no one can find you. From now on you're to talk to only me, and on a cell phone I'm going to give you."

"What's wrong with my cell phone?"

"Give it to me."

"Huh?"

"Give me your cell."

She complies, slowly, and I shatter it on the dashboard and throw it out the window. She gasps.

"Why did you do that?" she cries.

"I suspect they placed a tracking device in it. From this moment on you have to live as if you're being hunted. Wherever you sleep, wherever you eat, you're not to use a credit card. Don't worry about money—I'll give you cash to live on. I'm going to get your new identity. Lisa Fetch doesn't exist."

"Why are you doing this?"

"I don't want you to end up like Jeff. Listen, you asked if I met with Ms. Brutran. I did, and I can assure you she's one of the most dangerous creatures I've met in my life. She threatened to kill me, and only let me leave IIC alive because she wants something from me."

"What?"

"I don't know, we didn't get that far. She's not a normal woman, and that's not a normal company. You know this already. You can't go back there. You can't call to tell them you're quitting. Just vanish, for now, until I'm able to figure out what they're doing and how to stop them."

"You speak of them like they're evil."

"They are. Listen, this morning I was in Texas. The same man who murdered your ex, Randy, was contracted to kill a teenage girl named Shanti Garuda. Does that name ring a bell?"

"You asked me about her earlier. I told you I don't know her."

"IIC paid for a high-level hit man to kill this girl. I was lucky I was able to stop him. But IIC was in a hurry that she die. Can you think of any reason, even a crazy reason, why they would want her dead?"

"Wait . . ." Lisa pauses. "No, that can't have anything to do with it."

"What is it?"

Lisa is thoughtful. "I told you IIC's performance in the market has dropped in the last two years. They asked me to correlate groups of numbers with the drop, to see if I could detect a pattern. The cause wasn't obvious, because on the surface it appeared this number helped inflate their earnings."

"I don't understand. What do you mean by 'groups of numbers' and 'this number'?"

Lisa shrugs. "That's just it, I don't know what the numbers stand for. But they were always five-digit numbers. Initially I thought they represented stock symbols. But later I thought they might be IIC's way of listing people. Actual employees in the company."

"How could an individual both help and hurt their earnings? It seems they would either do one or the other."

"That was the puzzle. That's why they couldn't answer it without my help. But I'm a mathematician, and using advanced algorithms I was able to spot a trend where this number—or person—helped boost the revenue from a small group of stocks, while causing other numbers—or other people—to mess up when it came to a large list of stocks. Do you follow?"

"She gave answers that helped her performance but hurt others."

"Exactly. Although I have no idea how she could do such a thing."

"Shanti went to work for IIC two years ago."

"That is a curious coincidence. Do you know the exact date?"

"I can find out."

Lisa hesitates. "This last task they gave me at work, it made me wonder if I was finally working on what they call the Array."

"I was wondering the same thing."

"Do you know what it is?" she asks.

"Not yet."

"Do you have a theory?"

"I have lots of theories. We need facts. These people are messing with your life, and now they're messing with mine. Do you know the night after you visited me, someone showed up at my house and tried to kill me?"

Lisa is shocked. "IIC didn't know we were there!"

"Like I said, they may have had a tracer on your cell phone."

"Why didn't you check? Why did you just toss it out the window?"

"Nowadays, devices like that can look like anything. They can be built into the cell's computer chips. I threw the phone away because every minute we kept it made us that much more vulnerable."

"What if they put a tracer in my laptop?"

"Did you ever take your laptop to work?"

"No."

"But you took your cell, probably every day."

Lisa shakes her head sadly. "How come your assassin failed to kill you but had no trouble killing Jeff?"

"My house is equipped with elaborate security."

"Still, Jeff's a cop. He was armed."

"I'm sorry, Lisa. He's dead."

She is silent a long time. "I only have your word that all these things are true."

I pull over to the side of the freeway. I have tried to be

sympathetic, but now it's time for tough love. If the woman refuses to believe me, she'll die, it's that simple.

"That's the biggest crock of BS I ever heard. You and your boyfriend flew all the way out to Missouri to talk to me about your evil company even before I knew its name. Now you're trying to convince yourself everything is fine at work and your lover is going to magically come walking back through your door. It's time you woke up and faced reality. Jeff knew you guys were in danger when he was sitting in my living room. That's why he was there. And he's not playing a mind game with you today by not calling. He knows you'd be worried sick if he didn't check in. But he can't call you, Lisa. He's no longer with us. But IIC still is. They're hunting us both, and I have a feeling they won't let up until either we get rid of them or they get rid of us." I pause. "Are you listening?"

She wipes away a single tear. "Yes."

"Will you do what I say and lie low until we figure this out?"

"Why can't I help you? No, don't shake your head, Alisa. You listen. If what you say is true, they've murdered the two men I love most in my life. I can't just sit around forever, waiting for you to call."

"I understand. I would feel the same way. Let's make a deal. Give me a few days, and when I feel things have cooled down, I'll come get you."

"Then we can work as partners?"

I admire her grit. "Sure," I say.

• • •

I drive as far as Barstow, a godforsaken town in the middle of the desert. There I register Lisa in a Motel 6—under the name Lacey Jones, like they bother to check—and give her ten thousand in cash to keep her afloat. Lisa is reluctant to hand over her laptop, but I'm anxious to scan her notes on IIC. After all, she's been suspicious of her firm since she went to work for them. I might see something she's missing. In the end, she lets me take it.

I take her picture before I leave, and I e-mail a digital copy of it to a person in LA who's an expert at making fake IDs.

I drive back to Malibu and park not far from the IIC building. From there I hike into the hills that overlook the firm. By now the sun is near the horizon, but I see Ms. Cynthia Brutran is still hard at work in her office. I can see her through the reflective glass. Okay, I think, her building is her fortress, she made that point clear. I probably would have been shot down if I had tried to kill her this afternoon. But she cannot remain inside forever, and when she leaves . . .

Unfortunately, the woman appears to be a workaholic. She's on the phone, she types and reads on her computer, she calls in a second shift of secretaries and dictates letters. Midnight comes and goes, and I continue to sit nestled in the nearby hills while she shows no sign of fatigue.

I grow impatient. I consider storming the building.

Yet I hesitate. I have my reasons. . . .

With my telescopic vision, I can see Ms. Brutran's computer screens, and by shifting my place in the hills, I see another room where four security guards are devoting themselves full-time to three dozen screens that continue to pan the area around the building. The guards are all armed.

I can't hear them talking through the glass. Worse, I can't hear Brutran when she's on the phone. I'm familiar with most forms of soundproofing, but this is something remarkable. The only explanation is that the glass isn't just double-plated. Somehow they've managed to create a vacuum between the plates. Since sound needs a medium through which to propagate—such as air—these IIC people have created essentially a "dead zone" for any noise.

Why would they go to such extremes? For me? They just met me, and they didn't know I was coming to their office. Also, I'm not sure they know what I am. The number of guards and cameras and the vacuum windows are all very odd.

It's like they have armed themselves against another foe.

It makes me wonder if Ms. Brutran knows ancient Egyptian.

While waiting, I scan Lisa's laptop. It is not very helpful. The information she collected while working at IIC is mostly of a paranoid nature. When she started at the firm, she often wrote notes about how her boss gave her busywork that had nothing to do with her academic background. True, she was given the "reams of papers filled with numbers" that she told me about, and was ordered to search for patterns. But no patterns existed.

Her starting pay was ridiculously high, in the low six figures, but the firm appears to have kept her around in case of some emergency that never appeared. However, her boredom led her to investigate areas that IIC's upper management probably didn't appreciate. She befriended a woman named Michelle Ranker, who worked in accounting. It was Michelle who first told her about "the kids" and how she made sure they received their checks every month. Yet Michelle didn't speak directly about the Array.

I know of Michelle, of course. Marko killed her.

It was actually Lisa's ex, Randy Clifford, who gave Lisa and Jeff the most insight into IIC. I'm not surprised, since Lisa raved what a brilliant hacker he was. A pity he didn't cover his tracks better. His quick peek into IIC's files cost him his life, and now his death was part of a much larger pattern, now that Michelle and Jeff were also out of the picture.

What's the pattern?

IIC kills without hesitation—one could say they do so casually. By nature, I'm a predator. I do likewise, but nowadays I only hurt those who hurt others. IIC clearly craves money and power, that's obvious, yet I have no idea what their ultimate motive is.

Brutran can tell me. If she'd just go home, I could kidnap her and torture her at my leisure. I'm determined to make her talk after the way she taunted me this afternoon.

To my amazement, she doesn't leave her office all night.

The woman has takeout delivered to her office, and she stops for a few breaks to walk about the building and chat with the security guards and other hardworking employees who appear to share her work ethic. But she doesn't go outside, not even to catch a breath of fresh air.

Does she know I'm watching and waiting?

I move deeper into the hills as the sun rises.

I'm tired of waiting, but I'm not physically tired. I like an hour of sleep a day, but I can go a month without resting. I have a liter of Fiji water on hand; it keeps me from getting dehydrated. I prefer blood to water, naturally, but unlike the fictional fang figures that haunt so many modern novels, I no longer require it to live.

I still have the Glock that I took from the locker near LAX. I didn't take the gun into Ms. Brutran's office the first time. I was worried I might trip an alarm. But I won't confront her again without being armed. Even if she's surrounded by a platoon of guards, if need be I can grab her and use her as a shield. I assume her home will have security as well; that is, if she ever goes home.

I don't waste time as I wait for Brutran to leave. I'm on the phone making arrangements for Shanti's security. It takes work. I have to make sure each security guard assigned to her has a fake FBI identity that can be backed up by a local FBI agent. My people in the FBI have to labor overtime to help with the setup. But by the time the sun comes up, Shanti has at least four guards on her at all times.

That will be enough to discourage any human hit man. However, if IIC sends a fellow like the guy that tried to kill me, then no amount of guards will help. Shanti will die, probably along with her uncle.

I consider dispatching guards to watch over Lisa but decide she'll be safer relying on her invisibility. IIC has so much money, I fear they might have sources in the FBI like I do. The possibility makes me consider moving Shanti to another state. Yet I sense I can only push her uncle so far. Guards outside the door are one thing. But having to move . . . I don't think he'll go for it.

While I wait, I reflect on the last times I saw Teri and Matt. They each came to my house separately, which was good in a way. They were more open being alone with me.

Teri had located half the books I asked her to find, and she felt she'd have the rest by the end of the week. I reassured her she was doing a good job, but I could tell she still felt guilty about the salary I was paying her. She didn't feel she was doing enough to earn it.

"So far I'm just being a gofer," she said. "Anyone could do that."

"Don't think that way. Before you finish working with me, you will have helped in ways you can't imagine."

"I'll believe it when I see it."

"Believe it now. The way I work, I ramp up the further I get into a piece. By the time I finish this book, I'll be working day and night, and you'll be begging me for a break."

We talked in my kitchen, drinking peppermint tea with raw honey. I was only beginning to realize how strict Teri was with her diet. She seldom drank and never took drugs. The same could not be said for her boyfriend. She confided that Matt liked to smoke hashish soaked in opium.

"He only does it occasionally, so I don't worry," she hastily added.

"That's interesting. Did you know that was the drug of choice for the American soldiers who served in Vietnam?"

"No."

"Where does he buy it?"

"I don't ask and I don't want to know. But if Matt wants something bad enough, he gets it. You should see his house. He has an amazing collection of rugs from all over the world. They're a hobby of his."

"An unusual hobby for a budding rock star."

Teri groaned at my mention of his music.

"He's still acting like a goat when it comes to your offer to help him put together a record. He can be stubborn, and this is definitely one of those times. He feels like he has to make it on his own or it doesn't count."

"To who?"

"I asked him the same thing. Who is he trying to impress? It can't be me, because he's just annoying me with his male ego. I told him as much, but he didn't respond. That's another bad habit of his. He's hard to argue with. He clams up and says nothing. I suspect the only way we're going to get him to go to New York or LA is if he decides to go on his own. And chances are he won't tell us if he goes. He'll just vanish one day. That's the way he is."

"Does he disappear often?"

"Not too often, not now. But before he got these gigs, he could take off for a week without warning. And before you ask, no, I don't think he's seeing someone else."

"I'm glad you have that faith in him."

"It's not his style to cheat. He despises hypocrites."

"Do his quirks frustrate you?"

She sighed. "Yeah. But I try to stay focused on my own goals."

"What's your main goal now? To get into medical school?"

Teri hesitated. "That's on my list, but it's not at the top."

"You were serious the other day when you said you wanted to compete in the Olympics."

"Yes." She paused. "You said you've seen me run before."

"I've seen two of your races. When Truman competed against Chapel Hill and Ohio State. You ran the 5K against Chapel and the fifteen-hundred-meter against Ohio. You won both races—I was impressed."

"Thanks. I don't know how much you know about track. The season's almost over, and the NCAA finals are about to start. The woman I beat at Ohio, Frances McCormick, won the NCAA championship last year in the metric mile. That's another name for the fifteen-hundred-meter race."

"Wasn't Frances on the U.S. Olympic team four years ago?"

"Wow. You have an amazing memory."

"I told you, I remember everything. But you're not just interested in competing in the Olympics. You want to win a gold medal."

She blushed. "It's a dream, I know, a crazy dream. I'm not in the same league as the Africans. No one is. The trials are only two weeks after the NCAA finals. I've been training like mad. I spend more time at the track than I do in class or with Matt."

"Is he supportive?"

"He acts a hundred percent supportive. But I think he resents the time commitment. And now that I'm working for you, I'll probably see him even less."

"Why didn't you tell me about this dream the other day?"

"The day we met, you saw Matt play, and I'd be the first person to admit his talent is a lot more interesting than my ability to run around a track."

"Don't diminish your gift. I love track and field. There's no sport more primal than a race. At the dawn of civilization, I'm sure cavemen used to boast to one another, 'I bet I can run faster than you.' Or, 'I know I can run farther than you.' You laugh, but it's true. The first sport on earth was racing. That's why the Olympics never get old. And that's why I admire your desire to compete at the highest level."

"Thank you. It means a lot to me to have your support."

"You mean my money."

"No! I mean—"

"I know what you mean, Teri. Relax, I was just teasing."

"Well, frankly, your money helps. If I went back home, I'd be forced to work full-time and I wouldn't be able to train as much. But if I can stay here, when classes get out I'll have all the time I need to work on the track."

"You said before your coach wants you to train on the track. But you don't like it."

"Coach Tranton insists on the interval training. But he's a genius when it comes to developing runners. It's one of the reasons I decided on Truman. It's a small college, but every year we compete for the NCAA championship. He's an expert on the mile. My time keeps dropping. It's all because of him."

"I envy you, Teri. You know exactly what you want. Now all you have to do is go get it."

She laughed. "And beat out a hundred other women who will be competing for the three spots on the Olympic team."

"My intuition is almost as good as my memory. I have a sneaking suspicion you're going to make it."

That made her smile. Teri has such a lovely smile.

But I don't know why I told her that.

It wasn't like I was going to give her a pint of my blood.

No way. It was out of the question.

However, I did want her to make the team. . . .

The next day Matt stopped by. He used the excuse that he was looking for Teri, but we both knew how feeble it was. He wanted to see me, and of course I wanted to see him. He's such a pleasure to look at. He came from the gym, dressed in shorts, Nikes, and a sleeveless sweatshirt. He smelled of sweat, but to me it was a great smell. I offered him a bottle of beer and he took three. He said he was thirsty after his workout.

"And you like to drink," I said as we settled in my living room. He sat on the couch beside me. Our feet were inches apart.

"Did Teri tell you that?"

"I saw you at the club last Friday, remember?"

"Did I drink much that night? I don't remember."

"Six Scotch and Cokes, before the second show."

"I must have been drunk then."

"Liar. I don't think you can get drunk." It was true what I said. He seemed like one of those rare people who can function with a large amount of alcohol in their system. Nevertheless, I knew I could drink him under the table.

"I notice you kept up," he said.

"I was just being sociable. What brings you here this evening?"

"I told you, I was looking for Teri."

"Uh-huh. Now tell me the real reason."

He smiled. "You never give a guy a break, do you?"

"Not guys like you. You don't need them."

"That sounds like a backhanded compliment."

"It's a plain insult. Why are you here?"

He shrugged. "I wanted to talk, get to know you better. It's hard for me to loosen up sometimes when Teri's around. As I'm sure you've already guessed, she's more proper than I am."

"She's a sweetheart."

He stares at me and nods. "She's also innocent. She has an IQ through the ceiling, and it sometimes hides the fact she's only a year out of high school."

"Are you worried I'm going to take advantage of her?"

"That's not your style. I can see that already."

"Then what's bothering you?"

"You. You're the mystery woman."

"Don't tell me I inspired that song you sang the other day."

"Maybe. Let's be blunt, Alisa. You're clever at getting people to talk about themselves, but you don't volunteer much about yourself. You know, we have no idea where you were born, where you went to school, who your friends are."

"Do you really give a damn about that stuff?"

He holds my eye a moment longer before smiling. "I guess not. Shit like that doesn't tell you who a person is. Still, my point is valid. You've burst into our lives in a big way. But who are you?" He reached out and touched my bare foot. "Tell me who you are, Alisa."

"Careful. Touch them and you have to rub them."

He didn't hesitate. He pulled my feet into his lap and started massaging them. "Talk," he said.

"Or you'll pull out my toenails?"

"Something like that."

I took a slug of my beer. "My past is complicated. I don't like talking about it because I can give people the wrong impression. Let's just say I'm not the person I used to be."

"Do you have a criminal record?"

"Maybe. Do you?"

"No. Where were you born?"

"I thought that didn't matter to you."

"I changed my mind."

"India. In the north."

"You don't look Indian."

"I'm one of the original Aryans."

"How did you get so much money?"

"How do you think?"

"I figure you must have inherited it."

"Not true. I'm a great saver, and I know how to invest."

"Do you play the market?"

"I love to play . . . it."

My remark might have been suggestive, I don't know. He pulled me closer and began to massage my calves. He had such strong hands and his touch was . . . well, it was ridiculously sensual. I felt myself getting aroused, and I would have had to be blind not to know he was excited. I swore I wouldn't kiss him. I knew if I did I wouldn't stop. Still, he kept rubbing me higher, harder, and deeper.

"You like this?" he asked.

"Stupid question."

"You know, I've never cheated on Teri."

"I believe you."

"But you're thinking there's a first time for everything."

"I didn't ask you to massage my feet."

"Yes, you did."

"I didn't ask you to massage my legs."

"Do you want me to stop?"

I leaned back. "Maybe you should."

He leaned closer. He kissed me on the cheek, or else I averted my lips, I wasn't sure. He spoke in my ear. "Who the hell are you?"

"I'm a phantom. I'll be here for a while and then I'll disappear. You don't have to worry. I won't hurt Teri."

He sat back and stared deep into my eyes. "I think that's the first time you've lied to me."

I wanted to argue with him. I couldn't.

Looking back, I realize Matt is obsessed with protecting Teri. He is attracted to me. His flirting is genuine. Yet he uses it for a deeper goal. To pry the truth out of me. And he's good at it. He got me to reveal something I had no intention of revealing, and as a result he now knows I'm dangerous.

I wonder if he will warn Teri to stay away.

I suppose I couldn't blame him.

I call Lisa Fetch last, at nine in the morning, and with Brutran still hard at work at her desk. I don't worry my call can be tapped. I have a device on my cell that makes it 100 percent secure. Claire, my FBI friend, gave it to me.

Lisa sounds tired, and I doubt she got much sleep. I feel bad about having turned her life upside down, but I can't think of another way to keep her safe.

"I still haven't located Jeff," she says.

"Did you call his house?"

"What do you think?"

"I think that might be a bad idea."

"Look, Alisa Perne, or whatever your real name is, he may be dead to you, but I still have hope."

"You have to take my advice seriously. Hope can be a good thing in many situations, but you have to admit it's a bad sign he hasn't left a message on your home voice mail, which I'm sure you've checked a hundred times."

She's tired and she's hurting. It's all there in her voice.

"You don't have to keep rubbing it in," she says.

"Okay. Let me ask you a question. How often does Ms. Brutran work around the clock at her desk?"

"What do you mean?"

"I'm sitting outside your building. I've been here all night and she's never gone home."

"That's weird."

"I take it this is weird even for her?"

"As far as I know. When the day is done, she usually goes home with the rest of us. At least as far as I could tell. I didn't keep close track of her schedule."

It is as I fear. Ms. Brutran is staying at work because of me.

"I'll give her another night, see what she does," I say.

"What are you going to do? Kidnap her the way you kidnapped me?"

"There's no use whining, Lisa. I gave you plenty of cash. You can go home if you like. But I wouldn't want to bet on your odds of being alive next week."

Lisa's tone softens. "I do appreciate what you're trying to do for me. It's just hard, you know, to be here all alone, not knowing what's going on. Without Jeff."

"I understand. I promise to call you tonight and give you an update. But for now, try not to use the phone to call anyone other than me. Okay?"

"I hear ya," Lisa says.

We exchange good-byes and I stretch out and wait.

TEN

That night, finally, not long after sunset, Brutran leaves her office and heads for her car. I run for mine. It's a mile away, but I set a world record getting to it. I'm not unduly worried about losing her in traffic. My ears are acutely attuned to every sound in IIC's basement, where the firm stows their cars. Fortunately, the garage isn't equipped with vacuum-plated glass, and I'm able to hear Brutran not only start her car, but say good night to the garage attendant.

To my surprise, Brutran heads north on Pacific Coast Highway, not south into Los Angeles. The road is winding, the traffic sparse. I hang back a mile. The woman drives a white BMW, one of the six brands of cars I sacrificed to the sniper and his Gatling gun. As I follow, I try to envision what type of security I will find at her home, and what I'll have to do to defeat it. My heart beats with anticipation, and I realize how anxious I am to get my hands on her, to get to the truth of IIC and its mysterious Array.

The woman has a remarkable ability to control her mind, but I'm confident I can break her. There's a limit to how much pain any human being can stand. Plus her cavalier attitude toward assassinating innocent people angers me, and when I'm angry, my behavior knows no limits.

Brutran drives north along the coast until there's a break in the hills on our right and she's able to take a country road across vast farmland. From there she accelerates and races into the hills overlooking Ventura. I'm not surprised to see her turn up a long driveway that leads to a mansion sitting atop its own peak. The architectural style of the residence is the opposite of her workplace. This house belongs on an old Spanish plantation. Although technically one story, it's spread over an acre of shifting terrain, giving it a half dozen different levels.

The view is beautiful: the glittering lights of the city below, the dark expanse of the far-off ocean. But what strikes me most as I sit in my car down the hill from her driveway is the silence of the spot. I hear a garage door open and close. Brutran turns off her engine and enters her home. Yet she talks to no one, because no one's there. For the moment I'm bewildered. There's no husband present, no children, no security guards.

I remember the conclusion I came to earlier, when I spoke to Lisa. That Brutran must have stayed at work because she was afraid of me. The idea seemed logical at the time. The woman and I had a tense conversation, and then she went out of her way to spend the next thirty-six hours locked in her fortress. But now she's come out in the open, and returned home to an empty mansion, without a soul around to protect her.

There's something here I'm missing.

Yesterday afternoon, I was unable to read Brutran's thoughts. Yet when I did catch a faint glimpse of her mind, it felt like a tight capsule of consciousness that intimidated even me. She wasn't simply disciplined and calculating. It was her coldness that struck me the most. It was like she had been born without a conscience, or else had had it surgically removed from her brain because it no longer suited her goals.

I know nothing of her likes and dislikes, but I do know she'd leave nothing to chance. Yet she has met me, face to face, and felt the danger I represent, the same way I sensed the danger she represents, and now she's left herself wide open to attack.

It worries me. No, it scares me.

What I'm missing is the unexpected.

Carefully, I park in a cluster of trees and get out and hike around the ridge where the house stands. I search for hidden cameras, scanning lasers, infrared sensors—any type of high-tech surveillance equipment. But I find nothing, which is odd. Nowadays, virtually anyone rich enough to own such a mansion would have installed a basic blanket of electronic security. It's like Brutran's so confident of what's inside her that she's no longer worried about what's outside.

I hear Brutran turn on the TV. CNN.

My head tells me to wait, to learn more, to see what she's up to. My heart burns with impatience. I not only want the truth, I want revenge for all those she's so casually killed.

I step to a sliding glass door at the back of the house. It's locked. I snap it quietly using brute force. Then I'm inside, my Glock in my right hand, the safety off, moving silently toward the sound of the TV.

Suddenly a little girl, with big green eyes, stands before me.

I'm stunned—I didn't hear her approach.

"Who are you?" she asks.

I kneel beside the child. "A friend of your mommy's."

She holds up her doll. A beat-up clown with a sad smile.

"Mr. Topper can't sleep. He's having nightmares. He keeps waking me up."

I pat the doll's head. "Mr. Topper just needs a big kiss from you. Then his bad dreams will go away."

"You promise?"

"I promise. Now go back to bed. I have to talk to your mommy."

The girl nods and walks away. Strange little thing. Silent as a mouse.

I continue my hunt. Around a sharp corner, in an open living room with windows that reach from the floor to the ceiling, I see Brutran munching on a fruit salad and watching the news. There's no sign of her husband. Then again, I never saw

Mr. Brutran in his office the last two days. And it was easy to identify his workplace. His office is next to his wife's. I have to assume he's out of town.

Her food is fresh, with slices of strawberries, bananas, oranges, apples, kiwis, and melons. I realize I'm starving. I don't know whether to shoot her or to ask her for a bite.

Brutran lifts up the control and lowers the volume.

"Are you going to stand there or join me?" she asks.

I assume she heard me talking to her daughter, although we were both whispering. Of course, nothing about this woman makes sense. I decide to join her. Crossing the living room, I sit in a chair beside her, keeping a grip on my Glock but letting it lie in my lap. She's changed out of her work clothes and taken a quick shower, and now she wears a fluffy white bathrobe. Most people would say she looks relaxed. But I'm blessed with an arsenal of subtle senses, and I've only to gaze into her dark eyes to know she's not let her guard down an inch.

She gestures to the TV, leaving the volume down low.

"Do you keep up with worldly affairs, Alisa?" she asks.

"I watch the news and read the *New York Times*."

"Do you like CNN?"

"I think they do a pretty good job of reporting."

"IIC owns CNN. Of course, they don't know that, and wouldn't believe it if I told them. But they never make a major programming decision without input from the people we put on their board." She points to the black newscaster. "We're thinking of promoting this man. He's smart. He appeals to middle-aged women."

"It must be intoxicating to have so much power. Or is it frustrating that you don't get to brag about it?"

"I feel no need to brag."

"Except to me."

She shakes her head and reaches for a strawberry. "You misunderstand me. I'm trying to give you a sense of our reach, not to impress you, but so you can better understand us."

"You brought me here to educate me?"

"In a manner of speaking."

"Why didn't you educate me yesterday when I was in your office?"

"Too many people were watching and listening."

"Was your husband one of those people?"

"He's not important."

"It's my understanding he's president of IIC."

"In name only. I run the company."

"Does he know this?"

She shrugs. "He's a man, he thinks he's in charge. I let him think that. It changes nothing. I'm in charge of a unique company, and I'm always on the lookout for unique individuals."

"Don't tell me you're offering me a job."

"The title's irrelevant. I'd like us to work together. That is, if we can come to an understanding."

"The best way to gain my cooperation is to tell me what I

want to know. Then I relax. But when I feel confused, I . . ." I gesture with my gun. "I react badly."

"I understand. Unfortunately, there's a limit to how much I can tell you before I know I can trust you."

"What do I need to do to earn your trust?"

"You can kill Shanti and Lisa for me, for one thing."

"You're joking."

"No."

"Why do you want them dead?"

"Lisa knows too much about the inner workings of IIC. She's a loose cannon. And Shanti . . . well, it would be hard to explain the threat she poses to my company. Just accept that the threat is real. She has to be neutralized."

"What if she just stops working for you?"

"That won't stop the damage."

"The damage to what? She's a teenage girl with a severe handicap."

"On the surface. Beneath that, she's the center of an infection that makes the AIDS virus look benign."

"I don't have a clue what you're talking about. Explain."

"Not yet. I told you, I have to trust you first. I have to know you're loyal."

"I can be very loyal to those I care about."

"Is that why you won't kill Shanti?"

"It's one reason. Besides the fact she's done nothing wrong."

Brutran stares at me. I feel the power in her cold gaze. It

is as if a massive magnet scans me from head to toe, although her eyes never leave my face. I'm surprised when I feel a sudden wave of dizziness. It's usually I—my ancient eyes—who makes people swoon.

"I didn't expect you to be so sentimental," she says.

"I take it you've been studying me."

"From a distance."

"Tell me what you know about me."

"I know you're very old and very strong."

"Go on."

"I know you live and act alone. That's what puzzles me most."

"Why?"

"It makes you unique."

"Why?"

She acts surprised. "You honestly don't know, do you?"

"I'm not sure what you're talking about."

She nods again, to herself. "Interesting."

"Did you send an assassin to my house last week?"

"No."

"Who did?"

"What makes you think I know?"

"For someone who is trying to win my confidence, you're not very forthright."

"I'd like to win your confidence. But to do that, you insist I confide in you, when I keep telling you I need to know if I can count on you. We're obviously bumping up against what people call a catch-22. One of us is going to have to make a good-faith gesture. I think it should be you."

"I disagree."

"I thought you would say that." She reaches for the TV control and raises the volume a notch. "They're talking about the tension in the Middle East. Some experts believe Iran already has the bomb, while others say they are still a year away from having enough purified uranium to build one or two nuclear weapons. What do you think the truth is?"

"I don't know. But I'm sure you do."

"Iran already has the bomb. Not one they built on their own, but a dozen they bought on the black market. Saudi Arabia also has the bomb. They have hydrogen bombs, a hundred of them. You might wonder how I know this when the president of the United States doesn't. The reason is simple. I can write a check for a hundred billion dollars and he can't. Not without the approval of the House and the Senate."

"You're saying these countries bought their bombs from Russia?"

"Saudi Arabia did. When the Soviet Union collapsed, the Saudi royal family looked north and figured the Russians couldn't possibly keep track of the thirty thousand warheads they were supposed to decommission. No doubt some smart nephew of the king figured that with a hundred billion euros he could buy an already-made nuclear arsenal. Of course, somewhere along the line the king must have agreed to the plan." She pauses. "You see my point?"

"You're saying money can buy anything."

"Yes."

"Where did Iran buy their bombs?"

"From North Korea. They charged a lot less. Then again, their bombs don't always work. Iran has to remember that if they go to war against Israel. Speaking of which, they have their own nuclear arsenal. One we sold them."

"Everyone who goes on the Internet knows that."

"Yes. But they don't know why we sold them the bombs."

"We did so out of guilt. Because we turned our heads during World War Two and let six million Jews die."

Brutran nods. "Very good. Spoken like a wise observer who lived through those turbulent years."

"What makes you think I'm so old?"

"Intensive research. For such a rich lady, you have no birth certificate. Nor do you have any death certificates. You'll laugh at that last remark and say, 'Of course, I'm still alive. Why should I have a death certificate?' But let me give you a taste of the advice I can pass on to you if we agree to work together. You should have let your old identities die. It would have covered your tracks better. None of your earlier aliases were ever buried. That's one of the main ways we were able to track you."

Her advice is sound. I have been careless at killing off my

earlier incarnations. Before the computer age, it wasn't necessary. Now I see I'll have to adjust my lifestyle to include regular funerals.

Brutran has scored a point.

"How old do you think I am?" I ask.

She studies me. "Our data reaches back four centuries. You're at least that old. But sitting with you now, I sense we've barely scratched the surface of who you really are."

"Interesting."

"Now you sound like me. Good."

I shake my head. "I'm not like you. You may be right about certain worldly events, but I'll never believe money can buy everything. IIC can accumulate all they want, but when the public becomes aware of what you're up to, there will be such an outcry, your wealth will be useless."

"How is anyone going to know what we're up to?"

"No secret remains secret forever. Even now, there are cracks in your veil."

She brushes my words aside with her hand. "We own CNN and your beloved *New York Times*. Within five years we'll control all the major media outlets. Events don't make the news, the people who own the news companies do. Why, I could make you famous in less than a month, Alisa Perne. Or should I say Lara Adams? Talk about cracks in my veil. Your veil is paper thin. I don't have to physically touch you to destroy you. You have more secrets than any of us."

I play with the gun in my lap. "Are you sure you want to threaten me?"

"I'd rather reason with you. But threats have their place." She adds, "By the way, you can't harm me with that gun. Out of respect, I thought I should warn you."

"So a bullet through the brain won't bother you?"

"You'd never get that far."

"You sound pretty confident."

"I am." She slowly smiles. "Let's not fence. We have much to offer each other. We should form an alliance."

"So far I haven't heard what you can do for me."

"Let's say I know who sent that assassin after you. How would you feel if I told you I can stop your enemies from sending another?"

"Who are my enemies?"

"Don't answer a question with a question. How would you feel?"

"I can take care of myself."

"That man nearly killed you."

"How do you know how close he came?"

"To escape you had to blow up your house. He must have come damn close."

"And you promise to keep the bad guys away?"

"Yes. Among other things."

"Such as?"

She nods to the news on TV, where there are images of

Arabs and Jews killing each other. "IIC has a greater goal than wealth and power. Our higher purpose is to save mankind. Yes, I know that sounds grandiose. But the truth is mankind needs saving. You'd be hard-pressed to find a scientist who wouldn't agree that we're destroying the earth with global warming, pollution, and overpopulation. You'd have trouble finding a politician who doesn't believe we're heading for a major war in the Middle East or with China."

"And you have a magic pill that will make people behave?"

"In a sense, yes."

"The Array?"

She blinks. "What do you know about the Array?"

I gamble to keep her talking. "I know it's begun to malfunction. You can no longer count on making your usual percentage in the stock market. I wonder. Has the magic gone out of the pill?"

I have hit a nerve. The woman's face darkens.

"It seems a part of your nature to taunt us mere mortals. Perhaps if I'd lived as long as you, I'd do likewise. But I must warn you, I find the quality annoying."

"That's the second warning you've given in two minutes. Has anyone told you it seems a part of your nature to threaten people when you're in the midst of asking for their help?"

Her expression remains flat, distant. "I'm asking you to join us in a great cause. To use your special abilities to help save mankind."

"And I can start by killing two innocent young women?"

"I explained to you why they must die."

"No, you haven't." I pause. "Not yet."

"Is that a threat?"

"Yes." I raise the gun and point it at her face. "I believe it is."

She shrugs. For some reason she uses her remote to lower the volume. I see her push the mute button, and the sound stops. For the first time I realize she hasn't let go of it since I entered her house. Indeed, she was holding the remote even before I entered the living room. If it's a weapon, I assume she would have to point it at me for it to work—something I won't allow. At the same time, the device looks harmless.

But she doesn't put it down. She stares at my gun without the slightest trace of fear. "Are you going to shoot me?" she asks.

"I will if you don't start answering my questions."

"You'd kill me knowing I can protect you?"

"I know nothing of the sort. Tell me about the Array."

Her smile widens, yet it's a joyless expression.

"Why tell you about it when you can have a demonstration?"

"Huh?" I manage to mutter before I feel a sudden pressure at the back of my head. The sensation distorts my balance. I try to stand, to get away from what's causing it, but I have no control over my legs. It's as if someone else has taken charge of my central nervous system. The pressure escalates rapidly until the pain itself almost blinds me. I feel as if a metal claw fresh from a furnace has clamped down on my skull at the top of my neck. My cervical vertebrae make loud popping sounds. They feel close to rupturing.

"I think you will shoot yourself before you shoot me," she says.

I shake my head, trying to shake free of the invisible but all too real vise that squeezes me. The internal pressure is so great, I fear my brain cells will explode.

"No!" I gasp.

"Shoot, Alisa. Shoot yourself in the head."

Fearing she has somehow hypnotized me, I tear my gaze away from her eyes and try blocking out her voice. My right arm shakes. The hand that holds the gun twitches. With each passing moment, it twists the gun closer to my head. I don't understand what's happening, I only know I'm unable to resist it.

"No!" I cry.

"It will stop if you shoot. Just shoot yourself, Alisa."

I force myself to focus on the TV, anything to drown out the wicked suggestions she continues to force-feed my agonized mind. But on the screen the rival Arabs and Jews no longer fight each other. Instead, I see close-ups of children pressing guns to their temples and firing. As their innocent skulls shatter, their brains splatter the screen, and three-dimensional images of gross gray matter drip from the TV. I smell it, the bloody pulp, and I, who have killed thousands, feel sick to my stomach.

The next child who appears on the screen is Shanti. Beautiful Shanti—it's an image of her before her fiancé threw acid in her face. I'm confused. Where did such a picture come from? Is it real? Holding a gun beside her mouth, she begs for me to save her life.

"Shoot yourself and I'll live," she cries.

"No!" I shout back.

"Please, Alisa?"

"Shanti!" How does she know my name?

"I don't want to die," she pleads, before she puts the gun in her mouth. I cannot help her any more than I can help myself. My hand keeps twitching, and soon my gun is pointed at my face the same way hers is. Only I won't open my mouth, I refuse to open my mouth.

"Save me!" Shanti mouths a mumbled cry as the barrel of the gun slides past her lips.

"Don't do it!" I cry back.

"Sita!" she moans, calling me by my childhood name.

"Shanti!"

She pulls the trigger. The impact of the bullet hurts me as badly as if the bullet entered my own skull. The bullet ricochets around inside the girl's mouth, ripping out her right eye, tearing off her right nostril, bursting through her cheek and leaving a gaping hole. It's like the acid all over again.

Incredibly, the Shanti on the screen doesn't die. Her face covered with blood, she calmly puts down the gun and speaks to me in the hissing tone I'm familiar with, only amplified tenfold.

"You promised to protect me," she says.

I feel myself weep. "I'm sorry."

Shanti is suddenly bitter. "Why, you can't even protect yourself. Go ahead, pull the trigger and get it over with."

"No!"

"Put the gun in your mouth and do it!" She stops to grin as blood leaks from the hole in her face. "Who knows, you might survive and look like me. It's not so bad."

"Please, no," I beg like a frightened child.

"In the mouth," she insists.

I cannot resist her command. No matter how much my will strives to say no, my mouth begins to open, and my hand steers the barrel of the Glock into my mouth. I feel the cold steel scratch the top of my teeth. My tongue tastes the residue of the gunpowder inside the barrel from the last time I fired the weapon. I don't remember when that was, who I killed, but I know with a sickening certainty that this will be the last time I fire any gun. How ironic my long life should end in suicide.

"Oh, God!" I cry.

Shanti's grin causes her face to tear open further. More blood spills out, like black oil from a cracked engine. "That's a secret lesson the Array never had a chance to initiate you into. There's no God, Sita. He's nothing but a childish illusion. There's only power. The power over life and death." She stops and giggles like a hysterical witch. "Now pull the trigger and die!"

For some reason, hearing the final instruction of my doom from the image of a child I know is devoted to God causes me to think of Krishna. It's sad but true—in my life I've never known for sure if he was God. But like Yaksha once said, it didn't really matter if he was God or not. God was just a word. Krishna was simply too powerful to disobey. And now that my life is about to end, I see him in a slightly different light, and I would have to say it doesn't matter what we call him—he was just so loving, I have to love him in return.

If only I could say his name before I die. To die with Krishna's name on my lips means I'll go to him after I draw my final breath. That's what the ancient scriptures promise. But the gun is stuck deep in my mouth, and I can't speak. I can only think of him, and the dark blue light of his unfathomable gaze. Maybe death won't be so bad if it means I will see him again.

I hear his mantra vibrate inside my soul.

Om Namo Bhagadvate Vasudevaya.

A wave of peace washes through my chest.

As if from far away, I hear myself coughing. Gagging.

I pull the trigger. The bullet explodes in a vision of blue light.

I die, I am dead. Yet I have not lost my vision of Krishna.

I open my eyes—I don't remember closing them—and see I have shot out the TV. Somehow, I must have pulled the gun out of my mouth at the last second.

Brutran stands above me, her face creased with fear. A white trail of smoke rises from the tip of my fired weapon. She looks down, thinking she should grab it from me before I recover. Or else she considers reaching for another gun before I shoot her in the head. It's odd, but suddenly her thoughts are crystal clear to me. Her protective veil has been ripped away.

Only I know the effect won't last. Krishna promised me that I would have his grace, his protection, if I obeyed him. And even though I've gone against his word on more than one occasion, he has chosen to save me again. However, he helps those who help themselves, and I know I have to get out of this house as quickly as possible. Before the Array returns.

Standing, unsteady on my feet, I slip the gun in my belt.

I stare at Brutran, who's pale as a ghost.

"Impossible," she whispers.

"That I continue to live? Or that there could be a God?"

"Yes . . . Yes."

My reply is strangely sympathetic. "I've pondered those two riddles all my life. For me, the answer is knowing that I'll never know the answer. I have to take it on faith that both miracles are true. I suppose that's why I'm still alive." I pause. "And that's why your Array can't kill me."

The woman appears resigned to death. She doesn't grovel.

"Kill me then. I can't stop you," she says.

"Why did you try to murder me if you wanted my help?"

"I decided I could never trust you."

"When?"

"Just now."

"You're right, you can't trust me. I'll probably kill you later, and you won't stop me." Turning, I head for the door. "Until then, leave my friends alone. Understand?"

She doesn't speak but nods.

I suppose that will have to do.

I leave her as shaken as I feel.

ELEVEN

At home, I have much to consider. Most of my thoughts focus on the cryptic comments Brutran made. It's true the woman contradicted herself repeatedly. She'd say she didn't know something and then talk about it minutes later. That didn't matter much to me. That's her way; she is by nature a manipulative bitch.

Ironically, the point that impressed me most about my meeting with Brutran—besides the attack of the Array itself—was her honesty. It was unfortunate I couldn't read her thoughts, but I still have a truth sense without my telepathic gift. I know that most of what the woman said was accurate.

Yet I'm not sure if I understand what she meant.

There's a fine difference between the two, and it's a testament to the subtlety of Brutran's mind that she was able to lead me on without revealing what I wanted to know. The woman's a master at dropping hints. She said enough to keep me wanting more, but not enough to betray her position.

Even though she tried to kill me, I still feel like she's trying to recruit me to her cause. It's possible she used the Array to test me. It was probably a test she figured I'd fail, but now that I've passed, she wants me even more. I sensed that as I left her house.

I'm pretty sure she's going to test me again.

I dread the thought of the Array returning, especially now that I'm back home with Teri and Matt. I still don't know what the damn thing is, whether it's tied to Brutran's presence or not. Do I have to be in the same room for her to psychically attack? Is she the channel through which the power comes? In the end, one thing worries me the most. . . .

Can the witch, at a distance, force me do something I don't want to do?

I hate to admit it, but I'm afraid of the Array. It scares me worse than the assassin that came for me. At least he was a visible foe. True, he was a virtual superman, but he was alive, in a physical body that I could kill, and kill him I did. But my one-time resistance of the Array counts for nothing.

I know I didn't damage it. Besides, it was only by an act of Krishna's grace that I survived the initial attack. I have no doubt that if I had not thought of him at that last instant, I'd be dead now. Somehow, Krishna heard my prayer and answered.

The fact deepens my faith and my confusion. I remember,

in ancient India, how famous Krishna was for his mischievous nature. So he helped me ward off the Array this one time. It's unlikely he'll help me again. There's one thing I've learned in my long life. You can't count on grace; it doesn't follow a schedule. I'd be a fool to think God's going to keep saving my ass.

I can imagine Krishna laughing at me this instant.

It's your problem, Sita. Deal with it.

I warned Brutran to leave Shanti and Lisa alone, but I doubt she'll obey. Out of fear for their lives, I bring the women to Missouri and move them into a nearby condo. Shanti's uncle protests his niece's relocation until I explain that—besides being an FBI agent—I'm super wealthy and can afford to pay for reconstructive surgery on her face.

Lisa and Shanti form a tight bond. It's Lisa who accompanies the girl on her trips to a superb clinic I've found in Memphis. Shanti's doctors schedule a dozen preliminary surgeries, but cut the number in half when they see how fast she heals. Of course, they have no idea, nor does Shanti, that I often rub a diluted form of my blood on her face in the middle of the night when she's asleep. There's no chance it will change her into a vampire, but it might give her a chance at a normal life. Even I'm surprised when sight begins to return to her right eye.

Despite the care Lisa showers on Shanti, I find it difficult to keep our resident mathematician happy. I understand how the woman feels. She's lost her boyfriend, she's been uprooted from her home, and she's hiding from an enemy she's not fully convinced will attack her. However, I know Brutran wants Lisa dead. I tell her that her boss told me so, but she only half believes me.

To calm her restlessness, she gets a part-time job tutoring math students at Truman College. She does so under her real name. I've dropped the whole hiding routine. I'm convinced Brutran knows exactly where we are and there's no point in pretending otherwise. That's not to say we won't hit the road again in the future, if the need arises. For now I rely on Brutran's fear of my ability to resist the Array to keep the woman at bay.

We've created a dangerous balance that can't last.

A day will come when one of us will attack the other.

I hear from my sources that Joe Henderson of Fairfield, Iowa, is dead. His arm got caught in a machine that harvests corn and tore the limb off. He bled to death in his wife's arms. The local authorities are convinced it was an accident. I beg to differ. To me, it's another example of Brutran destroying an unnecessary tool.

Marko's death is a reminder of the woman's cruelty.

I ask Shanti to keep my FBI dealings secret from the others, and she does so without question. She's not naive, she simply trusts me. I even tell Shanti my real name. Lisa's another matter. She's too intellectual to blindly follow someone else. I have to keep reminding her not to discuss IIC around Teri and Matt.

The problem is, all five of us have become friends. The situation has its positive and negative sides. It's nice to have a family of sorts around me. For the first time in ages, I don't feel lonely. I love listening to Matt's music, staring at his magnificent body. Just as I enjoy sharing in Teri's dream of going to the Olympics. Plus it brings me incredible happiness to see Shanti's face healing. Even hard-to-handle Lisa is a welcome addition. Besides being a math genius, she has a sharp wit. Fortunately, I'm the only one who notices the major crush she has on Matt.

But how can I blame Lisa? I'm in the same boat.

He's so damn handsome, and talented, and charismatic. Other than his stubbornness, he's practically perfect. But if he knows about the effect he has on us poor lovesick girls, he's a master at playing dumb. He just goes about his business, writing music, playing his nightly gigs, taking care of Teri. One afternoon, on the spur of the moment, I swing by their place and catch them making love. I'm amazed at how jealous I feel.

He's a big help to Teri when she hits the track. He times each 400-meter and 200-meter interval she runs, and records her progress in a daily diary. When she finishes working out, he always gives her a long massage, carefully kneading out any cramps, so she can recover faster and train even harder the next day.

Yet he cannot give her the edge that I can.

Should I give her my blood or not?

I debate the matter furiously.

The NCAA championships, a prelude to the Olympic trials, arrive soon. They're in Chicago, and we all travel to watch Teri run the metric mile, the 1500-meter race. Shanti's in between surgeries and feeling sore, but the night before we leave for Chicago I rub an extra dose of blood on her incisions, and she awakens without pain and decides to accompany us.

Giving Shanti a few drops of my blood is an act of mercy. It aids her recovery and frees her of the majority of her suffering. Simply by gazing at her as she lies in bed, I make sure she remains asleep while I administer my blood.

But to substantially improve Teri's mile time, I'll have to put my blood directly inside her veins. I can do this without her knowledge by hypnotizing her, as long as Matt is not around. However, I struggle over the morality of the act. Teri wouldn't want to win by cheating. I've heard her harsh words against those who use steroids to improve their times. Yet I feel too much like her mom to let her go down in miserable defeat.

I decide to do nothing until after the NCAA finals. If she does badly there, I tell myself, she doesn't deserve to make the team. Of course, I lie to myself better than most people.

Teri fails to win the race. Indeed, she's lucky to finish third against the best college students in the country. Since she's just a freshman, her coach is happy with her performance, and we all congratulate her as we gather around and admire her medal.

But I can see the look of disappointment in her eyes. Later, that night, she comes to my hotel room to talk. She comes alone. She says Matt is asleep.

"You should be sleeping after such a hard race," I say.

She plops down on my bed and sighs. "I suck."

"You ran your best time under enormous pressure. How can you say you suck?"

She rubs her weary legs. "Because even the winner of today's race, Nell Sharp, isn't going to make the Olympic team. At the trials there's going to be half a dozen women who can beat her. Along with yours truly."

"You don't know that for sure."

"The clock doesn't lie. I ran as hard as I could and didn't break 4:25. It'll probably take 4:12 to win the Olympics."

"That fast?"

"Yeah. It's going to take a world record."

Teri wants the gold medal. I see that now. Making the team isn't good enough for her. Unfortunately, right now making the team's a pretty stiff proposition. I cross the room and sit beside her on the bed. At moments like this, I feel so close to her it's difficult not to hug her. Running a hand through her lovely blond hair—which looks and feels so much like my own—I stare deep into her blue eyes.

"How much do you want it?" I ask.

"What?"

"You know."

"The gold medal? I'd give anything to win."

"But you wouldn't cheat?"

"Are you talking about steroids?"

"Something else. Something secret."

She shakes her head. "Don't even tell me. I don't want to know. A medal would mean nothing to me if I knew I'd cheated to get it."

I admire her integrity. But it's ironic—as she swears she'll never cheat, it makes me more determined than ever that she win. Adding power to my gaze, I speak in a soothing tone.

"You're exhausted. Let's talk in the morning. Right now, you need to rest." Her eyes suddenly grow heavy—she struggles to keep them open. "Just close your eyes and lie down. Sleep."

Teri is asleep before her head hits the mattress.

Using my nails, I open the vein on my left wrist and do likewise with her wrist. Pressing the veins together, I let my blood pump into her. I give her thirty seconds' worth, no more, before I return her vein to her wrist. I close the incision with a few drops of my blood carefully spread over the wound. The operation doesn't leave a scar.

I let her sleep an hour before carrying her back to her room. I'm reluctant to wake her. I can feel my blood strengthening her system and know it's best she sleep through the change.

Outside her door, I listen and hear Matt snoring softly. I'm able to slip inside—using her key—and deposit Teri on the bed without waking either of them. I kiss her good night. I almost kiss Matt, but I figure I've played with fate enough for one night.

The Olympic trials for track and field are two weeks later, in Eugene, Oregon. The school year ends for Teri, and once more, as an oddball family of five, we fly to the west coast to see if our budding star can compete at the next level. On the IIC front, all remains calm, and my source in the FBI who has flown off to Switzerland has yet to uncover any new leads on Claudious Ember.

I'm too old, though, too experienced, to be lulled into a false sense of security by the lack of activity. My enemies are still out there, biding their time. The fact—and to me it is a fact and not a guess—adds to my guilt at having Teri and Matt in my life.

Shanti and Lisa are different; they are already involved with IIC. They are safer with me than without me. But my daughter—I cannot help but call Teri that—and Matt would be more secure if they had never met me. Yet when I contemplate moving to another state and walking out of their lives, never seeing them again, I feel a terrible sadness. Plus—and I know it goes against all reason—I feel it would be a mistake. My intuition keeps telling me that I've met them for a purpose.

Teri has to go through two preliminary races before she can compete for a place on the U.S. team. In those races something miraculous happens. She twice runs under 4:20. Afterward, excited, she gushes about how strong she feels. The press shares her enthusiasm. Her success in the opening rounds makes her the favorite to win the trials.

But Matt is cautious. Indeed, his concern borders on suspicion.

"She shouldn't be running this fast," he says when we're alone the night before the final. "She's burning herself out."

"She says she felt strong at the end of each race."

He shakes his head. "She shouldn't have won the races. I told her to just take third and advance to the final."

"You know how tricky the fifteen-hundred-meter is, especially at the end. If she hung back, she might have gotten boxed in. Look at what happened to Sharp, the woman who beat her at the NCAA championships. She didn't even make the final."

"Sharp had an off day. That can happen to anyone."

"Coach Tranton told Teri to stay near the front."

Matt looks doubtful. "Yeah, but he didn't want her to go to the front and stay there the whole race."

"I'm surprised at your reaction. I would have thought you'd be more excited about her times."

He stares at me. "You don't know her body like I do. Push her too far and it'll backfire."

"She pushes herself, Matt. I have nothing to do with it."

"Sure," he says, but he doesn't sound convinced.

Matt's reaction puzzles me, and I'm tempted to peep inside

his mind and see if there's something else bothering him. But it goes against a vow of mine not to eavesdrop on the thoughts of those I care about. My attitude is somewhat superstitious, I know, but I see my telepathic ability as a gift that Krishna bestowed on me to keep me safe. The last thing I want to do is abuse it.

Also, I know how disappointing it can be to gaze into another's mind and discover they're not as wonderful as they appear on the outside. I'm the first to admit I fantasize about Matt. I'd hate to ruin my dreams by putting his thoughts under a magnifying glass and discovering he's really a shallow jerk. The same with Teri. The best gifts are those we leave wrapped.

The final for the women's 1500-meter arrives. The race is run in the cool of the evening. It's the last race of the day, and the stadium is tense. No one appreciates track like the citizens of Eugene. It's like they've never let go of their native son, Steve Prefontaine, who died having never won an Olympic gold medal, a sad fact I fear I might have had something to do with.

In the early seventies, before the Munich Olympics, I was living in Oregon—where I later met Ray—and I happened to bump into Prefontaine when he was out for a ten-mile run. Since I had on shorts and tennis shoes, and had always admired the guy, I decided to run along beside him.

At the time, I meant no harm. But what I didn't realize was that Prefontaine was stunned at my ability to keep up with him. From my side, I was just getting in some exercise and saying hello, but he was trying to beat me. By the time I realized my mistake, he was gasping for air. Naturally, when I finally saw how weary he was, I feigned exhaustion and begged to stop. But it was too late—the damage had been done.

Steve Prefontaine went off to the Olympics knowing that he had been beaten by a girl. I often worried if that's why he tied up in the straightaway of his race and was passed by three people, finishing fourth without a medal.

In the final, against Matt's and Coach Tranton's advice, Teri pushes to the front and sets a brutal pace. I understand what drives her. She's feeling the fire of my blood. Yet it's a fire she doesn't know how to control, and I finally see that Matt's fears are not unfounded. I have seldom shared my blood with mortals, and I've never done so to make someone a better athlete. Have I given her too much blood? Could she really burn herself out? She runs through the first lap in sixty seconds, faster than a world-record pace.

I shout over the roar of the crowd.

"Teri! Slow down!"

It's as if she hears me, which should be impossible. She turns in my direction. Our eyes seem to meet, and I try to convey to her my fear for her safety. Since I gave her the transfusion, I have felt closer to her. I should not be surprised. We no longer share just the same genes, but the same blood, too. In that instant I feel a psychic bond stretch between us, like a golden thread capable of conquering any distance.

She suddenly slows down.

Teri wins the race by a full second, two seconds shy of a world record. The crowd gives her a standing ovation as she runs a victory lap. There is no longer any question in the minds of the experts. She is now the favorite to win the gold medal at the Olympics.

Afterward, when I hug her and congratulate her on making the team, I feel her flesh still shuddering from the effort she put it through. And I don't know whether that means she needs more of my blood or less.

TWELVE

The Olympics are two months away. Our gang returns to Missouri, and Teri continues to train in earnest, while helping me with my novel, which I begin to work on with more enthusiasm. The tenor of my book has shifted. Now I'm focused on creating a futuristic civilization inhabited by two types of human beings—those who have subjected their bodies to nanotechnology, which boosts their physical and mental abilities far beyond normal, and a small minority of people who believe it's best to remain the way nature intended. At the start of the story, the Nanots—as I call them—are in firm control of society. Indeed, it seems that normal humanity is about to become extinct.

I have no idea where the novel is going but don't mind. I enjoy writing it, and that's enough for me.

Shanti continues to get her surgeries, and her progress is

so rapid that when her uncle pays her a surprise visit he doesn't recognize her. The poor man breaks down and weeps with gratitude when he holds her in his arms.

Lisa's state of mind improves when she gets a full-time teaching job at Truman College, taking over for a math professor for the summer semester. It's apparent to the rest of us that Lisa is at heart an academic type and feels more comfortable in a university setting than in the marketplace.

After Teri makes the Olympic team, I see Matt less often. He excuses himself, saying he's busy with his music, but I know he's purposely avoiding me. His absence saddens me, but I don't dwell on it. It's almost a relief he's not around. It makes me crave him less.

The Olympics are in London, and it's been many years since I've left America. Although I was born in India, that country has changed so much in five thousand years it no longer feels like home. Nor does Europe. I came over to the New World with the Pilgrims, and although I've been back to Europe many times, if asked I would have to say I feel like an American.

I wonder if that's why I feel unsettled at the prospect of traveling to London. The sensation comes over me after Teri qualifies for the team and grows as the date of our departure approaches. There's no logical reason for my sense of dread. I simply feel that if I leave America, I won't return.

It's this feeling that pushes me to see Seymour Dorsten.

Ah, my beloved Seymour, I could write an entire book about him and still not express my feelings for him. As I mentioned before, although we've never physically met, Seymour's written several novels about me, most of which have been fairly accurate.

It's a long story, and I know when we meet he'll want an answer to the mystery of our relationship. Of course, he'll have trouble accepting the truth of our psychic bond, because I have the same difficulty. My relationship with him is a puzzle words cannot explain.

I know where Seymour lives, in Manhattan. Even without checking with my sources, I'm always aware of his location. I just have to close my eyes to see through his eyes. It's been that way since I first contacted him when he was a senior in high school. Naturally, Seymour later wrote that we became friends during that period, but I say it again: We've never met.

I tell the others I'll be gone a few days. I don't say where I'm going. It's my way. When I land at JFK, I half expect Seymour to be waiting to pick me up. I suspect he feels me near, because I've mentally sent out the thought that I'm coming. This fact is puzzling, I realize. He doesn't have to believe I exist in order to read my mind. When I deliberately link with him, he starts daydreaming about me, but he imagines the thoughts are his alone.

I'm acquainted with every detail of Seymour's life. Fifteen years ago, on the verge of dying of AIDS, he lucked out when scientists developed the protease inhibitor. Like millions of people infected with HIV, practically overnight he went from someone with an expected life span of a few months to a relatively healthy young man. That's not to say he doesn't still have the virus. Seymour has to swallow a twenty-pill-a-day cocktail to stay healthy. But he's alive, that's what matters, and he's had a remarkably successful life.

Like me, he's a writer, but he's a lot more famous, although for some reason he refuses to write under one name, on top of never using his real name. He's adopted a half dozen pen names. When he writes teen thrillers, he's Carol Kline. He publishes adult horror under Mike Fresher. Lately he's begun to put out a mystery series under Harold Boxter, and he recently wrote a nine-hundred-page love story that reached number one on the *New York Times* bestseller list as Debra Singer. When he writes a Hollywood script, he always uses the name James Hart.

With each pen name, he has a different agent represent him. Because the agents don't know he has so many identities, he avoids any legal issues. He's unquestionably the most diverse writer on the planet. His muse knows no limit. His imagination puts my own to shame, and I've lived a hundred times longer.

However, despite the millions of books he's sold, the scripts he's had made into popular movies, he's never made a single public appearance. He never does book signings, and his picture has never appeared on one of his novels. His privacy obsession is the one quality we share above all others.

Sometimes I think it is I who dreamed him up.

As I taxi into Manhattan, it's lunchtime, and I know Seymour is buying a turkey sandwich and french fries at a deli not far from his austere condo, which is located near Central Park. He has millions in the bank but seldom touches them. He's not into stuff. He enjoys movies, TV, books, long walks. He has a limited social life. In the fifteen years we've been connected, he's had only one serious relationship, with a young woman named Linda Johnson. Not surprisingly, she looked a lot like me. But she left him, the fool, I don't know why, and he's dated little during the last ten years.

I spot Seymour as he leaves the deli, carrying his sandwich in a brown paper sack into the park. This is part of his routine. It's not unusual for him to circle the park twice on foot in the same day. I follow at a distance, trying to figure out how to introduce myself. I eventually give up. I'll just say hello and take it from there, what the hell. If I give him a heart attack, I can always carry him to the nearest hospital.

He sits on a relatively secluded bench overlooking a wide grassy area. It's a Saturday. Children play with kites in the distance. Couples hold hands and pass by without thinking twice who he might be.

He's not classically handsome, but to me he's perfect. He's skinny, because of his illness, and his brown hair desperately needs a stylist. He cuts it when it starts to bother him, not before. He has full lips and long lashes, giving him a slight cherub look, and there's sorrow to the lines on his face that comes more from his depth than from any specific tragedy. There's also a warmth in his brown eyes I see in few people. As I stand nearby and study him, I feel his loneliness as strongly as his empathy, and know one has given birth to the other. A high IQ didn't make him a brilliant writer—it's his heart. No one I've ever met has Seymour's heart.

And he's never met me.

I walk over and sit beside him on the bench.

He turns and looks at me and blinks.

"Hello," I say.

He has to find the word. "Hi."

I offer my hand. "I'm Alisa. Mind if I join you?"

We shake. "Seymour. No, I don't mind."

"Thanks." I take back my hand, almost swooning at his touch. For an instant I felt as if I was in his body as much as my own. He, too, looks rattled. I add, "Do you come here often?"

"Almost every day." He tries to keep eating, to act casual, but clearly my appearance has shaken him. Yet he does not guess who I am. How can he? I'm a character in a story he wrote long ago—I don't exist. "How about you? Are you from around here?" he asks.

"No."

"Just visiting?"

"I have a friend who lives nearby."

"It's an interesting city. You meet the strangest people."

"Do you fit into that category?"

Looking down, he shakes his head. "Not really. But hang around the park and you'll run into lots of writers, actors, and artists. You just have to be careful to separate the true crazies from the moderately insane."

"Which category do you fall into?"

"Oh, I'm completely nuts. You don't want to talk to guys like me after dark. It's not safe."

"I know how to take care of myself."

"You sound pretty confident."

"Yeah."

He frowns. "Alisa, forgive me, this is going to sound silly. But have we met before?"

"Why do you ask?"

"You remind me of someone."

"An old girlfriend?"

"Not exactly. Have you been to New York before?"

"Sure. Our paths might have crossed. You look familiar to me."

"Really?"

"Yeah. To be blunt, it's the reason I sat beside you. I thought, I don't know, like we could be friends."

"I don't think your boyfriend would approve of that."

"Who said I came here to see a boyfriend?"

"Oh, I'm sorry, I just assumed."

"At the moment, I'm completely unattached."

"The way you look, I'm surprised you're ever alone."

I reply in a serious tone. "I'm used to being alone. I've been alone most of my life."

He looks over and studies me. "Why?"

"It's the way I am." I shrug. "I could ask you the same question."

"How do you know I'm such a loner?"

"I can tell by the way you sit here. You like to hang out in the park and watch people walk by and imagine what's going on inside them. At the same time, your mind can be light years away, and you don't see anyone."

He's forgotten his food. He's a long time answering.

"You're a mind reader, Alisa."

"So are you, Seymour."

"Why do you say that?"

"It's true, isn't it?"

"Maybe." He pauses. "What's your last name? If I may ask."

"That's a dangerous question."

"I'm sorry, I didn't mean to pry."

"Pry away, that's not what I'm worried about."

"I don't understand."

"I call myself Alisa Perne. But that's not my real name."

He frowns. "Is Alisa Perne a stage name?"

"Sort of. Few people know my real name."

"Are you an actress?"

"I'm acting right now."

"What do you mean?"

I reach over and touch his arm. "It's been a long time."

He feels the connection we share, it's impossible to deny. Yet he denies it anyway. "It's been a long time since what?" he asks.

"You really don't recognize me?"

"Like I said, you look familiar, but—"

"You recognize my name," I interrupt.

He goes very still, turning to stone, inside and out. I feel his shock as if it were my own. But he's not crazy. He's smart and rational. He knows I can't exist, so he doesn't let me exist. Yet he has a problem. I'm sitting right in front of him.

The pressure is too great. He goes to stand.

"I'm sorry, I have an appointment I have to keep. It was nice meeting you."

I reach out and yank him back down. I use my strength—he feels it.

"You're not going anywhere," I say.

I have scared him. He rubs his arm where I grabbed him. I might have squeezed him too hard. "What do you want?" he asks in a harsh tone.

"You don't have to be afraid," I say.

"You think I'm afraid of you?"

"Aren't you? Seymour Dorsten."

"How do you know my last name?"

"I know all about you."

"Who the hell are you?"

"I told you, you're not listening."

"What do you want from me?"

"To look at me. To listen to me. You know me as well as I know you. You might even know me better than I know myself."

He stands. "You're crazy."

I stare up at him and speak in a softer voice. "I'm sorry."

"I'm going now." He turns away. "Don't follow me."

I talk to his back. "Seymour?"

He stops. "What?"

"Please don't go. I want . . . I just want to talk awhile."

Turning, he puts his hands on his hips. "Why did you get all crazy on me?"

"I don't know. I suppose I'm kind of nuts."

"You seemed all right at first."

"I was trying to shock you into recognizing me. I guess it didn't work."

"How can I recognize you when I don't know you?"

"Would you sit down?"

"No."

"Please. I won't grab you again. I'm sorry I hurt your arm."

He rubs his arm as he sits back down. "How'd you get so strong?"

"That's a long story."

"How do you know my last name?"

"Another long story."

"Alisa—"

"But it's a story you know. You're the one who wrote it."

"You're starting to act nutty again. I'm going to leave."

I offer my hand. Not to shake, simply to hold. He stares down at it a long time, then looks in my eyes. "You have beautiful eyes," he says, finally taking my hand.

"Thank you. Do they remind you of anyone?"

Again, he lowers his head. "It's not possible," he whispers.

I squeeze his hand gently. "At the end of your story, you wrote how you wished it was possible. That I really existed."

A tear appears on his cheek. He wipes it away and another appears.

"I wrote that a long time ago. It was my first book, about a girl who thought she was the last vampire on earth." He takes back his hand and rubs his damp eyes. "How did you get a copy of it?"

"You think I read it?"

When he speaks next, his voice cracks. He's getting close.

"You must have read it. To invent that stage name."

"I'm not an actress, not really. And I never stole a copy of your book. I never read it, not in the usual sense of the word."

"Tell me your real name."

"Sita."

He gasps. "No!"

"It's true, it's me." I put my arm around his shoulder and

move closer. He's trembling, his eyes keep watering. Leaning over, I whisper in his ear. We sit together in a silent bubble. His thoughts speak to me as if they're my own. "We wrote the books together. When we join like this, you can read my mind and I can read yours. But we don't have to be physically close for it to happen. Years ago our minds bumped into each other, and you couldn't stop thinking about me. That's why the books you wrote about me were mostly true. I'm the last vampire, and you're the one who told my story."

He struggles to breathe. "I never published those books."

"I know."

"I printed out a copy, just one, then erased the file. It's locked inside my desk drawer."

"I know."

"You weren't at my high school. I never saw you there."

"You made that part up. You wanted to put yourself in the story. A lot of writers do that. We never met, but I was there, at your school. I came for Ray. Remember? You wrote how I met his father, how I killed him, and why I needed to find out who hired him to spy on me."

"Yaksha?"

"That's right." I keep whispering in his ear, but it's almost as if I don't speak at all. There's no need, our connection is so tight. "Yaksha came for Ray and me. He tried to kill us, but in the end he let us go. You wrote it all down, every detail. For a long time, your mind and mine were linked. You followed me to Los Angeles, where I met Eddie. You were there when Ray died, and when I stopped Eddie."

"You chopped off his head in a freezer?"

"That's right. Then I changed Joel into a vampire, to save his life. But the FBI came after us, followed by the army, and Joel was captured. An old lover of mine, Arturo, was working with them. I didn't know that at first, not until it was too late. Joel died and Arturo died, and things got messed up for a while. I made mistakes. Arturo left equipment behind that allowed me to become human again, and I used it on myself. I didn't know I was pregnant with Arturo's baby, and I gave birth to a daughter named Kalika."

Seymour speaks as if in a trance. "Kali Ma."

"She was a lot like the Goddess Kali. I didn't know whether she was good or evil. When I changed into a human being, it was like I fell into a weird dream. I thought Ray was alive again and that he was living with me and my daughter. She grew at a rapid rate—she kept needing more blood. I captured a boy and kept him locked in a room and used his blood to feed her. It was never enough. Then, when she got older, she tried going after the baby of a friend of mine."

"Suzama."

"The baby belonged to a woman named Paula. She reminded me of Suzama because they were both visionaries. They could see the future. To stop Kalika from hurting Paula's child, I changed back into a vampire. But my daughter was too powerful; it was like nothing could stop her. That's when I made another mistake. I sought out the help of a cult that knew about Suzama's prophecies. They believed she was supposed to be reborn in this time, and that her baby would be a divine child. When I joined forces with them, they pretended to help, but it was all a bunch of lies. Their leader was bent on sacrificing the child in a satanic ritual, and he would have, except Kalika helped me stop them. Remember what you wrote; it was all true. Kalika gave her life to stop them by sharing with me the last of her blood. She wasn't evil."

Seymour pulls back, his eyes fixed on me, his gaze bright. My voice, my words, have hypnotized him, but his trance is one of discovery. I know he feels as if he's staring into a mirror framed with the pages he wrote about me, because that's how I feel. As I relay the events of my life, it's like I live them once again. It's painful to speak of Kalika; I miss her to this day.

"Then you traveled into the past," he says.

I shrug. "Perhaps. My mind went into the past, even if my body stayed here. There was an evil man, a sorcerer, named Landulf of Capula, who had stolen my blood in order to create a race of monsters. I was sent back in time to stop him from using the blood. It was like I was given a second chance to correct a major mistake. And I was successful."

"Then you returned to the present?"

"Yes."

He shakes his head. "Wait. That's not what happened. You

tried to come back, but your body died in the present and you stayed in the past, in India, where you were born. You met Krishna, and he gave you a chance to live a normal life. To have never become a vampire."

"That's what you wrote, and maybe in some other universe that's true. But that's where your mind and my mine deviated. I returned to the present after I defeated Landulf. Then I went on with my life."

Seymour is doubtful. "How could I get so much right and yet be so wrong in the end?"

I stroke his hair. "Our thoughts got so entwined, you reached a point where you didn't know if you were writing about me or yourself. You had an advanced case of AIDS. You were dying. I'm not surprised you chose to kill me at the end of your story. You probably felt we should die together." I pause. "But you didn't die. The scientists developed those amazing drugs, and you got better. And as you continued with your life, I left you alone for a long time. I stopped sending you my thoughts."

"Why?"

"Because I'm a vampire, and so much of my life is about death, even though I'm immortal. I wanted you to be free of the burden of my long life. Free to write stories of your own. Free to love girls who didn't want to drink your blood."

"Do you really drink blood?"

"It's what I am, a vampire."

"The last vampire?"

Finally, I let go of him and look away. "I don't know. I thought I was, but I have been wrong in the past, and maybe I'm wrong now. It's one of the reasons I've sought you out. I need your advice."

He is silent for a long time.

"I want to believe you. But it's crazy, you know."

I point to two skyscrapers at the far end of the park. "What if, tonight, I leap from that building to that one. Will you believe me then?"

"I'd have to."

"Okay."

"Okay what?"

"I'll do that tonight. You can watch. Then will you help me?"

"You know from the books how much I love to give you advice."

"I need it now more than ever."

He stands and throws his sandwich in a nearby garbage can. He stretches in the sunlight and smiles. "I have two conditions, Sita."

"What?"

"If you turn out to be the real thing, then you have to let me come with you. And you can never leave me, not until I say so."

I stand and offer my hand. "Deal."

THIRTEEN

Eight weeks later, I sit in a hotel room in London with Seymour. We are discussing blood, a subject I like to think I'm an expert on, yet we wouldn't be talking about it if I knew what to do next.

The heats for the women's 1500-meter races start in three days. The final is five days off. With two heats set immediately before the final, the schedule couldn't be more brutal. But for Teri the challenge is especially difficult. Coming off the high of making the team, she has reacted with a frustration bordering on horror as her interval training has steadily gone to hell. For all practical purposes, she's back to where she was before I gave her my blood.

"It must feel weird to run like a god one month and a mortal the next," Seymour says.

"I should never have given her my blood in the first place."

"Didn't you once say regret was the most useless of all emotions?"

"A character in one of your books said that."

"Oh. Well, it's true. There's no going back."

I pace in front of him as he sits lazily on my bed.

"I have to give her more blood," I say.

"You swore to me you weren't going to risk that again."

"I have no choice. She's going to get her butt kicked."

"So what? It's just a stupid race. It's not worth the risk."

"It's the Olympics!"

"So? It's a bunch of stupid races. Two months from now, no one will remember who won what. Nor will they care."

"The last transfusion didn't hurt her. Why should this one?"

"For one thing, you don't know it didn't hurt her. Also, I know how attached you are to her, and how your mind works. You just said it—you're afraid she's going to get her butt kicked. That's why you're going to give her more blood this time."

"That's crazy. I'll give her the same amount."

"No way. You're so transparent. You're going to give her every advantage you can."

"If I give her a few more ounces, it won't make any difference."

Seymour groans. "Oh, brother."

I shove his leg out of the way and sit beside him.

"You have no idea how much this means to her," I grumble.

"Gimme a break. I see her every day. It will break her heart to lose. But I'd rather have that happen than she have a heart attack. Your blood is like fire in her veins. An extra ounce might push her over the edge. And for what? A stupid gold medal?"

I smile at him. "You have a crush on her, don't you?"

He shakes his head and reaches for a cigarette. He smokes—he never used to smoke, not in my stories, at least. "That's bullshit," he mutters.

"You love her because she's the closest thing you've found to me."

"I just found you and I don't love you."

"Liar."

"What are you trying to do, set me up with her?"

"You think she'd want you after being with Matt?"

He lights up and blows smoke in my face. "That's what I love about you. The way you make me feel so special."

"I need your help."

"I know."

"What do you know?"

"You need me to get Matt out of the way while you give her your blood."

"Can you do it?"

"Sure. But don't you think it's weird how he clings to her when you're around? I mean, I haven't known him long, but it's like he doesn't trust you with her."

"It started in Eugene, Oregon."

"Oh, yeah, you carried her back to her bed. Maybe he saw you."

"He was sound asleep, I know that for a fact. But the sudden change in her mile times, I think that shook him up. The guy's more sensitive than he acts."

"You have a crush on him, don't you?"

"Please, let's not start that again."

"You don't do a very good job hiding it. Teri's looking to you for moral support right now, but one of these days she's going to take your head off."

"Teri knows I would never betray our friendship."

"Not unless you could get away with it without her knowing."

"Christ, you're a pain in the ass. You're not at all like the Seymour Dorsten in your books. Now, there was a sweet guy."

"There was a loser, you mean." He pauses. "When do you want to do it?"

"Tonight. The longer she has to adjust to my blood the better."

"You should have given it to her before we left the States."

"That would have been too soon. Some of the effect would have worn off by now. How are you going to get Matt out of the way?"

"I have a better idea. Wait until Teri returns to the Olympic Village this evening, then sneak in. I assume you can get past their security. This way you won't have to worry about Matt.

Also, if you're going to give Teri an extra dose of blood, it's better if she stays in bed and doesn't move for the next twelve hours."

"That's clever. How'd you get so smart?"

Seymour puffs his cigarette. "If I was so smart, I'd figure out a way to talk you out of this crazy scheme."

Breaking into the Olympic Village proves to be a snap. I steal a badge from a blond pole-vaulter who looks like me and give the guard at the gate a hard stare when he checks my ID. I could have been a guy with a beard and he would have let me in.

Teri's awake when I reach her room, although it's after midnight. The girl's normally an earlier riser—she must be tense. She wants to know how I got into the Village, but I just wave my hand.

"I have that kind of face. Guards trust me."

Teri doesn't dwell on the mystery. She shows me a list of the intervals she ran this morning. "I did ten quarters. I didn't break sixty-five seconds in one of them."

"Good. You should be tapering. The first heat's Tuesday."

Teri rips the page in half. "You don't understand. My legs felt heavy. I was struggling when Coach told me to cruise. I couldn't find my rhythm. I was breathing hard the whole time."

"That's okay. In fact, it might be a good thing. Do you remember that interview you read with Frank Shorter where he said that your average runner will have a great day only one third of the time?"

"Yeah."

"Your body's going through a bad cycle right now. That's all. You should be grateful. It means you're going to slip into a good cycle when it counts."

Teri stares at me, then smiles. "That's the most pathetic logic I've ever heard. The weird thing is, coming from you, it makes me feel better. Why is that, Alisa?"

"Because I know you're going to win."

"How do you know?" she asks, serious.

"I operate more on intuition than you might realize. It works better for me than logic, or else it's a higher form of logic I can't explain. Just accept that when I see you in the finals, I see you winning. That's the way it's going to be."

"I wish I had your confidence."

"It goes beyond confidence. It's faith."

"Faith," Teri whispers, then shakes her head. "They say the first thing a medical student loses is any belief in God. Do you know why?"

"Of course. Gross Anatomy 101. You dissect a human cadaver, and no matter how close you look, you can't find a soul. But that doesn't mean there isn't one."

"But where's the proof? Please, don't misunderstand me, I'm not trying to attack your faith. I envy it, especially when I hear you talking to Shanti about Krishna."

"I never chose to believe in Krishna."

"Then how come you worship him?"

"I don't worship him. It's more like I feel he's near."

"Why? Talking to you, reading your work, I know you have a vast scientific background. How can you obey a deity that almost surely never existed?"

"Oh, he existed."

"There's no proof Krishna or Christ or Buddha ever walked the earth. You've read the arguments. All these god men—their lives are like carbon copies of each other. That's because they were born of the same mythologies. You're too smart not to see the pattern."

"Krishna came first, five thousand years ago. Is it possible the other god men might have copied his life story?"

"Is that what you think?"

"It's just an idea. I never met Christ or Buddha. I'm in no position to judge them."

"But you feel Krishna's just around the corner?"

I think of Paula and her son, John.

"He might be a little farther away than that. But I suspect if he was here, he'd tell you that you need to get into bed." Lowering my voice, I catch her eye. Now is not the time for lengthy philosophical discussions. "Look at me, Teri, let me see your eyes. You look exhausted, you need to sleep. Lie down, let your head hit the pillow. That's good, close your eyes and relax."

Teri responds to my gaze and suggestions as fast as before,

and soon she's so deeply asleep she doesn't feel the prick of my nail as I slice open the vein on her wrist. Seymour knows me well—I cannot help but give her an extra jolt of blood. This is, after all, the Olympics. The competition will be far stronger than it was in Oregon. Teri will need every advantage I can give her.

I'm finished in ten minutes and on the verge of leaving when she suddenly jerks in her sleep. It's like she's having a nightmare, which surprises me. I assumed she was too deep to dream. My surprise increases when she raises her arms over her body, as if trying to push away a rapist.

Yet I have underestimated the nature of Teri's dream.

"Yaksha!" she cries softly, before her arms drop down by her side and she falls into a soundless slumber. I have never uttered his name around her, and yet she has just cried out to the creature who created me. I'm unable to tell if she cried out in fear or for help.

The final is scheduled for nine o'clock at night. The stadium is packed. I have spent freely on scalper tickets, and Matt, Shanti, Seymour, and I sit twenty rows from where the race will finish, at the end of the straightaway.

Unable to leave her teaching job, Lisa has not come with us to London. Nor have Teri's parents. They feared they would add to her pressure. The four of us watch as Teri stretches and warms up. Coach Tranton is down on the field, but he keeps a distance from his star pupil.

We sat in the identical seats during her two heats, which were spread over the previous two days. In both races Teri ran hard, but far from wisely. In the first heat, she broke to the front of the pack and stayed there for the bulk of the race. No doubt the fire of my blood was partially responsible for her haste, but the pressure was equally to blame. She was a mass of nerves, and was chased down by two Africans on the straightaway and was lucky to finish third.

In the second heat, she listened to her coach and Matt and didn't make a move until halfway through the race. But again she ran too hard for too long and was fortunate to again finish third. Yet the experience has helped her and Coach Tranton mold a strategy for the final. She plans to hold back until the final lap, and then let it rip. It sounds good in theory, if she is able to control her emotions.

"She looks tired," Matt complains.

"She looks fine," Seymour says.

"She has bags under her eyes," Matt says.

"I don't think many of these girls slept last night," Seymour replies.

"I don't like it. She's been having nightmares," Matt says.

"How do you know?" Seymour asks. "You're not staying with her."

"She tells me about them," he replies impatiently. Matt and Seymour are not the best of friends.

"Nightmares about what?" I ask.

"She doesn't say. But whatever they are, they're awful. They keep waking her up."

"It's the stress," Seymour says.

"She looks pale. She doesn't look like herself," Matt adds.

"She's running fast, that's all that matters," I say.

"Is it?" Matt asks me.

The starter calls the women to their lanes. Since she barely qualified for the final, Teri is assigned an outside lane. Yet the starting line is curved to make up the distance, so it hardly matters. The starter is experienced and quickly lines up the women.

The starter raises her pistol in the air. At the last instant, Teri glances in our direction. I smile and she smiles back. Then she turns her focus back on the track. The starter fires her gun. The women leap forward.

The noise of the crowd is deafening. That is one thing that is lost on TV. We have to shout at each other to be heard over the roar. At least the others have to shout. Even with all the noise, I can hear the rhythm of Teri's breathing, the sound of her footfalls. She's running smoothly, and I'm glad. She's off to a good start.

Teri comes around the track and completes the first lap at the back of the pack. That doesn't bother us. The leader of the race is running too fast and is bound to fade. Also, the pack is tightly bunched. In reality, Teri isn't far from the leader, at most five meters behind.

Teri moves up slightly. Now she's running in the second lane, which forces her to run farther on the curves, but none of us can blame her. The African and European women are more aggressive than their American counterparts. They don't mind pushing and shoving their way into a more favorable position. In Oregon, in the trials, we never saw a woman use her hands or arms against another runner. Here, the only person not fighting back is Teri.

The second lap follows the pattern of the first, only Teri pulls closer to the front. It bothers me that she has run another lap in the second lane. She won't feel the extra distance until the end, but then it could be crucial. The leader—a sacrificial Kenyan rabbit if I ever saw one—continues to push a world-record pace. I feel sorry for the woman, because I know she's been chosen by her coach and teammates to forgo any chance of winning so the favorites on her team can win medals. The greatest burden is always on the leader of the race, especially in the metric mile. The leader breaks the air resistance for those behind her.

Going into the third lap, Teri finally manages to slip into the first lane. This is both good and bad. She is well sheltered from any stray breeze. She is running the minimum distance. But now she has entered the frenzy of skin-scraping spikes and swinging elbows. The toughest women in the world are inches apart and running almost flat out. I'm amazed no one has tripped and gone down so far. But there's time—the last lap sometimes resembles a boxing match.

At two and a half laps the rabbit falters, and her teammates sweep past her. The Kenyans and Ethiopians make up half the field. A twenty-five-year-old Kenyan named Radhur Jamur pushes into the lead and quickly opens up a five-meter lead. Her ability to accelerate catches the others off guard. Yet they should have been wary of her. Jamur is the world-record holder at the distance and has already won a gold medal in the 800-meter race.

Jamur is still in the lead when they swing around in front of us and the bell sounds. In the screaming stands, the four of us look at each other and shake our heads. Teri is still running fast in the middle of the pack, in the first lane, but now she's boxed in. She has no choice but to fight her way to the outside. It will cost her energy and time, but she'll lose if she stays where she's at.

While Matt and Seymour shout at the top of their lungs, I close my eyes and go still. I let myself feel Teri, her pain, her anxiety, and I dissolve so deeply into her I feel as if my mind is closer to the track than to the stands. Yet the pain is nothing to me, I have suffered tortures much worse than what Teri's going through. And her nerves—I feel as we blend together, a sudden upsurge of confidence washes away all her petty fears. She has not come this far to lose, neither of us has, and if she has to kick some butt to win, then so be it. The gold medal is hers, it will be hers.

Teri—or is it me?—accelerates through the two women in

front of her. The fact they are inches apart doesn't matter. They are in her way, and they had better get out of her way. Teri thrusts her arms forward to widen the crack, and then pushes the women apart. She accelerates, moving from eighth place to fifth in a single stroke.

It's not enough. There's only half a lap left. I see that Teri must return to the outside, to the second lane, to be able to pass everyone left in front of her. Teri sees what I see—maybe she reads my mind. Without hesitating, she jerks to the right and accelerates sharply and comes up on the shoulder of the woman in third place.

There are two women directly in front of her: Radhur Jamur and Olga Stensky from Russia. Jamur runs like a sleek gazelle. Olga has legs as thick as a shot-putter. If she's not injecting herself with steroids in the off-season, then both her parents were weight lifters and forced Olga to haul boulders on her back when she was in grade school.

So far Teri has run on nerves and fear and excitement. Now she enters the realm of real pain, the type even I have to respect. Her lungs feel as if they fill with molten lead. Steaming cramps radiate from her shoulders down into her chest and arms. Her legs, the most crucial part of her anatomy for what she must do next, keep jarring. The muscles are stiffening up, and she can't let them. Somehow, she must will her legs to move faster no matter how much they hurt.

They enter the final turn. Olga pulls up on Jamur's shoulder, and Teri crowds Olga. Teri knows Olga will wait until the final straightaway to make her move. To try to pass Jamur on the curve will be foolish. It will cause her to run farther and use up the last of her reserves.

Yet Jamur stumbles, and like a true warrior Olga pounces. To hell with the extra distance, the Russian thinks. Olga swings out and passes Jamur and begins to pull away from Teri and the world-record holder. Teri freezes for an instant—she doesn't know what to do. But I know, and I mentally push Teri to go after her.

Olga and Teri hit the straightaway. The gold medal waits at the end of the orange track—eighty meters away. Olga has cut back into the inside lane to block a possible spurt from Jamur. But she sees Teri out of the corner of her eye in lane two and recognizes her as the final threat.

Olga's legs are riddled with scars from wounds caused by countless encounters with spikes. She is used to the trenches; she probably prefers them. As Teri stretches forth with her magnificent stride, throwing the last shreds of her strength into an agonizing sprint, Olga suddenly moves into the second lane and bumps Teri with her right hip. Then, to finish off the cocky American upstart, she rams her elbow into Teri's side.

Teri falls back a step. Olga runs for the gold.

"Destroy her," I whisper quietly in the stands, knowing the words, the idea, is flying across the track faster than either of the women can run. Teri catches my meaning, and the five-thousand-year-old blood I secreted into the marrow of her bones finally ignites. She burns with hatred, with revenge, and most of all she burns with the desire for glory.

Teri lets loose the full length of her beautiful stride and begins to eat up the gap. The finish line is twenty meters away when Teri draws even with Olga. The Russian sees her victory slipping away and does the only thing she thinks can save her, never mind that it's against every rule in the book and might get her disqualified. She swerves into the second lane again, trying to either trip or block Teri before she can reach the finish line. But Teri sees this impending disaster through either my eyes or her own. Teri swings to the inside lane, and Olga misses her by inches and loses a full stride.

Teri flies like an eagle toward the finish line.

The victory tape breaks across her chest.

The board flashes a new world record.

Teri collapses in Coach Tranton's arms twenty meters beyond the finish line. She didn't know to stop running. In the stands, Matt, Seymour, Shanti, and I all hug for a long time. I'm glad they hold on to me. I'm filled with joy, but like Teri I'm ready to collapse.

FOURTEEN

The president of the United States wants Teri to come to a party he's having for the Olympic gold medalists. The message comes in the middle of a party I'm holding for Teri. I've rented out a small ballroom at the hotel where I'm staying, and Teri has invited two dozen friends from the American track team.

But the presidential invitation changes everything. It says that he loved her race and wants to congratulate her in person. The invitation also says she can bring a guest, but just one. Shanti and I beg off, and her old coach is wise enough to know that this moment belongs to Teri and her true love. Yet our star feels guilty about leaving. As is often the case, she turns to me for advice.

"What do you think?" Teri asks. "I feel guilty leaving all my friends. You're the ones who made this all possible."

"The president will meet with you for a few minutes and send you on your way. You can always come back here. This party has plenty of life in it."

"All right." She hugs me and turns to leave, but something keeps her by my side. "Alisa?"

"Yes, Ms. Olympic Champion?"

"Thanks for that smile at the start of the race."

"I'm amazed you saw us in the crowd."

"I knew where you were sitting. But it's not that. When you smiled at me, it's funny, I felt everything was going to be all right. That I was going to win."

"You had faith?" I tease her.

She smiles. "Maybe." She turns serious. "It was deeper than that. I felt you ran the race with me. At the end, when the pain was overwhelming, I had this moment of doubt. I thought, I can't do it. Then I saw your face again in my mind, and my doubt vanished."

I brush her long hair from her eyes, a habit of mine.

"We were all with you, Teri. But you were alone on that track, and you faced that fear alone. Don't forget that. It will give you a special kind of strength that will stay with you for the rest of your life."

She hugs me. "I feel like I've changed inside."

I squeeze her in return but stay silent.

Teri and Matt leave the party and go off to Matt's room to change. Teri is famous for taking forever to dress and fix her makeup. Seymour, of course, acts like he should get to meet the president.

"He's a fan of my books," he says.

"Under which pen name?" I ask.

"All of them."

Shanti goes off to bed. Seymour and I sit alone in a corner and drink wine and smoke cigarettes. I've taken up the habit to keep him happy, but only smoke in his company. He nods in the direction Teri disappeared.

"How does she feel?" he asks, and I know what he means.

"She's going to be all right."

"You're sure?"

"She pushed herself to the limit but not beyond it."

"You know you have a problem now."

"What's that?" I ask.

"Her coach is already talking about the next Olympics. Between now and then Teri expects to break the world record a dozen times. How's she going to feel when the magic wears off?"

"Disappointed. But she'll never forget tonight."

Seymour shakes his head. "I think that 'fifteen minutes of fame' bullshit is overrated."

"How would you know? You're afraid to come out of the shadows."

"So says the world's last vampire."

I touch my wineglass to his. "Touché."

Then I feel it. I hear it. I sense them.

Seymour sees my face change and asks what's wrong, but I gesture for him to be silent. However, he follows as I hurry from the party out into an empty lounge area. There I sit cross-legged in a leather chair and close my eyes. My subtle hearing spreads out into the night, like a vast fishing web thrown over a dark sea. I cannot see the predators that await me, but I'm suddenly convinced they are there.

Four powerful heartbeats. Four pounding pulses—of a type I have only heard once before in my life, the night the assassin Claudious Ember came for me. They approach from four separate directions. They're still miles away and appear in no hurry to reach me, probably because they're confident they already have me.

Opening my eyes, I explain my dilemma to Seymour.

"How can I help?" he asks when I'm finished.

"Get out of here. It will only distract me if I have to protect you."

"I'm not going to leave you."

"Then give me a brilliant idea that will allow me to stop them. Make it quick."

"Are you sure there are only four?"

"Four in a ten-mile radius. Beyond that, I can't tell."

"Are you armed?"

I gesture to my leather coat. "I have a Glock .45 semi-automatic."

"How many spare clips?"

"Three."

"Can you tell what they're carrying?"

"I hear their weapons banging into each other. They're carrying some kind of bags. We have to assume they're more heavily armed than I am."

"What if you run as fast as you can in one direction? Can you kill one of them and keep from getting boxed in?"

"I doubt it. They increased their pace the moment we came out here. That means they must have me under observation, in this hotel, by a normal person. If I try to flee from this trap, they'll just spring it that much faster."

"How many do you think you can take?"

"Based on the last guy, maybe two. If I'm lucky."

Seymour suddenly holds up a hand. "Wait a second."

"I hope what you have is extremely good."

"It's perfect. We're not vulnerable at all. In fact, we've never been so invincible."

"I'm dying to hear what you have to say."

"The president's hotel. It's down the block from here. Teri and Matt just left to go there, but you know how long she takes to get ready. They won't get there for half an hour. You won't have to worry about exposing her to harm."

"I'm not following you."

"I'm talking about the secret service. The president will have at least a hundred agents with him. More like two hundred. This is the Olympics, a prime terrorist target. If you can get inside his hotel, you'll be surrounded by a wall of the best-trained guards on earth. If these monsters try to attack you, they'll be cut to pieces. If they just try to sneak weapons into the president's hotel, they'll be arrested."

"You can't arrest creatures like these."

"Then they'll be killed. But you'll be safe."

I consider, then nod. "Clever. I like it. But what if the four surround the hotel and try to take me hostage? In that case Teri and Matt would be in danger."

"I doubt it will come to that. Whoever this group is, they've sent four superhumans to get you this time. They want you. They're not going to leave without you. Trust me, they'll do whatever it takes to get inside that hotel."

I stand and kiss him on the lips. "I owe you."

"Make me a vampire. That will make us even."

"You're perfect the way you are. I hate to ruin a good thing."

He kisses me. "We'll talk about it later. Run, Sita, and kill them. Kill them all. It's what you do best."

I'm outside a moment later. I walk briskly toward the president's hotel, but I don't break into a run. My pace appears to determine the speed of my assailants. Since I know they cannot hear as well as I can, I must assume their human spies still have me in their sights. If I increase my pace even slightly, they do likewise.

The night is warm and humid, London in August. Although it's late, a party atmosphere fills the city. I hear people drinking and carrying on. The Brits love track and field, and many are still celebrating Teri's race, among others.

The president's hotel is a five-star Hilton. Even before I catch sight of my first secret service agent, I dispose of my gun in a tree. I'm sure I'll have to go through a metal detector. I can get the weapon later, if need be.

Two hundred yards from the Hilton, I see my first wave of agents—the outer perimeter. A few are dressed as athletes, others as tourists. It's their job to stop anyone who looks remotely suspicious. I guess I pass the first test.

At the door to the hotel, I successfully go through a metal detector, but then I'm stopped cold. I don't have an athlete's badge, and I'm not on their list. I don't have time for subtlety. From each direction, I hear my assailants accelerate. They now know what I'm up to, and they don't like it. I hear them break into a run. They must be a blur to people out for a late-night stroll.

"My name's Linda," I say to the secret service agent who stands before me. He's of Asian descent, and I can tell by the way he holds himself he's an expert in martial arts. His neck is thick and his fingers are blunt. Ordinarily I would say he has intense eyes, but they melt as I focus on them. I continue, "Let me inside. It's important I see the president."

He begins to perspire. He checks his list again, hoping it

will bring relief. "What did you say your name is?" he asks.

I move beside him so I can read the list. There's a Lindy Addage near the top, who works for the *LA Times*, and I point to her. "That's me. Now please let me inside."

He shudders under the assault of my burning blue eyes and powerful suggestions. He must have remarkable self-control. He should have caved in the instant our eyes met. Finally he nods and steps aside.

"You must see the president," he mumbles.

"Thank you. You have been most kind."

I pass inside and find the president's party on the second floor in a ballroom twenty times larger than the one I rented for Teri. A few people have on tuxes, but overall the dress is casual. Many athletes wear the national suits they were issued when they made the team. Since the purpose of the affair is to celebrate American victories, there's plenty of red, white, and blue. I have on black pants, a white silk blouse, and a gray jacket.

The president has yet to arrive.

There is no sign of Teri and Matt, either. Good.

I focus in on the secret service and the four who are converging on the hotel. Seymour was confident the latter would try to break in, but I have my doubts. Like I told my friend, they can bide their time, lay siege to the hotel, and wait for the agents to leave. If I was them, that's what I would do.

I don't know the extent of their mental powers. It's possible they have none, and the only way they will be able to get by the guards will be to use force. Yet with two hundred agents focused on protecting this room and its occupants, it would be a desperate strategy. All agents are equipped with handguns, but a small number will have Uzis—handheld machine guns.

Two of the four reach the door. To my surprise, I discover they're women. I listen as they try to bluff their way inside. Their technique is a virtual replay of my own. It's a fact then—whoever they are, they possess at least basic telepathic abilities. I watch as the women slip past the guards, and I feel depressed. I had hoped to have shelter for a while, time to plan my next move.

The women are tall, sleek, with copper skin and dark brown hair so thick it would intimidate any modern stylist. They look like figures lifted from an ancient Egyptian pyramid wall. Their dress, however, is plain, and I understand why. They wear coats like mine, but they've made a mistake by bringing guns into the president's ballroom. In the bulges of their pockets, I see signs of their arrogance. However, I'm surprised they were able to get the weapons past the metal detectors.

I hear two men at the door persuading the agents that they, too, are invited guests. It won't be long before all four are inside. I have to move fast. Acting scared, I approach three female agents.

"Excuse me, but I think you have a problem," I say.

The shortest of the agents studies me. "What's wrong, ma'am?"

I nod to the two females, who stare at me from the other side of the room. If looks could kill . . . Their eyes are so cold I think of them as witches. Between them, they make rapid hand gestures, employing a subtle form of sign language no one else would notice. They're smart—they know if they speak, I'll hear them. Of course, they can hear what I'm saying, there's no point in being too coy.

"You have a security breach. Those two women standing over there got in here without presenting any form of ID. They're armed."

The short agent is amused. "I hardly think that's likely, ma'am."

"You have no reason to believe me, but please, check them out and you'll see what I mean." I catch the woman's eye and light a fuse between her synapses. I raise my voice. "For God's sake, look at them. Their coat pockets are bulging. They look like goddamn terrorists. Do you want to be the first secret service agents to be directly responsible for the death of a president?"

Shorty turns to her partners. "Janice, Debbie—approach the women from the front. Ask for ID and try to establish what door they came through. Be polite. I'll be behind them, ready to take action if necessary." Shorty glances at me. "Satisfied?"

"Thank you. Be careful, those witches are the real thing. They'll start shooting the instant they feel cornered. I'd bring more backup."

"We know what we're doing," Shorty says.

The agents move off, and I silently wish them good luck. It's against my nature to send humans after monsters. But I don't know what else to do. I can't die, I can't surrender, not when I don't know what these strangers are capable of.

The male half of the foursome makes it past the agents at the door and heads directly for me. They've seen me point out their partners. Before they reach my part of the room, I cower behind two agents, one tall and well built, a guy in his thirties, the other thin and close to retirement. I gesture to the men who are after me.

"Those guys have guns," I say quickly, in a panicked voice.

The older of the two agents frowns. "How do you know that?"

"I was behind them when I arrived here. They weren't frisked. They weren't required to go through a metal detector. The guard at the gate did whatever they told him. Are they part of the secret service?"

The old guy glances at his partner, then at me. "No, they're not. May I ask what your name is and why you're here?"

"Lindy Addage. You'll find my name on the guest list. I'm here with the *Los Angeles Times*. I was hoping to get a quote from the president about his feeling about the games. But I got here early and got stuck in the line with those two goons. I'm telling you, there's something creepy about them."

I notice the two males have stopped and are watching me.

The old guy is undecided. "Did you actually see their guns?"

"Definitely. They're carrying them inside their coats." I can see the weapons bulging through their jackets from where I stand. "Please, talk to them at least, check their IDs. What harm can it do?"

The old guy nods. "What do you think, Ted?"

"Like the lady says, Mike, it can't hurt."

"Let me go with you," I add.

"What?" Mike exclaims.

"I'm the one accusing them. Let me do it to their faces."

"She has a point," Ted says. "It's not like we can't protect her."

Ted is making a joke, but the irony of his remark weighs on me as we head toward the assassins. I fear to leave the agents alone, afraid they'll be killed. I wish I could have accompanied the women agents, but I had to alert the secret service to both groups of killers.

I have no idea how the assassins are going to react.

"Prepare for a fight," I say to Mike and Ted as we near the males, adding power to my voice. "They've come to kill, and they're not afraid to die. Put a hand on your guns now."

Mike and Ted jump at my command. They obey.

I note they're wearing bulletproof vests. Good.

I glance in the direction of the female agents and the witches. The group is having a casual conversation, and I worry the latter have already used their mental powers on the women. There's nothing I can do about it at the moment.

"Gentlemen. How are you doing this evening?" Mike says as we stop before the assassins. They bear no resemblance to their female counterparts. Both are tall, blond, and blue-eyed, with clearly marked Nordic bloodlines. They wear the same type of watch that Claudious Ember did, the one that worked as a communication device. I notice they both angle the watches so they're pointed at me. More people are watching this party than meets the eye.

The male on the right frowns. His partner forces a smile. It's curious how clumsy both expressions are. These two don't get out much; they have no social graces. Smiley speaks first.

"We are having very good time, thank you," he says.

"May I ask your names, please?" Mike asks.

"Why?" the sullen male responds.

His happy buddy smiles some more. "My name is Edward Simmons. This is my partner, Thomas Freeman. We are with the press, the *Times*. We have identification. Would you like to see it?"

"Love to," Mike replies, concerned. "You say you work for the *Times*, but you're obviously not Brits. What's that accent I hear?"

"I'm from Norway. Thomas is from Holland. Perhaps I confuse issue. My English not so good. We both employed by *Amsterdam Times*." Mike hands over two ID badges, adding, "We here to cover Olympics."

Mike studies their identification, still keeping a grip on the gun on his hip. "This looks legit," he says, handing back the badges.

"Thank you, sir," Edward says.

"Now may I see your invitation for tonight's event?" Mike says.

"Pardon?" Edward mutters.

"As I'm sure you know, this is a presidential event. Only those who have been personally invited by the White House are allowed here tonight. You must have shown your invitation at the door. Otherwise, they wouldn't have let you inside."

Edward glances at his partner, loses most of his smile. He gestures in my direction. "Excuse please, does this woman have an invitation?"

"He's trying to distract you," I say. "Don't let him. They're pros. Look at the bulges in their coats."

"Are you carrying weapons?" Mike demands.

Edward tries to catch his eye. "No, sir. We are unarmed."

I wave my hand in front of Mike's face. "He's using hypnosis on you. Don't look into his eyes. Frisk them, force them to surrender their guns."

Mike shakes his head as if feeling a sudden pain. Seeing his distress, Ted moves closer to Edward and draws his gun. "I'm going to ask you two to step to the corner of the room," Ted says.

Edward stares at the gun, smiles, then tries to catch Ted's eye. "There is no need for the gun," he says softly.

Ted blinks, sways slightly on his feet. "No?" he mumbles.

"Don't listen! They'll kill you!" I shout.

Mike recovers his wits swiftly. He draws his gun and points it at Edward. "Raise your hands! Now!"

Edward spreads his hands as his smile turns cold. Once more he gestures to me. "We are not your enemy. She is your enemy."

"Get your arms up!" Mike orders.

Edward refuses to raise his arms. So does his partner. They stare at Mike and Ted, who has shaken off the psychic attack at least enough to keep his weapon pointed at them. Yet Ted is struggling. He's pale and his hand is shaky. Mike is more in control.

Still, I dislike the direction things are going. There are too many variables I can't control. On my far right, the women agents have not surrendered to the witches, but the agents have yet to draw their guns. I wouldn't be surprised if they're already under the spell of the evil women.

I see now why the four didn't hesitate to enter the ballroom. The secret service don't intimidate them. They still see this contest as four against one. The surrounding humans don't factor into their thinking. Edward makes this clear when he responds to Mike.

"I do not take orders from you," Edward says flatly.

"Call for backup," I say firmly.

Mike speaks into a pin on his lapel. "This is G49. We have

a code red. I repeat, a code red. Request immediate backup." He shakes his gun at Edward. "Put your goddamn hands in the air or I'm going to put a cap in your head. I'll count to three. One . . ."

Edward is amused. "Count to a hundred. Call a hundred men. It will not change a thing."

Mike cocks his gun. "Two . . ."

Edward and Thomas simultaneously lash out with their feet, kicking away Mike's and Ted's handguns. In their position, I would have done the same. But I've anticipated their move and respond in turn.

Switching into hyper mode, crouching down, I sweep under Thomas's and Edward's legs as they kick away the agent's guns. Caught on only one leg, my foes are especially vulnerable, and they hit the floor on their backs. But they're well trained. Even as they fall, they reach for their weapons.

After my sweep, I end up standing beside Thomas and kick away the handgun he draws. Unfortunately, Edward has also drawn a gun, and even though he's lying on his back, he has it pointed at my head.

"Stay," he says with authority.

It's difficult, even for me, to dodge a bullet at such a short distance. Also, I suspect Edward isn't carrying ordinary ammunition. Chances are his bullets are enhanced with gunpowder sprinkled with nitroglycerin, if not something more exotic. Plus his reflexes are above normal. If by some miracle I manage to escape his first shot, I know his second will find me.

Five thousand years. Thousands of encounters with death.

And I cannot for the life of me figure out what to do next.

But maybe Krishna's cloak of protection still holds.

I hear a shot. Red blossoms in the center of Edward's chest.

He drops his gun and lies back on the floor.

Everything happens so fast, in a dimension where mortals are not usually of any help. In the brief moments I've spent with Mike and Ted, I have come to admire their professionalism, but I didn't expect them to be able to protect me. Certainly Thomas didn't believe Mike had a backup weapon. I never noticed it. I suspect the agent didn't see my move. His instincts just took over and he fired. Good for him.

But I'm far from safe. It's still three against one, and I'm not armed. The death of Edward doesn't slow Thomas. So I've kicked away his gun. He pulls out another and aims it at my head. I only have to look in his eyes to know he's not interested in my surrender.

If he's as fast as Claudious, I don't have time to kick his gun out of his hand. Fortunately, his shoulder is only a third of the distance from the tip of my boots. I strike there, with all my strength, and jerk my head to the side. The blow is brutal. It causes the muscles in his upper arm to explode, even as his passing bullet flips my hair from my ear. Blood pours through his coat. The nerves to his hand must be severely damaged. Yet he manages to hold on to his gun. He fights to get off a second shot.

I use the slight delay to my advantage. Going briefly airborne, I slash out with my left foot and knock away his gun. As my left leg recoils, I do a scissor kick and strike his temple—the thinnest part of the skull—with my right foot. I hear multiple cracks and know splinters of bone have fragmented into his brain. His eyes fall shut, and I don't believe they will ever reopen.

All this transpires in a matter of seconds. Nevertheless, other secret service agents are beginning to look over. Nothing like a couple of gunshots to catch someone's attention. The agents focus on the two guys on the floor but not on me, not yet. I estimate I have a narrow window of ten seconds to stop the others. Then I'll probably be arrested.

My eyes seek the witches. Like their male partners, they're well trained. They shifted position while I struggled with Edward and Thomas. I don't see them immediately, but I note that all three of the female agents they were talking to are on the floor. Since I didn't hear any gunshots from their direction, I assume the witches simply knocked the women out.

My scan reveals nothing. But when I kneel to collect Edward's gun—the one gun I haven't kicked away—I hear a gunshot and feel a bullet split the air where my head was an instant before. What blind luck, to dodge a round I didn't even see coming. I know more are on their way.

I leap straight into the air, rising high, ten feet off the floor. I'm trying to dodge the next bullet, but I have another reason for going airborne. While in the air, I present an easy target, however, I also have a better view of the crowd. I can spot the witches even if they have taken cover behind a group of people.

I spot one of the assassins in a crowd as she shifts her aim from the floor into the air. She's the one who just shot at me. I return the favor and shoot back. We're separated by a hundred feet, and she uses the distance to partially dodge the bullet. She moves fast—my bullet is lucky to catch her at all, in the shoulder rather than in the head.

The round has plenty of kick to it. I was right to assume they have brought along fortified bullets. My shot spins the witch around. Again, I take aim at her head.

Then I hear it, the faint click of a trigger being cocked.

It comes from behind. By fleeing to opposite sides of the room, they've made themselves difficult targets and even more efficient killers. Even as I whirl in midair, I know it is too late, that I will take a bullet, it's only a question of where.

I catch sight of the second witch the instant she fires. We're fifty feet apart, and I see the bullet as it heads straight for my face. I manage to get my left elbow up, but I know the power of these rounds, and I know my arm isn't thick enough to protect my head. Yet I'm Sita, the last of the vampires, and I don't die easily. As the bullet tears into my flesh, I simultaneously jerk my arm downward and redirect the bullet into the floor.

The audacity of my move startles my opponent. She hesitates, for an instant, she even blinks, and I unload two shots in her direction. One blows out her heart. The other cracks open her forehead.

I crumple as I hit the floor, from pain and cunning. The last of the two witches is wounded but still dangerous. I want to present the smallest target possible. However, as I turn toward her, I see she's made a line for the door. Drops of her blood litter the floor. I see them, smell them, and even when she vanishes I can still hear her hurried gait as she descends the steps outside the hotel. She's followed the frightened wave of humanity that's finally thrown off its shock and fled the ballroom. She may come from the same stock as Claudious, I think, but she doesn't have his courage.

Once more, I'm standing still. I've returned to the real world.

Mike and Ted take a step toward me.

Mike gestures to my arm. "You've been shot," he says.

"I'm all right," I say.

Ted shakes his head in dismay. "Does someone want to tell me what just happened? Because I sure as hell don't know. All I saw was a blur of Ms. Matrix here after those guys kicked away our guns."

"Quiet," Mike says to his partner as he steps to my side. I'm not only bleeding, I'm holding a gun, and there are dozens of secret service agents all around. None of that appears to bother Mike. He speaks in a low voice so that only I can hear. "Who are you?" he whispers.

"A friend. I came to stop these people."

"Who are these people?"

"Monsters. Seriously."

"Were they going to kill the president?"

"They came here to kill."

"Did one of them escape?"

"Yes."

He frowns. "What the hell am I supposed to do with you?"

"Let me go after her. I'm the only one who can stop her."

He looks around. "My superiors won't allow that."

"For some reason, I get the impression you're in charge of tonight's security," I say.

"That's true."

"Then if you and Ted say it's okay, I can go. No one will stop me."

He considers. "That I can well believe." He turns to Ted. "We're letting her go. Don't say a word."

Before leaving, I kneel beside Edward and take his second gun along with extra clips and his weird watch. I also find a pair of unusually strong handcuffs in each of the men's pockets and borrow them as well.

I'm grateful Teri and Matt have not yet arrived. And the president. I suspect after all these fireworks, the secret service is going to move him to another hotel. Chances are Teri will not get to meet him.

I cannot worry about that now—I have to capture the witch. She's my only connection to these people, and I'm not going to spend the next ten years of my life looking over my shoulder and waiting for another attack. I want it to end tonight.

I leave the hotel. No one stops me.

FIFTEEN

From the sound of the witch's pulse, I know she has procured a car and is driving south at high speed. There's a Porsche Carrera—a favorite of mine—parked down the street from the hotel, and I break the lock and hot-wire the engine and am soon in pursuit.

I have two points of focus as I drive. One, I pay close attention to the road. With my supernatural reflexes, I'm a better driver than those who compete at a professional level. But even I cannot exceed the limits of the vehicle and the terrain I happen to be on. Fortunately the roads are fairly deserted, and I'm able to keep my speed above a hundred miles an hour.

The pulse of the witch's heart is my homing signal. Listening closely, it tells me a few things about her. Her wound is worse than I thought. My shot must have torn an artery. She's still losing blood. It also tells me that these creatures, although strong, don't possess my regenerative powers. Claudious killed himself so fast, I was never sure of this fact until now.

My elbow heals as I drive.

The witch is three miles ahead of me when she stops at what I assume is the train station. Over the span of thirty seconds, I follow her with my ears as she boards a train and leaves the station. The train's departure is too much of a coincidence. They must have studied its schedule ahead of time, in case they had to flee, or in case they had me in their grip and wanted to get me out of the city before I could summon help. They might be operating under the erroneous belief that I have allies, I don't know.

The layout of the roads doesn't help me. I lose several minutes finding a freeway that's heading the right way. I suspect the witch's heading for the southern tip of England, which means she's probably trying to get out of the country. There are two ways she can escape—by driving under the English Channel or else taking a ferry across. I doubt the hovercraft operates at this time of night, but I'm not sure.

I push the Porsche up to a hundred and fifty miles an hour, its maximum speed. It doesn't take long before I have a policeman on my tail, but he can't catch me, not the way I'm weaving in and out of traffic. Still, the highway isn't busy, and for the most part I'm able to keep the accelerator to the floor.

The witch's train comes to a halt, and I listen as she departs and runs in the direction of what sounds like the harbor. The train station is adjacent to where the ships leave for France, and it's looking more and more like that's her destination.

I have to assume she knows the schedule of the ferries. It worries me. If she gets on a boat and it leaves the dock before I can arrive, I could be forced to follow by driving beneath the Channel. I doubt even my ears can track her with that much earth and water overhead. This is probably a part of her plan: to slip outside my radar, then make an unexpected move and vanish.

The watch I have taken from Edward continues to glow a dull green. It's an interesting device, and I would like to study it at leisure, but I don't trust it. They could be using it to track me. I throw it out the window.

I take time to examine the handcuffs and their matching keys. I don't recognize the alloy but know they brought them for me. For most of my life, I've had the strength of at least ten men, a factor that slowly increased as I aged. Fifteen years ago, when Yaksha and Kalika both died in my arms, they gave me their blood, and my powers increased another tenfold. However, despite my strength, I can't break these cuffs. It's a sobering thought. If they do manage to get them on me, I will be their captive.

The alloy is a product of a technology mankind doesn't possess.

Just like the acid that vaporized Claudious.

Damn it! The ferry leaves the instant the witch boards it.

I'm five minutes behind. I park at the harbor and rush to the water's edge and watch as the ship recedes over the black water. There's a good chance that driving under the Channel I can beat the boat to the other side and be in position to welcome her in France. Yet the prospect of losing track of her continues to haunt me. If she thinks I can no longer hear her, she'll do something drastic. For example, she could jump in a lifeboat and paddle back to Britain.

The cop who was chasing me pulls into the harbor parking lot. He has brought backup. I ran from the car so fast—he doesn't know it was I who was in the vehicle—but he's taken the Porsche into custody. A pity, the owner kept it in good shape and I enjoyed its speed. However, it makes my next decision easier.

Standing on the edge of the dock, I remove my coat and boots. I keep only one of Edward's guns—I assume it's waterproof—and the two sets of handcuffs. Already, the ferry's a fading silhouette in the night. I estimate its speed at twenty miles an hour. I can swim faster than that, for a short time, but even I will eventually tire. Plus each second I delay just makes the chase that much more difficult.

I dive off the dock and into the water.

Vampires dislike the cold. I suspect it has something to do with the fact we're related to yakshinis, mystical serpents. In the same way lizards or snakes are slowed by cold, it weakens me. But two factors come to my aid. August is the hottest month in

Britain, and the island's climate is moderated by what's called the North Atlantic Drift—a remnant of America's Gulf Stream, which flows up the East Coast before turning out over the Atlantic. For these reasons, the water is surprisingly warm, and I'm able to swim faster than usual.

It would be easier if I was naked, but I'm reluctant to give up my gun and the handcuffs. The witch may be wounded, but she's armed. There's even a good chance she can hear me coming. It's hard to hide the splashing sounds I'm making. If she starts shooting as I near the boat, I want to be able to shoot back.

I swim mostly freestyle, but occasionally alternate my strokes to use different muscles. The switching helps conserve energy.

Thirty minutes after leaving the dock, I close in on the boat. For a short while I let myself drift, catching my breath, listening. My foe has moved to the rear of the ship. She definitely knows I'm coming. That means she'll soon be taking aim at me in the water.

I decide on a bold strategy, and a difficult one. I hyperventilate for three minutes and then dive beneath the surface. I can hold my breath a long time, but it's harder when I'm running or swimming flat out. Yet the security of having thirty feet of water overhead is hard to resist. The witch can't shoot through such a barrier. Also, I suspect she won't be able to hear me coming. For the first time tonight, I'll fall off of her radar, even though I'll still know exactly where she is.

A funny thing happens as I near the boat. A herd of dolphins swims by and acts like they would like to play. I love dolphins, and my telepathic gifts have taught me they are far more aware than mankind realizes. But I admit I've never been able to decipher their complex language.

I think it's because they are conscious, but not the same way humans are conscious. It's almost like they live in a constant dream state. When I tune in to their minds, as I do now, I feel a profound peace. The feeling is one of floating, of drifting on invisible currents in a vast sea humans can't see with their physical eyes. I suspect we have only glimpsed the tip of the iceberg when it comes to such remarkable animals.

They appear to sense I'm aware of their thoughts and pull up beside me. It takes me a moment to recognize their offer. They know I'm tired and hungry for air, and they offer to tow me toward the ferry. There's a big one on either side, almost pressing against me. I just have to reach out and hold on. Ah, it's such a relief to rest. Again, it's silly, I know, but I feel as if Krishna is trying to help me. It's impossible not to believe in a benevolent creator while swimming in the company of such loving beings.

The dolphins swim away as I pull alongside the boat. Near midship, I surface and search for something to grab hold of, finding a portal at the waterline. Once again I relax, and catch my breath, yet I breathe softly. The last thing I want to do is alert the witch that I've reached the ferry. I go so far as to alter my heartbeat so it more closely resembles a normal person's rhythm.

Like on most ships, there are ropes hanging down from the deck, and I grab one and haul myself up. With the late hour, most people are inside the ferry. I stop to listen. The witch is waiting at the rear of the ship. She thinks I'm still in the water. I suspect the noise of the ship's engines have thrown off her hearing. The ferry is due for an overhaul. The turbines make a loud grinding noise as we plow through the water. All these factors work to my advantage.

I'm reluctant to get in another shooting match with the woman. I need her alive. Above all else, I can't let her commit suicide. I suspect it's a standard walking order when it comes to them: *Under no circumstances are you to let the nasty vampire interrogate you.* I don't know why they hate me so much. What did I ever do to them?

When I spot the woman, she's in the middle of an operation. Using a steak knife, she's attempting to dig out the bullet I put in her shoulder. She's doing a piss-poor job; there's blood all over the bench where she sits. The stuck bullet may be the reason she hasn't healed. I have trouble healing around impaled objects. But I suspect these people, for all their gifts, are more vulnerable than me.

A handgun rests in her lap, and her eyes don't stray from the water. Indeed, she has a pair of binoculars, and that makes me think she drove a prearranged car to the ferry. I wonder if she has other equipment on hand, though she should have packed a medical kit. Her people probably didn't think I'd put up such a fight.

Listening to her heartbeat, I know she is weak from blood loss. But that doesn't mean I underestimate her. These people are fierce. Even with her wound, she could kill a dozen humans in the blink of an eye. The fact that I want her alive adds to my difficulties.

She's alone, which is good, and I doubt her bench can be seen from the captain's control room. The noise of the engines also gives me cover. But I hesitate to approach her on foot. Her ears are too sensitive for that.

What to do?

I reconsider putting another bullet or two in her. That will slow her down and give me a better chance of rendering her unconscious. At the same time, I don't want her shooting back.

I must muffle the sound of my gun. I go in search of a restroom and steal a thick roll of paper towels. I check to see if Edward's gun is still dry, and am not surprised to find the weapon and its ammunition have weathered my long swim without problems.

Back on deck, I climb up to a second level that circles an enclosed snack bar. There are a handful of patrons inside. They pay me no heed. I can no longer see the witch—she's hidden by the walls of a lower lounge—but I know she's still on the bench. For a minute I stand still, calculating the wind, our speed through the water, the shifting waves.

Then I spring high into the air, straight up.

On the surface my plan may appear odd, but in reality it's simplicity itself, and probably the last thing she expects. What goes up must come down. While I'm in the air, the boat moves closer to its goal. However, I've timed my jump so that I'll land on the rear deck before the boat pulls too far away. Actually, I've timed my leap so that I'll land on the bench beside the woman.

Floating through the air, I shift my cocked pistol behind my roll of paper towels. I begin to descend before I see the woman. That's fine; I've timed everything perfectly. When she finally bursts into view, she doesn't even know I'm above her, and I'm able to take my time as I aim at her right knee.

I fire. The bullet, although silenced by the paper towels, still makes noise. It strikes its target, and the woman gasps in pain as the round shatters her kneecap. She tries to pick up her gun, and I let her. Then I shoot it out of her hand, crippling her right leg and hand in two quick strokes.

Landing beside her, I run into a problem. The bench wood is old and worn. It caves in and I have to struggle to stay upright. In my fight to stay on my feet, my arms shake and my aim falters. The woman has three bullets in her, but she's not ready to quit. With her left leg, she kicks both my legs out from beneath me and I fall toward the deck.

Only by spinning in midair do I manage to avoid landing in a helpless lump. Yet, as I spin, she pulls another gun from her jacket and aims it at my head. I'm lucky her gun hand is attached to her bad shoulder and her control is poor. Before she can cock the trigger, I put a fourth bullet in her left palm. Again, her gun goes flying.

I hit the deck. The woman stands, even with her bum knee, and kicks me in the face. The blow is impressive; it hurts. My nose breaks, and a jet of warm blood shoots from my nostrils. For a fraction of a second, my world is filled with twirling red stars and black holes, and I see her wind up for another kick. I have no choice. I shoot out her other knee. Finally she goes down, and I manage to get up.

"Don't move!" I shout as she lies facedown on the deck. This isn't exactly what I planned. If she has a suicide tooth in her mouth, she can use it now, and I won't be able to stop her. Yet this woman acts like someone who wants to live. Sort of.

"Shoot me and get it over with," she mutters.

"What's the fun in that?" Kneeling beside her, I yank both her arms back and snap the handcuffs in place. She tries to rise, and I grab her by her dark brown hair and smash her face in the deck. I apply the other set of cuffs to her ankles. If I can't break them, she can't. Pulling her upright, I set her on the end of the bench that's still intact. I rip off her weird watch and throw it overboard. Both our noses drip ridiculous amounts of blood.

"Are you in pain?" I ask.

She sneers. "What do you care?"

"Well, I don't care all that much. But if you're hurting, and you have medicine aboard, I'll give you some."

"We don't carry medicine to reduce pain."

"Too bad, you've got five bullets in you. It's going to hurt to dig them out." I frisk her as I speak and find another gun, a knife, and a stun grenade. These toys I decide to keep. She also has an assortment of canisters that resemble tiny spray cans. They're different colors, but otherwise they're unlabeled. "I assume one of these causes instant and agonizing death?" I ask.

"Why are you talking? Shoot me."

"I have no reason to kill you."

She glares at me but trembles with her pain and perhaps fear.

"You'll get nothing out of me," she swears.

"Maybe. Maybe not."

This is no place to banter. We'll be spotted soon. I have to get her below. Not all the people who boarded the ferry were on foot. The lower deck is loaded with cars, which approximately half the passengers are taking to France. My best bet is to find a suitable vehicle and stow the woman in the trunk and drive it off the boat. Border control between France and Britain is not a concern. The flow of traffic between the countries is pretty open. If I do get stopped at a checkpoint, I can always smile and bat my eyelashes.

Of course, my secret passenger must remain silent.

Reaching out, I grasp the two main arteries and veins in her neck and squeeze.

She loses consciousness almost immediately.

I get to work.

SIXTEEN

When I get to France, I immediately turn around and drive under the Channel, back to England. As a result, dawn finds me in London, in a poor section of town, where it's possible to rent a motel room and carry in a body and nobody asks any questions.

The van I stole to transport the woman belongs to an electrician. I'm lucky—it has several long rolls of electrical wire, in all gauges, in the back. The wire allows me to tie the woman to the bed. I wrap her up so thoroughly she looks like a generator waiting to be plugged in. The van also has tools I use to construct a wicked shocking device. I'm not a fan of torture, but I'm less a fan of dying, and these people are trying to kill me.

In France—before driving back to England—I dug out her bullets and her suicide tooth. I even sewed up a couple of her torn arteries in the rear of the van. Yet she's still bleeding as I tie her to the motel bed. She's in pain, moaning beneath the cloth I have taped over her mouth. I pull off the rag once we're settled and sit beside her on the bed.

"I won't gag you if you promise not to cry out," I say.

She nods weakly. "Thirsty."

The motel, despite its wretched exterior, has a well-stocked minibar. I hold a bottle of Evian water to her lips, and she gulps hungrily. I pull it away.

"Sip it slowly. You'll throw up."

She nods and slowly drinks the entire bottle.

"Would you like some more?" I ask as I toss the bottle in the garbage.

"I'm fine." She coughs. "Relatively speaking."

"So you have a sense of humor, good. I was beginning to wonder about you people."

"You know nothing about us," she says bitterly.

"That's why we're here, to get acquainted."

"That's not why we're here."

"No?"

"You're interested in only one thing."

"What's that?"

"Why do you play these games?"

"This isn't a game. I honestly don't know what you're talking about."

"Blood."

I smile. "You're joking. Who told you that?"

"You deny that you're a vampire?"

"No. It's not something I go around advertising, but I'm not a bloodsucker. In the last fifteen years, I've seldom drunk human blood."

"Liar."

"I'm aware of your mental abilities. I possess similar powers. But I can't read your mind, and you can't read mine. At the same time, I sense you know the truth when it's spoken aloud. So listen to me. I almost never drink human blood. I don't hunt people and drain away their blood and leave them to die. Now am I speaking the truth or not?"

She hesitates. "We know your history. We know you're evil."

"What's your name?"

"What do you care?"

"My name is Alisa. I—"

"That's not your real name," she interrupts.

"What's my real name?"

"Sita. Bloody Sita."

"I'm impressed. You do know something of my past. Who told you my name?"

"If I tell you, I'll be executed."

"Come on, I won't tell anybody."

"No."

"You can tell your pals I tortured the information out of you."

"They wouldn't care."

"Well, then, maybe I will have to torture you."

Her eyes widen. "You would enjoy that."

"It gives me no pleasure to hurt someone."

"I've seen you in action. You're a killing machine."

"Just because I'm good at it doesn't mean I enjoy it. You and your partners came to kill me. I was just defending myself."

"You're faster than us, stronger. You could have fled if you were only interested in protecting yourself."

"Bullshit. If I didn't set an example that I'm not to be fooled with, your people would never leave me alone."

"What kind of example are you going to make of me?"

"Answer a few questions and I'll call your people right now and tell them the address of this motel. They can pick you up and take you to their own private hospital."

She looks away. "We don't have hospitals."

"Because you're strong. You don't age."

"You may as well start the torture. I'm not going to answer your questions."

"Stop it! I don't want to torture you!"

"You are torturing me! My knees are shattered. My hands are broken! I can't stop bleeding. What else can you do to me?"

I soften my tone. "I know you're in pain, I can feel it. I can go to a hospital or pharmacy and get you bandages and medicine and clean up your wounds and remove the pain."

"If—"

"If you tell me your name."

She stares at me. "That's all?"

"Yes."

"My name is Numbria."

"That's a pretty name."

"You don't know what it means."

"But I do. It's not mentioned in any history books, but it's the name of the younger sister of the Goddess Isis. The mantra 'Om Numbria' used to be considered one of the most powerful chants on earth."

She's stunned. "How do you know this?"

"A friend of mine taught me the mantra. I used to chant it."

"You worship the Goddess?"

"Sort of. When I was young, I met Krishna. He touched me deeply. He told me that when a person worships him, they worship all forms of God. He said the form doesn't matter. Only the love matters."

She appears genuinely curious. "How does it matter?"

"He said worship cultures the human heart. That's why being a parent is the highest calling a human being can have. Krishna believed most parents worship their children."

"Huh! Most parents are cruel."

"Were your parents cruel to you, Numbria?"

She turns away. "I won't speak of them."

I squeeze her arm gently. "Do you want the medicine or not?"

Numbria casts me a weary glance. "You're not what I expected."

"Thank you." I stand from the bed. "On the drive here, I saw a clinic three blocks over. I can get you what you need there. I'll leave you ungagged if you promise to stay quiet. But if you call for help, I'll hear you and be back before anyone else can arrive. Do you understand?"

"Yes."

I turn toward the door. "I won't be long."

It's true I prefer to get the information I need without resorting to torture. I don't mind playing doctor to Numbria. But I have another motive in seeking out drugs. Sodium Pentothal is an established truth serum. From experience, I've found it to be effective. Yet I know if morphine and a small amount of dilaudid are added, the combination is much more potent, especially if the subject in question is in pain.

I have no trouble obtaining what I wish at the clinic. I accidentally bump into a young doctor in the hallway and work my magic on him, and a few minutes later he sends me out the door with a bag full of goodies. All free of charge. You have to love the British and their universal health care system.

However, a disturbing feeling sweeps over me as I prepare to leave the clinic. It's so strong it's close to a physical sensation. I feel like I'm being watched. Not by one set of eyes, either, but by a multitude. I remain still a long time, trying to get a fix on the source, to no avail.

I call Seymour on the cell phone I stole from the doctor. He's upset I didn't call earlier, but I apologize and we get down to business.

"How are Teri and Matt doing?" I ask.

"You mean, how do they feel about last night?"

"Yeah. Did they see anything?"

"They didn't see you. You lucked out in that respect. But there was gossip at the president's hotel about some superchick with blond hair who killed a dozen people. They both saw blood on the floor, and Matt kept asking where you were."

"Why?"

"Like you said, the guy's got an antenna. Maybe he's worried you were the superchick."

"They don't even know I was at that hotel."

"I guess."

"What did you tell him?"

"That you were tired and went to bed."

"Did Teri get to meet the president?"

"No. His secret service was too spooked to throw another party."

"A pity."

"I take it you killed the four?"

"I killed three of them. I've taken one of them captive."

"What are you going to do to him?"

"Her. I'm going to interrogate her."

"You're not answering my question."

"I'm going to do whatever it takes to get her to talk."

"That's what I was afraid of."

"If I don't figure out a way to stop them now, I'll never have peace. The rest of you could be in danger as well."

"More reason to make me into a vampire."

"More reason not to. Numbria has already admitted she knows what I am."

"Who told her?"

"That's what I have to find out. It's going to be a long day."

"The longer you're gone, the more suspicious it will look to Matt and Teri."

"What are they doing now?"

"Sleeping. It's still early and they went to bed late. Tell me where you are."

I give him the name and address of the motel. "Don't come here unless I call for you," I warn him.

"Fine. As long as you answer when I call."

"Agreed. Is the secret service searching for me?"

"I don't think so. I know they haven't linked you to Teri. They haven't questioned her."

"A secret service agent named Mike saw me kill the three and still let me go."

"Did you cast a spell on him?"

"No. He seemed to grasp that the people I killed weren't

normal. And that I should be left alone to deal with the rest of them."

"That's a hell of an insight on his part."

"I think Mike's what people call an old soul. You run into them if you live long enough. He has a rare form of intuition. He won't report me."

"You meet the strangest people."

"I hooked up with Teri so I could have some normal friends."

"Then juiced her up with vampire blood and pushed her into the Olympic limelight, where she shattered a world record."

"Are you saying it's my fault they came after me last night?"

"I don't have to say it."

That's what I love about Seymour. No one can cut to the chase like him. I tell him about my feeling of being watched. He's worried.

"They must have picked up your trail. Finish with your captive and get as far away from her as fast as you can. Let her live. Send her back to them as a goodwill ambassador."

"She's bleeding an awful lot to be an effective ambassador."

"They don't heal like you do?"

"No. But they're very strong, very fast. I could let her go and she could turn around and try to kill me."

"It's your call."

"There's something else that bothers me about this feeling of being watched. It reminds me of the IIC group."

"The Array?"

"Yes."

"That gold medal is costing you in more ways than one."

"That's not fair. Teri deserved to fulfill her dreams."

"Bullshit. She cheated, even if she doesn't know it."

"That wasn't her fault."

"It doesn't matter. Look at the attention it's brought. The vampire I wrote about was obsessed with staying in the shadows. What's gotten into you?"

"How do you know I didn't plan this? Look how it's flushed my enemies out into the open."

"As far as I can tell, you're the one who's out in the open."

I don't know what to say, so I say nothing.

"Let me help you," Seymour continues. "Let me come there. I can help you question the woman."

"You're too squeamish."

"Listen to me, Sita, please. I have a bad feeling about this."

"Go back to sleep. I know what I'm doing."

"Famous last words. If you begin to feel the least bit odd, call me."

I promise. I hang up and drive back to the motel. Numbria hasn't tried to escape. She must know more about the strength of the handcuffs than I do. I start out by showing her the labels on the two bottles I hold in my right hand: dilaudid and morphine.

"I'll give you a shot to take away the pain and then bandage you," I say as I fill the syringe. "I can set your broken bones, too. I don't need an X-ray. I assume once everything is set, you'll heal much faster than your average person?"

"Why are you doing all this?"

"There's no reason for you to suffer."

"You're a hypocrite. You're going to make me suffer if I don't answer your questions."

"A hypocrite says one thing and means another." I find a vein and insert my needle and inject her with the opiate solution. Her face relaxes almost instantly. "I haven't lied to you."

"You're Bloody Sita," she mumbles. "You want my blood."

"I'm not interested in your blood," I say, although I must admit I have seldom encountered blood that smells so vibrant. It makes sense. Their power must be derived from their blood. I imagine drinking it would be a rare delight.

Yet I push away such thoughts as I clean her wounds with alcohol and hydrogen peroxide. For her size, I have given her a strong shot. She appears to float on euphoric waves, even as I dig out fragments of bone from both her knees and sew up my incisions. The bones in her palms are also a mess, and I wonder if she will need a specialist and a series of operations to recover.

When I'm finished attending to her injuries, and before the narcotics wear off, I give her a shot of Sodium Pentothal. She doesn't notice. There are still enough opiates in her system to potentiate the truth serum. Her eyes fall shut, but I don't mind. As long as she can hear me.

"You hear my voice, don't you, Numbria?"

"Yes."

"And you know my name?"

"Yes."

"What is my name?"

"You have many. Alisa Perne. Lara Adams. Your oldest name is Sita. Bloody Sita."

"Why do you call me Bloody Sita?"

"Because you are a vampire. You are evil."

"Who told you I am evil?"

"The Source."

"Is the Source an individual? Or a group of individuals?"

"A group."

"Does this group have a leader?"

"Yes."

"Is it like a secret council but with a president?"

"Yes."

"How old is the Source?"

"It goes back to the beginning of time."

"The beginning of history?"

"Yes."

"What does your group call itself?"

"The Telar."

"Are the Telar connected to the IIC?"

"I don't know what that is."

"Do you know what the Array is?"

"No."

"Do you know a woman named Brutran?"

"No."

"Have you heard her name mentioned?"

"No."

"Can the word 'Telar' be translated into English?"

"Roughly."

"Translate it for me."

"It means the Immortals."

"How old is the oldest Telar?"

"I don't know."

"If you were to guess, what would you say?"

"Ten . . . twelve . . . thousand years old."

I have been standing as I question her. Now I have to sit down. It is hard for me to imagine any creature on earth older than myself. It's just so ingrained in me that I'm the oldest.

"How many Telar are there?"

"I don't know."

"Roughly."

"Five thousand. Maybe more."

"Are many Telar over ten thousand years old?"

"No."

"How old are you, Numbria?"

"Eight hundred years."

"Where were you born?"

"In Italy. In the Dark Ages."

"You were alive when the plague spread over Europe?"

"Yes."

"Did any of the Telar catch the plague?"

"Many did. Many died."

"Did any members of the Source catch it?"

"They saw it coming. They hid away. They survived."

"Did the Source instruct you to hide?"

"Yes. But when I heard, it was too late. Azol was sick."

"Who is Azol?"

"My brother. He died from the plague."

"Was he Telar?"

"He was my brother."

"Did the original Telar form a civilization?"

"Yes."

"What was it called?"

"The Egyptians."

"But modern archaeologists say the ancient Egyptian society only goes back five thousand years. How could the Telar be older?"

"Modern archaeologists know nothing."

I don't argue the point. I fled India for Egypt five thousand years ago, and it was a thriving civilization. That's when I met Suzama. It was largely wrecked by a group called the Setians, before I left, although I heard it quickly rebuilt itself.

"Do the Telar have records of a group called the Setians?"

"Yes."

"How do the Telar describe them?"

"As a race of demons."

Fair enough, I think.

"Do the Telar have records of a priestess named Suzama?"

"Yes."

"How do they describe her?"

"As a divine oracle."

"Was Suzama Telar?"

"Suzama was mortal. The Telar are immortal."

"Was Suzama aware of the Telar?"

"The Source cannot be sure what Suzama knew."

"Do the Telar have any record of me in ancient Egypt?"

"Not that I am aware of."

"When did the Telar become aware of vampires?"

"I don't know."

"Was there one vampire in particular who made the Telar aware of them?"

"Yes."

"What was this vampire's name?"

"Yaksha."

My heart skips in my chest. Simply to hear his name spoken by this stranger disturbs me. "Did Yaksha know about the Telar?" I ask.

"Yes."

"How can you be sure?"

"He married a Telar."

I almost swoon. My maker, Yaksha, not only knew of this race of immortals—a race he never told me about—but he was close to them. Hell, he married one of them. I don't know why, but I suddenly feel betrayed.

"What was his wife's name?" I ask.

"We do not speak of her."

"Why not?"

"She betrayed the Telar by being with the vampire."

"Did she become an outcast? Yaksha's wife?"

"Yes."

"Was she killed?"

"Yes."

"By whom?"

"The Source. The high priest of the Source."

"You mean the boss?"

"Yes."

"Did this boss try to kill Yaksha?"

"Yes."

"But he failed."

"Yes."

"Why did he fail?"

"Yaksha . . . Clever. Powerful. Impossible to kill."

"Yaksha must have been angry the Source killed his wife."

"We do not speak of it."

"Did he take revenge? Did he wipe out your Source?"

Numbria takes a long time to answer.

"The Source is eternal. It cannot be destroyed."

"What is the goal of the Telar?"

"To survive. To control."

"Are there members of the Telar in high positions in society?"

"Yes."

"In politics?"

"Yes."

"In business?"

"Yes."

"In science?"

"No."

"The Telar avoid scientific positions because they wish to avoid sharing their scientific knowledge with the rest of mankind. True?"

"Yes."

"Do the Telar wish to help mankind?"

"No."

"Why not?"

"Human beings have spread across this planet like a plague. They poison it. They must be stopped."

"How do you plan on stopping them?"

"There are ways."

"Tell me of some of these ways."

"The Source has not revealed what it will do next."

"But you're convinced the Telar want to exterminate mankind?"

"Not exterminate."

"You will allow some humans to survive?"

"Yes."

"Why?"

"To study them. To learn from them."

"What could you possibly learn from a human being?"

I'm shocked when the question provokes an extreme response. First Numbria doesn't answer, and I make the mistake of thinking she has not heard the question, that she has dozed off. But when I repeat it, with more force, she gets agitated. She begins to thrash in the bed, threatening to open the wounds I've worked so hard to close. Obviously I have struck a nerve. I have no choice but to sedate her further, and soon she is asleep.

For a long time, I sit and ponder how I could have shared a world with the Telar and yet been unaware of their existence. To make matters worse, Yaksha clearly didn't trust me with the knowledge of their existence. True, I only saw him at the end of his life, but he could have warned me.

Was he afraid of what I might do to them? Or was he trying to protect me from them? Maybe he felt if they didn't know where I was, then it would be better for all concerned.

"But they know about Bloody Sita," I say aloud as Numbria sleeps.

Who was this Telar that Yaksha married? She must have been a remarkable woman to have captured his heart. Here, in my arrogance, I always imagined I was the only one he loved. The truth is sobering. No, worse, much worse, it breaks my heart. I don't even know her name. I only know the Telar killed her to punish her for being with Yaksha.

Long ago, I was his lover. But that was before Krishna entered our lives and forced him to take a vow to destroy all the vampires—including me. Krishna asked me to take a vow too. To make no more vampires. In return, he promised I'd always have his grace, his protection. Thus Krishna gave Yaksha and me contradictory vows. Leave it up to the Lord of the Universe to make our life's purpose impossible.

I'm weary. It's been a long time since I've rested, and my battles with the Telar have exhausted my reserves. I crave sleep but fear to stretch out on the floor and black out. Instead, I lock the windows and the door and sit in a chair facing Numbria, with a gun on my lap.

Long ago I learned to half sleep, where my mind empties itself of thought and my metabolism slows down, but I still hear what's going on around me. The practice has saved my life on more than one occasion.

Turning off my cell, I close my eyes and rest.

The devil does not exist. I do not believe he exists. Nor do I believe the old saying that the devil's greatest accomplishment was to convince the majority of mankind that he does not exist. For me, Satan and a literal hell are fables born of Christianity's desire to control humanity by increasing its fear of death. After all, I'm five thousand years old and I've never met Satan.

Until now, I fear. I feel he is close.

I do not feel like I'm dreaming.

It's all . . . too real.

Fire and brimstone. I choke on red smoke and squirm from the heat of surrounding flames. My eyes are neither open nor closed. I sense a number of creatures around me, but when I try to focus on them, something else takes their place.

I feel as if I stand on a precipice above an abyss filled with lava and demons. Yes, real live demons, who torture thousands if not millions of souls who have sinned during the course of their short lives. This precipice—I feel like I've been shepherded there by a being greater than myself. A malevolent being who knows all my sins and who can hardly wait to make me suffer for them. Far below, I hear demons applauding with ravenous anticipation when they see me waiting to be shoved inside.

Inside where? Hell. I'm standing at the gates of hell.

"No!" I cry. "Don't put me in there! I don't belong in there!"

My cries make the demons explode in laughter. They know that no one who has been brought to the gates of hell ever returns. The reason is simple. It's their master who chooses who enters this accursed region, and their master is never wrong because—even though he's opposite of Almighty God—he's almost as old as God. He's the alpha and omega, the one and the many. His names are endless—Devil, Satan, Old Gooseberry, Beelzebub, Old Nick, Lucifer . . .

For some reason, in this place of darkness and pain, the name Lucifer, "the Light Bearer," haunts me the most. I recall how in the beginning God created heaven and the earth, and in heaven he created the greatest angel of them all. Greater even than Michael and Gabriel. His name was Lucifer, and God placed him above all the angelic hosts by endowing him with the light of the Holy Spirit itself. With this light Lucifer felt he was the equal of God, and thus was poisoned with arrogance, the first and most damning of all his sins, for it led to all his other crimes.

It was because of arrogance Lucifer strove to replace God in heaven, and rallied the bulk of the angels to his side by promising them a share of his light. These angels who joined him did so because Lucifer was so bright, so enchanting, and the Lord had never promised to grant them such a wonderful boon.

When the war began, Lucifer had numbers on his side, but when he rose up against God, the Lord chose not to fight. Instead, God bid his servants to save heaven and earth. He commanded Michael and Gabriel, and other archangels—whose names have long since been forgotten—to strike down Lucifer and his rebels.

How long this battle waged, no mortal was ever to know, for it was fought in a realm outside of time and space. But eventually Lucifer fell into the pit that God had prepared for him, and those angels who fought with him also fell, and became known as demons, and they hated the pit almost as much as they hated their master, who had promised them glory but instead led them to eternal damnation.

But it is said by Michael and his brothers that they did not defeat Lucifer, for he was too powerful. Lucifer was defeated for another reason. As he fought to claim heaven for his own, he had to call more and more upon the light of the Holy Spirit for strength, and the deeper he dove into the light, the more he realized the light had its origin in God.

Therefore, Lucifer realized a terrible irony. In his quest to destroy God, he saw that he was fighting against himself, for his light was not only of God, but his very being had been created by God. And Lucifer saw he was God, as were all those fallen ones who fought beside him.

Yet in the end, rather than share this truth with his demons, he chose instead to descend into the pit. It's said he traded eternal bliss for endless agony, all because he could not stand to admit the truth to anyone else.

It is this same Lucifer who stands before me at the gates of hell. He asks if I understand why I'm here, and I cry out, "No!"

He laughs as he replies, "But Sita, you have also fallen.

Even when you have seen that my light is no different from the light of your precious Lord?"

I try to answer but cannot speak. My fear is too great. I scream as his shadow engulfs me, and weep as he throws me into the pit.

But God does not hear my cries. For I am forsaken.

I awaken on the floor of the motel to the screams of Numbria. She thrashes on the bed in agony. She cries for another shot. As if in a dream, I reach for the needle and fill it with opiates. Yet as I turn back to her, I can't help but notice the blood soaking through her bandages. Its smell seems to penetrate to the core of my brain, and I feel I have reverted to a yakshini, a devil from the deep, a reptile consumed with hunger. There's no sympathy in me. How can there be? After all, Lucifer is right, I am forsaken.

"Sita, help me," Numbria cries. "There's something wrong with my mind. There's something inside me. I can't stand it. It's killing me!"

I sit beside her on the bed and lick my lips and smile.

"Do you want me to stop the pain?" I ask.

She glances at the needle in my hand. "Yes! Stop it!"

I raise the needle in front of her eyes and squirt out a few drops.

"But the pain adds a certain sweetness, doesn't it?" I ask.

Numbria stops thrashing and stares. "What are you talking about?"

I squirt out more of the drug, wasting it on nothing.

"It sweetens the blood. There's nothing like a meal when the victim screams for mercy, before they realize there's no chance. The pain is only going to get worse." My grin widens. "You must know that by now?"

She shakes her head. "This isn't you talking. It's this thing in my head. It's in your head too. Listen to what you're saying. You're not a monster."

I grip her wounded arm and twist it so that she cries out.

"But I am, the worst monster of all. I'm a demon. That's why I've lived so long. That's what he told me. I live in his light and I feed on his darkness." Pulling at her arm, I use my nails and rip off a chunk of skin. Her blood flows so bright, so warm, so dripping, I can hardly wait.

"No, Sita! Don't do this! I don't want to die!"

I open my mouth and lick. I bite and laugh out loud.

"Then you should never have been born!"

It's been too long since I've fed. Her screams make it so sweet.

There's an explosion at the motel door. Blinding light pours in, and for a moment I cannot see. A person, it is a human being, rushes to my side and grips my shoulders. I don't know who they are or what they want, but I hate to be interrupted, and I'm going to kill them. How dare they touch me!

"Sita, it's me, it's Seymour. Can you hear me?"

I smile, my face cracking with dried blood. I don't know why it's dry. I feel as if I was feeding only a moment ago. No matter, I will feed again off this one.

I giggle. "Yes! I hear you. I know you. Seymour, lovely Seymour." I reach out a hand and stroke his face. Such a pretty face it is. Too bad I will have to rip it to pieces to get what I want. "My, you're so warm, so tasty. Can I have a little bite?"

"No. Sita, you're caught in a spell. You're—"

"Yes!" I scream as I yank him closer. "You're supposed to say yes to me. No one says no to me! Certainly not a pathetic mortal like you! Do you know what you are? You are meat! Bloody meat!"

He does not struggle the way the other one did.

His eyes remain calm as he stares into my eyes.

"Krishna," he says. "Think of Krishna and it will stop."

I feel as if I have been stung by something burning.

I strike him, and he flies across the room and hits the wall, crumpling on the floor. His eyes stray to the motel door. For the first time I realize there is another one there.

"Shanti," Seymour gasps. "Run."

But this Shanti creature does not run. Instead, she walks slowly into the room. Her eyes remain focused on me—she doesn't even glance at the meat on the bed. At first I'm annoyed, but then I'm glad she's there. The more the merrier. She is smaller than the male. I'll eat her first, in front of him, draw out his terror, and then start . . .

"Sita?" this Shanti says.

"Ah." I grab her by her shoulders and shake her roughly. But she shows no fear, and that annoys me. It does something else to me. I feel suddenly dizzy and weak. She's draining my power! I raise my hand to strike her, to kill her . . .

But she reaches up and strokes the side of my face.

Her touch stings. Like that damn Krishna word.

"It's all right, Sita. Don't be afraid. I'm here. I love you."

"Stop it!" I yell. I will kill her, she's hurting me. But I can't keep my arm up. All the strength falls out of it and it drops to my side. She continues to stroke my face. Her hands don't feel as awful as they did a moment ago. Actually, it's kind of nice, her touch.

"That's right, Sita. It was just an evil spirit, and it's leaving."

I blink, I recognize her. "Who are you? What are you?"

"Shanti, your friend. Seymour's here too. We both love you so much."

"But you're . . . you're meat!"

Shanti shakes her head. "The spirit told you that. It lied to you. Let it go, let it leave. Remember Krishna and it will go."

I grip my head. "No! Don't say that word. It hurts."

"Krishna is soothing, like my touch. You know him. Tell me something about him."

It's a question I hate to answer. But I don't want her to stop touching my face. It lessens the pain inside. So I say a few quick words. "He carried a flute. He played it. . . . I remember. . . . The music was nice."

"What else do you remember?"

"His eyes. They were blue. A beautiful blue."

Shanti puts both hands on my head. "Say his name aloud. You're almost back. You're coming back."

"Krishna. Krishna." The warmth of the name and her palms washes over me like a healing balm. So soft, so soothing, so comforting. I feel as if my mind, which was locked in a black box, has suddenly been returned to me on a gold pillow.

"Shanti," I whisper.

"That's me."

"Seymour."

"Over here," he says from his place on the floor. "You okay, Sita?"

I feel a smile on my face. "Yes. I'm fine. I'm Sita."

Then I'm all the way back inside my body.

I sense a black cloud flee the room. It leaves behind a faint stink, but the more I focus on who I am, and my friends, and Krishna, the more I sense a perfumed odor fill the room. I remember everything.

The memory gives me the strength to look at the bed.

At what remains of Numbria.

A mass of torn flesh. It leaks onto the floor.

I feel I will be sick. "No," I moan.

Shanti and Seymour both hug me. I hear him talking.

"It wasn't you, Sita. It was the Array. Brutran and her cronies waited until now to attack."

"But why? How?"

"I don't know how," Seymour says. "But I think the why is becoming clear. All this time we've assumed we were dealing with a single enemy. We were wrong. The IIC is composed of normal people who have stumbled onto some great power. These others . . ."

"They call themselves the Telar. They're immortals."

"The Telar are their enemies. It makes sense. That's what Brutran was offering you in her home. Protection from the Telar. But you turned her down, and it pissed her off."

"I wonder what she wants in exchange for her protection?"

Seymour turns and steps toward the open door. He's going to close it.

"Whatever it is, it can't be good," he says. "Anyone who would focus the Array on you and force you to do something like this has got to be pretty sick."

I put a hand over my eyes, to shield them from Numbria's remains.

"Wait till you meet her," I say. "She's cold as ice."

"I hope to God I never meet her," Shanti says.

I hear Seymour closing the door. Then it bursts open.

"Alisa?" I hear Teri's gentle voice. "Are you there? Matt and I didn't mean to pry, but we decided to follow . . ." Her words trail off, and she screams. "Oh, God! Alisa! The blood . . . What's that on the bed? Oh, no!"

I leap to my feet, see Teri and Matt standing in the doorway, frozen in shock, their faces pale as ghosts. Teri's eyes are the worst. The horror inside them, I don't know if I can bear it.

"Teri! Matt! It's not how it looks!" I say, even as my lips crack on the dried blood that covers my mouth. "I was attacked by a group. They're the same ones who are harassing Lisa and Shanti. It's a long story, but I swear to you I didn't do this. Tell them, Shanti. Tell them, Seymour."

"It's true, she didn't do this," Shanti says.

"Listen to her," Seymour says.

Matt stares at them. "You guys just got here. What do you know?"

"We know she's telling the truth," Shanti says.

"Matt! Damn it! Just listen to her!" Seymour snaps.

The setting is too sick. The gross mass on the bed wipes away any chance at reason, as do my blood-soaked face and clothes. I hold out my hands, trying to calm the air, and speak in a gentle tone.

"Matt, get Teri out of here. But please let me explain later. It will all make sense then. I promise you, this is not how it looks."

Matt steps in front of Teri, who's on the verge of fainting, and pushes her outside the door. Then he turns to me, and I can't help but notice how cool he remains in the face of such horror.

"It makes sense now," he says. "There's no need to explain." Taking Teri by the arm, he turns his back on me. "Stay away, Alisa. Stay far away."

They walk away. I hear a car start.

Red tears pour over my bloody cheeks.

Deep inside, I feel a pain in my heart I have never known.

But I cannot call on Krishna to fix it.

Lucifer was right about one thing.

I deserve this pain . . . for I have sinned.

SEVENTEEN

A week later, Seymour and I sit on the deck of a massive ferry and gaze out at the blue-green beauty of the warm Mediterranean. To our left and right are a handful of rocky islands, but our boat's next destination is straight ahead—Santorini, one of the most lovely spots in the Aegean Sea.

The sun is bright and hot and has the effect of making me sleepy. But Seymour is charged with energy. Today is a dream come true for him. Years ago he wrote about a Hispanic woman, Paula Ramirez, who gave birth to a remarkable baby named John. Now Seymour's finally going to see the child. In describing John, Seymour and I went so far as to hint the child was divine, a possibility that is still very much open to debate. What I can say with a clear conscience is that John is special. He gives off the greatest vibe. Sitting with him is like bathing beneath a waterfall of peace.

"How old is the boy now?" Seymour asks.

I yawn. "He should be sixteen."

"You tired?"

"Just feeling lazy. The sun, you know."

"We can go inside."

"Not at all. You like it out here, and the water is beautiful."

"It's so clean and clear. I can't wait to go swimming."

"You mean you can't wait to visit the nude beach and check out the scenery."

He nods. "Nothing wrong with that. I can swim afterwards."

"I hope you don't expect me to go skinny-dipping."

"It's the main reason I came here. Since when are you shy?"

"I'm not shy at all. Except around you."

"Why?"

"It's a secret."

Seymour smiles. "When was the last time you saw the boy?"

"He was a toddler. They were living in Tahoe at the time."

"At least I got that part right."

"You got most of the story right."

"I don't suppose you used his blood to bring me back to life?"

"True, that was your version. It was me Kalika impaled with a sharp stick. It went through my heart. I should have died. But when my daughter left me for dead, I injected myself with a syringe of John's blood—directly in my chest—and I lived."

"That should be proof enough he's no ordinary child."

"I never said he was ordinary. But is he Christ? Is he Krishna? Those are much more serious questions."

"You always speak of them as the same."

"To me they're one and the same. They taught the same thing. They lived similar lives. They even died the same way. To skeptics like Teri, this means they're nothing but fables. I was lucky I had the advantage of meeting one of these fables."

"I thought Krishna died from an arrow to his heel, like Achilles."

"History has a habit of mixing fables and facts. There is a story in India that says Krishna was completely divine, except where his feet touched the earth. It was only there he was vulnerable—hence his death from an arrow to the heel. But if you travel in India today, you'll find a number of ancient paintings and murals that depict Krishna as being crucified between two criminals."

"I didn't know that."

"In the West, people have trouble with the idea there might have been more than one divine incarnation. Indians accept the concept easily. It's seems logical to them, and less dogmatic. They have a word for such beings. They call them avatars, or 'those who descend.'"

"Where do they descend from?"

"I was sitting near Krishna when he was asked that question. I actually spent more time with him than you described in your books. His answer was fascinating. He said between earth and his realm were fifty levels, with earth being the lowest and his being the highest. He said a few of the older races in the galaxy had evolved through these fifty levels. When I asked if there was a chance I could move on to these higher worlds, he said yes, but first I'd have to pay the price of my long life here on earth."

"What did he mean?"

"I don't know, I was afraid to ask." I lower my head, feeling a sudden powerful desire to be with Krishna. "Sometimes I feel I can't keep paying."

Seymour hugs me. "Teri will forgive you. She loves you."

"I think I terrify her. Besides, Matt won't let me near her."

"The Sita I know wouldn't let anyone stand in her way."

"The Sita you know doesn't exist. Besides, Matt's right, she's safer away from me."

"Hey, how come you don't worry about my safety?"

"You're just a writer. All you do is make up shit. That makes you expendable."

Seymour laughs. He doesn't disagree.

Soon after, we dock at Santorini. The ferry slides into the harbor like a hand into a glove. The entire lower level of cars exits in minutes. From the Athens airport, we've brought with us an Audi convertible. Even I, a creature of darkness, have to admit you should never visit the Greek islands and drive around with a roof on.

There's too much to see. Besides the sparkling ocean, which is seldom out of view, the stark countryside and the whitewashed brick buildings create a timeless aura. I visited Santorini a century ago, and it hasn't changed. I'm not surprised Paula Ramirez sought out such a peaceful environment to raise her son in.

Yet I'm disappointed she moved here without telling me her address. Paula's another person who thinks I'm dangerous. I had to use my CIA and Interpol contacts to locate her. I understand, though—I probably would have done the same in her position. I've saved her child a couple of times, but he's the one who's supposed to save the world.

If Suzama's prophecies are accurate when it comes to John.

That is a big *if*.

I let Seymour drive to Paula's house. He notes my reflective mood. "Does she know we're coming?" he asks.

"No."

"Will we be welcome?"

"The wolf at the door is never welcome."

"Would you stop that crap. John's alive because of you."

"He almost died because of me. Paula knows me as well as you do. She sees how violence stalks me. She hasn't gone out of her way to keep in touch."

"Why are we going to see her?"

"We're going to see John."

"Why?"

"I told you about that lead I found in Numbria's bag. The address in Arosa, Switzerland. I'm pretty sure Yaksha spent time there, with his wife. Now that's he's no longer there, I think the Telar have a base in Arosa." I pause, knowing I have yet to answer his question. "I have to check it out."

"Cool. I'll go with you."

"No."

"You can't stop me from coming."

"Can't I?"

"You took a vow in Central Park. You said you'd never leave me."

"Then you have to release me from that vow. Numbria said there are five thousand Telar on earth. How many do you think there will be in Arosa? There's no way I would be able to protect you."

"You talk like you're walking into a death trap."

"It's a possibility."

"Then don't go, Sita. Leave Europe, run and hide. You've spent most of your life in hiding and it's worked out pretty well. I'll go with you."

"The Telar are fixated on me. They won't leave me alone until I'm either captive or dead. Plus they're a danger to humanity. This has gone way beyond me and my personal safety. It's the same with Brutran and the IIC. They might be worse.

Look at the way the Array twisted my mind, and Brutran and her cronies weren't even in the same country. Imagine if they aim their weapon at the president of the United States."

"Who says they haven't?"

"Ain't that the truth."

Seymour is thoughtful. "It puzzles me how Brutran was able to focus the Array on you even though Numbria was in the same room. Your mind was obviously more powerful than hers. Yet you lost all control, while she remained relatively sane."

"It puzzled me for a long time, ever since I was in Brutran's home in California. I think I've figured out the answer. When I first visited IIC, they didn't know I was coming that day, but they were probably worried I'd show up eventually. They had killed Jeff Stephens, Lisa's boyfriend. They had killed Randy Clifford too, Lisa's ex. Randy was the one who'd hacked into their files and discovered they were collecting info on me. It didn't sound like they knew what I was, but they suspected I was older than any normal person. Putting all these facts together, they must have assumed there was a strong chance I'd force my way into their Malibu office. So they set a trap."

"You told me about your first meeting with Brutran. You two hardly talked."

"You're right. On the surface it didn't seem like much happened. But then I began to examine my entire visit there. When I burst in and demanded to see Brutran, they didn't throw me out like you'd expect. They told me to sit and wait and the boss would be with me in a few minutes. They kept me waiting a long time. Eventually a woman came in with her daughter, and we talked in the waiting area. Then the woman did something odd. She asked if I'd watch her daughter while she went to the bathroom."

"How old was the girl?" Seymour asks.

"Three or four."

"The woman had known you about ten minutes?"

"You see why it was strange. Of course I said, sure, no problem, I'll watch your kid. But the woman had barely left and the kid started moving all over the place. She was out of control. She lifted up a vase and smashed it on a glass table. She cut her hand pretty bad. I was picking out the shards of glass when her mother returned. Well, you would have thought I was choking the child. The woman went nuts and grabbed her kid and bolted out the door. Yet there was no real reason for her to leave. She was supposed to have this important meeting with Mr. Brutran."

"What was the setup?" Seymour asks.

"Oh, it was brilliant. You know how careful I am with my blood. To get it, you practically have to kill me. But by using this child to collect it, they made me drop all my defenses. I had nothing to pick the glass out of the girl's hand with except my fingertips. I pricked my own skin in several places. By the time the woman fled with her kid, several of my fingers were bleeding. I ran to the restroom and washed away the blood and bandaged my hands. The cuts healed quickly. But the damage was already done."

The light dawns for Seymour. "They had samples of your blood from the drops on their floor. They might even have siphoned blood from the pipes in the restroom, if they had prepared their plumbing ahead of time."

"Make no mistake, the pipes were prepped to catch my blood. The whole thing was planned down to the last detail."

"How did they get the child to break the vase on cue? They could have trained her, but that would have taken time."

"They didn't have time and they didn't need it. They have the Array. They must have briefly focused it on the girl. Even before she broke the vase, she was fidgeting."

"How does having your blood allow them to focus the Array on you?

"Since I don't know what it is, I can't answer that question. But I'll give you another reason why I know that stealing my blood is the key to understanding that first meeting. When I finally got in to see Brutran, we talked briefly before she cut our meeting short. I could tell she wanted to talk more, only later, away from the prying eyes inside that building. At the same time, she felt secure there. No one sees her without having guns aimed at them."

"But you said she didn't have security at her own house."

"Exactly. I expected her house to be a fortress, like her

work. But she lives alone, with her kid, maybe a husband. None of it made any sense. Then I realized something odd about the timing of our second meeting. After we first met, she stayed inside her office two days in a row. I know because I watched her from a spot back in the hills. I had her under observation the whole time. She never went home—she just kept working."

"She's obviously a workaholic."

"I said the same to Lisa. But Lisa told me she'd never seen Brutran stay at the office overnight. Don't you see? Brutran knew I was watching. She knew I was waiting for her to leave the building so I could get her alone. Only the next day she wasn't afraid to be alone with me."

"I'm sorry, I don't see what this has to do with your blood."

"I think the woman needed that extra day to load the Array with my blood so it could be used as a weapon against me. That's why she wasn't afraid to meet with me the second time, after two days had gone by. At that point, she knew she could focus the Array on me."

"You're making some pretty big leaps in logic here."

"You wouldn't have thought so if you were with me. She didn't blink when I walked into her living room. She knew she had the upper hand."

"But you beat her. You escaped."

"Barely. And look what happened to Numbria."

Seymour hesitates. "What did happen?"

"I was gripped by a overwhelming compulsion to drink her blood. To eat her alive. To torture her to death in the most painful way imaginable."

"The compulsion gripped you within seconds?"

I frown. "Not exactly. It seemed to start while I was asleep. Only I wasn't asleep."

"What do you mean?"

I take Seymour's hand. "You know, I've never believed in the devil. The last two thousand years, all the time the church was talking about Satan, I assumed they were trying to create a bogeyman to scare people into doing what the church wanted. Now I'm not so sure. The thing that came into that room—the only way I can describe it is to say it was demonic."

"Did you actually see a demon?"

"It was more like I was given an insight."

"Into what?"

"Into Lucifer." I let go of his hand and press my palms against my closed eyes. I feel a headache coming on. I need to change the subject. At the same time, I have to express my fear. Seymour's the only one who can understand it, and I can see even he's struggling with it.

"What was the insight?" he asks gently.

I fight to get out the words.

That the Light Bearer knows he's the same as God.

But they don't come. I can't speak them.

"It was not important," I whisper.

"Did you feel the same way in Brutran's house?"

"The evil element was stronger when I was with Numbria. And I felt . . . what it made me do was sacrilege. Like I defiled myself by being unable to resist it."

"Nonsense. You did everything you could to resist it."

"Did I? Or was there a part of me that wanted to drink her blood?"

"Listen, you're a vampire, it's natural for you to crave blood. But that doesn't mean you wanted to hurt her."

"I wish I could believe that."

"Is that why you want to see John? Are you looking for absolution?"

It's hard to admit. "Perhaps."

"Sita. You've done more than anyone else in the world to try to protect people."

"Protect them from what? Myself? Other vampires like me?"

"I'm not a priest, but don't they say there can be no sin without the intention to do wrong? The fact that Numbria died . . . It sounds cold, but she was just collateral damage."

"Try telling her that. But you can't, can you?"

I've gone too far. Seymour can't accept what I'm saying.

"Do you honestly think the Array is connected to Lucifer?"

I shake my head. I can't argue anymore. My headache is worse. We're outside beneath a crystal blue sky, weaving through the beautiful hills of Santorini, the shimmering waters of the Aegean Sea never more than a mile away. Yet I somehow smell the odor of fire and brimstone, and still hear the cries of the damned.

Paula lives near the airport, another artery through which visitors come to the island. She supports herself by renting low-powered motorcycles, the most popular way of getting around on the islands. She has a large stock, a hundred bikes, and makes more money than she can spend. I know all this from the spies I hired to find her. Paula and John have lived on Santorini for over a decade.

Her home is a block from her shop, a modest one story with a clay tile roof and brightly whitewashed walls, which makes it indistinguishable from 90 percent of the houses on the island. She's quick to answer the door when we knock. She smiles when she sees me, but I feel the expression is forced.

"Hello, Sita. Hi, Seymour," she says.

Seymour gushes. "I didn't know you knew my name."

"Sita's told me all about you. Come in, please."

Paula wears white shorts and a pink top. Her legs are deeply tanned. She's aged since we last met, which is only natural after fifteen years. Yet I can tell most of the lines on her once-smooth complexion are due to stress. Nevertheless, she is still striking, with her long black hair and large dark eyes. She has incredible lashes; she can convey a dozen subtle moods in the way she bats them. She also has one of the most lovely voices I've ever heard. She can disarm most people with a few words.

We sit in her living room. In the back, I hear John playing a computer game—the firing of electronic weapons, the howls of the special-effect villains as they die. I don't know what I expected John to be doing when we arrived, but playing games was not one of them.

"This is a pleasant surprise," Paula says when we're all seated with cups of tea. She's an expert when it comes to herbs. Her teas are not only tasty but healing. "Why didn't you call and say you were coming?"

"I was afraid you'd say no," I reply.

"Sita, you're one of my oldest friends."

"I'd say she's definitely your oldest," Seymour puts in.

Paula smiles. "I can't argue there."

"Is John here?" Seymour asks.

"He's in the middle of a computer game. You don't want to interrupt. He gets . . . annoyed. He should be done in a few minutes."

"How has he been?" I ask.

"Fine."

"Yourself?"

Paula shrugs. "Life doesn't get much nicer than Santorini. We've been very happy here."

"I'm glad," I say.

"Tell me about your life," she asks me.

I hesitate, then glance at Seymour. "Tell her. The last three months."

Seymour gives a brief summary, starting with my meeting with Teri and Matt and finishing with my catastrophic interrogation of Numbria. Paula listens closely, although she shifts her focus in three directions: on Seymour, on me, and out the window. The last disturbs me, because I know when she gazes into nothing she sees the most. I suspect her unpredictable power to see the future has suddenly awakened.

A chill runs through the room. In the back John stops playing, and there is only silence. I feel it and it scares me. It's not why I came to see her. I'm not there for a reading. I wouldn't mind some comfort, of course, to be told everything is going to be all right. But I don't want the truth, no, never, no one wants to hear that.

For some reason, a quote of Krishna's comes back to me:

"No one awakens in the morning thinking they will die that day. Not a saint or a sinner. Not even a condemned killer. We all know we're mortal, and yet we all believe we'll live forever."

Suzama would have known I'd come to see her out of fear. And when Paula looks at me, I sense she sees the same thing—that I'm afraid I'll die in Arosa.

When Seymour finishes, Paula sits quietly. John has finished with his game but hasn't come out to greet us. His mother gestures for Seymour to go to him.

"He's waiting for you," she says. Seymour, suddenly unsure of himself, glances at me and then retreats to the back room. Paula stands and slips on a pair of sandals. "Let's walk to the beach."

The sea isn't far, but when we reach it, Paula removes her sandals and heads north, letting the waves wash over her bare calves. I do likewise; the water feels wonderful. We walk a ways, but at one point she takes my hand and steers us up a dusty path that leads into a sheltered cove where a few old pillars lie worn and broken. We sit on a boulder beside the relics. They are too big, too heavy, to steal.

I continue to feel tense. Paula lets go of my hand and looks at me and shakes her head. "Why did you do it?" she asks.

Seymour's summary was short but detailed.

"Why did I give Teri my blood, or why did I say hello?"

"From the moment you said hello, you were going to give her your blood."

"That's not true." I pause. "At least, I didn't plan on giving it to her."

"Talk to me about it, Sita."

Her simple request shakes me to the core. "You have a son. He's your whole life. He fills your days. I had two daughters. Both were taken from me. More than anyone, you know about my loneliness."

"You've been lonely all your life. Why try to fill the void now?"

"The older I get, the more I feel the need for comfort."

"That's no answer."

"It's the truth. What else do you want me to say?"

"You knew that bringing Teri into your life would bring risk."

"Yes."

"It's unlike you to be selfish."

"I don't know. I can be the most selfish person on earth."

"Sita . . ."

"What?"

"Why?"

"I don't know! She was there, she was beautiful, and I knew she was related to me. She even looked like me. I couldn't resist. Of course, I knew it was a mistake to talk to her, that it would only lead to us getting involved. I'm not saying it was innocent. I planned to have a relationship with her."

"One you began with a murder."

Seymour had told her about Danny Boy.

I harden my voice. "I killed that guy to protect her."

"It sounds like Matt can protect her."

"I had to be sure. Besides, the guy was a rapist and a murderer. What difference does his death make? The world is better off without him."

"You haven't changed, have you? You're still so confident in your ability to judge. I'm surprised you still come to me for advice."

I go to snap at her but then remember who I'm talking to, who she might be. I feel Suzama so near when I sit beside Paula. Their voices, their words—they echo together inside me. There's a gentleness to her manner but a harshness to her gaze. Sitting so close to her, I feel pinned beneath a microscope. I cannot lie to her, there would be no point.

I lower my head. "I'm lost. I need your help."

"You want me to peer into your future?"

"No. I know you hate doing that."

"I don't hate it so much as I can't control what I see."

"Don't you always see the truth?"

Paula shakes her head. "The future's in flux. I see possibilities." She gestures to the worn pillars. "From our point of view, nothing is set in stone."

"Krishna could see the future. One future."

"His point of view was wider than mine."

"Maybe I should talk to John."

"If he'll talk to you."

"Did he know we were coming?"

"I didn't ask. But I knew."

I mock her. "So it wasn't really a pleasant surprise."

"Seriously, Sita, if you've come for my advice, then you should heed it. Leave Teri and Matt alone. Let them live their lives."

"What will happen if I don't?"

"What always happens to those you love."

"But, for good or bad, I've already opened the door. They're exposed. The Telar and probably the IIC know about them. They need my protection."

"Were you able to protect Ray? Joel? Your own daughter?"

"Kalika died trying to protect John! In case you've forgotten!"

"He only needed protecting because you showed up."

"That's a lie. I bumped into you by accident."

"But after that you sought me out. Why?"

"You know why. You reminded me of Suzama."

"Suzama's dead. That was another life. You have to stop living in the past. Seymour knows that. The only reason you had Kalika was because of Lalita. And the only reason you want to talk to John is because you once met Krishna."

"To hell with that and to hell with you! I need help! Help me!"

"Shanti can block the Array."

I stop. "In London, when she walked in the room and touched my face, the spell broke. But Seymour didn't tell you that. How did you know?"

"Why do you think IIC wants her dead?"

"How does she do it?"

"It doesn't matter. She can protect you from the attacks."

"I can't take Shanti with me to Switzerland."

"The Telar are located there?"

"I have a couple of leads that point in that direction."

"You can be sure they left the leads behind on purpose."

"Don't you think I know that? I'm probably walking into a trap. How can I take Shanti with me?"

"You decide. Brutran and the IIC are one issue. The Telar are another."

"They appear to be enemies. Brutran said as much. I was thinking if I could pretend to help one side, and do the same with the other side, I could stir up a war between the two. Let them annihilate each other."

"The Telar are ancient. They won't fall for anything so obvious."

"Did you know about the Telar?"

"Yes."

"How come you didn't warn me about them?"

"The world is filled with sleeping enemies. Should I wake them all up so they can come chasing after you?"

"The Telar are devotees of Suzama. They study her prophecies."

"Suzama never spoke about them. On purpose."

"But she spoke about John. Doesn't that worry you?"

"Many seers in the past and the present have predicted the Second Coming. Why should that bother me?"

"I told you, the Telar take Suzama seriously. If that's the case, they're probably interested in John."

Paula waves her hand. "John can take care of himself."

"You should have told my daughter that."

Paula stares at me in shock. "You can't blame us for that. Everything that happened, it was either your choice or hers."

"I didn't choose for Kalika to die."

"Kalika did what she had to do to protect John. But Teri hasn't been given a choice. If you stay on your present course, she'll die, or worse."

"What could be worse?"

Paula stands. "That's all I can tell you at this point. Let's go back."

When we reach the house, I'm disappointed to see Seymour sitting on the front porch. I know the verdict before he speaks.

"John's started another game. He doesn't want to be interrupted."

Paula holds up a hand before I can speak. "The games are important to him. He's trying to tell you it's not a good time, Sita."

The rejection stings. "Can we come back later?" I ask.

Paula catches my eye. "That depends on you."

She hugs us good-bye, and even gives Seymour a kiss on the cheek. When we get in the car, I drive. He looks too blissed out to grip the wheel.

"I take it you had a pleasant visit," I say, unable to hide my jealousy.

"He was wonderful."

"Did you promise not to write any more crappy novels in exchange for his grace?"

Seymour tries to comfort me. "You'll see him later."

"Did he say that?"

"It's a feeling I have."

"Swell. Everyone on this island knows the future. Except me."

"Sita—"

"Why the hell does he play computer games all day?"

"I'm not sure."

"At least tell me he's good at what he plays."

"Sure. But it's a tough game."

"Are you saying he plays the same one over and over again?"

"Yeah."

"What's it called?"

"Cosmic Intuitive Illusion." He pauses. "CII."

"IIC spelled backwards?"

"It could be a coincidence."

"What's the goal of the game?" I ask.

"Survival. But all games are about that. It starts on earth and you have to fight your way out of here to higher, more exotic worlds. The ultimate goal appears to be to reach the center of the galaxy."

"How far does John usually get?"

"He hasn't gotten off the earth yet. He keeps getting killed."

"But it's a game, right? It doesn't mean anything."

Seymour shrugs. "He takes it awfully seriously."

EIGHTEEN

Another week goes by. Shanti and I have traveled to Arosa together and are staying in a cozy bed and breakfast. She carries a cell so I can reach her at all times in case I begin to "feel weird." Shanti understands the IIC can send out a mental wave that can affect people at a distance. I've explained what it's like without going into detail.

I've finally told the girl I'm a vampire. Considering her religious upbringing, she took the news well. She still loves me and trusts me. After what she saw in London, I'm beginning to think nothing can break her faith in me. The feelings run both ways. I'm as devoted to her as I am to Teri.

I don't hide from Shanti how dangerous our mission is. She appears unafraid. There's a kind of magic about her, a light in her aura, that makes me feel protected, although I'm supposed to be the strong one. I trust Paula is right, that the Array cannot attack while Shanti is near.

Shanti's face is almost healed. I cannot take the credit. My blood helped, but the plastic surgeons did the heavy lifting. With makeup, most people don't even notice that she was once disfigured.

We've been in Arosa three days and no one's knocked at our door. The town's extraordinarily peaceful. I hope it's not a deception. A lake sits at its center, and is surrounded on three sides by snow-capped mountains. Arosa itself is a mile above sea level. The place is supposed to be busy during the skiing season, though this summer it's almost deserted. To me, it's the perfect spot to collapse and rest from the traumas of the last few months.

I have come to Arosa in search of the Telar, and to see what I can learn of Yaksha's past and his connection to this mysterious group of immortals. Of course, I don't have a photograph of Yaksha. There were no cameras in existence when we hunted together. But I have a photographic memory, and I've studied under many skilled artists. I'm able to paint a picture of Yaksha that could pass as a photograph. I carry it with me each morning and evening when I go for a walk around town, and ask people if they remember him. I know this makes me an easy target for the Telar, but I'm not going to hide from them anymore.

Not all of Arosa's population lives in the town proper. There are a few hotels located at the tree line, approximately fifteen hundred feet above their main street. One hotel in particular catches my eye as I take a long hike on our third evening in town. So far I've had a dozen of the old locals tell me Yaksha looks familiar, but they've been unable to say when they last saw him, or where he lived.

The instant I step into the Pratchli I smell him, and I know he didn't just visit the hotel, he came here often, and might even have kept a room in the building. His odor is unique, strong, and—make no mistake—exciting.

I walk up to an elderly man at the front desk.

"Grüezi val," I say. Hello, how are you?

"Grüezi. Sprechen Sie Deutsch?"

"Ja."

The man smiles. "But you prefer English?"

I smile back. "I thought my Swiss Deutsch was flawless."

He shakes his head. "I'm afraid not, dear. You've spent too many years in America. It's spoiled your accent."

"A pity." I offer my hand. "Lara Adams."

"Horace Reinhart. Pleased to meet you, Ms. Adams."

"Lara, please. I've heard your name mentioned in town. You own this hotel?"

"My wife and I do. It's been in the family two hundred years. Are you looking for a room? Our rates are very reasonable this time of year."

"Possibly. Your hotel is lovely. That's quite a view you have out back."

"Thank you. I've always felt Arosa looks like a painting from above. You might be surprised to discover you can see over into the next valley from the top floor."

"Then I must definitely take you up on your offer and stay here a few nights." I remove my small painting of Yaksha from my coat pocket. "But this evening I'm here on business. This man is an old friend of mine and I know he spent time here. I was wondering if you could tell me anything about where he lived or who his friends were?"

Reinhart recognizes Yaksha immediately. I don't have to be told. However, even though he nods at the picture, he frowns as well.

"Does your friend have a name?" he asks, testing me.

"He went by Yaksha when I knew him."

"He asked us to call him Yak." Reinhart sets the picture aside and studies me. "That was fifteen years ago. You can imagine why I'm puzzled."

I chuckle softly. "I'm older than I look, Herr Reinhart. May I ask how long Yak stayed here?"

Reinhart gives me a penetrating gaze, trying to decide what secrets I know, and which ones he should share. "A long time. You understand?"

I keep my voice even. "Yes."

"He kept two rooms in the hotel. One on the top floor, overlooking the valley. Another in the basement. That's where he spent most of his time."

"What did he do in the basement?"

"He wrote. Day and night. A very large book. At first he told me it was a fantasy tale. Later, he said it was the story of his life. I never did get to read it. When he wasn't writing, he kept it in a vault he constructed in the basement. The safe was a remarkable technical achievement. I had an expert out from Zurich to examine it after Yak was gone for over ten years, and he was unable to break into it. Understand I only took this step when I became convinced Yak wasn't going to return. But a part of me prayed that if he was gone, that he had made arrangements for someone to visit us who knew the combination."

"Herr Reinhart, I may be that person. Can I see the vault?"

"Certainly. But before I show it to you, may I ask if Yak is still alive?"

"I'm sorry to say he's dead."

He bows his head in respect. "Some kind of accident?"

"It was more complicated than that."

Reinhart is genuinely sad. I can tell the two were good friends. I also know the hotel owner was acquainted with Yaksha for many years and never saw him age. Yaksha must have trusted the man a great deal to give away such a secret.

Reinhart leads me to a floor that is actually two levels beneath what the staff would call the basement. The entrance to these deeper levels is sealed tight with hefty wooden doors and large steel locks. Reinhart has with him a bulky set of keys I suspect he hasn't made use of in years. The stairs down to the hidden basement are covered with a fine layer of dust. Yaksha's odor, strong in the reception area, almost overwhelms me the deeper we go.

The bottom floor has no electricity. Reinhart carries a flashlight and halts before a varnished door with a dome-shaped top. He takes out a key as large as my hand and struggles to fit it in the lock. He's old and his hand trembles. For that matter, his pulse is shaky, even though I can tell he has a pacemaker buried in his chest to keep his heart beating.

"My wife has never been down here," he says.

"Why not?"

He smiles. "She thinks it's haunted."

"Why was this floor built? It couldn't have been for guests or staff or storage."

Reinhart shakes his head. "My great-great-grandfather left a diary. He said this floor was only to be used in the event of an attack. Otherwise, it was to be left deserted."

"But you let Yak stay here?"

"*Ja.* I did so because he knew about this place without being told. When I asked him how he knew, he replied, 'I'm here to make sure you're never attacked.'"

"An odd remark," I say, although it makes me think of the Telar.

"*Ja.* Yak reminded me of what was in the diary. For some reason, I felt God was trying to tell me something."

"Are you a man of faith, Herr Reinhart?"

"Very much so. And you, Lara?"

"I believe the universe is a mysterious place."

Reinhart finally gets the door open, and I'm treated to a suite that is much larger and well furnished than I expected. The quarters are immaculate. Indeed, except for the fact the sofa, desk, and chairs are antiques, I could be looking at an expensive suite in one of the finest hotels in Zurich.

Only there are no lamps, no lights of any kind. Does Reinhart know this secret as well? That Yaksha—like myself—had no need for them?

"It's beautiful," I say.

"Can you believe I've only been down here twice since Yak left us?"

"You wanted to preserve it the way he kept it. You never stopped hoping for his return."

"You are a wise lady. How old did you say you were?"

"I did not say, Herr Reinhart. Where did he build the safe?"

"It is this way. On the other side of the restroom." Reinhart leads me through the bathroom, which is equipped with a large tub, and into a narrow hallway made of red bricks. The transition in the decor is sudden. The hall dead-ends in a stone wall.

Not speaking, but with a faint smile on his lips, Mr. Reinhart waits for me to make the next move. I see he's testing me. I study the stones—they're far from polished. On the far right and left the tips of two rocks protrude like doorknobs. I note how worn they are. Quickly, I grip them and press them together, and envision a disk overlaying the stones. Nothing happens until I try rotating them clockwise, and then counter-clockwise.

That does the trick. The upper portion of the stone wall slides to the right, disappearing into God knows where. A gray vault with a large gold dial stares back at us, twenty-four numbers etched on its face.

"I am impressed, Lara," Reinhart says.

"Are you sure you don't know the combination?"

"Quite sure. Otherwise the temptation would have been too great to look at Yak's masterpiece."

"How do you know it's a masterpiece?"

"He was a brilliant man. It could not be otherwise." He removes a second flashlight from his pocket. "Do you want to have a go at it?"

"You act like I'll succeed. I'm confused, where does your faith come from?"

"I have not been completely frank with you, Lara."

"Oh?"

"Yak told me about you."

"About Lara Adams?"

"He said your name could be anything. But I would recognize you because of your beautiful blue eyes, and your strength, and your grace. I must admit I had given up all hope of ever meeting you. But here you are, and yes, I'm sure you know the combination to this lock. You just have to remember the time you two spent together."

"Did he say that?"

"I say it." He turns on the extra flashlight and hands it to me. "Take as long as you need."

"Thank you."

When he is gone, I consider opening the safe by force. But when I grip the gold dial, I realize other metals have been mixed in with the gold and it is impervious to even my great strength. The same with the rest of the vault. It looks like steel, but it's something else, possibly an alloy similar to that used to make the handcuffs I bound Numbria with.

Turning off the flashlight, I stand in the darkness and think. It does not matter that there is no source of illumination—I can see perfectly. It is odd, but my vision becomes more acute in the dark. All matter gives off a faint glow. Humans are simply unaware of it.

I spin the dial and listen for imperfections in the mechanism.

There are none. Did the damn thing not wear down at all?

I contemplate the dial and its twenty-four numbers. The English alphabet has twenty-six characters. It would have been easier to speculate on a combination if there had been two more numbers on the dial.

However, when I was young, and together with Yaksha, neither of us knew English, because it didn't exist. We spoke

Sanskrit, not the modern version known in India today, but a type many of the ancient scriptures were written in. That Sanskrit had twenty-four characters.

That can't be a coincidence. I don't believe in them.

I try to imagine what word or series of words Yaksha would use as a password. "Krishna," I gasp, convinced I'm right. "It's got to be Krishna."

I spell Krishna several ways. First, I go to the number that represents *K*. Then I go to *R*, followed by *I*, and so on. When that doesn't work, I try approaching the *K* by spinning the dial clockwise, then I search for the next letter by spinning it counterclockwise.

Again, I'm sure it will work. Yet the vault remains locked.

I try Yaksha's name, racing through the variations. Next I use Sita. No luck. Frustrated—patience is definitely not my strong suit—I sit in the dark and fume. I talk to myself.

"Sanskrit has got to be the key. He didn't choose that number of digits by chance. But if there are Telar here, and he was hiding his book from them, he wouldn't have trusted in the antiquity of the language alone to protect his secret. They might know the language. Hell, they might have invented it." I pause. "The code must have been deeply personal to Yaksha. What did I ever say to him, or what did he ever say to me that . . ."

Suddenly, I know what the code is.

I dial the code by starting with a clockwise spin—to the

number that corresponds to the letter I'm seeking—followed by a counterclockwise turn. I work fast, and a minute later the vault opens. Inside is a thick manuscript, overflowing with beautiful penmanship.

The code, as I take the book into my hands, makes me blush.

I love you, Sita.

The words must have meant a lot to him.

NINETEEN

Reinhart is stunned at my success. He is less enthusiastic when I ask if I can take the book for the night.

"It's thick. You won't be able to read it all in one night."

"I'm a fast reader." I want to take it so I can make a copy of it.

"I would feel more comfortable if you read it here. After all, Yak left the manuscript in my care. I feel responsible to make sure no harm comes to it."

"I understand. I'd feel the same way. But you did mention that Yak said I might show up one day. And I was able to figure out the combination to the vault."

"May I know what the combination is?"

"I prefer to read his book first before divulging that secret."

Reinhart frowns. "You ask me to trust you, but you do not return the favor."

"The book is not mine to give away."

"But you said Yak is dead."

"It still belongs to him."

Reinhart sits behind the front desk. "You drive a hard bargain for such a pretty young lady."

I nod but say nothing. Silence is often the strongest weapon in a tense negotiation. Reinhart is reluctant to let the book go, but seems to sense my determination. He finally nods.

"I will be at this desk at eight tomorrow morning. Do you promise to return the manuscript by then?"

"Yes," I say, without mentioning that I might stick it back in the vault before he arrives.

"Very well. Promise me you won't make a copy of the book."

"I wouldn't think of it."

I take a cab back to the bed and breakfast where I am staying. I'm anxious to start reading. Yet I take time to borrow a copier from the strict Swiss woman at the front desk. She refuses to let me take the machine to my room until I slip her five hundred euros. Then she's all smiles. She calls on her strong sons to lift the bulky copier to my room, and gives me ten extra reams of paper, which I need. The pages are not numbered, but the book is a foot thick. I estimate it's five thousand pages long.

The word count is staggering. The text is in Yaksha's own personal handwriting, in Sanskrit, and no one ever taught him the virtue of double spacing. His penmanship is neat and tidy but compressed. Indeed, it would be hard for a human being to read it without a magnifying glass. I'm sure the size is not accidental. After what Reinhart said, I feel Yaksha wrote the book "for my eyes only."

I copy and read at the same time. Multitasking doesn't affect my concentration. I assumed the book would be an autobiography, and I'm not disappointed. I tremble as I begin to read. . . .

> I will not start with the night I was born, although I remember it well. Nor will I begin with the summer when I realized what I was, or the time I murdered my first human being, or even the painful evening I proclaimed my love to Sita. I must start with the instant I met Krishna, and asked myself if he truly was God, if such a being did indeed exist. . . .

Yaksha's first lines don't surprise me. I might have started my own story the same way, if I had been the first one to tell it, instead of Seymour. Nor does his reaction to Krishna shock me, for we both felt the same awe, reverence, love, terror, and, most of all, confusion around him.

However, Yaksha's faith that Krishna was divine seems

stronger than mine. Certainly he embraced his vow to Krishna, to destroy all the vampires he'd made, with a true believer's zeal.

The first part of his story deals with that gruesome task, and how much he hated killing each member of his extended family. I had almost forgotten how close Yaksha was to many of the vampires. Witty and beautiful Sadrai. Powerful and sincere Apon. Brilliant and loyal Jamune. It was Jamune who was his closest friend, next to me, and it was Jamune who first understood what Yaksha was up to, and organized the other vampires to resist him.

This part of his life I barely knew, because I fled Vrindavana not long after meeting Krishna. But I find it fascinating to read how Jamune captured a human fort not far from modern-day Madras, on the east coast, and set about strengthening it to resist Yaksha's attacks. The move was clever, because even though Yaksha had many times their strength, Jamune had numbers on his side.

Yaksha estimated Jamune had two hundred vampires in the fort, and despite repeated attacks he was fortunate to kill a dozen of our kind and escape with his life. Jamune was quick to train each vampire in the art of archery. He knew that a stake through the heart was the best way to destroy our leader.

Yet Jamune was hampered by two weaknesses all young vampires possess: The need to drink blood regularly and an allergy to sunlight. Of course, the myth that a vampire will burst into flames in the sun is silly, but at midday a vampire of less than twenty years is not much stronger than your average human.

Yaksha sought out help in a bizarre place. He convinced the local raja that the fort in question—Samir, it was named—had been taken over by a band of demons. He called upon soldiers who had been stationed at Samir to testify, and naturally, not wanting to look like cowards, they told the raja they had been defeated by monsters possessing superhuman strength.

Yaksha had the raja take a tally of all the deaths in the region around Samir, and the king quickly discovered that not only were his subjects dying in unusual numbers near the fort, they were being drained of all their blood. It did not take Yaksha long to make a believer of the raja.

Yaksha himself managed to escape suspicion. From birth the bright sun had bothered him, and he tried to avoid it whenever he could. At the same time, it didn't cause him to swoon, and he was able to hide his aversion to it without much effort. Likewise, he could go for a long time without drinking blood. He made a point to stay in the raja's castle, where hundreds could watch him, and that alleviated any fears that he might be a vampire himself.

But he did demonstrate to the raja what a powerful swordsman he was in battle, and the king put him in charge of an army of five thousand soldiers and ordered him to bring back the head of every vampire that had infected Samir. To further enhance his advantage, Yaksha attacked the fort at midday.

Jamune was not caught unawares. He was too shrewd. Using a treasury of gold he had collected over the previous fifty years, he solicited spies about the land. He knew the day the hammer was to fall, and he took precautions. He was able to repulse Yaksha's first attack. It was not until Yaksha brought out catapults, fueled with oil-soaked bundles of sticks, that the tide of the battle changed. Surprise in a fight usually gives the advantage. No one had ever seen the catapult before, because Yaksha had invented it. Plus fire can destroy a vampire as easily as a stake through the heart.

The day Yaksha attacked, Jamune lost the fort and half his followers, but it was a testament to his planning that he didn't lose everyone. He had made provisions for defeat. He had a large sailing ship waiting for him and his people in the warm waters of the Bay of Bengal. Jamune and his followers escaped through a secret tunnel and raced to the coast. Yaksha had no sooner taken the fort than he realized he had lost his best chance to fulfill his vow.

Yaksha reached the shore in time to see the ship disappear over the horizon, but he had no idea where Jamune was headed. He had heard rumors of Europe, we all had, but he had no concept of the New World.

Yaksha felt he had no choice but to return to Krishna and beg to be released from his vow. At that time, Krishna was reputed to be in the north, near Delhi, where the two most powerful factions of India were at war with each other.

I stop reading at this point, because I find myself reentering Yaksha's tale almost without knowing it. For I, too, was at the Battle of Kurukshetra, when the five Pandava brothers—Arjuna, the most famous of all—fought against Dhuryodhana and his ferocious army. It was said before the battle that Arjuna was offered the choice of having Krishna's army as an ally or Krishna himself. To the dismay of Arjuna's soldiers he chose the latter, and during the famous battle Krishna served as Arjuna's charioteer.

I stood on the battlefield, before the fight began, hoping to catch a glimpse of Krishna, not knowing that Yaksha did likewise. Now I tremble at my desk in Arosa, because I realize I'm about to have one of the greatest mysteries of my life either confirmed or ridiculed.

I remember that day well, and how confusing the start of the fight was. With Krishna by his side, Arjuna rode out to accept battle from his rival. Yet Arjuna stopped before he reached his foe and threw down his bow and arrow, saying out loud, "I will not fight."

Besides Yaksha and Krishna, I must have been the only one on the battlefield to hear his words. To say I was dismayed was to put it mildly. Arjuna represented Krishna, and vice versa, and if one was a coward, then what was the other? All my faith in Krishna teetered.

But then Krishna spoke to Arjuna. I should have been able to hear, but I could not. However, their dialogue was to become the main Indian scripture for five thousand years. In the next twenty minutes Krishna gave to Arjuna the Bhagavad Gita, *The Lord's Song*, the Indian equivalent of the Bible.

Through some mysterious power, Krishna was able to cloak his voice from me, and since I left the continent soon after, a thousand years were to pass before I was able to hold a copy of the Gita in my hands, and read it.

Still, I was never to know for sure if the book was an accurate record of what was said. Until now. Because Krishna did not block Yaksha from listening, and in Yaksha's book I see a word-for-word rendition of what he heard before the battle began. A wave of joy washes over me as I realize it was all true—the Bhagavad Gita is a precise reproduction of Krishna's conversation with Arjuna.

For a Christian, it would be like discovering that every word of the gospels was true. Yet, since I'm neither Christian nor Hindu, one might wonder why the revelation means so much to me. To be frank, I don't know. Like most people, even Vedic pundits, I don't understand most of the Gita. Krishna's words, I must assume, were meant to lift Arjuna into an exalted state of God consciousness. They were not designed to be dissected and grasped by the intellect.

Yet it comforts me to know that at least one scripture on earth wasn't man-made. To this day I don't know if Krishna was God, but whatever he was, he was not human.

Yaksha fought with Arjuna and helped him win the battle.

His tale resumes after Kurukshetra, when Yaksha meets with Krishna and is told two amazing secrets. Krishna warns Yaksha that Jamune and the rest of the vampires have traveled to an unknown continent on the other side of the ocean and set up a culture of human sacrifice. Krishna also warns him about an even more dangerous group of immortals called the Telar. He tells Yaksha they're based in Egypt.

"Do I need to destroy them, as I do the vampires?" Yaksha asked.

"You won't be able to destroy them," Krishna replied. "But try to contain them."

"How?"

"They have forgotten much of what they once knew. They have even lost the secret of their origin. But I will give it to you, and this will give you a powerful advantage over them. Do you know the legend of the Hydra?"

"Yes," Yaksha said.

"It has its origin in the Telar. The Hydra is a many-headed monster, and it does not matter if you chop off one head, it simply grows another. No single head of the Hydra is very strong. That is its weakness. Yet when all its heads are aligned, no power on earth can stop it. That is its strength. Do you understand?"

"Yes," Yaksha replied.

"No!" I shout at the manuscript. I don't understand what Krishna is saying, and I need to, because this Hydra sounds a hell of a lot like Brutran's Array. Yet it's the IIC that has the Array, not the Telar.

At least, as far as I know.

Damn!

Now I'm more confused than before I started Yaksha's book.

I'm also a lot more paranoid.

I stop reading and finish making a copy of it and contact one of my European handlers. Then I summon Shanti to my room. I place the copy of the book in my carry-on suitcase and hand it to her. It's the middle of the night, and Shanti's eyes are sleepy. Yet she listens closely as I speak.

"This book's important. It might be the most important book on earth. I believe it contains the secret of what the IIC are up to, how they were using you and other kids like you. I need you to take this copy back to America tonight. A helicopter will land at the end of the block in half an hour. It will take you to Zurich, where you will find a private jet waiting to take you to JFK. Give the book to Seymour—I'll give you his cell number in New York. He'll pick you up, and you're to stay with him until you hear from me. Do you understand?"

She nods. "What about you? You said you can be attacked if I'm not around."

"I'll have to take that risk. Our situation's just changed. It's because of this book. It might hold the key to all our problems. Tell Seymour to find a Vedic scholar who can translate it for him. Tell him to first study the part after the Battle of Kurukshetra."

"My uncle knows Sanskrit."

"Can he read most Vedic scriptures?"

"That's all he does in his spare time."

"Perfect. Put him and Seymour together."

Shanti is curious. She's from India, after all—she knows about the battle. "Is the book about Krishna?" she asks.

"Parts of it are. Have Seymour read you those parts, but only those parts. Otherwise, I want him to keep its contents private." I pause. "Now go get ready. The helicopter is already on its way. It will set down for a moment—you'd better be ready to jump aboard."

There are tears in Shanti's eyes. "I feel you're in danger. Why can't you come with me?"

"There are some things in life that get worse the more you run from them. This is one of those. That's all I can tell you. Now get dressed and packed, I'll walk you to the helicopter."

I try to read while Shanti packs, but I'm too anxious. Stepping outside, I visually scan the area and listen for the sound of Telar heartbeats. The moon shines bright on the snowy mountaintops. The air is utterly silent. I hear nothing and wonder if I'm overreacting to Krishna's secrets. My head says yes, my heart says no. Somehow, I'm convinced, the Telar know about this book and want a copy of it.

I hear the helicopter before I see it. The pilot is skilled. He swoops around a mountain and lands at the end of our road beside the lake. I'm the one who insisted on an immediate landing and takeoff, in case someone unseen should wish to interrupt Shanti's escape.

I whisper Seymour's cell number in her ear and make sure she memorizes it. I don't let her write it down.

"I love you," Shanti says as she hugs me good-bye.

"You are love, child." It hurts to let her go, as much as it hurt to see Teri leave.

The helicopter rises and vanishes into the night.

The pilot has orders to call me when Shanti is safe on the jet.

Back inside, I begin reading again.

I finish the book two hours after dawn, in time to keep my promise to Reinhart. Feeling tired from the intense night, I take a cab up to the Pratchli. True to his word, the hotel owner is at the front desk at eight o'clock. He smiles when he sees me.

"Did you enjoy it?" he asks.

"It's very interesting."

"Ha! There's no way you read it all in one night."

"I'm not saying I read every word."

Reinhart gestures to a young couple waiting for his help.

"I'm busy at the moment, Lara. Can you find the vault without me?"

"Sure." I turn toward the stairs that lead to the basements.

"Take a flashlight!" he calls after me. "And please don't lock it in the vault. Fair is fair—it's my turn to have a peek."

"I hear you," I call back, although I'm not going to listen. Following the creaking stairway down three levels, I eventually reach the suite where Yaksha wrote the book. It appears the same as yesterday, except the vault is wide open. I place the manuscript inside and close the door and spin the gold dial. At the same time, I hear a click from the direction of the hallway.

I find the door to the suite closed. Locked.

A tiny TV monitor comes to life beside the door. Reinhart stands outside the door. His voice comes through a speaker.

"Not very sporting of you. Locking the book back in the vault."

"Is that why you've locked me inside here?"

"No," he replies, and I notice he's lost his Swiss accent.

So many things become clear to me in that instant.

The pacemaker he wore—just part of his disguise.

"You're Telar," I whisper.

TWENTY

They leave me alone for two days. I spend the time giving my cage a thorough but useless examination. Behind every wall is the same metal alloy that was used to make Numbria's handcuffs. The door itself is composed of the metal, although they wisely hid that fact from me by covering it with a layer of varnished oak. The smell of the varnish kept me from smelling the alloy. They thought of everything.

Yet a part of me is not surprised I've been captured. Coming to Arosa, I knew it was likely. As Paula said, the fact Numbria had her home address on her was no accident. I'm just happy I sent Shanti away when I did. I pray all my friends are safe.

I find myself thinking of Krishna a lot. Perhaps because I feel I have reached the end of the line. From reading Yaksha's book—and I read every single word of it—I have a clear idea how formidable the Telar are. They do whatever is necessary for their survival, and they appear devoid of any moral conscience.

Except for Umara, the female Telar Yaksha married and had a son with. According to his story, she was the kindest person Yaksha ever met. He loved her, he said, as much as he loved me.

It's childish, I know, but I feel jealous of Umara.

Yet those were my favorite parts of Yaksha's book.

I read them with great relish. A few times, actually.

At the end of my second day in captivity, the suite lights go on.

I have a visitor.

His name is Haru. He is Umara's brother. Indeed, he's the ruler of what the Telar call the Source. He's the one responsible for the death of Umara and her son, a boy Yaksha named Keshava. If Yaksha's tale is accurate, Haru had the two burned alive. It seems Haru didn't approve of Telar marrying outside their own kind.

Haru is an odd duck. He's squat and heavily muscled. His torso is 50 percent longer than his legs. He has black hair, which he wears short, and copper skin that smells of exotic oils. His skin is unlined, but his nose and mouth are big even for his large head. His dark eyes are small and beady, always staring, probing. He sits before me on a stool, four guards at his back. They carry rifles that look like lasers. Their aim never wavers from my head or heart.

Haru's voice . . . it does not sound entirely human. Deep and soft, it has a faint metallic timbre that makes it seem robotic. On the surface, to a mortal, it might feel soothing, but I sense nothing but manipulation.

He wears a black suit, a dark red shirt. His hands are small, his fingers blunt but strong. When he speaks, his mouth barely moves. He could be a ventriloquist who uses his own body as a puppet. Yet that is almost certainly an illusion. He's ugly, but that doesn't dampen the power he radiates. This is a man no one says no to.

"It's a pleasure to meet you after all this time," Haru begins. "I've heard so much about you. You've led quite the life."

"Yaksha didn't tell you about me. Who was your source on my life?"

"You must know we have spies all over the world. Not all of whom are Telar." Haru shrugs. "I've read Seymour's manuscript."

"You did so without his permission. Or mine."

"I doubt you would have given it."

"True. But you Telar, you seem to do whatever you want."

"That surprises you?"

"It annoys me."

"Doesn't our age count for something? Our experience? Our wisdom? If I'm not mistaken, you have done whatever you wanted to do all your life."

"I've lived a life that's pleased me, yes. But not at the expense of others."

Haru smiles thinly, his white teeth small and numerous. "So says the last vampire, who has fed off the veins of thousands, if not millions."

"Few people died taking care of my hunger, especially after I matured. The vast majority of those I've killed were of questionable moral character. Like the assassins you sent to kill me."

"They were sent to capture you, not kill you."

"You should have told that to Claudious and his Gatling gun."

"We sent Claudious to test you. If I'd wanted you dead that night, I would have sent a dozen like him."

"Why test? When you've heard so much about me?"

"To see if the stories were true. I saw everything that happened that night. You were most impressive."

"You watched from here? With remote equipment?"

"Naturally. I have not lived so long by taking unnecessary risks."

"What if I told you that you're in danger now?"

"How so?"

"You're sitting rather close. Do you have any idea how fast I am?"

"If you attack me, you die. I don't think you want to die."

"My life might be worth spending to kill a monster like you."

"Again, I'm surprised at your attitude. I would have thought you'd feel more kinship toward our group. We're roughly the same age. We've lived similar lives. Staying in the shadows, observing the evolution of mankind, only interfering when necessary."

"That's not what Yaksha said."

"You have me at a disadvantage. I've only had the book two days. I haven't had a chance to finish reading it."

This time I'm surprised. He appears to be telling the truth.

"You mean, with all the advanced technology you possess, you weren't able to break into a simple vault?"

"It only appeared simple on the surface. Yaksha designed it with my sister's aid. He blended the finest elements of his knowledge with ours. Of course, we could have broken the lock using force, but we feared damaging what was inside."

"The book means that much to you?"

"Let me finish the book and I'll let you know. I assume you enjoyed reading about your master's life. It's my hope, in the days to come, that we can discuss it at length. There's much we can learn from each other."

I have to laugh. "Gimme a break."

His voice hardens. "Excuse me?"

"Do I need to point out that I'm your prisoner? All this talk about what a pleasure it is to meet me and how much we can learn from each other is sort of silly, don't you think? I suggest you drop the bullshit and cut to the chase. What do you want from me?"

Haru stares at me a long time. His gaze is far more powerful than Brutran's, and I feel him attempting to probe my thoughts. Still, I'm able to block him by emptying my mind. The blankness, which comforts me, seems to annoy him, and I feel his psychic tentacles retract.

"Very well, Sita. You want blunt, I'll be blunt. I'm going to ask you a series of questions. I suggest you answer them. If you don't, I'll be forced to make you answer them."

"You'll torture me?"

"Only if you push me. We're not animals."

"Surely you must know I'm capable of resisting any form of pain."

"Not the type of pain I'm talking about. You mention our superior technology. It's true—we possess instruments mankind can only dream of. For example, we have a machine that taps directly into the pain and pleasure centers of the brain. We call it the Pulse." He pauses. "You have not known agony until you've experienced the Pulse."

"Bring it on. I love new toys."

"For your sake, I hope that won't be necessary. Whenever we've interrogated someone with the Pulse, they've always ended up . . . well, shall I say, not themselves."

"It causes brain damage?"

"Severe damage."

I quickly reconsider his offer.

"If I answer your questions, will you let me go?" I ask.

"If you answer all of them honestly, yes."

He's one smooth customer. His mind is much more disciplined than Numbria's. He has impenetrable psychic walls. I can't tell if he's lying or not.

"Ask your questions," I say.

Haru glances at his guards. They back off a few steps.

"The IIC employs a tool called the Array. It allows them to compete in the stock market in such a way that the majority of their investments make money. The Array can also be used as a psychic weapon. It can force people to do things they don't want to do."

"I've heard about it."

"Have they used it on you?"

"They've tried."

"How many times?"

"Once."

"Tell me what happened."

"I was in Ms. Brutran's living room. I assume you know who she is?"

"Yes. She invited you to her home?"

"I went in the back way, so to speak."

"Did she have security?"

"No. At first I found that odd."

"She uses the Array as security."

"Yes." I pause. "You have sent your own people after her."

"Of course."

"I assume none of them came back?"

His face darkens. "Tell me what happened to you."

"Brutran asked me to have a seat. She offered me a job. She didn't go into detail, but she assured me we could help each other."

"She must have given you incentives?"

"She gave me the impression I could help her rule the world. She also said she could protect me from you guys."

"Did she mention us by name?"

"Not exactly. But she seems to know all about you."

"Then what happened?"

"I told her I wasn't interested. Then I felt a strong pressure at the back of my head. My vision blurred, and I felt sick to my stomach. Then I felt this strange compulsion to take my gun and blow my brains out."

"Why do you call it strange?"

"It was like nothing I had ever felt before in my life."

"Continue."

"I was able to resist the compulsion. That seemed to surprise Brutran. I don't think she'd ever seen that before."

"Did you try to kill her at that point?"

"No."

"Why not?"

"I figured it would be a waste of time. Another person in IIC's inner circle would just take her place."

"You showed remarkable restraint, especially considering

how abusive she was. From our research, that's not a quality we would have expected of you."

"I guess you've been talking to the wrong folks about me."

"What happened the next time they used the Array on you?"

"Who said there was a next time?"

Haru studies me. "You're a superb liar. One of the most skilled I've ever met. But even Yaksha couldn't lie to me without my knowing." He pauses. "You were with Numbria the second time you were attacked. What happened?"

"Why ask? You seem to know what happened."

"Answer me or we'll attach your brain to the Pulse."

"After your people attacked me at the president's hotel, Numbria escaped, and I chased after her across the English Channel."

"Numbria was in contact with us at that point. She said you missed the ferry."

"I swam after it."

"You can outswim a boat?"

"Yes. I reached the ferry, boarded it, and attacked Numbria. When she finally came to, I had her tied up in a motel in London. I questioned her about the Telar."

"You mean you tortured her for information on the Telar."

"Numbria was hurting from wounds she received when we fought. But I didn't use pain to elicit information from her. On the contrary, I bandaged her injuries and gave her pain medication."

"Along with Sodium Pentothal."

"The drug is a humane way to extract information."

"What did Numbria tell you about us?"

"A few interesting facts. She explained how old you were, how many you are, how you control most of the major governments on earth. She told me how you started in ancient Egypt but went to great lengths to stay hidden, behind the scenes. She gave me the impression you watched mankind closely, but when I tried to question her why, she got upset, and I had to sedate her."

Haru's eyes are black as coal. Cold as space.

"Continue," he repeats.

I shrug, trying to act casual but feeling far from it. Just the memory of what happened in that motel room makes me shake. "The Array came. It . . . It was stronger than before. It forced me to kill her."

Haru nods. "It upset you."

"Wouldn't it upset you? It made me lose control."

"How did you kill her?"

"Why do you need to know the details? Do you get off on them?"

"Answer the question."

"Like a vampire kills. Like an animal. I ravaged her until there was so little of her left you couldn't tell she'd once been human. Or Telar. Are you happy now?"

"No. I sense you're leaving something out."

"What?"

"How were you able to resist the Array the first time but not the second time?"

"I told you, it was stronger the second time."

"It frightened you more?"

"Yes."

"You do not frighten easily, Sita. How was it different?"

"It felt . . . evil."

"I'm not sure I understand."

I lower my head and sigh. "That makes two of us."

Haru stands and walks around the room. He straightens a painting, fixes his hair in a mirror, pulls a book from the shelf. Having spent days in the suite, I know all the books Yaksha has on hand. Haru picks up a copy of the Bhagavad Gita.

"Sita. You have been surprisingly open with me," Haru says in a flat voice. "I want to thank you for that."

"You can thank me by letting me go."

"Soon. There are still a few things to discuss."

"I don't know anything about the Array. How Brutran and her cronies at IIC got it to work is beyond me. Why don't you capture some of her people and question them?"

"We have. Only her inner circle knows about the Array. And those people are not easy to get to. For now you're our best lead. You must have a theory on how it works."

"I don't."

"You're sure?"

"You've studied them for years. I just became aware of them. I should be the one asking you these questions."

"What did Krishna mean when he told Yaksha about the Hydra?"

"He was talking about your people. You should know."

Haru walks toward me with the Gita in his hands. "Five thousand years ago the Telar were based in Egypt. You're the only living person who was in India when Krishna was alive. You were given a chance to see how he taught. To understand how his mind worked."

"I doubt Arjuna or Radha or all the gopis combined had a clue how Krishna's mind worked."

Haru stands over me. His voice remains cold but grows hard.

"The Hydra is a monster with many heads. Chop off one and it grows another. That's the key to its power. That's what Krishna told Yaksha. What does it mean?"

"I don't know."

"I want you to guess."

"I don't have a clue what he was talking about."

Haru shoves the Gita in my face. "Were you there at Kurukshetra?"

"Yes."

"Did you hear the recitation of the Gita?"

"No."

"Why not?"

"I don't know. Krishna blocked my hearing somehow."

"But Yaksha heard. He said the Gita I hold is accurate."

"Yes."

"So one day Krishna explains to Arjuna how humanity can realize God. And the next day he tells Yaksha how my people can be destroyed."

"I wouldn't take it personally."

"How can you joke about such a thing?"

"Krishna wanted Yaksha to kill all the vampires. And Yaksha did as he was told. You must have read the part in the book where he followed Jamune and his people to the New World and discovered the advanced Aztec culture. They were advanced because of Jamune. That would be the first Aztecs, not the tribe that moved into their pyramids after the others vanished overnight." I pause. "At least now we know what happened to the original Aztecs."

"I'm not interested in solving archaeological riddles."

"I'm merely pointing out that Krishna saw the Telar and vampires as enemies of mankind. He wanted us eliminated. What's so surprising? If I was in his shoes, I'd probably want the same thing."

"Except for you, Yaksha rid the world of vampires. But he was never able to destroy us."

"There were thousands of you, and only one of him. Why weren't you able to kill him?"

My question was designed to anger him. Yet Haru's voice remains flat.

"Yaksha was a very powerful creature, much stronger than you. He was also well informed. First Krishna gave him insights into our history, then my sister made the mistake of confiding in him. If those two had not meddled in the matter, we could have handled Yaksha. I suspect he might even have joined us."

"I doubt that. Yaksha was not exactly a team player."

Haru slaps me in the face. My nose breaks as blood drips onto my shirt. Even with his henchmen and their laser rifles, he risks a lot. I almost give him his hand back, minus a few fingers.

"Don't mock me. Ever," he says quietly.

I hold his icy gaze. "Don't strike me again."

My threat doesn't bother him. He changes the topic. "You promised not to make a copy of Yaksha's book. But you went ahead and made one anyway."

"Like Herr Reinhart was completely forthright with me."

"You sent your friend off with the copy. Where is she now?"

I'm grateful they don't know where Shanti is, but I'm not surprised. They had to be careful to stay out of Arosa until after they'd trapped me. Otherwise, I would have spotted them with their unusual heartbeats. It's not as if the whole gang could have walked around wearing pacemakers.

"I can't answer that question," I say.

"You will answer it."

I can only take so much. Then I lose my patience.

"Why? So you can take more people hostage and torture

them? You say you're not animals, but that's exactly what you are. Only a beast could live for so long and learn so little. I pray I'm able to decipher the secret of the Hydra that Krishna taught Yaksha. The day I do, I'll turn it against you and grind you all to dust."

Haru acts like I didn't say a word. "What do you know about the Suzama prophecies?" he asks.

"Never heard of them."

"You lived in Egypt the same time she did. You knew her."

"Whatever."

Haru crouches beside me. "You don't understand how the Pulse works. First we drill holes in your skull. Then we stick fine wires and fiber optics deep inside your brain. These wires and optics transmit special codes that activate the neurons and synapses inside your neocortex and limbic system, and even down into what scientists call the R-complex, the reptilian part of the brain. Working on all these levels, we're able to create tidal waves of pain. Those who have experienced it and survived to talk about it have described the agony as being in hell." Haru stands. "Long ago you spoke to Krishna. Perhaps on that day you believe you spoke to God, I don't know. But I can assure you that once the Pulse starts to work on your brain, you're going to feel like Lucifer himself is torturing you."

I think of my nightmare in the motel room with Numbria. "It won't be the first time," I say.

Haru puts his hand on my shoulder. He squeezes gently.

"I don't want to do this, Sita. Strange as it might sound, I admire you. I hate to think of you sitting in this chair, a few hours from now, a slobbering vegetable. But that's all that will be left of you when the Pulse has finished frying your brain."

"So why don't we skip that part," I suggest.

"I will, if you answer just one question. I promise you won't have to answer any others. You know, I can hear the truth when you speak, the same way you can hear the truth when I speak. I'm not lying when I say I'll let you go unharmed if you tell me this one thing."

Haru is telling the truth. Yet, if anything, my deliverance feels even more distant. "What do you want to know?" I ask.

"Where is Paula, and her son, John?"

"Beats me."

TWENTY-ONE

The moment Haru and his bodyguards leave the room, I black out. I don't smell any gas in the ventilation system, but it must be strong to knock me out so fast. When I awake, I'm in the same chair as before, only I'm chained down and the chair has been bolted to the floor.

Worse, there are IVs in both my arms and an assortment of wires and what feel like glass tubes sticking in my skull. My shirt is splattered with blood and tiny fragments of bone. My cranial bones. Haru was not bluffing. He's drilled a half dozen holes in my head.

The wires and what I assume are fiber-optic cables lead to a relatively simple box. It has an on and off switch, and a dial that goes from one to ten. I have a bad feeling about what number ten will feel like.

They have placed a bright light in my face and have

mounted a digital camera nearby. Telar, male and female, come in and out of the room, but I pay them little heed. I still feel groggy from the gas and I have a headache.

My mind clears minutes later when Haru reappears. He's dressed in green doctor scrubs, as if he knows he's going to get splashed with bodily fluids. He even has on disposable slippers, like the floor is soon going to be slippery. None of these signs soothe my already taut nerves. I wish I had listened to Shanti and gotten on that damn helicopter. Right now, I could be enjoying a warm bath at the Plaza and ordering room service. Instead I'm bracing myself for waves of transcendental pain.

Haru sits off to my right, beside the control box.

"The less you move, the better. Several of the wires are in deep, and we have a fiber optic attached to your core brain. You can minimize the damage by remaining still. And you can avoid the pain by answering my questions honestly. A few I have already asked. Even if you feel you answered honestly the first time, I'm asking again because I'm looking for certain fine points in your answer. Understand?"

"Yes."

"I want a more detailed explanation of what you asked Numbria."

I tell him as much detail as I can remember. It feels repetitious to me. I get bored. I don't know what he's looking for.

Yet I start to get an idea when I recall the questions I asked Numbria about the Telar's role in modern society. I listen to my own answer, studying it for clues as to what he wants.

"Numbria said the Telar were involved with business and politics at the highest levels. But they disliked sharing their scientific knowledge with mankind. Then I asked why the Telar were still interested in humanity. That's when she got upset and I had to sedate her."

"You are skipping something here," Haru says.

"What?"

"You tell me."

"Can you give me a hint?"

"Yes." Haru reaches over and turns the dial.

The pain is instantaneous and unlike any pain I have ever known. I don't feel it in a particular part of my body. It's like my mind is filled with pain. First it feels like nerve pain, then a burning sensation. It changes as it grows. I keep trying to get a handle on it, to block it, but I can't because it's too deep. My thoughts of the pain are made of pain. I feel I no longer have a name. I've lost all sense of identity. I exist only to experience pain.

Far off, I hear someone screaming.

It takes forever to realize it's me.

The pain suddenly stops. It is just gone.

I open my eyes and wince in the light. Blood drips from my lower lip, where I bit it. My heart pounds, and I gasp for air. Haru speaks in his calm, cold voice.

"That was three, Sita. You see the dial goes up to ten. No one has ever experienced ten and been able to talk afterwards.

The brain, whether it is human, or Telar, or vampire, cannot stand such a level of torment. As it is, you were thrashing around, and we had trouble holding you down. You may have damaged your brain already. My advice is for you to stop lying and answer my questions to the best of your ability."

"Did you do this to Yaksha?"

"Yes."

"No wonder he killed so many of you." For the first time since being captured, I feel despair. The Pulse is more powerful than I imagined. I doubt I can resist it. To willingly invite another twist of the dial would be insane. I can't block even a portion of the pain. The reason is both subtle and obvious. The device appears to have the ability to obliterate a person's sense of "I" and replace it with pain. Therefore, there is no one left to try to resist it. Haru senses my despair and smiles faintly.

"Enough. What did Numbria tell you about our interest in humanity?"

"She said you have no desire to help humanity. That you see them as a plague spreading across the planet. A plague that has to be wiped out."

"Did she tell you how we plan to do this?"

"No. But she said you wouldn't exterminate everyone. She said you would keep a few alive, to study, to learn from them."

"That's not true."

"I'm repeating what she said."

"What she said isn't true."

"You would know."

Haru stares at me. "How do you feel about our plan?"

"I told you, Numbria didn't explain your plan to me."

"Forget that. Should we destroy humanity or not?"

"You're seriously asking for my advice?"

"I'm curious how you feel about the matter."

"Your plan is monstrous. No one knows people better than I do, their strengths and weaknesses. But this is their planet. They have a right to life. You can't just wipe them out like you would a swarm of mosquitoes."

"That's where you're mistaken. Several times in the past, we have destroyed the bulk of humanity. In fact, Numbria told you about the plague. We were the ones responsible for it."

"But why?"

"Humans breed like rats. What better way to halt their growth than to use rats?"

"Are you going to use disease again?"

"Not necessarily. Whatever method we use, the earth cannot bear the weight of seven billion people. You know the story. The poles are melting. The oceans are polluted. The ozone layer has a hole in it. If we don't act soon, and decisively, the earth will be ruined forever."

Odd. Brutran had given the same speech.

"Then work with humanity to help clean up the planet. You obviously possess tremendous scientific knowledge. But you're few in numbers. They can help you if you point them in the right direction. You know, I've lived a long life, I've seen everything. But I've never seen a case where mass murder has led to a higher standard of living."

"I respect your arguments. But the decision has been made."

"By who?"

"The Source."

"You're the head of the goddamn Source." When he doesn't respond, I ask, "How are you going to do it?"

"That's irrelevant."

"When are you going to do it?"

"Soon."

"God," I whisper.

"Do you believe in God? That is one of my questions."

"You can't be serious." Haru reaches for the dial. "Wait! Okay, you are serious. I'll answer as best I can. I don't know."

"You met Krishna. You were deeply moved by him. Surely you must have thought he was a divine being."

"He radiated extraordinary love and power. He was definitely not a normal human being. But to say someone is God, what does that mean? I honestly can't say."

"But you feel an obligation to do his will?"

"I wouldn't put it that bluntly. I've disobeyed him on occasion."

"When?"

"I promised him I wouldn't create more vampires. But I made two."

"Why?"

"In order to save their lives."

"Are these two still alive?"

"You read Seymour's books. You know they're both dead."

"Still, we come back to the original question. Do you feel compelled to obey Krishna?"

"I try to follow the example he set. I don't always succeed. Why?"

"You know why. He told Yaksha to kill as many of us as possible. If I let you go, I assume you'll try to do the same."

"Not if we can come to an understanding that benefits us both."

"What do you have to offer?"

"You know my abilities, and you know I'm no friend of Brutran and the IIC. Perhaps we can work together to put them out of business."

"Do you have a plan to destroy them?"

"I'm working on one."

"How can you get near them when they've got the Array?"

"Is that the main thing holding you back?"

"Answer my question."

"I've discovered a way to block the Array. I'll be happy to share it with you if you release me."

"Share it with me now."

I hesitate. "I can't."

Haru turns the dial on the Pulse.

I scream. I cannot stop screaming.

The pain cannot get any worse, and yet it keeps getting worse. I lose all concept of time. My agony feels eternal. I cannot recall a time when there was no pain, because the pain has wiped my memory clean. Yet I manage to remember the name of the machine. The Pulse, he calls it the Pulse, as if it were designed to generate waves of pain. But that's a lie, because there's not the slightest gap in the torment.

All that exists is pain and a desire for it to end.

Finally, it stops. My body is racked with spasms I can't control. I fear to open my eyes. I know I'm a mess. I've vomited on my shirt and urinated in my pants. And if my bowels had not been empty, I would have shit myself.

"Sita," I hear Haru say.

"Stop," I whisper.

"You want me to stop the pain?"

I keep my eyes tightly shut. "No more."

"I'll be happy to stop if you will just answer my questions."

"I'm trying."

"Not hard enough, I'm afraid. You have no real desire to join forces with us. Granted, the IIC is your enemy as much as ours, but you're the same as Yaksha and Krishna. You see the Telar as something that must be wiped out."

"Only because you're talking about . . ." I feel too weak to finish.

"Wiping out humanity? I told you, we've reduced their

numbers before and they've survived. Think of what we intend to do as a deep pruning. With the bulk of humanity gone, the planet will have a chance to heal. It's the only chance it has. You can talk all you want about humanity joining us to repair the damage they've caused, but it's a dream. Mankind won't take any serious steps until it is too late. Humans are bound by the silly political institutions they've created. Every elected official in every country has to show immediate improvements to his constituents or else he's voted out of office. For that reason alone, your leaders are unable to plan ahead. No, Sita, earth is our home too, and we're not going to stand by and let it be destroyed."

I manage to open my eyes. "There must be a middle ground."

"It's those Telar who have urged compromise that have pushed us to the edge of this present catastrophe."

"You mean you're not all of the same mind?"

His hand lingers over the dial. "Are you trying to annoy me?"

My disgust helps to restore my strength. "Are you so utterly devoid of compassion that you can bury seven billion bodies?"

"The Nazis incinerated six million Jews and didn't lose any sleep."

I grasp his hidden meaning. "You helped them!"

"We have been behind every great war humanity has fought."

"But why?"

"To keep human beings in their place. We were surprised the Cold War lasted so long. It was supposed to heat up with the exchange of a few nuclear warheads. Mankind surprised us there, by keeping the genie in the bottle."

"There! You admit they're capable of great acts. Come out of the shadows, Haru, and give them a chance. The worst that can happen is you'll have to fall back on your original plan."

"Now you're behaving like a cheerleader for your precious humanity. You know as well as I do that when people learn we're immortal, they will have only one goal—immortality for themselves."

"I'm glad you brought that up. It's key to what I'm proposing. Living short lives has made most people complacent. Why should I bother about the environment? I'm going to be dead in a few years. Yet that will all change if they see that they can live forever. Share your gift of long life with them and they'll do everything in their power to preserve the earth."

"So says the vampire who refused to share her blood with another soul for five thousand years."

"You know why I fought to keep my blood to myself."

"Because Krishna told you to."

"Yes."

"That's pretty weak, Sita."

"It's the truth. You keep saying you want the truth."

"What I really want is for you to join us. You're right, you could be a help in our battle against Brutran and the IIC, especially if you've discovered a weakness in the Array."

"You can hear the truth. You know I have found a hole in it."

"But you refuse to share it. How can I trust you enough to release you when you won't answer a few basic questions?"

"You don't trust me and I don't trust you. I fear that whatever I tell you will just expose my friends to greater danger."

Haru nods. "It is a paradox."

"I didn't intend to kill Numbria. I was going to let her go."

"Because you knew she was insignificant."

"I felt sorry for her. I had no desire to kill her."

"Useless human emotions. After all these centuries, I'm surprised you haven't outgrown them."

"If I didn't still have feelings, I wouldn't be bothered to get out of my coffin every night."

"You don't sleep in a coffin."

"I was trying to lighten the mood with a joke."

"This is no time for jokes. Unless you can convince me of your value, I'm going to kill you. Here, in this room, tonight."

"Go ahead."

"It won't be that easy, Sita. A moment ago I turned the dial to five. If I decide to kill you, I'll turn it to ten and leave you here, and you'll die in an agony so terrible, you'll leave this world cursing Krishna. You understand?"

"Sure. You're a sadist."

"I told you, it gives me no pleasure to see you suffer. But I need you to understand the penalty of disobedience."

"You've zapped me twice. I screamed my head off. I'm covered in vomit and piss. I think I have a pretty good idea what the penalty is like."

"Then you're ready to answer my next question."

"Ask."

"How does the Array work?"

"I don't know."

"Tell me what you do know."

"They use children to make it work. And teenagers."

"How do they use them?"

"They ask them questions over the phone."

"What kind of questions?"

"Yes or no questions."

"About stocks?"

"I think so."

"Do you know any of these children?"

"One. The girl who came with me to Arosa."

"What's her name?"

"Shanti Garuda."

"Why did you befriend her?"

"She's very sweet, kind, and compassionate. She's suffered in her life, but she doesn't complain. I admire her."

"Why did you bring her to Arosa? You must have known it could be dangerous."

"I brought her with me for protection."

"Who are you protecting her from? Us?"

"The IIC. And she protects me from them."

"I don't understand. Clarify."

"She can block the Array from attacking me."

"That's ridiculous. How does she do that?"

"I don't know."

"You're going to have to do better than that."

"All I can say is the instant she touched my head in that motel room in London, where Numbria died, the Array's compulsion stopped."

"Is she psychic?"

"I don't think so. She's kind."

"You said that already."

"Yes. But I just realized something. Maybe that's the answer."

"I don't understand."

"Is it possible the Array doesn't work in the presence of kindness?"

Haru acts impatient. No, actually, he looks a little . . . spooked.

"That's ridiculous," he says.

"I'd say it's a reasonable theory. At least until you come up with a better one."

"She's a kid. Do you know how many psychically trained Telar we sent against Brutran and the Array? Hundreds. You were right, most did not come back. But those we were able to recover had to be killed. Their minds had been ruined."

"How so?"

"They were like zombies. They ran around trying to eat the brains of whoever they saw."

"Gross."

"I'm not satisfied with your answers when it comes to Shanti."

"I've told you what I know."

"Shanti took a copy of Yaksha's book when she left here."

"Yes."

"Where did she take it to?"

"Seymour Dorsten."

"Where is he? Give me his address."

"I can't. I only have his cell number. I arranged it that way so that I wouldn't know where they were in case I got in a situation like this. But I suppose there's no harm in telling you that Shanti has instructions to call Seymour as soon as she lands in New York. He's supposed to pick her up and take her somewhere secret."

"In the city?"

"Seymour's too smart to stay in New York."

"But you know his number. If you call now and ask where he is, he'll tell you his location."

"He has instructions not to tell me where he is."

"Then how will you find him?"

"He'll find me. A part of him always knows what I'm doing."

"How?"

"We have a telepathic bond."

"So that part of his books was true?"

"Yes."

"I've never met a human who was a true telepath."

"You've never met Seymour."

"But everything you say means you know where he is."

"It's not like that. He can block me when he wants. I can do likewise. He has orders to block me now."

"We'll come back to him later. Right now I want to talk about Paula Ramirez and her son, John. Are you ready to divulge their location?"

I feel pain and he hasn't turned on the Pulse.

It's like he has burned it into my brain. I'm scared.

I sigh. "I don't know."

"Do you need more pain?"

"No!"

"Do you believe John was born of a virgin?"

"No."

"But Paula said she didn't have sex before John was born."

"Paula never said she was a virgin. And as far as when she last had sex, before John was conceived, I had trouble with that part of Seymour's story."

"Why?"

"Everyone lies about sex. It's human nature."

"Do you believe Paula's the reincarnation of Suzama?"

"I don't know."

"I'm not asking what you know. I'm asking what you believe."

"It's possible, I suppose."

"Has Paula shown psychic abilities?"

"Yes."

"Has she accurately predicted future events?"

"Yes."

"When did you last see her?"

"A week ago."

"Where?"

I hesitate. "I can't tell you."

"Why not?"

"I can't let you get to John."

"Sita. You understand if you don't tell me, I'll have to use the Pulse. And this time I will turn the dial up to eight. Do you want that?"

"No."

"Then answer my question. Where are Paula and John?"

I feel tears in my closed eyes. "I can't tell you."

He turns the dial, I hear him turn it, the click of the numbers, eight in a row, eight steps down the ladder that leads to hell. But an instant before the pain starts, I think of Krishna and his deep blue eyes. It is said, in the hidden scriptures in India, that to focus on the eyes of the Lord is the highest spiritual practice a human being can perform. It's supposed to be equal to the greatest act of charity, which Jesus describes in the Bible as sacrificing one's life to save the life of another.

The Vedas, the Bible, it's true, they overlap a lot.

Maybe gazing into Krishna's eyes . . .

Pain . . . Pain . . . Pain . . .

Is equal to Christ's sacrifice.

I'm only suffering this pain to protect John. It doesn't matter that he won't see me. I still love him, I will always love him. And in this exquisitely agonizing moment, I realize he refused to see me because he wanted to force me to see him inside. Ah, that's the key! This practice of visualizing that I'm staring into Krishna's blue eyes, I've done it before.

But this is the first time I see him staring back at me!

The agony comes, and it does not get transformed into bliss.

If anything it is worse than before. Except for one thing.

The pain does not obliterate my sense of "I."

I'm still Sita, the last vampire.

I manage to open my eyes and look at Haru.

"You're a cold bastard, you know that," I whisper.

He stares back, shocked. He reaches for the dial, then stops. He calls to one of his assistants. "You placed the wires on the wrong lobes. No one can defy me under such duress."

"She was breaking down a few minutes ago."

"She's not breaking now!"

"Her brain must be wired different from human beings'."

Haru stands. "I don't have time to argue. Fix the problem and call me when you're ready."

"It doesn't matter what you do with your silly wires," I call after Haru. "I gave you the answer to all your questions, and you didn't hear it. No, you heard it, but you rejected it because it scares you. You already know what's stronger than the Array and your Pulse, and it frightens you, because you've lost the capacity to care for another person. Your coldness has turned you into a coward. It's made you lose your control over me. It's done all these things because it's the truth. Yes, you're finally getting the truth that you've been begging for. Love and kindness are the answers. Without them you'll always be afraid of the Array. And you'll always be running from your own shadow."

Haru grabs a laser rifle from a guard and strides toward me. He pushes a button and a row of lights turns red on the side of the weapon. I assume that means it's ready to fire. He puts the barrel to my head.

"I don't need pain to make you beg," he says.

I smile and prepare to say what I assume will be my last words.

Then I hear a noise in the hallway. No, it's on a level above us. It seems to be coming from the stairway. I hear a high vibration followed by a sizzling sound, as if meat were being cooked at an extremely high temperature. I pick up an odor that I immediately recognize as burned human flesh. Ironically, the smell is sweet, far from unpleasant.

The vibration switches on and off, in quick succession, and I hear Telar screaming for help. I can hardly believe it. Someone is trying to rescue me.

TWENTY-TWO

Chaos reigns supreme. Haru shouts for his people to kill the intruder. A half dozen rush out the door, male and female, all armed with their strange rifles. Yet they're no sooner past the threshold than a series of ruby beams slices the length of the hallway.

The Telar are tightly bunched. The rapid laser fire proves devastating. Chests are scorched, amputated arms fly through the red-soaked air. A head is severed at the neck and tumbles to the floor and rolls into our room. It belongs to the technician who was helping Haru torture me.

A female Telar with a ghastly abdominal wound staggers into Haru's torture chamber. Blood gushes over her legs. A fried hip bone protrudes through her burned flesh. Haru catches her in his hands.

"Who?" he demands in ancient Egyptian.

"The Abomination," she gasps in the same language.

"Impossible!"

"He's alive. He's coming." The woman dies, and Haru drops her as if she were a sack of garbage. He turns to his three remaining guards. As a group, they continue to speak in the same lost tongue. "Can we seal this room and gas the entire hotel?" Haru asks.

One of the guards checks a weird watch on his wrist, the kind Numbria and Claudious wore. "No," he says. "He's already neutralized our defenses."

"How is that possible, Dakor?" Haru asks.

"He must have schematics of this structure. Our only way out is through the tunnel."

More screams erupt from the hallway as the laser fire increases and the floor outside begins to steam with boiled blood. Whoever is coming is faster and stronger than the Telar. Haru shakes his head at Dakor's suggestion.

"Stay here with your men and slow him down. I must return to the Source and warn them."

Dakor gestures to me with his laser rifle. "What about her?"

Haru turns in the direction of the vault, ready to leave. He calls over his shoulder. "Use her as a shield if you have to, but don't let her escape. She's as dangerous as the Abomination."

"Bye," I call to Haru.

He turns and glares at me. "You will die," he says in English.

Then he is gone, and it is a relief.

The guards lock the door. They're scared, but not terrified the way a group of humans would be. Working quickly, they barricade the entrance with furniture.

"The Abomination's dead," the second guard tells his buddies.

"Asep must have been mistaken," the third guard agrees.

"He's here," Dakor says. "Besides us, there's a dozen of our people stationed at this hotel. You hear them dying. Someone's killing them. It has to be the Abomination."

"This suite is shielded with Neutra," the second guard says. "There's no way he can cut through the door."

"Not unless he has a disruptor," the third guard says.

Dakor is clearly in command. He acts annoyed. "He didn't stroll into the Source and check out a disruptor. Anyway, the weapon's still in the testing stage."

"Then we should be safe," the third guard says.

Dakor doesn't answer. He looks at me. He has been studying me throughout my interrogation. He has a strong face; it's blunt and worn, but I find him handsome. He has a thick mop of black hair. A wicked scar runs from his right ear to his jaw. One thing for sure, he's been through a hell of a lot in his life.

"Are you in league with the Abomination?" Dakor asks me in English.

"Can't say I ever met the guy."

"Can you help us stop him?"

The question surprises me. He wants my help?

"I'm not sure. Probably. I'm stronger than your people."

"Are you mad?" the second guard cries at Dakor. "She's a vampire. Release her and she'll tear us to pieces."

"We can't disobey the Source," the third guard says uneasily. "If Haru finds out, he'll wire us to the Pulse. We'll die in agony."

"Haru left us here to die without a thought," Dakor snaps. "We owe him no allegiance."

"We just tortured her," the second guard argues. "Why should she help us?"

Dakor studies me. "It's a reasonable question. How do we know you won't turn on us?"

"You don't know. But since you seem certain the Abomination's going to get in here and kill you all, you may as well release me. I'm your only chance of stopping him."

Dakor considers silently. Then he pulls out a set of keys. "Before I release you, you need to know not all of us approve of Haru's approach. Many of us were against taking you hostage."

"Are you a member of the Source?"

"No. I was close to the Source. Until Haru had me demoted."

Outside, the cries stop, and the sudden silence is more intimidating than the fighting. Outside, someone walks the hallway alone. The others hear him. He appears to be collecting weapons.

Dakor stands near me. "I'll take out the wires and fiber

optics before I undo your chains. It's safer this way. But you must remain still."

"Dakor. Think what you are doing," the second guard pleads.

"I have," Dakor says. He slips on sterile gloves and reaches for a tray of surgeon tools. He begins to tug on the implants in my skull. He works fast, but his touch is delicate. I feel pain, but it is mild.

"Are you a doctor?" I ask.

"I am many things."

Dakor is almost finished unhooking me from the Pulse when the top hinge on the door begins to sizzle and smoke. All of the guards begin to sweat, but it is the third guard who shows the most fear.

"He has a disruptor," the man gasps.

"No," Dakor says. "He's gathered our lasers together and focused the beams on a single spot."

"The Neutra won't melt," the second guard says.

"He's not trying to melt it," Dakor says. "He just has to soften it."

"We should flee, back through the tunnel," the third guard says.

Dakor shakes his head bitterly. "Do you think Haru's left a shuttle for us? He's sealed the tunnel behind him."

"You don't know that for sure," the second guard says.

"Go check if you don't believe me." Dakor finishes working on my head. He kneels and pokes a key into a heavy lock that fastens the chains that bind my feet and legs.

The second of three hinges on the door begins to sizzle. The four of us, almost frozen in place, watch with morbid curiosity. Two more minutes elapse. It's hard to imagine an alloy that can withstand the heat of a dozen laser beams—lasers that can slice a human in half. But I know Dakor is right. The Abomination doesn't have to melt the hinges. He just needs to weaken them enough to where he can . . .

The second and third guard cry out.

In a cloud of smoke and fire, the door explodes inward!

The fumes are so thick, I can't see through them. However, our foe has sharper eyes. A blast of ruby light darts from the cloud and strikes the second guard in the chest. His heart explodes and his sternum rips apart. The blast leaves a massive hole in his torso and fills the room with a steaming red mist.

Kicking the chains from my feet, I struggle to stand. But my upper body is still tied to the chair, and Dakor has dropped the keys and reached for his laser. I can't really blame him. In the red haze of bloody smoke, a dark figure emerges.

"Put down your weapons and you will live," a voice says.

It's no ordinary voice. I recognize it.

"Matt?" I call, more confused than I have been in my entire life.

"Stay still, all of you, no one else has to die," Matt says quietly, taking another step into the room. He's dressed in black, in an assault uniform, and looks pretty beat-up. He's bleeding from a dozen wounds. The burned incision across his belly looks serious. I'm amazed he's on his feet. Most of the hair on the right side of his head has been singed away.

Yet these changes are superficial. It is as if he has thrown off a cloak and let his true nature shine. The power of his presence is immense. It feels like a tangible mass that shakes the foundation of the hotel. His face is hard, I could even say cruel, but it's stamped with a confidence that only comes from a long, painful life. His every gesture conveys that he's in control.

"So you lie!" Dakor swears at me as he puts his laser to my head. "All this time you've been waiting for the Abomination to rescue you."

"I don't know anything about your Abomination," I snap. "I never heard of him until a few minutes ago. This man is a friend of mine named Matt."

"Lies. All lies," he whispers in disgust.

"She's telling you the truth, Dakor," Matt says. "She knows nothing about my past, and she knows little about the Telar. She only attacked you because you attacked her. It has all been a terrible misunderstanding. Why don't you put down your weapons and we can talk."

"Even if she's innocent, you most certainly are not," Dakor replies. "I won't surrender to you, and if you do shoot me, my hand will spasm and squeeze the trigger and blow her brains out."

It's a dilemma. I realize I made a mistake when I revealed

that we know each other, although it was an innocent mistake. I still can't get over how blind I've been to who Matt really is. Actually, I still can't say I know what he is. How was he able to kill so many Telar at once? Even I couldn't have done that.

"Our history is painful. I won't pretend otherwise," Matt says. "But it happened a long time ago. We can start over. I heard you talking to Sita and your partners about Haru. You know he took control of the Source by force, and he's leading the Telar down a fool's path. You can help me stop him."

Dakor shakes his head. "How can I help a monster like you?"

"I'm not a monster."

"No? Who killed my father?"

"Your father died trying to kill my father. He died in battle, bravely, but he knew what he was doing. He was not innocent."

"No Telar would ever join you in a fight against Haru. You have too much Telar blood on your hands, Keshava. It can never be washed off. Kill me if you must, but I'll never join you."

My head spins as the revelations fly.

Keshava is Yaksha's son!

He is supposed to be dead.

Matt is a vampire-Telar hybrid.

No wonder he's so powerful!

Wearily, Matt takes aim at his old friend, or enemy. "There must be a better way," he says. I realize he's not talking to

Dakor, he's talking to me. Dakor has the muzzle of his laser pressed to my temple. He's forgotten that he loosened my legs, or else he doesn't think it matters. If Yaksha taught his son anything about me, then Matt must know my feet are more deadly than my hands.

I slowly turn my head and look up at Dakor.

"I wish you would listen to him," I say with feeling.

His voice is empty of hope. "I wish you hadn't lied to me."

Dakor is not waiting. He goes to pull the trigger.

He doesn't have my speed. I slam my head forward, onto my chest, so it's no longer in the path of his laser. Simultaneously I lash out with my feet, kicking his left leg away from me while hooking his right knee and pulling it toward me. From head to toe he twists like a pretzel, but he still manages to fire. The shot goes wild. Now I have him, in the grip of my bone-crushing legs. But I pause—I don't really want to hurt him.

It doesn't matter. Matt knows Dakor better.

The situation must be hopeless. Matt shoots him in the chest.

Hot, dark blood drenches me. Dakor falls, and a moment later the third guard joins him on the floor. Matt hurries to my side and picks the key ring from the slime. He unlocks the last of my chains. Soon I'm on my feet, but I sway like a slender tree on a windy day. He supports me with a strong arm, and for the first time in a long time I feel safe.

"Keshava," I say. "You really are Yaksha's son."

"That's why I came for you."

"I thought you were angry at me."

"I am mad at you, but right now we have to get out of here. More will come."

"Tell me Shanti reached Seymour. That they're both safe."

He helps me to the door. The hallway is a veritable butcher's block of blood, flesh, and fat. We have to walk over a mass of scorched entrails to reach the stairs. The sight seems to drain Matt. He's no casual killer. He speaks in a tired voice.

"They're safe for now. But you opened a door coming here. Now the Telar know I'm alive, and with you. They will hunt us until the day we die." He pauses. "This is the last thing I wanted for Teri."

I answer with a sigh. "I know. I know."

TWENTY-THREE

A helicopter waits for us in the hotel parking lot. It is not an ordinary helicopter. I have seen its like before, when Joel and I were fleeing the U.S. military over the Nevada desert. It is an Apache helicopter, one of the most deadly flying machines on earth. It comes equipped with duel Gatling guns and has a rocket launcher capable of firing shells large enough to blow up a tank, and missiles that can destroy a large house. As Matt helps me into the front seat—I'll have to get used to his real name—I ask where he got the Apache.

"On eBay."

"Seriously."

"You'd be surprised at the toys my dad collected."

It warms my heart to hear Yaksha referred to as Dad, but I'm still jealous of Umara. She got to have his child and I didn't, because—except for a short time when I was human again—I'm barren, like all female vampires.

Matt sits in the rear, the pilot's seat, which is elevated slightly above the forward cockpit. Jammed around me are the weapon controls. I study them as we lift into the air and circle a mountain peak before we leave Arosa behind. He appears to be an experienced pilot. It's midnight, but the moon is bright, and I catch Matt giving it a worried look.

"Does Haru know we're airborne?" I ask.

"He will soon."

"What will he do?"

"Try to have us shot down before we reach the airport."

"Is that our destination? Do you have a jet waiting?"

"I have a very fast jet waiting, but our destination is flexible. It all depends on how fast the Source reacts." He pauses. "I should never have let Haru escape."

"He fled using a secret tunnel."

"I know about the tunnel. I could have blocked it, but . . ." He doesn't finish—he doesn't have to. He had to make a choice between saving me or killing Haru, and he made his choice.

"How long have they considered you dead?" I ask.

"Shanti told us you read the book. Three hundred years."

"The book said you were dead."

"Well, that's what Yaksha wanted the Telar to think."

"Is Umara alive as well?"

He hesitates. "Yes. But I haven't seen her in ages."

"Why?"

"Staying apart doubles our chances that one of us will survive." He glances over. "How's your head?"

"Healing. Slowly. That Pulse is awful."

"I know."

His answer surprises me. "They had it three hundred years ago?"

"They had a version of it. It was bad enough." He pauses. "Did you break?"

"I came close."

"I'm impressed. So Paula and John are safe for the time being."

"How do you know about them?"

"Seymour told me. Yesterday."

"You told him who you were?"

"He figured it out."

"How?"

"He said he saw clues in the book. The guy's a genius. Right now, Seymour and Shanti are with Teri. They're in Colorado."

"What's in Colorado?"

"A safe house."

"How safe is safe?"

"It's practically a fortress."

"Good. Where's Lisa?"

"She's still in Missouri."

"That's bad."

Matt swings around another peak, staying near the tree line, probably trying to evade radar. He flies at full throttle, over two hundred miles an hour.

"There's an abridged learner's manual on the computer on your right," he says. "Study it, learn the basics of how to fire the Apache's weapons."

"I have a good idea by looking at the controls."

"Still, use the program. I wrote it for you."

"You planned my rescue carefully."

"Sure. Run in, kill everyone, and run out."

"No, seriously, I want to thank you, Matt. Strapped to that chair with all those wires in my brain, being tortured by that egomaniac, I thought it was over, finally. I couldn't see any way out."

"You no longer felt protected by Krishna's grace?"

"Actually, I thought I would be talking to him soon." I pause. "I am grateful. I owe you one. I owe you everything."

Matt is silent a long time. "The last time my father and I spoke, he told me to protect you," he says.

"That's funny. He went to Oregon to kill me."

"He was never going to kill you."

"But he made a vow to Krishna. . . . He almost killed me."

Matt shakes his head. "He loved you too much. He could never have hurt you."

"I wish he had told me about you."

"He had his reasons."

"But I was with him when he died," I say, feeling sad.

Matt appears to sense my mood. "Do you want to talk about it?"

"Did you read Seymour's books?"

"He just shared them with me in the last few days."

"Then you know what happened."

"It sounded like he was at peace at the end."

"He was. He was radiant. He was convinced he was going back to Krishna." I pause. "You know, I have a million questions for you."

"I can imagine."

"Why did you seek out Teri?"

"To find you. My father had told me you were fond of spying on your descendants, and that you occasionally made contact with them."

"Why were you looking for me?"

"I was curious. Growing up, I had heard so much about you. At least when my mother was not around. You were not a favorite topic with her."

"You had to have been driven by more than curiosity."

"True. We're not all that different, Sita."

He's saying he was lonely, like me.

But for some reason, the sentiment stirs a faint doubt inside me.

"Did you plan on falling in love with Teri?" I ask.

"It was the last thing I wanted."

"How did you find her?"

"My father had records of your descendants. He shared them with me. But I can promise you the Telar never saw them. If they had, they would have found you much sooner."

"How did they find me?"

"I assume they got a lead on you when Lisa, her boyfriend, and her ex hacked into IIC's computers. Once Lisa and Jeff went looking for you, the Telar were not far behind."

"The first Telar to attack me showed up the same day as Lisa."

"That's interesting."

"It was the same night I met you."

"The Telar were not spying on me. I would have known."

"How?"

"I would have been dead."

"But you have to admit it's a curious coincidence."

"Not at all. Lisa and Jeff were not professional investigators. The Telar have been following everyone who works at IIC's Malibu office. I wouldn't be surprised if the Telar bugged Lisa's apartment. Once Lisa heard about you from her ex, it couldn't have been long before the Telar also knew about you."

"Why are the Telar so interested in IIC?"

"You're kidding, right?"

"Indulge me."

"The Telar have run the world for the last ten thousand years. Now suddenly there's a new player in town—that no one knows about—who's steadily taking control of every major company in the world." He pauses. "You know this. What are you really asking?"

"IIC's power is based on money."

"Their money is secondary. IIC's strength is based on the Array. And you know that." He stops. "Wait a second! You're testing me!"

"I'm sorry."

"Here you sounded so grateful a minute ago. Jesus."

"Matt . . . Do you mind if I call you Matt?"

He grumbles. "Matt is fine."

"Did you see the movie *Marathon Man*?"

"I assume you're referring to the part at the end when Dustin Hoffman's character is being sadistically tortured by Lawrence Olivier's character—a Nazi dentist. The guy keeps saying to Dustin, 'Is it safe?' But Dustin doesn't crack under the torture, because he doesn't know what the hell the question means."

"The part I was referring to comes right after that."

"I know. I was getting to it. Then Dustin appears to be rescued by a friend. He's driven around the city and asked pretty much the same questions he was asked while being tortured. But it's all a charade to win Dustin's confidence. His friend is really working with the Nazi, and when he's done with Dustin, he drives him right back to the German."

"It was an interesting movie."

"Do you honestly think I killed all those Telar, and rescued you, just so you would break down and tell me your secrets?"

"It's an interesting theory."

Matt is annoyed. "What a bitch. You don't trust me."

"Did Seymour tell you where Paula and John are?"

"No. I suppose he doesn't trust me, either."

"What did Krishna mean when he told Yaksha the story of the Hydra?"

"No idea. I never heard of the story until yesterday when Seymour shared parts of the book with me."

"Your father never showed you the book?"

"I saw him working on it, but he never let me read it."

"That's convenient."

"It's the truth. Can't you hear the truth when it's spoken?"

"From your mouth? Gimme a break. You're a Telar-vampire hybrid. You probably have powers I can't imagine. There's got to be a reason the Telar are so afraid of their . . . Abomination."

"I never much cared for that name."

"You're not doing a very good job of defending yourself."

"Defending myself from what?"

"That you're a spy who's working for the Telar. Everything that's happening right now could be a charade."

"Tell that to the dead I left behind. By the way, besides Dakor, some of those people used to be close friends."

"You sacrificed them to save me."

"No, they faked their deaths. They lasered open their guts and burned their organs and sliced off their limbs just to make it look real." Matt snorts. "I don't know what my dad saw in you."

That makes me laugh. "Look, Matt, I'm ninety-nine percent certain you're telling me the truth. Actually, I think the main reason I'm taunting you is because you faked me out for so long. I feel embarrassed. I'm not used to having someone put something so big over on me."

Matt stews for a while. "I'm not going to try to get rid of your last one percent of doubt. Frankly, I don't give a damn about it. It's your problem."

"A little doubt can be a good thing. It's kept me alive a long time."

We swing around another mountain peak, and a wide lake stretches out beneath us, shining white under the blazing moon. Matt warns me to hang on and dives toward the water. He races the helicopter less than five feet over the surface, our four-bladed propellers kicking up a cool mist and a dull roar.

I study the weapons' control program.

We don't speak for fifteen minutes.

"Do you still think we're being followed?" I finally ask.

"Haru hates to be embarrassed. He'll do whatever it takes to stop us. But we have one big advantage—we surprised them. Still, we have a narrow window in which to escape."

"You sound so convincing."

"Would you stop that!"

"As soon as you prove you're not a spy."

He reaches forward and tugs on my earlobe. "I'm stronger and faster than you. If I wanted, I could break your neck before you could blink."

I remember the carnage back at the hotel.

"I believe you," I say.

"Not that I don't think you have a lovely neck."

"Ha! You've been lusting after me since the night we met."

"I'd say the reverse is closer to the truth. Remember, I knew what you were. You had no idea who I was."

"How were you able to disguise yourself so well?"

"I have precise control over my bodily functions. It's easy for me to breathe like a human being. The same with my heart. Whenever we were together, I caused it to beat like a normal person's."

"Yaksha must have told you about Krishna."

"Sure. Krishna meant everything to him."

"Then why didn't he tell you what the Hydra story meant?"

"You really think that story explains the Telar's weakness?"

"Yes," I say.

"My dad's book doesn't say what it meant?"

"It drops hints. Krishna liked to operate that way. The Bhagavad Gita is like one long hint on how to find God. Krishna seldom came out and said anything clearly."

"Perhaps my father meant to tell me the big secret. After he saw you."

"I told you, his visit was no social call. He came to kill me, and then he planned to die."

Matt shrugs. "Believe what you want. The fact you're alive proves my point. He said good-bye to me, but it didn't sound final. I think he planned to see me again. At least once more. I know that he wanted to say good-bye to Umara before he died."

"Did he get to see her?"

"I don't think so."

"You must miss her a great deal."

"I miss both of them." He pauses. "Being with Teri has helped."

"You got angry at me at the trials and the Olympics because you knew I gave her vampire blood."

"Of course. My father warned me that you were reckless, but I had no idea. Your blood was too strong for her. It caused her to push herself too hard. It also thrust her into the limelight, when I was trying to maintain a low profile. Why did you do it?"

"She wanted to win. It meant so much to her."

"You didn't use her to flush the Telar out of hiding?"

"I would never have used Teri that way."

Matt nods. He appears to believe me. He's only a thousand years old. He's a youngster compared to me. He hasn't developed my cynicism.

I'm reluctant to ask my next question.

"How did Teri react to seeing what I'd done to Numbria?"

"I convinced her that you hadn't done anything to her. That you must have been attacked with the other woman and beaten up. Only not as badly."

"That's pretty weak. She believed it?"

"I made her believe it. You know what I mean."

"I do." He used psychic powers on her. "I'm sorry I put you in that situation."

"It wasn't your fault. Seymour told me how you were attacked by the Array."

"How long have you known about it?"

"My father became aware of the IIC not long before he went to see you. His knowledge of them was sketchy, but I know he saw them as dangerous. One of the last things he said to me, when we were talking about the IIC was, 'The Hydra returns.'"

"But Krishna said the Hydra was connected to the Telar."

"I'm quoting Yaksha word for word."

"That's the most interesting thing you've said all night."

"I'm glad I'm not a boring spy."

"I'm not convinced you're a spy."

"You're not convinced I'm a hero, either."

"Trust takes time. You turned my world upside down when you walked into that torture room tonight."

"Who were you expecting?"

"Godzilla. Kalika. I don't know."

"You really thought it might be your daughter?"

My throat feels tight. "I was just running through a mental list of who could be so powerful."

"You miss Kalika. Her loss caused you to seek out Teri."

"Now you sound like Paula."

"The seer? I would like to meet that woman, and her son."

"They're well hidden. In fact, I wouldn't be surprised if Paula has moved since my last visit. She wasn't overjoyed to see me."

"Did she give you guidance?"

"Nothing I wanted to hear."

"What's the kid like?"

"I don't know. He refused to see me."

Matt is surprised. "Why?"

"I guess I'm unworthy. But he saw Seymour."

"I figured it was John who told you to go to Arosa."

"I was chasing down a lead. But I thought there was a chance I'd end up confronting the Telar."

"That really worked out well."

"The hell with you! If you had just told me who you were, you could have saved me a lot of misery."

"You would never have gotten the book if you hadn't gone to Arosa."

"Yeah. But now the Telar have a copy. I can't imagine that's what your father wanted."

"It's possible they already had a copy. That they were

playing you. Hoping you would give them some insight into what my father meant with certain passages."

I shake my head, trying to clear my mind. My skull continues to ache from the Pulse. Yet I feel close to a major breakthrough. It's not like I can fit all the pieces of the puzzle together, but at least I know which ones belong on the board. I try bouncing a few ideas off Matt.

"Do you think the Hydra and the Array are related?" I ask.

"I don't know. The Telar sure as hell don't have their own Array. And they seem helpless against what the IIC is able to throw at them."

"You heard what Brutran did to Haru's special ops?"

"Yeah. There are a few Telar who still speak to me. I heard most of them died. And the ones who lived went insane."

"Haru told me they turned into zombies."

Matt shook his head. "That's horrible."

"Let me suggest an idea you might not have considered. Krishna told Yaksha the Telar had forgotten much of what they once knew. Is it possible they had an Array in the past, but in the present they've lost the knowledge of how to construct one?"

"How could you forget something that important?"

"That's what I thought at first. But you know better than I do how old the Telar are. Like any group, they must have had their ups and downs. Do we even know for sure that any of the original Telar are still alive? What did your mother tell you?"

"She said the original Telar were all dead."

"Did they die of old age?"

"From upheavals, internal fighting, external wars. My mother is the oldest Telar alive."

"Haru is absolutely convinced she's dead?"

"He was. He'll change his mind now that he's seen me."

It takes me a moment to absorb what he's saying.

"I'm sorry, you really did risk everything to rescue me," I say.

"It wasn't your fault."

"You said it yourself, I was reckless. Rescuing me put your mother in danger again."

"You did what you had to do. I did the same."

There's pain in his voice that can't be faked.

I drop my last doubt. He's not a spy for the Telar.

"Can you find her? Talk to her?" I ask.

"There's a way. But I'm not ready to go down that road yet."

We fly another fifteen minutes in silence. Clouds pour off a nearby mountain range and the moon is blocked from the sky. The dark deepens, and it seems to comfort Matt. He continues to race from one valley to the next, seldom riding high in the sky.

I continue to study the helicopter's elaborate weapon system. Matt was wise to write me a program. The guns, cannon, and missiles all work together as an integrated whole. The system is more complex than just aiming and firing. I have to admire the men and women who train for years to master such controls.

We're halfway to Zurich, and the airport, when an alarm sounds.

"What is it?" I ask.

"Check your C-Scan. You'll see two jets closing in from the south."

"Are they Telar?"

"Pretty sure."

"They could be part of the Swiss Air Force."

"The alarm sounded because they've scanned us and are attempting to get a radar lock. They're about to fire on us. They're Telar."

"How much time do we have?"

"A minute. Maybe less." He pauses. "I didn't see them coming. They must have launched from a hidden airfield."

"Can we fire first?"

"They're behind us but closing fast. We'll come into range first. It's always easier to attack from behind."

"Maybe we should reverse course."

"No."

"Why not?" I ask.

"Trust me. I have my reasons."

"Will they try to hit us with heat-seeking Sidewinders?"

"That will be their first choice."

"You know what to do?"

"I hope so," Matt says.

His reason for not turning around and attacking is a small town up ahead. Our Apache is fast, but it's no match for a jet when it comes to pure speed. The helicopter's biggest advantage is it can stop and hover. I know what Matt's thinking. The jets that are chasing us will lock their heat-seeking missiles onto our hot engines. He's hoping to find an alternative heat source somewhere in the town that will confuse the weapons.

We both see the bonfire at the same time. It's at the center of town, at a junction of two large streets. I urge Matt to hurry toward it, but he heads for the trees on the mountain behind the town.

"Why?" I cry.

"I need them to commit to their attack plan before they see how we're going to respond."

A much louder alarm sounds. On my C-Scan I see . . .

"They've launched two missiles!" he shouts.

"One was not enough?"

"Hold on!" Matt suddenly changes course, and we drop at a frightening speed toward the town. It's a pleasant summer night, and there's a crowd—it looks like mostly teenagers—hovering around the flames. But when they look up and see our huge rotor blades, they quickly begin to disperse. Not fast enough to please Matt, though.

"I need to scare them off with our blades," he says.

"You need to hover in front of the fire until the missiles arrive."

"I'm not going to blow up a bunch of innocent kids."

"How long to impact?"

"Ten seconds."

I take hold of the Gatling gun's controls, and without asking Matt's permission, I open fire at a dark and empty pastry shop a hundred feet from the fire. I hold the trigger down a second, but it's enough to destroy the shop. The kids scream and flee from the street.

"Now get in front of that fire!" I order.

"Clever, Sita." He lowers the Apache between the bonfire and the rapidly approaching missiles. I can see them now, streaking red meteors in the night sky. They're coming right at us. Matt has nerves of steel. I would have veered away already, but he continues to hover in front of the fire.

The missiles swell outside our window.

They look close enough to touch.

Matt jerks the Apache to the right. For a few seconds we're turned at a ninety-degree angle to the ground, flying sideways. The bonfire explodes in a blinding ball of red light. The shock wave hits us so hard we tumble out of control, and our blades almost scrape the ground.

I don't know how Matt does it, but moments later we're stable and rising swiftly. "Lock a missile onto each jet and fire."

"Roger!" I yell, firing the missiles.

"Lock the machine guns into our radar tracking system."

"Already locked. Ready to fire."

"Excellent. Flyby will be in . . . three . . . two . . . one. Fire!"

Our missiles miss, and I'm not surprised. They're heat seekers, and the jets' engines are turned away from us and thus make poor targets. But by waiting to the last second to make an evasive move, Matt has lured the jets close to us. They fly almost directly over the main street, and as they do so I pound them with our high-speed Gatling guns. It feels great, the sensation of pure power at my fingertips.

I feel even better when both jets smash into the side of the mountain and explode. They hit above the tree line and spare the village a major fire. Indeed, they ram into a snowpack left over from the winter, and the intense heat of the explosions melts the snow and the steaming water extinguishes the flames.

No one on the ground appears hurt.

We fly away unscathed, toward Zurich.

"Still think I'm a spy for the Telar?" Matt asks casually.

"They could have been Swiss jets."

"Swiss jets would have politely called on the radio and asked for our flight plan number. They wouldn't have shot at us. The Swiss are civilized."

"You should know."

"What's that supposed to mean?"

"I'm just saying you know them well. After all, the Telar have their headquarters here."

Matt laughs. "My father lived here. That's the only reason they lured you to Arosa. They knew you would make the Yaksha-Switzerland connection."

"Where are their headquarters?"

"America."

"America's big."

"They're centered in Washington DC."

"Why am I not surprised?"

TWENTY-FOUR

Five days later finds us in Colorado, in an old mining town called Goldsmith. Matt says he chose the place for the clean mountain air and the privacy. Goldsmith has a population of fifteen hundred—on the weekends. The town is definitely far off the beaten track.

Matt owns the home, under a pseudonym. It's comfortable, and it is heavily fortified. It's also invisible from the road and strategically placed. It's ten miles from the town, hidden behind a grove of lush pines on one side and a granite ridge on the other. Furthermore, next door to the residence is an elaborate network of mines the frontiersmen carved out at the close of the nineteenth century.

Legend has it that one of the boarded-up mines—an obscure tributary of the main tunnel that stretches miles into the mountain—leads to a cavern sheltering a vein of gold so rich that dozens of skeletons can be found there, of the men and women who killed each other while standing guard over the treasure. The old-timers swear the mine is haunted.

It is now, in a sense. The Apache was not the only exotic toy Yaksha managed to get his hands on and leave to his son. Matt has equipped the house and mine with enough firepower to defeat a small army. He fears, when we're found, that's exactly what the Telar will hit us with. He spends his days training us on how not to blow each other up.

He spends his nights explaining to Teri our predicament.

Considering 90 percent of what he tells her sounds like science fiction, he does a decent job. Yet the truth is Teri has been in a daze since she walked in on me and Numbria in that crummy motel in London. All the talk, all the psychic massages we've subjected her to, have not brought back the sweet innocent woman Matt and I both fell in love with.

I see how it kills Matt, and I die with him a little each day.

He came out of hiding for me, to rescue me. He destroyed his life and the life of his true love for me. Those are facts, and they're regrettable. Yet we have bigger issues to contend with that make his personal sacrifices less significant. The Telar are about to crush humanity. Brutran and the IIC must surely be aware, and have plans to counterstrike. Which means the tempting shadows can no longer hide Matt, for he's caught in the middle of this battle. He's wise enough to know he has to take a stand and fight.

Nevertheless, I feel for the idyllic lifestyle he's sacrificed. For two years he's floated on his love for Teri, waiting for me to show up, while praying I never would. Yet I doubt it's by chance that we've all come together at the same time the storm has arrived.

So my guilt is tempered with responsibilities.

Lisa is another handful. She has refused to quit her teaching job in Truman and move with us to Colorado. Part of the blame lies with Matt. He doesn't trust her enough to explain what he is, and who I am. His decision is understandable—under ordinary circumstances. But to me, to leave her out in the wild, unprotected, feels wrong. Maybe the Telar and the IIC will see her as too insignificant and ignore her. Yet both groups have already proven that no one is too small to murder.

I can stand up to Matt. I'm the oldest—I should be our leader. But the roles have suddenly shifted, and I feel there's probably no going back. He is faster and stronger than me, and he was trained by Yaksha from childhood to fight the Telar. Even Seymour looks to him for protection.

But Seymour and I still look to each other for answers.

On our fifth evening in Colorado, the two of us sit on a summit above the mine and wait for the sun to set. The air is still and dry, suffused with peace and a feeling of timelessness. My head has healed from the Pulse, and yet I continue to feel an ache that's more psychological than physical. I'm not easily traumatized, but Haru did a number on me.

As always, Seymour seems to read my mind.

"Would you really have revealed our location?"

"I came close to breaking. It scares me how close."

"You once said that pain was only a state of mind."

"That machine erased my mind. That was the problem. It leaves you with nothing to fight back with."

"I hope they don't plan on mass-producing the device."

"Their physical technology is superior to the IIC. But the IIC has an advantage with the Array."

"It's probably naive of me, but I expected the Telar to have more knowledge of the mind."

"I have thought the same thing. But then we have Krishna's words: 'They have forgotten much of what they once knew. They have even lost the secret of their origin.' He said that five thousand years ago, and they were at least that old when he was on earth." I pause. "Seymour, is it possible they've lost the secret of immortality?"

"I don't follow you. Numbria was an immortal, even though she was born only a few hundred years ago."

"Yes, their offspring are still immortal. But could they have lost the key that gave them their longevity in the first place?"

"It's an interesting theory. Where does it come from?"

"Haru wanted something from me. I could feel it. He needed my help."

"He might have just wanted your blood."

"The Telar don't seem obsessed with vampiric blood, not as much as you'd expect. Look at the name they've given Matt.

The Abomination. No, they want protection from the Array. And they feel the answer might lie in Yaksha's book."

"I've only read a small fraction of it. Can you take the place of Mr. Garuda and translate it for me?"

"Sure. When I have time."

"Do you still feel there's a link between the Array and the Hydra?"

"Yes."

"But you don't know what either one is?"

"That's why I have you here. Our resident genius. You're supposed to figure these things out."

"I already know we don't have enough information on either group."

"That helps?"

"It helps me to know when I don't know."

"Matt's mother is the oldest Telar on earth, but even she didn't know the first ones, the old ones. They must have done something long ago, before recorded history began, that triggered their nervous systems into a higher level of functioning."

Seymour doesn't approve. "We can't make that assumption. What if the Telar did nothing? What if they're just genetically superior?"

"You mean, like they're a different branch of humanity?"

"Yes. For all we know, their DNA may mimic vampire DNA and be self-correcting. That alone would keep them from aging. It probably would enhance their strength."

"I'd consider that idea except for two facts: Krishna's words that they lost their secret. And Haru's desire for help. Believe me, I could see it in his eyes. He was a cold fish, but he's clearly facing an enemy he isn't sure he can defeat." I pause. "I wish I hadn't told him Shanti can block the Array."

"He was torturing you. It's only natural you let a few things slip."

"I didn't let it slip. I told him about Shanti deliberately. Anything to stop him from turning that damn dial."

"Sita, if Haru had shown me the box the Pulse came in, I would have broken down and told him everything I know about you. Don't be so hard on yourself."

I smile. "My darling Seymour. What would I do without you?"

"You love me that much?"

"You know I do."

"Then maybe you can do me a small favor."

"It's already done."

"What are you talking about?"

"You don't need to take all those pills every day. Last night, when you were asleep, I put a few drops of my blood in your veins. It killed the HIV virus."

Seymour brightens. "Why did you decide to do it now?"

"After Arosa, I realized I have fallen for Krishna's greatest illusion. I keep thinking I'm never going to die, but I could die any day. Even today."

He leans over and kisses my cheek. "Thank you."

"You're welcome. Now let's stay on topic. How could the Telar have lost their secret of secrets?"

"That's not so hard to understand. Chances are only a few knew the secret of how the Hydra worked. Those few would have wanted to keep it that way, because then they would have leverage over the rest of the Telar. Leverage they could use to stay in power."

"But if the bulk of the Telar revolted against the Source—"

"Then they might have killed one or more of the Telar who knew the secret of secrets. They must have had plenty of revolts over five thousand years."

I nod in agreement. "Or they could have had one huge revolt where the younger Telar ended up killing the original guys. Then the secret of the Hydra would have been lost forever. Until the IIC discovered it again."

"I'm still not sure the two are related. The links between the Hydra and the Array are weak."

"My gut tells me they are connected. In either case, we need to look into Ms. Brutran's history, and the backgrounds of those close to her. When IIC was originally incorporated, it listed five board members. Brutran's husband was one of them."

"When you were in LA, you didn't follow him. Why?"

"Lisa said the woman ran the company. Besides, I never saw him."

"You said she had a child in the house?"

"Yes. A daughter."

"How old?"

"Four or five. Why?" I ask.

"I was wondering what it would be like for a kid to grow up with such a creepy mother."

"When I first snuck in Brutran's house and ran into the kid, something about her creeped me out."

"Interesting."

"Who is the greater threat? The Telar or IIC?"

Seymour considers. "On the surface, you'd have to say the Telar. They're old, strong, deeply entrenched in society. But Haru confessed to you he threw hundreds of Telar soldiers at Brutran's house and none came back."

"A few came back as zombies."

"Lovely. My point is that the IIC seems to be gaining strength, while the Telar are stuck in a rut. If the IIC have accumulated trillions in assets, they could for all practical purposes buy governments."

"What about weapons of mass destruction?" I ask.

"I've quizzed Matt about that. He says the Telar have nuclear bombs and the means to deliver them. It might be how they'll wipe out humanity."

"But you don't think so," I say.

"Nuclear bombs are messy, with all the radiation and fallout they leave behind. The Telar still have to live here. I thought it was important that Haru bragged about how they started the plague. If I was them and I wanted to reduce the population below a hundred million, I'd develop a supervirus and then vaccinate my people against it. Then I'd release the virus at airports and in planes traveling to all parts of the globe."

"How hard would it be to create such a virus?" I ask.

"I bet our scientists have already done it. Take Ebola. If the smart guys and girls in white coats just tweaked it a little, so you could catch it through the air, then it could easily kill almost everyone on earth."

"You scare me. You weren't alive when the plague swept through Europe. I saw what it did to whole towns. One person would catch it, and you'd go back three or four days later and the corpses would be piled up in the streets. All black and swollen. In a week the village would be dead."

"I'm glad I missed that. A normal virus is difficult enough to stop from spreading. But if the Telar engineer a supervirus and release it in a few dozen major cities, then it would be virtually impossible to stop."

"You're making a stronger case that the Telar are more dangerous."

"Why is it important to decide which one is worse?"

I don't answer. There's no need—he will know in a moment.

Seymour pales. "You're thinking of joining one side. You're thinking of helping the IIC."

"It seems the logical thing to do."

"Sure, it's logical. To a sociopath."

"I know Brutran and her people are evil. But look at us, look at what we're doing. Nothing! We're hiding away in the middle of nowhere, praying neither of them finds us. Since Matt and I escaped from the Telar, Haru will be anxious to accelerate his plans. The only reason he told me what he did was because he thought I wasn't going to leave that hotel alive. But now he's got to be scared I'm going to run straight to the IIC."

"The enemy of my enemy is my friend."

"It's true sometimes," I say.

"It's bullshit. Hiding and doing nothing might be the smart move. Let them fight it out. They might end up destroying each other."

"I'd agree if we didn't have to worry about superviruses."

We fall into a tense silence just as the sun sinks below the horizon. Normally I find the rise and setting of the sun a peaceful time. Not now. Goldsmith reminds me of Arosa. Its peace is illusionary.

"We're ignoring the biggest question of them all," Seymour says.

"Paula and John."

"Did you try to reach her?"

"Sure. They've left Santorini."

"That's probably good."

"Paula didn't leave a forwarding number."

"That just means she'll contact you when she feels it's safe. I trust her intuition. You should too."

"It means she doesn't trust me."

"Sita. She has to protect John."

"Have you studied Cosmic Intuitive Illusion more closely?"

"I've played it a lot. It has a strong underground following. You can download it for free, which is strange. The game's high quality. It could easily sell for fifty bucks."

"What's the name of the company that puts it out?"

"Ascension."

"Sounds New Age. Tell me why John's obsessed with it?"

"I'm not a hundred percent sure. I told you the game starts on earth. You have to battle your way to a departing spacecraft. That's hard to reach. I haven't gotten that far. After that, you're supposed to fight your way through higher and higher worlds until you reach the galactic core."

"Why would it appeal to John?"

"The game's unusual in lots of ways. First off, it has nothing to do with how good your mind-body coordination is. It's not a shooting contest. To succeed at the game, you have to walk a moralistic tightrope where you make wise and compassionate decisions. In each situation you encounter, you have to decide whether to follow your head or your heart. For example, your character might get married and have a child. But three years later you meet someone else and you fall in love. Then you're forced to decide: Do I do the noble thing and stay with my wife and make sure my kid has a father? Or do I run away with my true love?"

"This is a computer game for teenagers?"

"I never said it was for teens. I just said John plays it all the time."

"I assume you'd advance faster if you sacrificed for your family."

"Sometimes that's true. But in other cases, depending on the previous decisions you've made, that can be a bad choice. Being with the wrong partner can ruin your life. You see, on one hand it's a game about making real-life decisions. But there are aliens and angels and demons in it too. They can help you or hurt you depending on how you relate to them. But here the game really fools with your head. Unless your character grows to a certain level, he's not even aware that angels and demons are whispering in his mind. The less awareness you have, the greater the chance is that you'll die before you reach the mothership."

"The mothership?"

"That's what takes you to the galactic core."

"It sounds incredibly complex."

"It's staggering. It must have cost a fortune to develop."

"Any sign Ascension is connected to IIC?"

"Just the coincidence with the game initials." Seymour shakes his head in admiration. "You have to hand it to John. When I was at his house, I had no idea how skilled he was at weaving his way through such a maze. If he isn't a divine incarnation, he at least has a high IQ."

The explanation leaves me feeling dissatisfied. I dislike searching for profound portents in everyday events. Maybe John is like any other kid who likes to waste time on computer games, and he plays Cosmic Intuitive Illusion because he likes it. End of story.

"I wonder why Haru is anxious to find him," I say.

"That's the biggest question of them all."

"Is it? I don't know."

"He swore he'd let you go if you'd tell him where they were."

"He was lying. He was never going to let me go."

"It still shows how desperate he is to find the kid."

"What are you getting at?" I ask.

"You can't understand your enemy without putting yourself in their shoes. What are they thinking? What do they want? We know the answer to the second question. Haru wants John."

As is so often the case with Seymour, he stimulates a fresh set of ideas inside me. He forces me to speculate. "Haru was bitter that Krishna gave Yaksha information that could help destroy the Telar. At the same time, he seemed impressed with Krishna's knowledge."

"Haru might be worried John is another Krishna," Seymour says.

"As you're fond of saying, that's a big leap."

"I disagree. The Telar are not atheists. The first one you killed, he died praying to the Goddess Isis. Numbria worshipped Isis too. Some of them believe in the supernatural. Look at their interest in Suzama. I think Haru gave you a big hint to his motivation when he brought her up."

"Explain," I say.

"Could they be lost? Could they be seeking guidance?"

"Seymour! They're preparing to wipe out humanity. They're as far from humbly seeking the truth as Hitler was when he invaded Poland."

Seymour is thoughtful. "It makes me wonder."

"What?"

"How it would feel to live so long."

"Ask me. I have lived that long."

"You're different. You're a vampire. No offense, Sita, but the Telar are more like human beings than vampires. I wonder what it's done to them to live all these years. And to know that they might live thousands of more years."

I think he's mistaken. I have far more humanity than Haru. Still, his words, his insights, have a powerful effect on me. "What do you mean?"

He flashes a sad smile. "The price of immortality might be higher than we know."

I hear a noise behind us. To my sensitive ears, everyone has their own unique gait, their own special way of breathing. I know it's Shanti running up the dirt path that leads from the back of our house. Seymour and I stand as she bursts into view. The flesh on her reconstructed face is rich with blood. Her eyes shine with fear, and her voice cracks.

"Matt says they're coming!"

"Who?" Seymour demands.

"The Telar."

"How many?" I ask.

"Too many!" Shanti cries.

TWENTY-FIVE

Matt insists Seymour take Shanti and Teri and hide in the mine, in a place Matt prepared. Seymour has spent the last few days learning to fire an M16 rifle and feels babysitting—his word—is too cowardly a role for him to play.

"You won't feel that way if you take a bullet in the gut," Matt says, helping Teri into a bulletproof vest. I do likewise with Shanti. "Besides, it won't be long before Sita and I are forced to follow you guys."

"Seymour will probably shoot you guys on your way in," Teri says. She sounds more alive than in a long time. She's scared, but I think the idea of battle has stirred her naturally competitive spirit.

Seymour is unhappy. "Let me at least guard that sniper hole you dug into the ridge. The one that looks down on the road."

"That's Sita's spot," Matt says. He snaps grenades onto his belt. These are not ordinary shrapnel balls. They have Telar explosives inside that make them especially deadly. Because they're perfect spheres and are able detonate every milligram of their explosive at the same instant, they can send out a shock wave equal to a case of dynamite. Most humans would not be able to throw one far enough away to avoid getting killed.

We have a mix of Telar and conventional weapons. Unfortunately, we have only four laser rifles. Matt insists that we hold on to them. That's just common sense. He knows he and I are going to do the real damage. That's why Seymour, Teri, and Shanti are all heading to the mine with M16s.

But I'm not knocking human weapons. I'm looking forward to turning the Gatling gun that Claudious used on me on his associates. I spent a small fortune having it shipped from Truman to Goldsmith.

"I was just teasing you," Teri tells Seymour. "I'd feel a lot better with you guarding us,"

"Me too," Shanti says.

Seymour isn't suckered in by a few kind words from pretty girls, but he knows when to accept his fate. He speaks to Matt. "What's the source of your info on this attack? Hiking back to the house, I didn't see a soul."

"A dozen vans and trucks just rolled into Goldsmith," Matt explains. "I've got people there—men I've bought—who called and confirmed the visitors are asking about us. The caravan will be here in ten minutes."

"I'm surprised they didn't swoop in with helicopters and bomb us back to the Stone Age," Seymour says.

"They want to take us alive," Matt says. "But believe me when I say you don't want to be taken prisoner."

Seymour tells the girls that he agrees with Matt. Of course, he knows about the Pulse. Teri and Shanti don't. They have no idea how preferable death is to sitting with that device.

"If heavy shooting starts, won't the police be alerted?" Seymour asks.

"The Telar have already taken care of the police," Matt says.

"How?" Teri asks.

"Bribes. Big ones," Matt says.

"We should have opted for a heavily populated area," Seymour says.

Matt shakes his head. "That wouldn't have stopped the Telar. More people would just have died."

"At least tell us we stand a chance," Seymour complains.

Matt pats him on the back. "Actually, I think we're going to kick butt. A small team dug in deep with plenty of ammo can hold off a platoon. I've spent years arming this house. I've mined the entire area. But if we have to escape, I've got a helicopter hidden on the far side of the mine. So we have options."

Seymour seems satisfied with Matt's answers and prepares

to leave. But at the last second Shanti corners me. "I need to stay with you," she says.

"The Telar are attacking, not the IIC," I say.

"The IIC knew when you were with Numbria."

"That might have been a coincidence. Besides, you heard Matt, we're going to make a brief stand, then fall back. I'll see you soon enough."

Shanti hugs me. "Whatever happens, I'm grateful for everything you've done for me."

"Jesus, Shanti. I've put you in terrible danger."

"You've kept me alive. You've fixed me."

I squeeze her tight. "Don't let them get their hands on you."

She hears the edge in my voice. "I understand."

Seymour hurries off with Teri and Shanti. Matt and I continue to load our weapons while he explains the pattern to the mines he's laid out.

"Delay detonating any mines as long as possible," he says. "I don't want them to know that's part of our defense. I have a feeling they're going to come in waves. Haru doesn't mind sacrificing his people. He won't stop until we crack."

"So we'll end up using the helicopter."

"Maybe not. Haru can't let the fight last forever. No matter how much privacy his bribes have bought, all the shooting is going to attract attention. At some point the police and National Guard will show up."

"How do you think the Telar found us?"

"I told you they would," Matt says.

"But so fast. I thought we'd have more time."

"They're here. There's nothing we can do about it."

"I hate leaving you in this house," I say. "One well-aimed mortar and you'll be history."

"They won't start with the big guns. They make too much noise. I'll know when to withdraw. How's your headpiece working?"

We have miniature walkie-talkies implanted in our ears so we can stay in contact over the noise of battle, which can get so loud it can block even our subtle hearing. We do a quick check—they are working perfectly. It's a pity the rock surrounding the mine blocks the signal, or we could stay in touch with the others.

Yet I have faith in Seymour. He's never been in battle before, but he's not scared. He's not afraid to die, and I wish I could say the same about myself. I feel confident—I'm actually looking forward to the fight—but a part of me senses that Haru has a surprise in store for us.

Matt must feel the same. His next remark worries me.

"I stowed gas masks in the mine and at the sniper hole," he says. "Put one on and keep it on."

"I can see them gassing the mine. But how are they going to gas the entire side of a mountain?"

"You're talking about a man who started the plague."

"Point taken."

Matt is all business. He hurries me out of the house. He wants me on the ridge because he needs my eyes as well as my cover fire. Now that the fight has come, I'm glad to let him take command. What I told him when he rescued me was insightful—he is his father's son. Haru will have his tricks, sure, but I suspect Matt has aces up his sleeve that none of us know about.

The twilight has deepened by the time I reach the ridge. Venus shines bright in the west, and Vega is visible overhead. A mile in the distance, from the direction of Goldsmith, I see twenty vehicles heading our way. Like Seymour, I'm surprised they're not using a surprise attack, but it could be a sign of Haru's arrogance. I can tell from the powerful heartbeats of everyone in the vehicles that we're facing strictly Telar soldiers.

Three of the trucks are massive.

I wonder what goodies they have stored inside.

I finish arming the Gatling gun. I have a ton of ammunition. I could spray them at this distance. But I obey Matt's instructions and let them get closer. I have two laser rifles and two sniper rifles. I plan to alternate. The weakness of the lasers is they quickly lose their charge. It's not an issue as long as I remain in the sniper hole—Matt's wired the rifles to heavy Telar batteries. But when we retreat to the mine, I'll have to leave the power supply behind. Then I'll have to count every shot I take with the lasers.

Matt speaks on my headpiece. "Do you see them?"

"Roger. They're almost to our driveway. They're showing no sign of slowing."

"Chances are they'll pass us by and hide their vehicles behind the bluff north of us."

"Sure you don't want me to hit them as they drive by?"

"Let them make the first move. And Sita?"

"What?"

"Put your gas mask on."

"It's stuffy."

"It could save your life."

"I can put it on fast if they gas us."

"What if they use something besides gas?"

He knows them better than I do. I put on the mask.

Matt's prediction proves accurate. The Telar convoy passes by and doesn't park until all their vehicles are hidden from view. I listen as their people climb out and scatter into the hills. Haru isn't a sexist. Half are males, half females. They chat with each other with their own headphones, but use a code I don't recognize.

"I wish I knew what they're saying," I say.

"I doubt it would change our plans."

"Matt, you have six Telar approaching from the east. Plus another six coming from the south, to the side of the driveway."

"Roger that. I see them."

"Cameras?"

"I've got the area wired. You have a dozen Telar on the west side, beneath you. Plus a half dozen climbing the peak at your back. They're probably hoping to shoot down on you."

"Roger that. Can I start shooting?"

"Hold. Do you have a clear view of the mine entrance?"

"Roger. No one's near the mine. But I'll keep an eye on it."

"Interesting," he mutters.

"What is it?"

"They're trying to cut my power."

"You have backup?"

"Roger that." His voice takes on a more urgent note. "Sita, change of plans. They're setting up several odd-looking projectors. They're probably powered by whatever they have stowed in their vehicles."

"They can project energy over a distance?"

"Yes." He's puzzled. "These might be disruptors."

"Dakor and his guards spoke of them. What are they?"

Matt sounds tense. "Nasty buggers. Let's switch gears. Kill as many soldiers as you can in the next sixty seconds. Force the rest to take cover. Then throw a dozen Telar grenades over the bluff."

"Roger that."

"Can your arm reach that far?"

"Hell, yeah. Bloody Sita is armed and dangerous."

The laser rifles come equipped with excellent scopes. They are infrared and motion sensitive. They even send out a sonic pulse that relays back the exact distance of a target. Because I'm worried about the projectors the Telar are setting up near the house, I try to defend Matt's back first.

The Telar due east of the house are embedded in the trees, but I catch quick glimpses of a head here, an arm there, a leg sticking out. I fire three blasts in succession, and hear three shrieks. I see one of the projectors Matt mentioned. It looks like a wide-angle lens on a tripod. I blow it away.

The Telar climbing above me are a threat to my position. I blast three, but the others manage to take cover.

The impact of the laser on my targets is fascinating, in a sick sort of way. If the beam hits a limb, it severs it. But if I hit a torso, the result's much more intense. The body is mostly made up of water. Even a brief laser blast will boil several quarts of water. As a result, several of my targets explode as they fall, the steam causing their guts to spew out. Not a pretty way to die. At least it's quick, I tell myself.

I kill two Telar who are hiking up the driveway, and an even dozen who are spread across the bluff that hides their vehicles and the bulk of their attack force. My sixty seconds is up, and I'm reaching for the grenades when my opponents start firing back. To my surprise, they're using conventional sniper rifles. They may not want the police to later find evidence of laser fire. Their choice of weapons is less lethal. Unfortunately, they're all superb shots, and their bullets echo around my hole. I quickly reposition dozens of sandbags to protect my head.

The most irritating soldiers are the ones I failed to kill above me. There are only three, but they're aggressive. To get them off my back, I turn my Gatling gun in their direction and set it on auto control. It starts firing sixty rounds a second while swinging back and forth through a twenty-degree arc.

The noise of the weapon is deafening. For one of the first times in my life, I use earplugs. Of course that means I take off my gas mask, and I'm in too much of a hurry to put it back on. The plugs also crush my ear implants. I hope Matt and I will still be able to hear each other.

The Telar above me scamper for cover. They stop shooting.

The special grenades are dense. As big as a softball, they each weigh over twenty pounds. Stacking them in a row on a rocky ledge, so I can throw one after another without pause, I study the controls. There's a tiny digital clock on the side of each one and an arming button. It seems pretty self-explanatory.

The question is, how long will they be in the air before they explode? Do I want half to land in the ravine and the other half to explode above the Telar camp? I like the idea. The grenades that explode in the air will send out a larger shock wave, although it won't be as concentrated as those that hit the ground.

I set half the grenades for four seconds, the other half for three. As I pick each one up, I plan to automatically push the arm button. I'm just about to throw them when Matt signals me. I barely hear him with my earplugs.

"Sita. You need to hit their trucks now."

"Roger. Have they turned on their disruptors?"

"I have a few seconds left. No more."

"Roger that."

I throw the grenades, one after the other, an even dozen. My delivery is so fast and smooth, all twelve are aloft before the first one explodes. I'm treated to a glorious sight—glorious for those who are closet pyromaniacs, which I believe a high percent of the population is. The grenades detonate in blinding blue-green balls of light. Their fire and concussive force batter the vehicles and the Telar beneath them, and a much larger wave of fire erupts. It is as if the valley beside us is suddenly swamped with lava. Orange flames two hundred feet tall whip the air.

I jump in the air, cheering. "Yeah!"

Then our house explodes in a red mushroom cloud.

"Matt! Matt!" I yell in my headpiece.

There's no answer. Of course there's no answer. He was in the house, and the house is gone. Two shock waves strike me. The one from our home, which knocks me down, and the emotional one, which keeps me down. Despite the fury of the Gatling gun, the Telar above me have resumed fire. I don't fire back. Tucking into a ball, I try to hide in the deepest part of my sniper hole.

"He can't be dead," I whisper to myself.

Matt leaps into the hole beside me and shakes his head.

"Ye of so little faith," he says. "Put on your gas mask."

I sit up and hug him. "How did you get out in time?"

"I saw it coming."

"What was it?"

"A disruptor blast."

"It looked like a nuclear bomb," I say.

"I'm not surprised. It works by splitting atoms."

"Then we'll die if we stay here. We have to get in the mine."

"Hold on." The weapon's fire from the Telar above us irritates Matt. He stands and, aiming faster than I could on my best day, fires his laser rifle three quick times. The shots stop. Matt turns off the Gatling gun and sits back down beside me. "Where was I?" he asks.

"We should get in the mine."

"We will. But this is only the first wave. The next will be worse."

In addition to his twin laser rifles, he has a laptop equipped with a joystick. He flips it open and scans the screen. I assume it's linked to his cameras, but I'm confused when I see a rapidly changing shot of this part of the state—seen from an altitude of a thousand feet. He pushes a button, and the view shifts to a rear shot of a dozen cargo planes.

"Damn," he says.

"What's wrong?"

"They're close."

"The second wave?"

"Yes."

"They're going to drop in on us, so to speak?"

"Oh, yeah. Hundreds of them."

I feel a wave of despair. "I should have joined the IIC."

Matt talks as he hooks his laser rifles into my battery source.

"They'll parachute in. Close enough to rush us on foot, but far enough away that we'll have trouble shooting them out of the sky."

"What's the range of our lasers?"

"If they have on body armor, three miles."

"I didn't know the beams dissipated that fast."

"This isn't *Star Trek*. These aren't phasers. But to kill us, they'll have to get close. We have the higher ground, and we're dug in. We can take out a lot of them before we retreat."

"Who's taking the picture of the planes?"

"It's not a who, it's a what. You'll see in a few minutes."

While we wait for the "second wave," Matt makes quick work of the remainder of the first wave. He fires without pause, like a robot. Apparently, his father taught him to shoot this way.

He kills the last of the nearby Telar just as the cargo planes come into view. They're at two thousand feet. They will have to pull their parachutes at six hundred feet or higher. Unfortunately, the planes are at least four miles away. They have anticipated us having laser rifles. A trail of dark figures pours out of a dozen planes. They're dressed in special-ops black, and after a quick ten-second drop, they pull their cords. I'm not surprised to see their parachutes are also black. Your average human wouldn't even see them in the night sky.

When they hit the ground, the Telar quickly pack their chutes and head toward us. For the most part, they appear armed with laser rifles and normal sniper rifles. But a few could be carrying disruptors—it's hard to tell from this distance.

"Haru's making more noise than I expected," Matt says. "You must have really pissed him off."

"Me? You don't see him calling me the Abomination."

"My mother pissed him off when she had me."

"I take it Haru wasn't invited to Umara and Yaksha's wedding?"

"Who says they got married?"

"You mean you're a bastard? Can I call you that?"

"Why not?" He splits his screen in four and studies each square. The air shot appears to be losing contact with the planes. Now he's more focused on the terrain the Telar are crossing as they advance toward us.

"How far out are the mines?" I ask.

"They start two miles out."

"How many did you bury?"

"Thousands."

"I'm surprised they're not scanning the ground for them."

"That would take time. Haru sees these soldiers as cannon fodder. He's willing to accept a high level of casualties to bring us in."

"The Gatling gun can hit them from this distance," I say, as I swing the tip of the weapon toward the advancing army.

"Its heavy rounds might trigger my land mines. Let me detonate them first, and then we'll turn it on."

The soldiers continue to approach, running fast. I count four hundred. Many are less than a mile away.

"What are we waiting for, damn it?" I snap.

Matt sets his laptop aside. "Start shooting. But remember, our goal is to back them up, slow them down, so they crowd together. That way the land mines will be more effective."

"Roger that."

We start shooting. The Telar immediately hit the ground and shoot back, using their lasers. This upsets Matt and for good reason. His mines are largely "Bouncing Bettys." A Betty, when triggered, tosses a shrapnel-filled bomb three feet into the air. That's the "Betty," and it's the main explosive component of the mine. Because it lifts off the ground, its shock wave and shrapnel spread in a large circle. But Bouncing Bettys don't work so well if the enemy is already lying on the ground.

Hundreds of lasers scorch our side of the ridge. But I'm surprised at their lack of effect on the granite. It must be because the rock is dry. The bush and shrubs catch fire, but we don't take any damage.

Matt pauses. "Sita, stop, I've changed my mind. We have to get them back up. Turn the Gatling gun on them and sweep it back and forth." He reaches for his laptop. "I'm going to call in help."

"You have someone on our side?"

"It's not a person. It's a machine."

"Great." I set the Gatling gun on high-speed automatic fire. After I'm sure it's swinging back and forth in a wide arc—over sixty degrees—I drop back in the hole and resume fire with my laser. I'm afraid to stay close to the Gatling. Already I see a hundred bolts of laser fire trying to take it out. The Telar are excellent shots, but the weapon is buried deep. Still, it's only a matter of time before one of them gets lucky and the thing explodes.

Matt is focused on his laptop, which annoys me—I could use some help. Especially when a heavily armed assault helicopter swoops over the mountain behind us. I expect it to riddle us with rocket shells. Instead, it opens fire on the Telar, hitting them with mortars, machine-gun rounds, missiles. Now, at last, I know where he's been getting his air shots from.

The Telar leap up and race toward us.

"Don't tell me that's our escape helicopter," I say.

"I have a spare," Matt replies. "Cover your ears."

"I'm wearing earplugs."

"Put your hands over them."

I stop shooting and do what he says.

Matt detonates the Bouncing Bettys. All of them, thousands of them. For a minute I imagine the earth's mantle for miles around has shattered and the lava beneath has been released. For the advancing Telar it's literally hell on earth, for they're caught in waves of fire. And buried in this terrible tide, hidden as smoldering black specks, are countless pieces of shrapnel. They rip into the Telar, their body armor notwithstanding, tearing them to shreds, to bloody meat, and it's perhaps the tragedy of my immortal life that I've lived so long that I'm forced to hear four hundred souls scream at once in agony.

I cannot bear it. I cannot look.

I feel Matt tugging at me, anxious. He has his gas mask on.

"We've got to go, Sita. We have to get inside the cave."

I gesture weakly to our annihilated foe.

"But they're all dead," I mumble.

"We can't be sure." He's pulling my mask over my face. "Put this on and let's get out of here!"

I feel dazed. My voice comes out muffled by the mask.

"What's wrong?" I ask.

He holds the back of my hand up to my face.

Blisters are forming on my skin. Some dark.

He rubs my skin and takes his hand away.

It's covered in blood.

"They've released something in the air," he says. "We have to get in the mine and seal it. The others will die if this reaches them."

"What is it?" I moan as I follow him toward the cave.

Seconds ago I felt physically fine. Now it's as if a thousand fireflies have landed on my skin and vomited gasoline into my pores. The burning sensation is matched only by an unbearable itch. I can't stop scratching, and the more I scratch, the more I bleed. Matt's next words sting as badly as our invisible ailment.

"It's what Haru's going to use to kill humanity."

TWENTY-SIX

We are at the mine entrance when I hear them. My ears might be the one part of my body that's stronger than Matt's. I have to stop him. He's preparing to arm Telar grenades and bring the walls down behind us, sealing us inside with the others.

"There are three Telar above us, on the other side of this hill," I say.

"I don't hear them."

"They're there."

"I don't care. Whatever's out there has to stay out there. We have to block the entrance."

I grab Matt's grenade to stop him. "What if it's not gas but a virus of some kind? We could already be infected. We could carry it straight to the others."

"It feels like an external agent."

"That's because it's driving us crazy. Listen to me. I never noticed these Telar before until we got this close. They must have been either hiding underground or they're wearing something that blocks their heartbeats and breathing."

"Your point?"

"I think they've been here awhile. They might have been given orders to observe the battle, and if it started to go against them, they might have had instructions to release this toxin or virus or whatever it is."

"More the reason to seal this door now."

"No. Think this through, Matt. We have to know if we're infected or not. I don't see anyone alive on the battlefield. I'm pretty sure these three just released this thing. That means they'll know what it is. They might even have a way to treat it." I turn. "I have to go after them."

He stops me. "If you're wrong, you're leaving Teri and the others open to a greater chance of contamination."

"Seal the entrance if I'm gone more than three minutes."

"I can't leave you out here." He wipes at my bleeding face, and I feel the pain of a dozen popping blisters. "You're sicker than me. I'll go after them."

"You know the Telar better than anyone, and you're stronger than me. I'm more expendable. It's a fact. We're talking about the safety of the world here. Let's stop arguing and let me go."

"Three minutes, no more."

"Agreed," I say.

Carrying a single laser rifle, I rush away from the mine entrance and scurry around the side of the peak. Now that I know the Telar are there, it's not hard for me to get a fix on them. I surprise them in a ravine not half a mile from the mine. The two females react instantly, firing lasers at me—continuous beams. I have to twist and turn to dodge them, but I finally manage to get off two shots that hit them square in the chests. Their hearts explode, and they go down. I'm on the third one, a guy who looks twenty, before he can shoot. He freezes when I appear—he appears to be the weak link in the group. He wears thick glasses and has a facial twitch. He is not exactly a poster boy for immortals. I don't care, I don't have a lot of time to talk. I point my laser at his head.

"Do you know who I am?" I ask.

He's scared. He seems younger than the rest. "Yes."

"You released an agent in the air a few minutes ago. What is it? A virus or a toxin?"

He stutters. "I . . . I can't talk about it."

I drop the rifle and grab him by the throat.

"You say you know me. You must know I'm a vampire. You must know I can make other vampires by putting my blood in people. I'm going to do that to you right now. Then you'll live in a constant tormenting thirst. You'll spend eternity craving blood. You'll walk the earth feeding from thousands, and it will never be enough."

I go to bite his neck. He screams.

"Stop! Please stop! I don't want to be a vampire!"

I relax my grip. "Then tell me what I want to know."

"If I do, will you let me go?"

"I might."

"That's no answer."

I squeeze him tighter. "Damn you! You will be a vampire!"

He bursts out crying. "I shouldn't be here! I'm a scientist!"

"Did you help develop this thing that's causing these blisters?"

"Yes. No! I just helped test it. I never thought it would be used."

"Tell me what it is. I'm running out of patience."

"You asked if it's a virus or toxin. It's both."

"How can it be both?"

"I can explain, but I need time. Look, it's extremely contagious. One part in a billion can cause your skin to blister. But when you inhale it, and it enters your blood, it begins to multiply."

I feel I'll go mad from the itching. I interrupt.

"Are you the one who released it?"

"No." He points to one of the women I killed. "She did."

"When?"

"A few minutes ago. Our commander ordered her to—"

"Shut up. You're not infected. Why? Do you have a vaccine? A cure?"

"This pathogen is unlike anything the world has ever seen before."

I feel my desperation rising. The illness affects my mental state, and I have to fight not to scream. "Damn it. Do you have a vaccine on you or not?"

"Yes." He points to the same dead women. "She has a vial of it in her pack."

I release him and search her backpack. She has a vial with a clear fluid with the label X6X6 on it. "Is this the vaccine?" I ask.

"That's the pathogen. Look in the other pocket."

The other pocket has a vial of blue liquid with the label T-11 on it. There's also a packet of syringes. I rip one free. "How much vaccine do I need to stop it?" I ask.

"Ten milligrams works on most humans."

"I'm not human. I'll try ten anyway." Stabbing the vial with the needle, I withdraw the milky fluid and prepare to inject it in my arm. "Is it better taken intravenously?"

"It will work faster, yes."

"You better not be lying." I shoot it into my vein and wait. I know I have no time, but I let a minute go by. Then I notice the itching is less and the blisters are shrinking. "How many can I treat with this vial?" I ask, waving the T-11.

"Fifty people."

I hold up the X6X6 bottle. "How many can I infect with this?"

He gulps. "A million people."

"Good God. How could you develop such a thing?" He goes to answer, and I stop him. No time. I pick up the laser. "You deserve to die."

He holds out his hands. "I've answered all your questions. Please don't kill me. I . . . I . . . I cured you!"

"So you have. Come with me."

"What? I can't do that."

"Come with me or die."

He decides to accompany me. We rush back to the cave. Matt is relieved to see me, although he's not happy I have brought company. His face oozes red fluid, and his grenade is covered in a film of blood from his blistered palm.

"I was just about to blow it," he says.

"I know. Matt, this is . . . Who are you?"

"Charles Legart. My friends call me Charlie."

"Charlie has a vaccine for us. It works. Let me give you a shot." I take out a fresh syringe and stab the vial of T-11.

"Wait! How do you know you can trust this guy?"

"He's a scientist. He doesn't belong here. Stick out your arm."

Matt does as he's told. He has large, healthy veins. I inject him.

Charlie pales as he stares at Matt. "You're the Abomination."

Matt smiles through his pain. "Everything you've heard about me is true."

"Are there any other secretly placed Telar in this area?" I ask Charlie.

"Not that I know of."

I turn to Matt. "Give me the grenade—I'm feeling better already. I'll set it."

Matt doesn't argue. He staggers as he herds Charlie deeper into the mine. I give them a head start, then set the timer for fifteen seconds and arm the grenade. Knowing the shock wave will be focused by the walls of the cave, I run after them as fast as I can. The blast is strong, deafening, I'm almost knocked off my feet. Charlie and Matt are flattened. I help them up.

"My blisters are beginning to go away," Matt says.

"T-11 is the perfect antidote for X6X6," Charlie boasts.

"Can you produce more T-11?" I ask.

Charlie looks nervous. "No. I mean, I never worked on the vaccine. That's a whole other line of research."

"You must have some idea of how it works," Matt says.

Charlie shakes his head. "I'm afraid not."

Matt turns to me. "Get rid of him."

Charlie perks up. "But I'm a chemist, a biochemist, and a geneticist. I can break it down to its component parts."

I look at Charlie and sigh. "We'll keep him alive for now. But if you fail us, I'll have you for supper."

"Dessert," Matt suggests. "Eat him alive."

"That sounds wonderful," I agree.

Poor Charlie is left speechless.

We reach our friends minutes later, and I give them each an injection of T-11. It's fortunate I went back for Charlie, for their sakes. Each of them is showing signs of the infection. Shanti, in particular, is suffering with the skin on the reconstructed portions of her face. Seymour questions Charlie but is not happy with his answers.

"No virus can incubate this fast," he says. "It's impossible."

"You're right," Charlie says. "But X6X6 has two components. It's a toxin and a virus. The blisters are caused by the toxic aspects."

"We're over a mile underground," Seymour argues. "How could it have infected us?"

Charlie frowns. "It's highly contagious. But I must admit I'm surprised you three show symptoms."

His answer is not reassuring.

Yet on the whole the gang is relieved. It shows in the way we casually chat as we hike toward the other end of the mine, where a carefully buried helicopter should be waiting for us just outside. We have withstood a brutal attack and emerged without casualties. It's true it will take me time to recover from the death cry of the Telar army, but I blame Haru and not Matt's thousands of land mines for those soldier's deaths. It's my hope we've given the Telar a black eye that will make them hesitate to go ahead with their genocide plan. If I was in Haru's shoes, I'd be uneasy knowing we had obtained samples of X6X6 and T-11. And he will know, once his people examine the area.

The mine proves to be more of a maze than I anticipated, with many twists and turns and changes in altitude. For the first hour we climb, then we reach steep sections where the human members of our party have to use ropes to get down. Matt isn't troubled by the dusty floor or the creaking walls and ceiling. He says the mine has lasted over a hundred years and it won't collapse on us now.

Finally, in the middle of the night, we turn a corner and find a small circular opening through which we see the stars. Minutes later we're outside and enjoying the fresh air of a thick grove of trees. I estimate we're at least six miles from Matt's old house. We hike a hundred yards down a slope to what appears to be a tranquil meadow. But Matt surprises everyone, except me, when he tugs on the grass and it pulls away like a carpet. Beneath it are a series of long boards, and under them is the helicopter.

Matt has thought of everything. There's a tall ladder the others can use to climb down. But now that we're out in the open, even in the pitch dark, Matt urges us to hurry. I take him aside as the others climb in the helicopter.

"What's wrong?" I ask.

"Nothing."

"Your mood has changed."

He taps his closed laptop. "I've lost contact with my other copter. I have to assume it was shot down."

I nod to the helicopter. "What sort of weapons does this baby have?"

"It's no Apache."

"We'll ditch it as soon as we're clear of the area."

Matt is doubtful. "I'd like to get to Denver. I have contacts there. It will be easier for us to disappear."

"We don't know what kind of arrangements the Telar made to launch those planes. For all we know the governor of Colorado works with them."

"Haru took a beating. I'm hoping he's busy with damage control."

"He's busy looking for us. Ditch the copter quickly. That's my advice."

The helicopter has the clean oil scent of having been recently serviced. We take off straight up, and once clear of the trees Matt heads north toward Denver. Mountains rise up in front of us and he's forced to climb, but like in Switzerland, he stays near the ground. For the most part we fly above the tree line.

There's a harsh beauty to the rocky terrain. The barren soil has a rusty tinge to it, and I'm reminded of photos I've studied of the Martian landscape. But the illusion is destroyed by the small lakes we frequently fly over. Wide sheets of ice float on the surface of these isolated ponds, and I know the water must be cold.

We're in the air an hour when an alarm sounds.

"What is it?" I ask, sitting beside Matt in the copilot's seat.

"Someone's trying to acquire us on their radar," he says.

"Is it a jet? Are they near?"

"Just a moment." Matt swerves behind a steep peak. The alarm stops. Matt slows into a hovering position. "For this peak to block their radar, they must be flying at a similar altitude. We're being chased by a helicopter."

"This type of radar . . . what is it?" I ask.

"Whoever they are, they're trying to lock on weapons."

"It's the Telar."

Matt nods, grim. "You were right. I should have set us down earlier." The alarm comes back on. "Damn."

I check outside the windows. "I don't see them. And it's hard to hear over our own rotors. How far back do you think they are?"

"Impossible to tell. They're not showing on our radar. I suspect they're in an Apache."

"Any way you can beat them in a dogfight?"

"None."

"Then the rest of us should get out."

"If I land, it will be like sending up a flare to our position."

"I'm not talking about landing." I raise my voice so the others can hear. "We're being followed. In a minute or two, we're going to circle a peak and drop off their radar for a few seconds. Then we're going to leap into one of those lakes below."

"The water down there is close to freezing," Seymour says.

"We don't have the choice of a nice warm desert lake."

Seymour understands. "You did this when you escaped with Joel."

I nod. "It worked then, it will work now."

"You're going to have to time your jumps perfectly," Matt says. "I can't slow down, or they'll guess what you're up to."

I speak in a soft voice to Matt. "You know what to do?"

"Leap out at the last second if they fire a missile."

"Yeah. Try to be over a lake. You can stay underwater, hug the floor until they leave the area."

"I'll be okay, Sita. Just take care of . . . the others."

"I will. Where should we meet?"

"Evanston. It's a small town due east of here. 1244 Pine Street."

"Got it. Good luck."

"Same to you."

Moving into the rear of the helicopter, I throw open the side door and huddle with the others. Charlie goes to complain, but I hush him. I need an unobstructed view of the night terrain. We're doing close to a hundred miles an hour. The wind howls, and the gang presses closer together to stay warm.

"This isn't as hard as it looks," I say. "I'll choose a lake deep enough to absorb our fall. The water will be cold, sure, it will be a shock when you hit the surface. But none of us will have to swim far to reach the shore. The cold can actually work in our favor. They can be straight above us and we'll be invisible on their infrared scopes. The main thing is we jump when I say jump. If just one of us hesitates, we can end up missing the lake and landing on rocks. Questions?"

"I can't swim," Charlie says.

"How old are you, Charles?"

"Two hundred years."

"Then it's time you learned. You're Telar. Paddle with your arms and kick with your legs and you'll be fine." We round a narrow peak and I see a lake two miles up ahead. Luck seems to favor us. The radar alarm falls silent. I point out the door. "That's our lake. Shanti, take my hand. We're going first. Teri, hold on to Seymour, and follow us. Charlie . . . try not to drown."

Seconds go by, the lake draws near, sprinkled with thin sheets of ice. Most of the surface is exposed, and I can see the lake floor. It looks plenty deep—I'm not worried. Shanti's fingers are cold in my warm palm. I hold on to her because I feel she's the most delicate.

"Scared?" I say to Shanti.

"A little. I'm glad I'm going with you."

I speak to Teri. "This is like the Olympic finals all over again."

Teri shivers. "This is worse."

We pass the edge of the lake. Matt slows slightly.

I raise my voice so everyone can hear. "Shanti and I will jump on the count of three. Teri and Seymour will follow immediately. Then Charlie. One . . . two . . . three!"

I yank Shanti out the helicopter and switch her into my

arms as we fall, cradling her like a child. Matt has brought us in low, fifty feet above the water. The short drop is not a problem—it's our forward momentum. In the last instant, I pull Shanti close to my chest and turn to absorb the impact.

We crash through a layer of ice and plunge down twenty feet. The ice is only an inch thick, but it's fortunate I hit it first. At this speed, it feels like a brick wall. The water's practically the same temperature as the ice. There's pressure, too; I have to pop my ears. But Shanti flashes me a thumbs-up in the icy darkness. She knows I will take care of her.

I steer away from the sheet of ice, and we reach the surface in seconds. Shanti can swim, but I insist on towing her on her back. In less than a minute, we're safe on the shore. But I have no time to warm her limbs. I hear moans coming from farther out on the lake and know Teri's in trouble.

"Stay here," I order Shanti as I run and dive back in the water. I reach Teri and Seymour quickly, but the situation is not good. Seymour is struggling to keep her head above the water, and Teri appears to be in shock.

"We separated in the air," Seymour gasps. "She hit the ice. I think her leg's broken."

Teri's right leg is not merely broken, it's shattered. Even in the night, in the black water, I see her thigh bone has pierced the skin. She's bleeding heavily. I fear the femoral artery that runs the length of the leg has ruptured. If that's the case, she doesn't have long to live.

"I need to take care of her," I tell Seymour. "Can you make it to shore on your own?"

He shivers badly. "I can make it. Don't worry about me."

Turning Teri on her back and slipping my arm around her chest, the same way I did with Shanti, I pump with all the strength in my legs. I'm so frantic to reach the shore, I send out wide waves across the lake. Shanti and Charlie are waiting for me where the rocky soil and the cold water meet. I stand upright and sweep Teri into my arms. Charlie points to the side of a nearby peak.

"There's a cave up there where we can take shelter," he says, pulling out a pocket lighter and handing it to me. "It's deep—you can light a fire and no one will see you. I'll collect driftwood and meet you there in a few minutes."

"Thank you, Charles. Please hurry," I say.

Holding Teri tight, I run to the cave, leaving Shanti behind. It has been used before by backpackers, but that was years ago. There are a few thin logs and dried branches buried in the back. Setting Teri down, I gather what wood I have and light it. The yellow light and feeble warmth are enough to wake Teri from her daze. I kneel on her right side, and she opens her eyes.

"Alisa," she says, groaning in pain. "It hurts . . . I'm so cold."

"I know, honey. You've broken your leg. But I can help you." I tear her pants leg in one swift stroke and examine her wound more closely. The break is ugly; the ends of the bone are jagged. She's bleeding heavily, but I suspect the femoral artery has not ripped in half, or she'd be dead already. Still, for her to be losing this much blood, it must have some kind of tear in it.

"I'm sorry," she moans. "I tried to hit the water. But there was ice. Ouch!"

"It's okay, Teri. You're going to be okay." I pull off my shirt and tear it into long strips. I tie three around her leg, at the top, near her hip, using the material as tourniquets. Immediately the blood flow slows, but it is nowhere close to stopping. Part of my problem is I don't know how much blood she lost in the water. I fear it was a lot. She's deathly pale, and for a human who usually has a powerful pulse, her heartbeat is weak. My daughter is an Olympic champion, after all.

I cannot help thinking she is mine.

I cannot bear the thought of losing her.

"Listen to my voice, Teri." I put my left hand over her forehead and gently touch her wound with my right hand. "Just listen to what I say. You might feel a magnetism in your forehead. That's okay, it's a healing energy, it will help take away the pain. Now close your eyes and imagine the pain is dissolving as your body does everything it can to fix your sore leg. This is a very old practice. We call on the body to heal itself, and the body responds. Can you hear me?"

"Yes," she mumbles, as if from far away. Her eyes are shut, and her breathing has taken on a better rhythm. Even her bleeding has slowed, but it has not stopped.

"Feel yourself fill with a warm yellow light. It's like the light of this fire. It's your fire, the fire of your life. It's the same fire that gives you the strength to run fast and far. Let this fire heal your leg."

"My leg," she whispers.

"Good, you're doing good," I whisper. But my psychic abilities can only help her so much. She needs surgery, and she needs my blood. Careful not to open her wound further, I slip my right fingers in the cut and feel for her pulsing artery. What I find devastates me. The trauma of the break has caused her artery to balloon. Besides having a slight tear in the artery, it's on the verge of popping. If that happens, she'll bleed out in seconds.

Quickly, I remove my fingers, bite the tip of each one so my blood drips out, and slip them back in the wound, around the injured artery. The small tear responds to my blood. I feel it struggle to knit together, to close. But the balloon portion of the artery pounds harder. The bubble of tissue grows. I don't understand it. It's like a portion of her body accepts my blood, while another portion rejects it. I'm not sure what to do. Pulling my fingers out, I sit back on my legs, my left hand still covering her forehead.

"How do you feel, Teri?" I ask gently.

Her eyes stay shut. She speaks in a faint whisper.

"Pain . . . Cold . . . Love."

I wipe away a tear. "You feel love?"

"I love you, Sita. I know that's your real name."

"I love you too, Teri. You're going to be okay."

"I feel . . . dying." Her voice fades. "Death."

She passes out. Carefully, I press the ends of her bone together and push them back in her leg, trying above all else not to add to the pressure on the artery. Then I take my remaining two strips of cloth and tie them around her leg, directly over the wound, hoping to hold the bone in place. Later, if I decide to give her more blood, I can remove the bandages.

Shanti and Charlie enter the cave carrying armfuls of what looks like driftwood. I have them put half on the fire and save the other half for later.

"Where's Seymour?" I ask.

"He's coming," Shanti replies. "He barely made it to shore. He's cold."

I turn to Charlie. "Go help him. Carry him if you have to."

Charlie runs out the cave. Shanti sits on the other side of Teri.

"How is she?" she asks.

"Not good."

"Will she live?"

"I don't know."

"Can you use your . . . powers to help her?"

Shanti knows I'm not human. But she doesn't know what I can and cannot do. "I'm trying. But I don't know if it will be enough."

"We have cells. They're still working. I can pick up a signal outside. We can call for help."

"The Telar will pick up any call we make to a hospital."

"But if it's a choice between Teri dying—"

"I know, Shanti, I know. Let me think for a minute."

Charlie soon returns with Seymour. My old friend is shaking badly. We stretch him out beside the fire. He has a bad case of hypothermia, but he's not injured. He points a trembling hand at Teri.

"Tell me," he mumbles.

"Her leg is smashed. She's lost a lot of blood. The artery in her leg is about to pop."

"Fix her," Seymour says.

"I don't know if I can."

"You can," he insists, before he blacks out.

Time is not on Teri's side. I have decisions to make. Standing, I ask Shanti to give me her cell, and I hurry to the cave entrance. From there I try to call Matt. He has two cells on him at all times. Two cells that can withstand incredible punishment without failing. The connection between our phones and his is secure. It can't be intercepted. But I can't reach him on either of his cells. That is bad. It means his helicopter was probably shot down, with him in it.

But I'm not willing to accept he's dead. He's Yaksha's son, and the child of the most ancient Telar. The clothes on his body could be burned to ash and he would survive. Even if his helicopter exploded all around him, he could take it. I must assume he's alive and that he's heading for 1244 Pine Street, Evanston.

I walk back in the cave. Teri and Seymour are both unconscious. I'm not worried about my old friend, but Teri continues to lose blood. She's going into shock.

I explain to Charlie and Shanti about Evanston, how it is twenty miles due east of our current position. I tell them to hike in that direction as fast as they can. I tell Charlie he can carry Shanti part of the way, if it speeds things up. Or if they run into campers, they can ask for help to reach the town. But I assure them that Matt will be waiting for them in a house there.

"What do we tell Matt?" Shanti asks.

"Describe Teri's condition. Tell him to get help and come here. Or, if he thinks it's safe, to get hold of another helicopter and fly it here." I turn to Charlie. "You haven't known us long, but I think you realize all the stories you've heard about us are lies."

He nods. "You seem like good people."

"You can call Haru when you locate Matt and be the big hero to the Telar. But as a group the Telar are sick, and I think you know that too. I need to hear it straight out, and I will know if you're telling the truth or not. Are you with us, or are you with them?"

He doesn't hesitate. "I'm with you."

I pat his back. "I'm proud of you, Charlie. Take good care of Shanti."

"I will, Sita. I promise."

Again, Shanti corners me before she leaves.

"Charlie can go without me. I'll just slow him down."

I shake my head. "Charlie likes you, I can tell. He's convinced he should help us, but if we leave him to wander alone in the night, he might change his mind. Your company gives him moral strength."

Shanti leans closer. "What if you're attacked?"

"I have to risk it."

"You keep risking it. Is that smart?"

"I have to be alone with Teri. I can do more if we're alone."

"But Seymour—"

"Go, Shanti. It's for the best."

She's doubtful. She has her own intuition. I sense it in her, and she has confidence in her own ability. What worries me is that it might be more accurate than my own, particularly in this case. Yet she obeys me, as usual, and leaves with Charlie.

I turn my attention back to Teri. I cannot leave the tourniquets in place forever, at least not this tight. They are cutting off the blood flow to her leg and the pressure on her artery, but her leg will eventually begin to die without enough blood. I'm caught in a catch-22. Whatever I do to help her can also hurt her.

I loosen the tourniquets, I do not remove them. But I take off the two bandages and again slip my fingertips inside to feel how the femoral artery is doing. The original tear has healed, but another has formed at the base of the balloon. That's terrible, it's absolutely the worst thing that could happen. It means the artery is going to burst and she is going to die.

"Teri," I cry. "What should I do?"

To my amazement, she opens her eyes. She is groggy, but she heard me, and she seems to understand my dilemma. "It doesn't matter," she says so softly even I have to lean closer to hear. She's so near death, the words could be thoughts.

"What doesn't matter, Teri?" I ask.

"What I saw . . . London."

"You mean at the motel. It doesn't matter what you saw there?"

"You're good . . . You strive for goodness."

"Thank you. That means a lot to me."

"But I cannot be you . . . like you."

I frown. "Do you know what you're saying?"

"Dying . . . Let me die."

"No. I won't let you die."

"Let me go. . . . I can't be like you. . . . The blood . . . No. . . . Never."

Those are her last words. She passes out, and I watch as tremors shake the length of her body. The fire is strong, but she has lost too much blood to get warm. Her pulse is ragged. Her heart doesn't have enough liquid to pump. Even if the artery doesn't burst, she'll die. Her breathing has switched back to a painful pant. Her organs are shutting down.

I tear the top of my fingers and slip them back around her artery. It's strange—before the trials, before the Olympics, her body gladly drank up my blood. But now it's as if her system is wary of me. As if her blood knows what she saw in London, and it recoils from the idea of being contaminated by a vampire. That's how the balloon in her artery reacts to my help. It pounds madly, likes it's threatening to pop.

To stop me from changing her.

She knows she's dying. She told me to let her die.

All who are born die. All who die will be reborn.

The wise do not grieve over the inevitable.

Krishna taught me that. Why can't I listen?

"Because I love her," I tell myself.

No. That's only part of it. The minor part.

"Because it doesn't have to be this way."

If I wait, if the artery pops, I won't have time to change her. She'll bleed out. She'll die in my arms. Teri, my daughter, will be dead, gone, finished. I can't imagine it, and maybe because my mind refuses to accept the possibility, I refuse to let it happen.

"But she asked you to let her be," I tell myself.

Those are my last words for the night. I can no longer speak, I can no longer think. My grief is too great. All I know is that if she dies, I'll never love again, and I'll have no reason to live.

The fire burns low. The night grows cold.

EPILOGUE

Seymour Dorsten hated funerals. He tried to avoid them whenever he could. He always said he wouldn't go to his own. Not that anyone ever laughed at the tired joke. The last funeral he had gone to had been his mother's. Before that had been his father's. Both had been sad affairs, but at least with them they had been sick and were looking forward to some peace.

But today's funeral, he knew, was going to be pure agony.

He had hoped that it would help to have Paula and John come. On Santorini, when he had been alone with the boy, he had been very moved. That afternoon they had done nothing more than play a computer game for an hour or so, but John had gotten to him. The weird thing was, he hadn't said more than a dozen words, certainly nothing profound.

But sitting in his company, Seymour had felt like everything was all right, and everything was going to be all right. That the final summation of this strange thing called life was peace and joy. At the time, Seymour hadn't been able to figure out how John invoked such a feeling. Actually, on that island, he hadn't cared how the kid did it. All Seymour had wanted to do was enjoy John's company. He still felt grateful to Sita for taking him to meet the boy.

Of course, he had felt like a jerk when Sita had tried to call Paula after her nasty trip to Arosa and she hadn't been able to get through because their number was disconnected. The truth was, John had given Seymour a private number to call him on if he ever needed help. He had kept it from Sita simply because John had asked him to. But he had still felt like he was betraying the love of his life.

Paula and John had arrived in Denver last night, in time for today's funeral. Seymour had tried to spend some time with John, hoping the boy could lift his spirits, but the stream of bliss had run dry. John could have been any other kid who was more interested in playing computer games than in the fact that someone had died.

Seymour heard a knock at his hotel room door.

He answered it. Shanti, it was always good to see Shanti. On the surface, you'd have to say she was a much brighter drop of sunshine than good old John. Then again, Shanti had hardly stopped crying the last two days.

She sniffled when she asked how he was doing.

"I'm okay. You want to come in? I just ordered breakfast."

"I'll come in, but I don't think I can eat," she said.

"You should have something. You're too skinny."

She forced a smile as she entered his suite. "I've read some of your books. Didn't you say a girl could never be too skinny?"

"Too skinny, too stupid, or too sexy. But it was a character of mine who said that, and the guy doesn't reflect my own personal view of the entire female species." He paused. "At least have some yogurt. I ordered three different flavors."

"For yourself?" she asked.

"I hate the stuff. But I was kind of hoping you'd stop by." There was another knock at the door, and Seymour answered it. "Here's our food. Don't you just love room service? You just pick up your phone and fifteen minutes later there's hot food at your door. The only reason I still write is so I have enough money to stay in nice hotels and order room service."

"Sita said you often drive to another city just so you can stay in a fancy hotel and watch TV all day and order room service."

"That's true." Seymour accepted the tray on the rolling cart, tipped the waiter handsomely, and closed the door. He pushed the food over to Shanti. She looked stunned at how much he had ordered: scrambled eggs, sausage, wheat toast, bacon, pancakes, yogurt, pastries, a pitcher of coffee, and a glass of orange juice. It was his usual order, not that he ever ate everything. On the contrary, he was not a big eater—he just liked to eat one of everything. One strip of bacon, one egg, one pancake, and so on. He explained his system to Shanti as she got comfortable beside him.

"So you waste most of the food," she said.

"I don't waste it. I usually bag it and give it away to the first homeless person I meet. But if the hotels would just let me order tiny portions, I'd do that instead."

"You know I grew up in India."

"Please don't tell me any starving kid stories."

"A meal this size could feed a family of four for a week."

Seymour poured his coffee and reached for a bear claw. "That may have been true in the past, but not now. The last time I was in India, I never saw so many fat men in dhotis and fat women in saris. Did you know that India exports more food than it consumes? When I read that, I decided to never donate another rupee to their starving children programs."

"Sita told me you donate most of your money to charity. That you like to act cheap, but behind everyone's back you give away your royalties."

"Another lie. You can't believe anything Sita told you."

Shanti's lower lip trembled. "I believe everything she told me."

Seymour saw he had upset her. "I'm sorry."

"Don't be. Say whatever you like. I love listening to you talk. You make me laugh. I'm just overly sensitive."

"Any girl who looks as beautiful as you has no right to be sensitive, shy, or even that bright."

Shanti giggled. "I heard you like your women stupid."

"All men do. They're just too smart to admit it."

The compliment worked wonders on Shanti. She fairly glowed.

"Do you really think I'm pretty?"

"Ask me when you turn eighteen and I'll prove it to you."

"You! You're a scoundrel."

"Eat your yogurt. You're gorgeous, but you need to gain weight."

It was while she was eating that Seymour noticed a few dark blisters on her face where the skin had been expertly grafted on. He had the same blisters on the back of his calves. They were smaller than the ones they had sprouted in the mine, and not truly black, but they were a bad sign. He tried not to think about what they meant. . . .

Like maybe the end of the world.

He had the vial of T-11 in his bag. Sita had given it to him.

It would have been nice to have a long breakfast and talk to Shanti for hours, but Seymour checked his watch and saw it was time to get out to the cemetery. He didn't know why most funerals were early in the morning. It was like people had this weird sense of etiquette where they felt it was impolite to leave a dead person sitting around all day—or lying around, as the case may be—while the living did other stuff. Personally, Seymour thought all funerals should be at midnight.

Shanti wept softly when the cemetery came into view.

Seymour felt his own throat constrict. He was not a big weeper by nature, but he knew he was going to have trouble keeping it together this morning. He was grateful there was to be no service at a chapel, no minister, and no open casket.

God, whoever invented the open-casket ritual should have been shot and put on display. It was no joke. How did it help people gain closure when they refused to close the goddamn box?

There was no minister and no chapel service because Seymour had paid for the funeral himself. He had even chosen the plot. It was nice, except for the fact it was surrounded by a bunch of dead people. The plot was at the top of a grassy bluff that looked out at the mountains.

Paula and John were already present, as was Charlie. Seymour was surprised to see the Telar was wearing a brand-new Armani suit. Seymour just had on an old suit off the rack, which he hated. Charlie was obviously taking the occasion seriously. In fact, he was doing everything he could to be accepted into their small family.

Lisa Fetch was also present. She stood beside Matt and a certain blond woman everyone knew but no one was talking to. It was kind of strange to be carrying a prejudice to a funeral. However, Seymour had to remind himself it was not really a prejudice—it was more a fear. He sought to throw off his own confused emotions by walking straight to Matt and his companion. But he stumbled when he saw the hole in the ground, the pile of fresh dirt, and the closed coffin.

It hit him then. It was no longer a story.

It was like that moment in Central Park.

It was too real. Too much.

Shanti hugged him close to her side. They kept each other upright.

Matt turned and looked at them, hiding every last trace of emotion. "Hi, Seymour. Hi, Shanti," he said.

"Hi," Shanti said quietly.

Seymour couldn't reply. Not even when Matt's blond and blue-eyed partner looked at him and sadly nodded her head. She looked more alert today, less dazed, and he supposed that was a good thing.

"Hello," Teri said to Seymour.

Three days before, when Seymour had awakened on that awful morning, the first thing he'd noticed was that Teri was asleep beside him. She was lying so still, though, that he went so far as to creep over to her on his hands and knees to make sure she was alive. He was relieved to find her breathing, although she was as silent as a mouse. He supposed that came from running a hundred miles a week.

However, he didn't check her leg. He occasionally wrote violent scenes, but when it came to the real thing, his stomach was nowhere to be found, unless it was over in the bushes barfing. He didn't mind that Sita had used his jacket to cover Teri.

He assumed Sita had kept him warm enough with the fire. She was good at taking care of people.

It was then he heard the talking outside. Only these people weren't having a friendly conversation, but a major argument. Putting on his shoes, Seymour hurried from the cave to see what was the matter.

Sita was sitting on a boulder near the cave entrance. Matt paced in front of her, a laser rifle slung over his shoulder. Seymour was pleased to see a helicopter parked beside the lake. At least they weren't going to have to hike out of this remote place. Last night, jumping into the frozen lake at a hundred miles an hour had given him enough of a thrill to last him the rest of his life.

There was something about the high Rockies on a sparkling summer morning. If only Sita and Matt weren't fighting, the scene would have been enchanting.

Seymour was half-awake. It took him a while to catch on.

"You had no right," Matt was saying. "You're not God. My father told me about your arrogance. I didn't want to believe it until the trials came and you juiced her up like a common junkie. I should have seen then that this day would come."

"Bullshit," Sita snapped. "No one could have seen this day coming except for you. Yeah, you, and don't look so startled. I did what I did because you put me in an impossible situation. Face it, Matt, the day you decided your privacy was more important than my safety was the day you killed Teri."

Seymour wanted to say Teri was alive but was afraid to interrupt.

"You were the one who exposed Teri to risk," Matt said.

"I did everything I could to protect her."

"You don't protect someone by making them a celebrity! You turn them into a target. That's why I kept my mouth shut around her."

"Oh, yeah, that's right. You're a master at the silent routine. Why didn't you say a word to me about the Telar, even when you knew they'd just sent an assassin after me?"

"I didn't know about Claudious until after the fact."

"You could have told me about the Telar a week after I killed him. Then I wouldn't have ended up in Arosa, which led to Goldsmith, which, by the way, led to here. It's here Teri fell. It's here her leg cracked open and she lost most of her blood." Sita paused. "I tried calling you, but you didn't answer. I was on my own. I had to make a decision."

"That's my point. It's not a decision she would have made."

"You don't know that. You weren't here."

"I didn't have to be here. I saw how she reacted to what you did to that woman in London. She would never have chosen to die and be reborn as a vampire."

Seymour finally began to see the light.

"I couldn't just let her die," Sita said, her voice cracking with emotion.

"Yes, you could have. It's what she would have wanted."

"You say that so easily. But you weren't here. I had to decide."

Matt halted his pacing and held out a threatening finger. "Now you lie. I hear the stink of lies all over your voice. Teri must have spoken to you at the end. She must have told you to let her go."

Sita stared at him. A watery tear ran from one eye, and she wiped it away. A bloody tear ran from the other, and she shook as if she was going to collapse. Seymour had never seen her in such a state. He wouldn't have thought it possible.

"You're right," she said. "What are you going to do?"

"I don't know."

"You can't kill her. It's done."

"It's not done. My father taught me it takes twenty-four hours to make a vampire." He paused. "We can stop it before it's too late."

Sita trembled. "You'll just march in the cave and shoot her? You think you can do that?"

He removed the rifle from his shoulder. "Yes."

Sita stood from the boulder. "No."

"You can't stop me."

"I can try. Believe me, I'll try."

"For God's sake, you're not even armed."

Sita strode toward him and shoved him in the chest. She hit him hard, but he didn't fall over, just took a step back. "I'll die before I let you kill her. And maybe when I'm dead, you'll look around, at the lake, at the sky, at my body, and you'll change your mind. It's a risk I'll take. So go ahead and shoot. Because I can't live without her."

Finally, Matt showed his pain.

"I can't live without her either! But now I'll never be able to let go of her. Because of you. Because of what you've done. She'll still be here, but it won't be her. She'll be—"

"What? A monster? A vampire? Your father was a vampire. You loved him. Why can't you love Teri the same way?"

"She won't be the same! Nothing will ever be the same again!"

"It's better than death. Anything is better than nothing." Sita reached to try to hug him. "Believe me, Matt, this way at least life goes on."

He hugged her in return, and they wept in each other's arms.

Seymour felt like he shouldn't watch. That he was prying.

He turned to leave. Then he felt a strange vibration in the air.

It came out of nowhere, but suddenly it was everywhere.

Seymour noticed a smell. A familiar odor used in childish stories to scare boys and girls and ignorant people into obeying whoever was telling the tale. Sulfur, burning sulfur, the stink of rotten eggs. It rushed his nose and kept going until it struck the back of his skull. Suddenly he had a headache, and there was a ringing in his ears, which scratched on his nerves, irritating them at a deep level. In the space of seconds he felt angry at everyone. But worse, a thousand times worse, he knew the hatred was going to last forever.

"Help," Seymour mumbled. "Help me."

But there was no one present who could help him. His friends were caught in the same psychic web. Sita was no longer weeping in Matt's arms. She was backing away from him, her face flushed with fear. Matt had his laser rifle in his hands, and the grin on his face, why, it belonged to the boy with the magnifying glass whose greatest joy was to sit in the backyard on a sunny day and focus his glass on ants, grasshoppers, butterflies, and even frogs, and slowly boil off their skin until they either turned to ash or else began to leak dark blood. Matt was that twisted child grown to stature, with the power of a sun in his hands.

He lifted the rifle and pointed it at Sita.

Seymour knew then that Matt was the focus, while she was the target. Seymour began to walk toward her. He had to help; he had to do something.

"You bitch," Matt said softly. "You think you can change my girl into a bloodsucking whore like you and get away with it. Well, you best think again. No woman of mine is ever going to leave my bed at night to go suck other men. After I burn your heart out, I'm going to take what's left of it to her and see if she bites. If she does, I'll do the same to her. And if she doesn't . . ." He chuckled obscenely. "I'll do her just the same."

"Matt, listen to me, this isn't you!" Sita cried. "It's the Array!"

Sita had not lost the power of her voice, and it hit Matt like a sobering bucket of ice water. For an instant he lost his sick grin and sank into painful confusion. His obscene manner vanished as quickly as it had come.

"My name's not Matt," he mumbled. "It's not Ray."

Sita implored him with every fiber of her being.

"It's called the Array! It's evil. Remember London. Remember what it made me do."

"No!" Matt held up a hand to hold her back. "I saw what you did! You ate that girl. You're the evil one."

Seymour continued to close on them.

Sita softened her voice but kept begging.

"You can fight this, Matt. Fight it for Teri."

Seymour saw it might have been a mistake to use Teri's name at such a delicate moment. Because even before the Array had struck, the name had been tearing the two of them apart. Now, tossed into this cauldron of madness that had possessed Matt's brain, the name threw a switch, but the wrong one. The slimeball returned with renewed bitterness. He raised the rifle.

"Shut up! You're the one who poisoned her with your filthy blood. You're a goddamn witch is what you are. A witch from hell who has to burn."

Matt pressed a switch on the side of the laser.

A row of red lights lit up. Seymour recognized them.

The weapon was now armed and ready to fire.

Seymour darted toward Matt. He had traveled maybe half a step when Matt reacted. He turned and focused the laser on Seymour.

"Why, the bitch has a pup," he gloated.

"No!" Sita shouted.

"Yeah!" he yelled and pressed the trigger.

The ruby beam lashed out. Seymour saw it, his own death approaching. He knew for a fact a laser traveled at the speed of light. What he didn't understand was how Sita managed to leap in front of it.

The beam hit her in the chest and burned through her sternum and melted a large chunk of her heart. But it didn't cause her chest cavity to rupture like the others. The laser punched a hole in her chest, and from both openings poured forth gallons of blood. Blood that turned to red dust the instant it touched the air. Dust that in turn changed to gold flakes, as a sweet-smelling breeze suddenly swept the area. As the gold sparkled in the sunlight, lifting higher and higher on a spinning funnel, Seymour realized the Array had switched off, or else had been turned off by a greater power.

"Krishna," Sita whispered.

Matt dropped the rifle and caught her before she fell.

Seymour ran to his side. They were too late.

Her empty eyes were fixed on the endless blue sky.

Sita, last of the vampires, was no more.

• • •

Seymour managed to nod when Teri said hello.

"You okay?" he said.

She lowered her head. "Okay," she replied.

The burial ceremony was brief. Each of them said a few words about Sita. How they had met. What she had done for them. When she had made them laugh. Why they had loved her. They went around the circle, and even Charlie said a few words. But Teri and John remained silent, and Seymour was not surprised.

As a final farewell, they each placed a red rose on top of her casket. Shanti said, "Good-bye, Sita. Miss you." Paula said, "Good-bye, Sita. Love you." The rest said similar things, except for John and Teri. But this time John did show some feeling. The dark-haired boy with the luminous dark eyes knelt at the head of her coffin and placed his own head on the sweet-smelling maple. He stayed in that position a long time, as much as five minutes. No one disturbed him. When he was done, he stepped toward Teri and took her hands and squeezed them. They were exactly the same height, and they stared at each other over a short distance that seemed to stretch as the seconds went by. Finally John smiled faintly and released her.

It was over.

Everyone left the cemetery except Seymour. Shanti assured him that Matt could give her a ride back to the hotel. Not caring that he was staining his suit with dirt and grass, Seymour sat on the ground and used the coffin for back support. It felt heavy considering it held a 120-pound woman. Of course, she had been no ordinary woman, not to him. She had filled his world and made it complete.

Now . . . he could not think of now.

He scratched at his blisters. They weren't too bad. Just itchy.

He did not know how long he sat there. It was nice just to be near her. The weird thing was he still felt her presence. He kept expecting to hear her voice. He had always loved her voice. He had loved everything about her. He was lucky in that respect, that their lives had crossed paths. He felt he was one of the chosen few. Yet to lose her this way . . . it was like a curse.

He supposed that was how the universe kept balance.

He remembered how she had said Krishna's name as she died.

According to the Gita, that meant she was now one with him.

Seymour hoped that was true.

After so much struggle, she deserved to find peace.

"Seymour," a voice called. It startled him, and he realized he might have been dozing. But he quickly stood when he saw Teri Raine walking toward him. Brushing off his pants, he noticed all the cars were gone except his. Teri would need a ride back to wherever Matt was staying.

It was supposed to be a secret. Matt was acting like a haunted man. Hell, he must be feeling like one. Who wouldn't? In one crazy stroke he had killed his father's true love. And now he was condemned to sleep with a vampiric copy of his own love.

"Teri. This is a surprise," Seymour said.

"How are you doing?"

"I've been better. How about you? Has the change been rough?"

"I felt confused the first few days. I didn't know where I was or what I was doing." She paused. "But everything became clear when I saw John."

"That's good. I thought it would be rough without having Sita to guide you. I'm happy for you. You know, I was just sitting and thinking that now you're the last vampire."

Teri stared at him. "That's true. Nothing's changed."

He wasn't sure what she meant. "Well, if you're okay with it, then I'm sure in time Matt will come to accept that you're still his girl."

"You're not hearing me. I'm not his girl. Nothing's changed."

He finally did hear her. Still, he couldn't accept it.

"What do you mean?"

She hugged him and buried her face in his shoulder. Then, as if telling him the secret of secrets, she spoke in his ear. "It's me, Sita. I'm still here. I'm in Teri's body."

ALISA LIVES ON. . . .

THIRST

NO. 4

SUMMER 2011

HERE'S A PEEK AT ANOTHER SERIES BY

Christopher Pike

REMEMBER ME

MOST PEOPLE WOULD probably call me a ghost. I am, after all, dead. But I don't think of myself that way. It wasn't so long ago that I was alive, you see. I was only eighteen. I had my whole life in front of me. Now I suppose you could say I have all of eternity before me. I'm not sure exactly what that means yet. I'm told everything's going to be fine. But I have to wonder what I would have done with my life, who I might have been. That's what saddens me most about dying—that I'll never know.

My name is Shari. They don't go in much for last names over here. I used to be Shari Cooper. I'd tell you what I look like, but since the living can see right through me now, it would be a waste of time. I'm the color of wind. I can dance on moonbeams and sometimes cause a star to twinkle. But when I was alive, I looked all right. Maybe better than all right.

I suppose there's no harm in telling what I *used* to look like.

I had dark blond hair, which I wore to my shoulders in layered waves. I also had bangs, which my mom said I wore too long because they were always getting in my eyes. My clear green eyes. My brother always said they were only brown, but they were green, definitely green. I can see them now. I can brush my bangs from my eyes and feel my immaterial hair slide between my invisible fingers. I can even laugh at myself and remember the smile that won "Best Smile" my junior year in high school. Teenage girls are always complaining about the way they look, but now that no one is looking at me, I see something else—I should never have complained.

It is a wonderful thing to be alive.

I hadn't planned on dying.

But that is the story I have to tell: how it happened, why it happened, why it shouldn't have happened, and why it was meant to be. I won't start at the beginning, however. That would take too long, even for someone like me who isn't getting any older. I'll start near the end, the night of the party. The night I died. I'll start with a dream.

It wasn't my dream. My brother Jimmy had it. I was the only one who called him Jimmy. I wonder if I would have called him Jim like everyone else if he would have said I had green eyes like everyone else. It doesn't matter. I loved Jimmy more than the sun. He was my big brother, nineteen going on twenty, almost two years older than me and ten times nicer. I used to fight with him all the time, but the funny thing is, he never fought with me. He was an angel, and I know what I'm talking about.

It was a warm, humid evening. I remember what day I was born, naturally, but I don't recall the date I died, not exactly. It was a Friday near the end of May. Summer was coming. Graduation and lying in the sand at the beach with my boyfriend were all I had on my mind. Let me make one point clear at the start—I was pretty superficial. Not that other people thought so. My friends and teachers all thought I was a sophisticated young lady. But I say it now, and I've discovered that once you're dead, the only opinion that matters is your own.

Anyway, Jimmy had this dream, and whenever Jimmy dreamed, he went for a walk. He was always sleepwalking, usually to the bathroom. He had diabetes. He had to take insulin shots, and he peed all the time. But he wasn't sickly-looking or anything like that. In fact, I was the one who used to catch all the colds. Jimmy never got sick—ever. But, boy, did he have to watch what he ate. Once when I baked a batch of Christmas cookies, he gave in to temptation, and we spent Christmas Day at the hospital waiting for him to wake up. Sugar just killed him.

The evening I died, I was in my bedroom in front of my mirror, and Jimmy was in his room next door snoring peacefully on top of his bed. Suddenly the handle of my brush snapped off. I was forever breaking brushes. You'd think I had steel wool for hair rather than fine California surfer-girl silk. I used to take a lot of my frustrations out on my hair.

I was mildly stressed that evening as I was getting ready for Beth Palmone's birthday party. Beth was sort of a friend of mine, sort of an accidental associate, and the latest in a seemingly endless string of bitches who were trying to steal my boyfriend away. But she was the kind of girl I hated to hate because she was so nice. She was always smiling and complimenting me. I never really trusted people like that, but they could still make me feel guilty. Her nickname was Big Beth. My best friend, Joanne Foulton, had given it to her. Beth had big breasts.

The instant my brush broke, I cursed. My parents were extremely well-off, but it was the only brush I had, and my layered waves of dark blond hair were lumpy knots of dirty wool from the shower I'd just taken. I didn't want to disturb Jimmy, but I figured I could get in and borrow his brush without waking him. It was still early—about eight o'clock—but I knew he was zonked out from working all day. To my parents' dismay, Jimmy had decided to get a real job rather than go to college after graduating from high school. Although he enjoyed fiddling with computers, he'd never been academically inclined. He loved to work outdoors. He had gotten a job with the telephone company taking telephone poles *out* of the ground. He once told me that taking down a nice old telephone pole was almost as distressing as chopping down an old tree. He was kind of sensitive that way, but he liked the work.

After I left my room, I heard someone come in the front

door. I knew who it was without looking: Mrs. Mary Parish and her daughter Amanda. My parents had gone out for the night, but earlier that evening they had thrown a cocktail party for a big-wig real estate developer from back east who was thinking of joining forces with my dad to exploit Southern California's few remaining square feet of beachfront property. Mrs. Parish worked as a part-time housekeeper for my mom. She had called before I'd gone in for my shower to ask if everyone had left so she could get started cleaning up. She had also asked if Amanda could ride with me to Beth's party. I had answered yes to both these questions and told her I'd be upstairs getting dressed when they arrived and to just come in. Mrs. Parish had a key to the house.

I called to them from the upstairs hall—which overlooks a large portion of the downstairs—before stealing into Jimmy's room.

"I'll be down in a minute! Just make yourself at home—and get to work!"

I heard Mrs. Parish chuckle and caught a faint glimpse of her gray head as she entered the living room carrying a yellow bucket filled with cleaning supplies. I loved Mrs. Parish. She always seemed so happy, in spite of the hard life she'd had. Her husband had suddenly left her years earlier broke and unskilled.

I didn't see Amanda at first, nor did I hear her. I guess I thought she'd changed her mind and decided not to go to the party. I'm not sure I would have entered Jimmy's room and then let him slip past me in a semiconscious state if I'd known that his girlfriend was in the house.

Girlfriend and *boyfriend*—I use the words loosely.

Jimmy had been going with Amanda Parish for three months when I died. I was the one who introduced them to each other, at my eighteenth birthday party. They hadn't met before, largely because Jimmy had gone to a different high school. Amanda was another one of those friends who wasn't a real friend—just someone I sort of knew because of her mother. But I liked Amanda a lot better than I liked Beth. She was some kind of beauty. My best friend, Jo, once remarked—in a poetic mood—that Amanda had eyes as gray as a frosty overcast day and a smile as warm as early spring. That fit Amanda. She had a mystery about her, but it was always right there in front of you—in her grave but wonderful face. She also had this incredibly long dark hair. I think it was a fantasy of my brother's to bury his face in that hair and let everyone else in the world disappear except him and Amanda.

I have to admit that I was a bit jealous of her.

Amanda's presence at my birthday party had had me slightly off balance. Her birthday had been only the day before mine, and the whole evening I remember feeling as if I had to give her one of my presents or something. What I ended up giving her was my brother. I brought Jimmy over to meet her, and that was the last I saw of him that night. It was love at first sight. And that evening, and for the next few weeks, I thought Amanda loved him, too. They were inseparable. But then, for no obvious reason, Amanda started to put up a wall, and Jimmy started to get an ulcer. I've never been a big believer in moderation, but I honestly believe that the intensity of his feelings for her was unhealthy. He was obsessed.

But I'm digressing. After calling out to Mrs. Parish, I crept into Jimmy's room. Except for the green glow from his computer screen, which he was in the habit of leaving on, it was dark. Jimmy's got a weird physiology. When I started for his desk and his brush, he was lying dead to the world with a sheet twisted around his muscular torso. But only seconds later, as I picked up the brush, he was up and heading for the door. I knew he wasn't awake, or even half-awake. Sleepwalkers walk differently—kind of like zombies in horror films, only maybe a little faster. All he had on were his boxers, and they were kind of hanging. I smiled to myself seeing him go. We were upstairs, and there was a balcony he could theoretically flip over, but I wasn't worried about him hurting himself. I had discovered from years of observation that God watches over sleepwalkers better than he does drunks. Or upset teenage girls . . .

I shouldn't have said that. I didn't mean it.

Then I thought of Amanda, possibly downstairs with her mom, and how awful Jimmy would feel if he suddenly woke up scratching himself in the hall in plain sight of her. Taking the brush, I ran after him.

It was good that I did. He was fumbling with the knob on the bathroom door when I caught him. At first I wasn't absolutely sure there was anyone in the bathroom, but the light was on and it hadn't been a few minutes earlier. Jimmy turned and stared at me with a pleasant but vaguely confused expression. He looked like a puppy who had just scarfed down a bowl of marijuana-laced dog food.

"Jimmy," I whispered, afraid to raise my voice. I could hear Mrs. Parish whistling downstairs and was becoming more convinced with each passing second that Amanda was indeed inside the bathroom. Jimmy smiled at me serenely.

"Blow," he said.

"Shh," I said, taking hold of his hand and leading him away from the door. He followed obediently, and after hitching up his boxer shorts an inch or two, I steered him in the direction of my parents' bedroom and said, "Use that bathroom. This one's no good."

I didn't wake him for a couple of reasons. First, he's real hard to wake up when he's sleepwalking, which is strange because otherwise he's a very light sleeper. But you practically have to slap him when he's out for a stroll. Second, I was afraid he might have a heart attack if he suddenly came to and realized how close he'd come to making a fool of himself in front of his princess.

After he disappeared inside my parents' room, I returned to the bathroom in the hall and knocked lightly on the door. "Amanda, is that you?" I called softly.

There was a pause. "Yeah. I'll be right out—I'm getting some kitchen cleanser."

Since she wasn't going to the bathroom, I thought it would be OK to try the knob. Amanda looked up in surprise when I peeked in. She was by the sink, in front of the medicine cabinet and a small wall refrigerator, and she had one of Jimmy's syringes and a vial of insulin in her hand. Jimmy's insulin had to be kept cool, and he'd installed the tiny icebox himself so he wouldn't have to keep his medication in the kitchen fridge downstairs where everybody could see it. He wasn't proud of his illness. Amanda knew Jimmy was a diabetic, but she didn't know he needed daily shots of medication. Jimmy didn't want Amanda to know. Well, the cat was out of the bag now. The best I could do, I thought, was to make a joke of the matter.

"Amanda," I said in a shocked tone. "How could you do this to your mother and me?"

She glanced down at the stuff, blood in her cheeks. "Mom told me to look for some Ajax, and I—"

"Ajax," I said in disbelief. "I wasn't born yesterday. Those are drugs you're holding. Drugs!" I put my hand to my mouth. *"Oh, God."*

I was a hell of an actress. Amanda just didn't know where I was coming from. She quickly put down the needle. "I didn't mean to—" she began.

I laughed and stepped into the bathroom. "I know you weren't snooping, Amanda. Don't worry. So you found the family stash. What the hell, we'll cut you in for a piece of the action if you keep your mouth shut. What do you say? Deal?"

Amanda peered at me with her wide gray eyes, and for a moment I thought of Jimmy's expression a moment earlier—the innocence in both. "Shari?"

I took the syringe and vial of insulin from her hand and spoke seriously. "You know how Jimmy's always watching his diet? Well, this is just another part of his condition he doesn't like to talk about, that's all." I opened the medicine cabinet and fridge and put the stuff away. "It's no big deal, is what I'm saying."

Amanda stared at me a moment; I wasn't looking directly at her, but I could see her reflection in the medicine cabinet mirror. What is it about a mirror that makes the beautiful more beautiful and the pretty but not exceptional less exceptional? I don't understand it—a camera can do the same thing. Amanda looked so beautiful at that moment that I could imagine all the pain she would cause my poor brother if her wall got any higher. And I think I resented her for it a tiny bit. She brushed her dark hair back from her pink cheek.

"I won't say anything to him," she said.

"It's no big deal," I said.

"You're right." She nodded to the cupboard under the sink, "I suppose I should have been looking down there."

We both bent over at the same instant and almost bumped heads. Then I remembered that Jimmy was still wandering around. Excusing myself, I left Amanda to find the Ajax and went searching for him. When I ran into him, coming out of my parents' bedroom, he was wide awake.

"Have I been sleepwalking?" he asked.

"No. Don't you remember? You went to sleep standing here." I pushed him back into my parents' bedroom and closed the door. "Amanda's here."

He immediately tensed. "Downstairs?"

"No, down the hall, in the bathroom. You almost peed on her."

Sometimes my sense of humor could be cruel. Jimmy sucked in a breath, and his blue eyes got real big. My brother's pretty cute, if I do say so myself. It runs in the family. He's the solid type, with a hint of refinement. One could imagine him herding cattle all day from the saddle, playing a little ball in the evening with the boys, taking his lady to an elegant French restaurant at night where he would select the proper wine to go with dinner. Except he would mispronounce the name of the wine. That was Jimmy. He was totally cool, but he wasn't perfect.

"Did she see me?" he asked.

"No. I saved you. You were about to walk in on her when I steered you this way."

"You're sure she didn't see me?"

"I'm sure."

He relaxed. Jimmy always believed everything I told him,

even though he knew what an excellent liar I was. I guess he figured if I ever did lie to him, it would be for his own good. He thought I was a lot smarter than he was, which I thought was stupid of him.

"What's she doing here?" he asked with a note of hope in his voice. I couldn't very well lie and tell him Amanda had come over to see him. When I had been in the bathroom with her, she hadn't even asked if he was home.

"Her mom brought her over. She's downstairs cleaning up the mess from the cocktail party. Amanda wants to ride to Beth's party with me."

"Why's she going? Is she a friend of Beth's?"

"Not really. I don't know why she wants to go." I had to wonder if Amanda had had time to buy a present, if she even had the money to buy one. She and her mom didn't exactly enjoy material prosperity.

"Is she still in the bathroom?" he asked.

"I don't know. You're not going to talk to her, are you?"

"Why not?"

"You're not dressed."

He smiled. "I'll put my pants on first." He started to open the door. "I think she's gone back downstairs."

"Wait. Jimmy?" I grabbed his arm. He stopped and looked at me. "When was the last time you called her?"

"Monday." He added, "Four days ago."

"That was the last time you talked to her. You called her

yesterday. You called her the day before that, too. Maybe you should give it a rest."

"Why? I just want to say hi, that's all. I'm not being fanatical or anything."

"Of course you're not," I lied. "But sometimes it's better, you know, to play a little hard to get. It makes you more desirable."

He waved his hand. "I'm not into all those games." He tried to step by. I stopped him again.

"I told her you were asleep," I said.

"She asked about me?"

"Yeah, sure." I wasn't even sure why I was so uptight about his not talking to her. I guess I couldn't stand to see Jimmy placed in a potentially humiliating situation. But perhaps I was just jealous. "We have to leave for the party in a couple of minutes," I added.

He began to reconsider. "Well, I guess I shouldn't bother her." He shook his head. "I wish her mom would tell her when I've called."

"Jimmy—"

"No," he said quickly. "Amanda really doesn't get the messages. She told me so herself."

I couldn't imagine that being true, but I kept my mouth shut. "I'll drop sly hints to Amanda tonight that she should call you tomorrow."

He nodded at the brush in my hand. "Isn't that mine?"

"Yeah, mine broke."

"You have a dozen brushes."

"They're all broken." I gestured to our mom's makeup table behind us. She never went out of the house without fixing herself up for an hour. Some might have called her a snob. I had called her that myself a few times, but never when my father was around. We didn't have a lot in common. "And mom wouldn't let me use one of hers."

"What did Amanda ask about me?"

"If you were getting enough rest." I patted him on the shoulder. "Go to bed."

I tucked Jimmy back in bed so that he could be fresh when his alarm went off at three in the morning and finished getting ready. When I went back downstairs, I found Amanda and her mom in the kitchen discussing whether a half-eaten chocolate cake should be divided into pieces before squeezing it into the jammed refrigerator.

"Why don't we just throw it in the garbage?" I suggested.

Mrs. Parish looked unhappy about the idea, which was interesting only because she usually looked so happy. Maybe I should clarify that. She wasn't one of those annoying people who go around with perpetual smiles on their faces. Her joy was quiet, an internal matter. But if I may be so bold, it often seemed that it shone a bit brighter whenever the two of us were alone together. I could talk to her for hours, about everything—even boys. And she'd just listen, without giving me advice, and she always made me feel better.

Jo, "Little Jo," had given her a nickname, too—"Mother Mary." I called Mrs. Parish that all the time. She was a devout Catholic. She went to mass several times a week and never retired for the night without saying her rosary. That was the one area where we didn't connect. I was never religious. Oh, I always liked Jesus, and I even went to church now and then. But I used to have more important things to think about than God. Like whether I should try to have sex with my boyfriend before I graduated from high school or whether I should wait until the Fourth of July and the fireworks. I wanted it to be a special moment. I wanted my whole life to be special. But I just hardly ever thought about God.

I'm repeating myself. I must be getting emotional. I'll try to watch that. Not everything I have to tell is very pleasant.

Back to that blasted cake. Mrs. Parish felt it would be a waste to throw it out. "Shari, don't you think that your mom might want some tomorrow?" she asked.

"If it's here, she'll eat it," I said. "And then she'll just complain about ruining her diet." I ran my finger around the edge and tasted the icing. I had already tasted about half a pound of it earlier in the day. "Oh, wow. Try this, Amanda. It's disgusting."

Amanda looked doubtful. "I'm not a big cake person."

Mrs. Parish suddenly changed her mind about saving it. "Maybe we should throw it out."

"You don't like cake?" I asked Amanda. "That's impossible—everybody likes cake. You can't come to Beth's party with me unless you eat cake. Here, just try it. This little piece."

I could be so pushy. Amanda had a little piece, along with her mother, and I had a slightly larger little piece. Then I decided that maybe there was room for it in the refrigerator after all. I didn't care if my mother got fat or not.

Mrs. Parish sent Amanda to check to see if our vacuum cleaner needed a new bag. For a moment the two of us were alone, which was nice. I sat at the table and told her about the party we were going to, while she stacked dishes in the dishwasher.

"It's for Big Beth," I began. "I've already told you how she's been flirting with Dan at school. It really pisses me off. I'll see the two of them together on the other side of the courtyard, and then when I walk over to them, she greets me like she's really glad to see me, like nothing's been going on between them."

"How do you know something *is* going on?" Mrs. Parish asked.

"Because Dan looks so uncomfortable. Yeah, I know, why get mad at her and not at him?" I chuckled. "It's simple—he might leave me and run off with her!"

I was forever making jokes about things that really mattered to me. I doubted that even Mrs. Parish understood that about me. I may not have been obsessed with Daniel the way Jimmy was with Amanda, but I couldn't stand the thought of losing him. Actually, I honestly believed he cared for me. But I continued to worry. I was never really cool, not inside, not about love.

"Is Dan taking you and Amanda to the party?" Mrs. Parish asked, carefully bending over and filling the dishwasher with detergent. She had an arthritic spine. Often, if we were alone in the house, she would let me help her sweep the floor or scrub the bathrooms. But never if anyone else was present. I'd noticed she particularly disliked Amanda knowing she needed help.

"Yeah. We're picking Jo up, too. He should be here in a sec." I paused. "Mary, what do you think of Dan?"

She brightened. "He's very dashing."

I had to smile. *Dashing.* Great word. "He is cute, yeah." I took another forkful of cake, although I needed it about as much as I needed another two pounds on my hips. "What I mean, though, is do you like him? As a person?"

She wiped her hands on her apron and scratched her gray head. Unlike her daughter's, her hair was not one of her finer features. It was terribly thin. Her scalp showed a little, particularly on the top, whenever she bent over, and she was only fifty. To be quite frank, she wasn't what anyone would have called a handsome lady. She did, however, have a gentle, lovely smile.

"He seems nice enough," she said hesitantly.

"Go on?"

"How does he treat you?"

"Fine. But—"

"Yes?"

"You were going to say something first?"

"It was nothing."

"Tell me."

She hesitated again. "He's always talking about things."

"Things?" I asked, even though I knew what she meant. Daniel liked *things*: hot cars, social events, pretty people—the usual. Since the universe was composed primarily of things, I had never seen it as a fault. Yet Daniel could be hard to talk to because he seldom showed any deep feelings or concern for anything but "things."

Mrs. Parish shrugged, squeezing a couple more glasses into the dishwasher. "Does he ever discuss the two of you?"

"Yeah, sure," I lied.

"You communicate well when you're alone together then. That's good. That was the only thing I was concerned about." She closed the door on the washer and turned it on. The water churned. So did my stomach. I pushed away the cake. I'd heard a car pulling up outside. It must be Daniel, I thought. I excused myself and hurried to the front door.

I found him outside opening our garage. Graduation was a couple of weeks off, but my parents had already bought me my present. I can't say what it was without giving the impression I was spoiled rotten.

It cost a fortune. It was fast. It was foreign.

It was a Ferrari.

Oh, my car. I loved it. I loved how red it was. I loved everything about it. Daniel loved it too, apparently. He hardly noticed my shining presence when I came out to greet him. He fell in love with my car at first sight.

He had taken longer to fall in love with me.

I had officially met Daniel after a high school play in which he played the lead. I have an incredible memory for facts, but I cannot remember what the play was about. That says a lot. He blew me away, and he wasn't even that great. He had forgotten several lines, and he'd been totally miscast. None of that mattered, though. He just had to strut around up there under the lights, and I felt I just *had* to go backstage afterward and commend him on his artistry. Of course, Jo had to drag me kicking and screaming to his dressing room. I was sort of shy, sometimes.

Since we went to the same school and were in the same grade, I naturally knew *of* him before we met after the play. I would like to record for posterity that the reverse was also true, that he had noted with approval my existence the four years we had spent together at Hazzard High. But the first thing he asked when Jo introduced us was if I was new to the area. What a liar. He didn't want me to think I was too cute.

But he asked me out, and that was the bottom line. He asked me out right there in front of his dressing room with Jo standing two feet away with her mouth uncharacteristically closed. Later, it seemed so amazing to me that I wondered if Jo hadn't set it all up beforehand. But she swore to the day I died that it wasn't so. . . .

I must talk about his dashing body. It was smooth and hard. It had great lines, like a great race car. Except Daniel wasn't red. He was tan. He hugged the road when he moved. He had legs, he had hips. He had independent rear suspension. We used to make out all the time in his bedroom with the music on real loud. And then, one warm and lustful evening, two weeks before Beth's birthday party, we took off our clothes and *almost* had sex.

I loved to think about sex. I could fantasize six hours a day and not get tired, even if I was repeating the same fantasy with only slight variations. I was a master of slight variations. But one can think too much. When we got naked together in bed, things did not go well. Daniel couldn't . . . Oh, this will sound crude if I say it, so I'll say instead that I shouldn't have overdone it comparing him to my Ferrari. Yet, in a sense, he was as *fast* as the car. I left the room a virgin.

He was *so* embarrassed. I didn't understand why. I was going to give him another fifty chances. I wasn't going to tell anyone. I didn't tell anyone, not really. Maybe Jo, sort of. But she couldn't have told anyone else and had enough details to sound like she knew what she was talking about. Unless she had added details of her own.

Daniel and I had other things in common, other *things* we liked to do together. We both enjoyed going to movies, to the beach, out to eat. That may not sound like a lot, but when you're in high school, it often seems like that's all there is.

Anyway, when I went outside to welcome Daniel, he was in ecstasy. He had turned on the light in the garage and was pacing around the car and kicking the tires like guys are fond of doing when they see a hot set of wheels. I didn't mind. He had on white pants and a rust-colored leather coat that went perfectly with his head of thick brown hair.

"Did you have it on the freeway today, Shar?" he asked.

"Yeah, but I didn't push it. They told me to break it in slowly over the first thousand miles."

"This baby could go up to one forty before it would begin to sweat." He popped open the driver's door and studied the speedometer. "Do you know how many grand this set your dad back?"

"He wouldn't tell me. Do you know how many?"

Daniel shook his head. "Let's just say he could have bought you a house in the neighborhood for the same money." He went to climb inside. "Are you ready to go? Can I drive?"

"We can't take it. Amanda Parish is here, and she's riding with us. And we have to pick up Jo."

Although Joanne had introduced the two of us, Daniel didn't like her. It would be hard to pinpoint specifically what she did that bothered him, other than that he was a boy and she had a tendency to make the male species as a whole feel inferior.

I had no idea what he thought of Amanda.

He showed a trace of annoyance. "You didn't tell me."

"I didn't know until a little while ago." The Ferrari had no backseat. "We can go for a drive in it tomorrow."

He shut the door, sort of hard, and I jumped slightly. To be entirely truthful, I never felt entirely comfortable around Daniel. He strode toward me and gave me a hug. His embraces were always unexpected.

"Hi," he said.

"Hi."

He kissed me. He wasn't an expert at lovemaking, but he had a warm mouth. He also had strong arms. As they went around me, I could feel myself relaxing and tensing at the same time. I didn't know if other girls felt the same way when their boyfriends embraced them. But when his kisses grew hard and deep, I didn't mind.

"Oh, sorry," we heard behind us a minute or so later. Daniel let go, and I whirled. There was Amanda, as pretty and as unprepared as when I walked in on her in the upstairs bathroom. Her big eyes looking down, she turned to leave.

"No, it's OK," I said, taking a step toward her, only mildly embarrassed. "We should be leaving. Stay here. I'll go say goodbye to Jimmy and Mother Mary. Be back in a moment."

Amanda stopped. "What did you say?"

I suddenly realized I'd brought up Jimmy. "If Jimmy's awake," I said quickly, the remark sounding thin in my own ears. "He was asleep a few minutes ago."

Amanda stared at me a moment. Then she muttered, "Say hello for me."

"Sure."

Jimmy was awake when I peeked in his door. He motioned me to come and sit on his bed. His computer screen was still on, and, as always, I found the faint green light hard on my eyes.

"Why don't you just turn it off?" I asked, gesturing to the CRT.

He smiled faintly, his muscular arms folded across his smooth chest, his eyes staring off into space. He was in a different mood now—more contemplative. "I might wake in the night inspired."

"The way you get around in your sleep, you wouldn't have to wake up."

"I was dreaming about you before I bumped into you in the hall."

"Oh? Tell me about it?"

He had just opened the window above his bed, and a cool breeze touched us both. Later, I thought it might have been the breath of the Grim Reaper. It was a warm night. Jimmy closed his eyes and spoke softly.

"We were in a strange place. It was like a world inside a flower. I know that sounds weird, but I don't know how else to describe it. Everything was glowing. We were in a wide-open space, like a field. And you were dressed exactly as you are now, in those jeans and that shirt. You had a balloon in your hand that you were trying to blow up. No, you *had* blown it up partway, and you wanted me to blow it up the rest of the way. You tried to give it to me. You had tied a string to it. But

I didn't catch the string right or something, and it got away. We watched it float way up in the sky. Then you began to cry."

Far away, toward the front of the house, I heard Daniel start his car. He wasn't a good one to keep waiting. But suddenly, I didn't feel like going to Beth's party. I just wanted to sit and talk with my brother until he fell asleep. I pulled his sheet up over his chest. The breeze through the open window was getting chilly now.

"Why was I crying?" I asked.

"Because the balloon got away."

"What color was it?"

"I don't know. Brown, I think."

"Everything's brown to you! What was so special about the balloon?"

He opened his eyes and smiled at me. For a moment I thought he was going to ask me about Amanda again. I felt grateful when he didn't. "I don't know." He paused. "Will you be out late?"

"Not too late."

"Good."

"What's the matter?"

He thought a moment. "Nothing. I'm just tired." He squeezed my hand. "Have fun."

I leaned over and kissed him on the forehead. "Sweet dreams, brother."

He closed his eyes, and it seemed to me he was trying to

picture my balloon a little more clearly so maybe he could answer my question about it a little better. But all he said was, "Take care, sister."

People. When you say goodbye to them for the last time, you'd expect it to be special, never mind that there's never any way to know for sure you're never going to see them again. In that respect, I would have to say I am thankful, at least, that my brother and I got to talk one last time before I left for the party. But when I got downstairs, Daniel was blowing his horn, and Mrs. Parish was vacuuming the dining room. I barely had a chance to poke my head in on her as I flew out the door.

"We're going," I called.

Mrs. Parish leaned over as if she was in pain and turned off the vacuum. "Did you bring a sweater?" she asked, taking a breath.

"Nah! I've got my boyfriend to keep me warm!"

She laughed at my nerve. "Take care, Shari."

"I will," I promised.

But I lied. And those little white lies, they catch up with you eventually. Or maybe they just get away from you, like a balloon in the wind.

ABOUT THE AUTHOR

CHRISTOPHER PIKE is a bestselling author of young adult novels. The Thirst series, *The Secret of Ka*, and the Remember Me and Alosha trilogies are some of his favorite titles. He is also the author of several adult novels, including *Sati* and *The Season of Passage*. Thirst and Alosha are slated to be released as feature films. Pike currently lives in Santa Barbara, where it is rumored he never leaves his house. But he can be found online at christopherpikebooks.com.